The Women Who Ran Away

Sheila O'Flanagan

The Women Who Ran Away

REVIEW

First published in Great Britain in 2020 by HEADLINE REVIEW
An imprint of HEADLINE PUBLISHING GROUP

1

Cataloguing in Publication Data is available from the British Library

ISBN 978 1 4722 5478 8 (Hardback)
ISBN 978 1 4722 5479 5 (Trade Paperback)

Map illustration by Yeti Lambregts

Typeset in Galliard by Palimpsest Book Production Ltd, Falkirk, Stirlingshire

Printed and bound in Great Britain by Clays Ltd, Elcograf S.p.A.

Headline's policy is to use papers that are natural, renewable and recyclable products and made from wood grown in well-managed forests and other controlled sources. The logging and manufacturing processes are expected to conform to the environmental regulations of the country of origin.

HEADLINE PUBLISHING GROUP
An Hachette UK Company
Carmelite House
50 Victoria Embankment
London EC4Y 0DZ

www.headline.co.uk
www.hachette.co.uk

The
Women Who
Ran Away

THE JOURNEY

DUBLIN

RINGASKIDDY

ROSCOFF

NANTES

LA ROCHELLE

BORDEAUX

PAMPLONA

ALCALÁ DE HENARES

TOLEDO

ANDÚJAR

CARTAGENA

GRANADA

N
W   E
S

Chapter 1

Grand Canal, Dublin, Ireland: 53.3309°N 6.2588°W

Even after she'd put her luggage in the tiny boot of the convertible, Deira still wasn't sure if she was going to go through with it. Which was crazy, she told herself, because this was the easy bit. The harder part had been the previous night, when she'd walked into the dimly lit underground car park and waited for the Audi to unlock automatically. Even as she'd told herself that nobody would take any notice of her, she'd expected one of the residents to suddenly appear and ask her what the hell she was doing. But the one person already there, a young man in head-to-toe Lycra, was more concerned with unchaining his bike than with Deira's actions.

Nevertheless, the familiar click as she slid her hand along the driver's door was comforting. So was lowering herself into the driver's seat and finding that it still moved automatically to her favoured position when she pressed the memory button. She'd been afraid it would have changed. But there was no lingering scent of an unknown perfume or a different shampoo. No sense that someone else had taken her place. Nothing at all was different. Her heartbeat slowed down. Everything felt normal. Easy. Right.

1

Driving slowly out of the apartment complex, she'd told herself that her criminal career was off to a good start.

Of course she had a key, which surely meant that taking the Audi wasn't actually a criminal act, no matter how anyone else might see it; but she wasn't supposed to be here, doing this. Deira didn't care. She was past caring. And being back in the car was comforting in a way she hadn't expected. So it was worth it.

Now, as she slammed the boot closed and walked back into the granite mews overlooking the canal, she felt a sudden rush of tears fill her eyes and clamped down hard on her jaw to try to stop them falling. It didn't matter that she was tired of crying; the slightest thing still set her off, blubbing uncontrollably and embarrassing both her and anyone around her. She rubbed her eyes with the back of her hand. If for no other reason than the sake of her skin, she needed to get over it. Her complexion was ruined from the salt of her ever-present tears.

She glanced at the clock on the kitchen wall and released a slow breath. Unless she was going to chicken out at the last minute, she'd have to leave soon. After all the trouble she'd gone to, missing the ferry would be a complete disaster.

But instead of picking up her keys and bag and heading back outside, she put a pod in the coffee machine and made herself an Americano. She sipped it slowly as she studied the tickets in front of her, making doubly sure that she had the right date. It would be idiotic of her to go on the wrong day, but over the last couple of months she'd done so many idiotic things that she didn't trust herself any more. She recalled the phone calls, the emails and – worst of all – the scene in the office, and she shuddered. She'd been made a fool of, but she knew she'd been a fool too. And that was hard to take.

She put the tickets back in her bag. She had the right date. She wasn't a complete idiot, no matter what other people might think.

Although the trip had been booked nine months previously, she'd totally forgotten about it until the direct debit for the balance had resulted in her account being overdrawn. She hadn't even realised she'd gone into the red until her bank card had been declined at her hairdresser's. It had been one more humiliation added to all the others. Naturally she'd burst into tears again.

It had been Gavin who'd first suggested taking the car to France, confessing a need to drive a stylish convertible along some decent motorways before people judged him a sad old fart and passed comments about his virility and the size of his penis.

Deira had laughed when he said that, and wrapped her arms around him.

'Nobody would think that of you, ever,' she'd told him. 'They wouldn't dare.'

Because Gavin Boyer looked at least a decade younger than his fifty-seven years. True, his hair, once even darker than Deira's, was now almost entirely silver-grey, but that only made him appear even more distinguished than when he was younger. He was still tall and broad, and even if his waist was thicker than it had been in his twenties and thirties, he'd managed to maintain his athletic build. Rather unfairly, in Deira's view, he achieved this without any great effort other than golf twice a week and an occasional visit to the swimming pool of the nearby gym. Metabolism, he'd say airily, when she complained that, at seventeen years younger, she put on weight simply by looking at a packet of biscuits. He made no comment at all about her monthly trip to the hairdresser to have her own increasing number of greys covered with an approximation of her natural chestnut brown.

Definitely not fair, she thought now. But life wasn't fair, was it? Because if it was, she wouldn't be standing here with a rapidly cooling cup of coffee in her hand wondering if he would set the police on her when he got home.

She took a sip of the coffee. There was no need to worry. He wouldn't set the police on her because he wouldn't know that the car was gone until the end of the following week, and even then he wouldn't know she was the one who'd taken it. Besides, even if he did suspect her, she'd be miles away and there'd be nothing he could do about it. Interpol would hardly worry about a missing car, after all.

She shook her head. Car thief. Interpol. None of that was part of her life. France was supposed to have been a holiday. For both of them.

Their original plan had been to explore Brittany for a few days before heading to Paris. Deira had told Gavin that if he was going to indulge in his dream of open-top cruising down the motorway, she wanted to be able to say she'd driven around the French capital in a sports car with the warm wind in her hair. When he'd looked at her in bewilderment, she'd explained that one of her late mother's favourite songs had been the haunting 'Ballad of Lucy Jordan', in which a thirty-seven-year-old woman feels so trapped in her life that she knows she'll never get to do just that. When Deira was old enough to understand the lyrics, she'd sympathised with Lucy Jordan and wondered if her mother had ever felt the same way. Now approaching her own fortieth birthday, she'd visited Paris on a number of occasions but had never driven an open-top car around the city's streets – and had never particularly wanted to until the day they'd collected the convertible.

Until recently, she would have felt enraged at the notion that any woman would feel washed up by the age of thirty-seven. But she'd come to realise that there was more to it than how you felt, and she knew there were things she'd previously considered unimportant that she'd never have the chance to do. And that, more than anything else, was why she'd cried every single day for the past two months.

She glanced at the clock again. She knew she was cutting it fine. It was a three-hour drive to Ringaskiddy, and she was supposed to be at the ferry terminal forty minutes before the ship sailed. Unless she was going to abandon her plan, she had to leave now. Yet something was holding her back. She wasn't sure exactly what. A reluctance to commit herself to all the driving? The knowledge that she was poking a hornets' nest? Fear of what people would say?

'If he rings, it's a sign and I won't go,' she said out loud, even as she knew he wouldn't ring, and that if he did, she'd be in a panic to get the car back before he realised it was gone. Even thinking about him ringing was a sign of her weakness, not her strength. Anyhow, she didn't believe in signs or omens, good or bad.

Life was life, she often said to her friend Tillie, who had a more open view on random signals as pointers for making important decisions. Seeing a white feather floating on the air or a sudden shaft of sunlight on a dismal day didn't mean anything more than the fact that a bird had flown by or there was a momentary break in the clouds. Tillie would shake her head and tell her that she needed to be in touch with her inner self a bit more. But Deira was afraid of her inner self. She wasn't sure it was a part of her that needed being in touch with at all.

Maybe the very fact that her account had been debited without her actually noticing it was a cosmic sign. Perhaps the fact that she'd had no problem taking the car was a sign too. Or the sign could simply be that the sun was shining in a clear blue sky and the drive would be lovely.

On the other hand, it was always possible there would be something on the way to Cork that would make her come to her senses and turn around again.

'Plenty of signs on the road to Cork,' she muttered as she picked up the car keys. 'Mostly telling you about motorway exits.'

She slung her bag over her shoulder, set the alarm and walked outside.

The morning air had warmed up and the bright sunlight dazzled off the canal water as she sat in the driver's seat and lowered the roof of the car. Truth was, she rarely drove it with the roof down. She lived in Ireland, after all. There was always a good chance that a torrential downpour would arrive out of the blue. And even on the sunniest of days, the wind-chill factor meant that it wasn't always ideal for open-top driving.

But today was perfect.

So maybe that was the sign.

Deira wondered if she should call Gillian and tell her what she was doing. But if she did, her older sister would want to know when she'd decided to make this trip and who she was

going with and why she hadn't said anything before and . . .
No, talking to Gill would definitely be a sign, Deira thought.
A sign that I've lost my mind completely.

She started the car and pulled away from the kerb. Her
phone rang almost at once, and her heart began to beat wildly.

'Are you on your way?' asked Tillie.

'I've just set off.'

'You'll be late.'

'No I won't.'

'No phone calls?'

'No,' said Deira.

'Everything will be fine,' said Tillie. 'Have fun.'

She waited for Tillie to remind her not to do anything
crazy, but when she didn't, Deira simply replied that she'd
do her best to have a good time.

'You deserve to,' said Tillie. 'I'll send you positive vibes
and keep in touch.'

'Thanks.' Deira ended the call and continued to follow the
canal before turning onto the industrialised Naas Road. The
traffic on a Saturday morning wasn't too heavy, and she
nudged her speed up a little. Her hair whipped across her
face and she tucked it behind her ears. My life hasn't been
wasted, she told herself, as she thought again of Lucy Jordan.
It really hasn't.

And yet as she drove on, she was regretting once again
the choices she'd made and the decisions she'd taken that
now meant that, in ways she'd pretended to herself didn't
matter, the last thirteen years of her life *had* been entirely
wasted. There was no point in thinking otherwise. Nothing
could change it. That was the thing. Not taking the car, not
driving to Paris, not telling herself that forty was the new

thirty. What had happened had happened and the worst part of it all was that she'd been complicit in it. Which really did make her an absolute, utter, complete fool.

'Of course you're not a fool.'

Tillie's words, spoken when Deira had first broken the news to her, came back to her.

'Yes I am,' Deira had told her. 'I'm the same kind of fool that all women are. Thinking they're doing what they're doing because that's what they want when really it's just because they're in love with the wrong man.'

Tillie had hugged her then.

And Deira had felt the rage and the hurt ball up inside her so tightly that she literally doubled over with the pain of it.

She felt it again now. A horrible feeling in the centre of her stomach. And the pain higher up too, the one that had made her think she might be having a heart attack. But she knew she wasn't. She knew it was simply her anger at being played. At allowing herself to be played.

She was angrier with herself than with him.

She blamed herself more than him.

But she blamed him too, and that was why she was going away and taking the damn car with her.

Chapter 2

Ringaskiddy, Ireland: 51.8304°N 8.3219°W

Grace Garvey was already at Ringaskiddy. She'd driven from Dublin the previous night because that was what she and Ken had always done in the years when they'd taken the children on their annual camping holiday to Brittany. Drive down the night before, stay in a guest house near the port and wake up refreshed and ready for the sailing. Also, Ken would say, there was no need to worry about breakdowns or anything slowing them down en route if they went ahead of time. They were where they needed to be.

Only once had Grace pointed out that if they had a breakdown in Ireland they'd be in big trouble regardless, given that they usually had at least a two-hour drive after getting off the ferry at Roscoff. But Ken had shaken his head and told her not to be a drama queen. Even though he was the one who made their annual holiday into a drama, planning it down to the finest detail and fuming if things didn't go exactly to his meticulous plan.

Grace always did her best to ensure that nothing interfered with the plan, without him ever being aware of it. Ken was a man who became stressed when things didn't turn out the way he wanted. This stressed Grace out too, although the children, Aline, Fionn and Regan, never seemed to notice the undercurrent of tension that surrounded the house in the week leading up to their departure. All they cared about was arriving at that year's chosen campsite and having a good time.

And despite the stress that Ken placed upon himself, their family holidays invariably were good times. Grace's memories of them were precious.

She sat on the bed in Portview House – the same guest house they'd used all their lives – and opened the laptop she'd brought with her. Ken's laptop. She hadn't intended to bring it, but at the very last minute, she'd gone back inside the house and grabbed it. She could have emailed the documents to herself, but she'd decided that perhaps the laptop might have hidden information on it that she might need. She hadn't yet found anything, other than the sent email she'd received three months earlier. And she didn't need to read that again. But having the laptop, knowing that it was Ken's, was important to her.

She gazed indecisively at the folder entitled *The Big Anniversary Treasure Hunt*. She'd opened it when he'd first sent the email and then closed it again, not willing to be part of a plan that she'd known nothing about. And not willing to have him tell her what to do. Not when he'd done something so truly dreadful that he'd shaken her faith in everything they'd had together. But here, now, she couldn't help herself.

She clicked on the folder. It contained eight documents, each with an individual title:

Nantes
La Rochelle
Bordeaux
Pamplona

Alcalá de Henares
Toledo
Granada
Cartagena

Each document was locked by a password. Grace had tried a couple of random passwords on them without any success. Then she'd concentrated on the Nantes document, because it was the first in the itinerary that he'd set out, bombarding it with memorable dates and other significant combinations. Frustrated by her failure, she'd moved on to La Rochelle. After her third incorrect guess, she'd got a message saying that she had seven further attempts before being locked out. She'd stopped then. Even if she wasn't sure she wanted to see the contents of the document, she didn't want to be locked out yet.

She'd gone back to the Nantes document, where it appeared she had as many guesses at the password as she liked, possibly because it was the first of the collection. That would be typical of Ken. Break her in easily before making things progressively more difficult. But she could almost feel his disgust at her not having been able to figure it out straight away. He'd known by the time he'd sent the email that he wouldn't be with her to help. So why hadn't he left her some sort of clue to start her off?

Maybe he had, she thought. And maybe she was too stupid to spot it.

Had he considered at all that she might not play his silly game? Or had he always known she'd do what he wanted no matter how ridiculous?

She snapped the lid of the laptop closed. Her brain was too frazzled to work on the passwords now. It was focused on getting to the port and boarding the ferry, as though Ken was sitting beside her telling her not to shilly-shally. He'd always made sure they arrived at the terminal exactly two and a half hours before the sailing. Once they'd even been the first car in the queue, which had pleased him no end. Grace didn't need to be first in the queue. But she didn't want to be late either.

There was no chance of her being late. She could see the ship from her bedroom window, tall and white against the blue sky and teal-green sea. She knew it was far too early to leave, no matter what Ken's voice was telling her.

She put the laptop into her overnight case and went downstairs.

Claire Dolan, the owner of Portview House, smiled at her and asked if she was planning to leave already.

'You'll need me out of the room shortly,' replied Grace.

Claire told her that there was no rush and that she was welcome to use the living room for as long as she liked. 'I know you've been coming here for years and you're accustomed to travelling, but it's the first time you've done it on your own,' she said. 'So take your time.'

'I'll be fine,' Grace assured her. 'There's no need to worry about me.'

There was an infinitesimal moment of awkwardness before Claire reached out and gave her a little hug, one arm around Grace's bony shoulder. 'I know you're a strong woman,' she said gently, 'but I'm sure it's been hard. I was surprised, to be honest, when you made the booking. I didn't think you'd want to go by yourself.'

'I hadn't planned to be by myself.' Grace gave her a rueful smile. 'My friend Elaine was supposed to come with me. But then her daughter went into a very early labour and her baby was poorly for a while, so I told her not to even think about me but to go to Megan. She lives in Canada.' Grace shrugged, as though Canada explained everything.

'Are you a hundred per cent sure you'll be OK on your own, though?' asked Claire.

Grace nodded. 'Absolutely,' she said, in a voice that was free of any doubt.

She'd said the same to her elder daughter, Aline, when she'd asked Grace that question too.

'I'm sure you'll manage,' agreed Aline, who'd dropped in on her way home from work to see how her mother was doing. 'But all that driving without anyone to share . . . I'm sure Dad didn't expect you to do it alone. He'd have imagined one of us would be with you. Maybe even all of us, like before. You could wait until that was a possibility. I don't want you to get too tired, and there's really no rush to—'

'I won't get tired,' insisted Grace. 'None of the stages are that long. And you know quite well that it would be impossible to get everyone together again this year. So I'm doing it and that's that.'

'It's asking a lot of yourself. Especially when—'

'When what?' Grace's clear blue eyes hardened as she interrupted her daughter again.

'When you're grieving.'

'I'm not grieving!' The words had come out more forcefully than she'd meant and she registered the dismay on Aline's face. 'I mean, yes, I'm grieving but I'm . . .' She was going to say she was too angry – and perhaps too guilty – to grieve, but she knew that would freak Aline out even more. 'I'm doing it for closure,' she said, quietly confident that she'd pressed the right button. Aline was big into closure. She'd had a closure evening for Ken before Fionn and Regan had left the country; they'd gone through his vast library of books, picked one each and then read a chapter out loud to each other. She'd played video clips of him at all their graduations, as well as at the family dinner for Grace's sixtieth birthday, where he'd called her his constant light. And then she'd recited 'My Memory Library' by Sarah Blackstone

Grace had smiled throughout, but her heart hadn't been in it, especially during Aline's recitation of a poem Grace knew Ken would have dismissed as sentimental nonsense. Ken had never liked poems that rhymed. So while her children were reading and reciting, she'd been remembering the week after Aline's graduation, when her daughter had packed her textbooks into a big box and donated them to a local education centre, saying that it was important to have them out of the house and in her past. Ken had been furious with her. He'd said that she'd need to reference them in the future even though she had her degree. She'd mentioned Google. He'd fumed quietly. Ken hadn't believed much in closure either. Until, perhaps, he had.

Aline celebrated birthdays and Christmas and Easter as waypoints in her life, always talking about marking new beginnings (tautology, Ken said, and when Aline asked what he meant, he told her to look it up. On Google, if it makes you feel better, he added). But even if their tastes in books and poetry differed, Aline and Ken were more like each other than they knew, mused Grace. Both of them brimming with self-confidence, both of them believing their way was the right way. Neither of them thinking of the consequences of

14

their actions on other people, always expecting they'd fall into line.

'I care about you.' Aline broke into her thoughts. 'We all do. We don't want anything to happen to you.'

'Things happen all the time,' said Grace, which elicited an even more shocked expression from Aline. 'But I'll be fine. I'm more worried about you guys, to be honest.'

'It's been really hard, but I've dealt with it,' said Aline. 'So have Fionn and Regan. I'm not sure you have, Mum.'

'I have. Honestly,' Grace lied.

'I'd be happier if Elaine was going with you.' Aline wasn't at all convinced by her mother's words.

'So would I,' said Grace, although that was probably a lie too. 'But she has other priorities. I'll be fine. Anyhow,' she added, 'I'll FaceTime you from all my destinations and let you know how it's going. You can keep me up to date too.'

'I guess so.'

'I'll be fine,' said Grace again.

She wasn't going to tell her daughter that there was a part of her that *wanted* to do the trip by herself. Aline would have been even more hurt by that. And, like the rest of them, she'd been hurt enough already. But since Grace had decided to make this journey, nobody was going to stop her. Despite some initial misgivings, she was looking forward to driving off the ferry in France and doing her own thing, as much as she could given the schedule he'd laid out for her and the requests he'd made.

'You couldn't simply leave it,' she murmured. 'You still have to organise me.'

She'd never acknowledged before how much Ken's desire to be in charge bothered her. Especially his determination to plan their holidays. Her own working life had been ruled by timetables and plans, which should have made it a pleasure, really, to leave the arrangements to him. But he never chose to fly to a destination. On a plane, she would inevitably have known more than him. She'd been a senior cabin crew member after all. She could have made things easier for them. But he didn't want her to. She knew nothing about ferries.

However, despite the stress he brought to it, Ken had been good at organising holidays. The children loved taking the ferry and the freedom of the campsites in France. They loved the excitement of living in a tent, and later, in a mobile home, enjoying the basic nature of it. So despite occasionally feeling aggrieved at her lack of input, Grace went with the flow.

She'd always been good at going with the flow.

Now she walked into the colourful garden of the guest house and gazed out over the ocean. The sun was higher in the sky and had turned the sea to a deep azure blue. It was a perfect day for the crossing. A perfect day to travel.

Chapter 3

Dublin to Ringaskiddy: 268 km

Deira didn't stop on her journey from Dublin to Ringaskiddy, and as soon as she arrived at the port she joined the queue of vehicles waiting to board. Embarkation had been under way for the past hour, but there were still quite a number of travellers ahead of her. From the vantage point of her car she could see people already walking around the upper deck of the boat, bright specks of colour against the white ship.

She allowed herself a sigh of relief as she handed over her ticket and was waved forward. Deep down, she'd half expected to be stopped and hauled off to be interviewed by the Gardaí. But the port officials clearly hadn't been alerted, and the other travellers were far too concerned about boarding the ferry to even notice her; although the male drivers of the heavily laden cars, camper vans and SUVs surrounding her occasionally shot envious glances at the low-profile convertible.

When she was safely parked, she made her way to the passenger deck, not bothering with the lifts, where families with children, babies, bags and buggies, were waiting, but taking the stairs instead. By the time she reached Deck 8, she was regretting it, thinking she was a good deal less fit than she'd fondly imagined. She waited for a moment to catch her breath, then walked the length of the carpeted corridor to find her cabin.

She pushed the door open and went inside.

Before they'd booked the holiday, she and Gavin had spent hours on the ferry company's website doing virtual tours of all the cabins and decks, so she knew what to expect. But it was still a relief to see that their chosen cabin – her cabin now – was bright and airy, with plenty of room for a table and chairs as well as the bed. It also had a patio door leading to a private balcony. 'Cruise-ferrying', the company had called its service, and Deira had to admit that the cabin was almost as good as the one they'd had on the only occasion they'd gone on a proper cruise. That had been for her thirtieth birthday. It didn't feel like only yesterday, yet it didn't seem like nearly a decade ago either. She still remembered the thrill of it – flying to Barcelona, from where the enormous ship was departing on its Mediterranean voyage; staying overnight in a flashy hotel; getting a taxi to the port the following morning. Feeling the joy of being away with the man she loved. It had been a fantastic holiday. One of the best of her life.

Now she was on a cruise ferry from Ringaskiddy. And this time she was alone.

She opened the patio doors and stepped onto the balcony. The breeze whipped her hair around her face and she tucked it behind her ears. Far below, she could see the huge ropes tethering the ship to the pier. Workers in hi-vis jackets were walking along its length, shouting information to each other. Beyond the enclosed area for passengers a crowd of people sat on a mound of grass looking up at the ship, waving from time to time. Deira didn't know if they were waving at people they knew, or if they were randomly waving because the ship was about to depart. It was nice to see them, though. Nice to think that people she'd never met before might be wishing her bon voyage.

She felt a shuddering sensation beneath her feet as somewhere within the depths of the ship the engines throbbed into life. The smell of diesel mingled with the tarry whiff from the jetty and the salty tang of the sea. Huge seagulls screeched and wheeled overhead. The workers began loosening the heavy ropes. The ship's vibrations increased. The people on the grassy bank waved again. And suddenly they were moving, slowly and ponderously, away from the shore, away from Ireland and out into the open water.

Although not immediately into the open water, she realised. The ship still had to negotiate the harbour and the long channel that led to the sea. But they were on their way. Nobody could stop her now. She'd done it.

Her mobile rang.

She almost dropped it overboard.

'Where are you?' asked Gillian when she answered. 'I got your automatic "do not disturb, I'm driving" message when I texted you earlier.'

'Is something wrong?' Deira felt a sudden fear in the pit of her stomach and thought of Gavin.

'I wanted to ask you a favour,' said Gillian. 'Bex is going to Dublin tomorrow. She has an interview for a summer internship later in the week and she was hoping to spend a couple of nights with you. Her friend Lydia is going with her.'

Deira stifled a groan. Her nineteen-year-old niece and

god-daughter, Gill's eldest child, often came to the capital and always assumed that there'd be a bed for her at Deira's for the duration of her stay. Gill invariably made the same assumption on her own visits to Dublin. And although Deira was fond of Bex and usually enjoyed her company (if not always Gill's), it drove her nuts that both of them invariably landed on her at the last minute, as though she didn't have a life of her own.

Though from Gill's point of view, she probably didn't. Not now, anyway.

'I'm really sorry,' she said as she watched the emerald-green shoreline glide past, 'but I'm away. So it's not possible.'

'Away? Where?' asked Gill. 'You didn't say anything about it last time we talked.'

You're not in charge of me now. I don't need to tell you everything I do. Deira steadied herself and bit back the remark.

'I wasn't sure I was going,' she told her sister. 'But then I decided I would.'

'Where?' demanded Gill again.

'France,' replied Deira.

'France! When did you go and when are you back?'

'I'm on my way now,' said Deira. 'And I won't be back for nearly a month.' That wasn't strictly true. She'd be home in less than three weeks. But there was no need to tell Gill that.

'A month!' Gill's words ended in almost a screech. 'How on earth can you take a month off, Deira O'Brien?'

'Because I had holidays due to me that I didn't take before,' Deira replied.

'Right.' There was a pause before Gillian asked her where she was staying.

'I'll be travelling,' said Deira.

'With who?'

'With whom, d'you mean?' Deira couldn't help herself.

'Grammar Nazi,' said Gill, as Deira had known she would. 'Who are you going to France with? Where will you be travelling to?'

'I'm on my own,' said Deira. 'I haven't planned my itinerary yet.'

Gill's next words were lost in a bellow from the ship's horn.

'What the hell was that?' she asked.

'The ship,' replied Deira.

'The . . . What ship?'

'I'm on the ferry.'

'But . . . I thought you were in the airport. Aren't you flying to Paris?'

'No. I'm sailing to Roscoff.'

'Why on earth are you doing that?'

'Why not?'

'Nobody takes the ferry to France on their own.'

'I have.'

'Jesus, Deira, have you lost your mind?' Although Gillian's words were harsh, her tone had softened. 'Look, I know it's been hard for you this last while, but there's no need to run away.'

'I'm not running away,' said Deira. 'I'm going on holiday.'

'Why didn't you pick something nice, like a fortnight on the beach?' demanded Gill. 'I'm sure you could've got a lovely all-inclusive in the Maldives or somewhere. You can afford it, after all. Or can you?' she added. 'Are there money problems?'

'I don't like beach holidays,' said Deira. Which was only partly true. She enjoyed a week on the beach with a few good books. But more inactivity than that did her head in. 'And I'm fine for money.' Which, despite the hiccup when the direct debit for the trip had hit her account, was currently true.

'Have you heard from Gavin?'

Deira's heartbeat quickened. 'No. Should I have?'

'I don't know,' said Gill. 'But let's face it—'

'I don't want to talk about Gavin.' Deira interrupted her. 'I'm off on my holidays. He's the last person I want to think about or talk about right now.'

'You should have told me you were going,' said Gill.

You would have tried to stop me. Deira didn't say this out loud either.

'I'll message you when I'm there. I think the signal will drop on my phone soon. We're nearly out at sea.'

'Message me every day,' said Gill.

'Whenever I can,' said Deira.

And she ended the call.

Back inside the ship, Deira visited the onboard shop, which was already crowded with people stocking up on French wines and special-offer spirits. Her only purchase was reflectors for the headlights of her car to redirect the beams for driving on the right-hand side of the road. Living it large, she murmured to herself as she paid for her solitary purchase. I really do know how to have fun!

She then made her way to the self-service restaurant, which was loud and noisy and, she realised, the last place she wanted to be. The sight of a mother feeding her tiny baby while at the same time spooning food into a toddler made her feel dizzy.

She turned away and almost bumped into a man carrying a tray laden with food.

'Sorry,' he said.

'My fault.'

He nodded at her apology and kept walking.

Are you on your own? she wondered as her eyes followed him. Are you the one? He was attractive, though not memorable. He would be suitable enough. Wouldn't he?

Stop, she said to herself. Just stop. She turned away and headed for the waiter-service restaurant at the other end of the ship. There was a queue here too, which was surprising until she realised that the frequent ferry travellers knew to get to the food as quickly as possible and leave the shopping and everything else until later.

When she finally reached the top of the queue, she asked the young Frenchwoman with a list in her hand if a table for one was possible.

'We have nothing until eight o'clock, madam,' she replied.

Deira wasn't hungry, but eight o'clock was a long wait. Nevertheless, she supposed the self-service restaurant would probably be full for most of the evening. And she deserved something peaceful and quiet. So she booked her table and then went back to her cabin, where she made herself a cup of tea. Then she stretched out on the bed and closed her eyes.

She was completely disoriented when she woke up, aware of the throbbing engines deep within the boat but not knowing what they were. It took a moment for everything to come back to her: the car, the drive, boarding the ferry – and the fact that she'd booked a table for eight o'clock. She looked at her watch. It was seven thirty.

She got up from the bed and used the small en suite bathroom to freshen up. Then she changed into the belted denim dress she'd put into her carry-on bag, glad that she'd added it at the last minute, because the white blouse she'd been wearing was crumpled from her unexpected siesta. She hadn't bothered with extra shoes; her wedge sandals went well enough with the dress. She brushed her dark curly hair, added some peachy lip gloss and sprayed herself with Jo Malone Grapefruit.

She looked at herself in the mirror, wondering if she'd done enough, or if she needed make-up to hide the pallor of her cheeks and the dark circles that had been under her eyes for the past couple of months. She'd never been much of a make-up person. She was always groomed and presentable for work, but she usually achieved her look with nothing more than mascara and tinted moisturiser to enhance her green eyes and high cheekbones. When they were younger, Gill had frequently told her that she'd drawn the lucky straw as far as looks were concerned. Not that you're beautiful, she'd say (in case Deira got notions about herself), but there's a bit of the wild Irish rose about you, what with your black hair and creamy complexion. No need to slap on anything more than a dollop of Nivea.

That had been then, of course, when neither of them had needed more than Nivea, and Gill had taken on the role of mother to her younger sister. She'd mothered their father and their brother too, even though Peter was five years older than her and didn't really want anyone to mother him at all.

But Gill was unyielding. She was the eldest girl and she was the one in charge. Deira had thought of her as overprotective when she was younger. Later on, she couldn't help thinking that Gill was inherently bossy and had enjoyed being the one who ruled the roost. She'd certainly enjoyed interfering in Deira's life, that was for sure.

Deira herself was ten when her mum passed away. Gill was fifteen, Peter nineteen. Peter had stayed at home for another year and had then headed off to London, where he'd got a job with one of the rail companies. It suited him perfectly – he'd always been mad about trains. They hadn't seen him for a few years after he'd left, but when the budget airlines arrived with their cheaper fares, he was back and forward a couple of times a month. Then he married Sarah, the girl he'd been seeing for the best part of a year. He still returned to Ireland regularly with her and their children, Tyler and Sian, but although she'd seen him earlier in the year, Deira had been too busy with an upcoming exhibition to meet him on his last visit.

He'd texted her when he'd heard about Gavin. She'd texted back to say she was fine. He'd sent her a thumbs-up emoji in reply. She hadn't heard from him since.

Deira didn't get back to Galway very often herself, and when she did, she preferred to be in the city centre rather than the suburbs with Gill. However, her sister came to Dublin at least half a dozen times in the year, staying in Deira's canalside mews every time. It had created tension between Deira and Gavin, who wanted to know why her relatives couldn't stay in a hotel like normal people. Why did they think it was OK to impose on them whenever they came to town? Wasn't Gill always boasting about how well her husband, Bob, was doing? At which point he'd wink at Deira and she'd laugh, because Bob, like Deira and Gavin, worked in life and pensions. But unlike Gavin, who was on the board of directors, he was stuck at middle management, with no chance of moving any higher.

She sat down abruptly on the bed, overwhelmed by the memories. Back then, it had been her and Gavin against the world. At least, that was how it had felt. Now her world had shifted on its axis. And – whether she meant to show it or not – Gill was quietly smug about it all.

Deira stayed sitting for a moment, her eyes closed, trying hard not to cry. Then she stood up straight, ran the brush through her hair again and stepped out of the cabin.

She hadn't come away to think about how things had been. She was here to think about how they were going to be. Even though, right now, there was nothing in her future to look forward to.

Chapter 4

Ringaskiddy to Roscoff: 580.2 km

When she arrived at the restaurant, Deira was led to a table for two near one of the large windows at the stern of the ship. The restaurant was nearly full, and most of the diners seemed to be excited Irish passengers on the outward leg of their holiday. Deira, accustomed to taking flights to wherever she wanted to go, hadn't realised that so many people did it differently, even though she and Gavin had joked about reducing their carbon footprint when they'd first booked the trip. Now, as she took the menu the waiter offered her, she thought that perhaps she might travel this way more often.

The choices on the menu were appetising, although she couldn't remember the last time she'd either eaten out or felt hungry. Which should, at least, have led to the upside of dramatic weight loss, except that avoiding food didn't include avoiding two glasses of wine and a few squares of chocolate every night. Comfort eating. And drinking. And she didn't care.

She decided to start with a salad from the buffet, followed by some seared tuna from the menu. The buffet itself was so extensive that some people seemed unable to limit their choices to one or two selections and had piled their plates with an assortment of meat, shellfish, salads, cheese and crusty bread. Deira could almost hear Gavin beside her, murmuring that a buffet always brought out the inherent savage in people. 'Clustering around as though they're never going to see food again,' he would have said. Because that was what he always said when they were away together and facing a breakfast buffet. 'It makes you lose all faith in humanity.'

She always agreed with him when he said that. She agreed with him on most things. It was why people said they were a great couple.

She put a little pot of prawns along with a small salad of green leaves on her plate. She brought it back to her table, then took her iPad from her bag. But although she opened it, she didn't click on any of her favourite apps; instead she simply ate her food and stared into the distance.

It took her a moment or two to register that the waiter was walking towards her again, and for a brief moment she wondered, irrationally, if she'd taken too much from the buffet. And then she saw that there was a woman with him – tall and graceful, clearly older than Deira herself but with fine features that gave her an almost ageless appearance. Her silver-grey hair was cut in a fashionable mid-length style, and she was wearing what Deira had realised was almost the uniform of many of the older women on the ferry – a navy and white striped T-shirt, white chinos and espadrilles. A necklace of turquoise agates hung around her neck. She looked so stylish that Deira immediately assumed she was French.

'This table,' said the waiter.

'Um – I booked a table for one,' said Deira.

'I'm afraid we don't reserve tables for one person,' said the waiter. 'You'll have to share.'

'If I'm disturbing you . . .' The woman's voice was clear and measured, her accent Irish.

'I . . . well . . . no . . .' Deira moved her iPad out of the way.

'Thank you.' The woman sat down, and the waiter took her order for a glass of Chablis, then left them alone.

'I apologise if I'm disturbing you,' the woman said to Deira. 'But it's always the case on the ferry that they plonk people down beside you. Everyone wants to eat at the same time, you see.'

'It's fine,' said Deira, who was saved from further conversation by the arrival of both the other woman's glass of wine and her own main course.

She busied herself with her food and her iPad, opening the book she'd been reading for the past month. Normally she managed a book a fortnight, but lately she'd been finding it hard to concentrate, and even though this one was well written, her attention kept wandering after a few pages. It had been recommended to her by Tillie, who insisted that she needed something inspiring, and was about a woman who'd suffered a major trauma in her life and gone trekking through the Andes in an effort to find her inner self. Deira wasn't sure if trauma was at the root of the more recent decisions she herself had made, although sitting in a good restaurant toying with excellent food said a lot about the inner self she still didn't want to embrace. I'm shallow, she thought. Too concerned about material things and creature comforts. But – and she smiled involuntarily at the thought – a car thief. So a bit out-there after all.

The woman opposite was also reading; she'd taken an old copy of Hemingway's *The Sun Also Rises* from her bag and had left it on the table while she'd gone to the buffet. Deira had written a critical analysis of Hemingway's most famous work for the English literature module of first-year college exams, suggesting that his casual anti-Semitism was shocking, his characters unlikeable and his dialogue stilted, a critique that had caused her tutor to look at her appraisingly and remark that when she'd written her own masterpiece, she might be in a position to pan a classic twentieth-century novel. Deira had responded by telling him that she'd been asked to write a critical essay, not simply praise the damn book. Hemingway's so-called masterpiece was full of male arrogance, she insisted, and she was entitled to say so.

The professor laughed then and told her that he liked people who could defend their own point of view, no matter how wrong it might be, so he would mark her highly for the essay even though he didn't agree with a word of it. It had been a turning point for Deira at college – until she'd locked horns with him, she'd been self-effacing and timid. But that day she'd become a more positive person, one who could stand up for herself. She'd stayed that person for a long time. But now she'd suddenly lost her again. Perhaps, she thought, this trip was the start of getting her back.

The woman opposite turned the pages of the book as she ate, but when she'd finished her smoked salmon, she closed it and pushed it to one side. She looked up and caught Deira observing her.

'It's kind of awkward sitting opposite each other without saying a word, and yet so many of us who want tables to ourselves aren't the kind of people to strike up friendships with random people,' she observed. 'However, it's rude not to at least know who you're sharing with. My name is Grace. Grace Garvey.'

'Deira O'Brien.'

Observing Grace more closely, Deira estimated she was in her mid fifties, or perhaps slightly older. But her complexion was smooth and almost flawless and hinted at real beauty when she was younger. In fact, thought Deira, she was beautiful now.

'Have you sailed on this ship before?' Grace asked.

Deira shook her head. 'My first time.'

'I think this is my tenth, maybe even eleventh.' Grace smiled. 'We used to do it every second year when my children were younger.'

Deira glanced around as though Grace's family would suddenly materialise.

'I'm on my own this year,' Grace said.

'Me too.'

It was a relief to know she wasn't the only person travelling solo. Seeing so many families on board was the most difficult part of the experience for Deira. Because if things had been different, if she'd been more sure of herself, she could have been part of the whole camping-trips-to-France scene. She could have been the one hustling her children through the interminable queues of the self-service restaurant, hoping they wouldn't make a scene; unlike the French parents, whose children seemed to have impeccable table manners, Deira knew that hers would have taken after both her and Gavin and been irrepressible. They wouldn't have wanted to sit still in these more formal surroundings. They would have been a nuisance.

No. She held back that thought. Her children might have

been boisterous, but they would never have been a nuisance. She'd have made sure of that.

'Where are you heading afterwards?' she asked Grace, who'd finished her salad but hadn't opened her book again.

'I'm driving to Cartagena in southern Spain.'

Deira looked at her in astonishment. 'From Roscoff? On your own? That must be a couple of thousand kilometres at least.'

'Seventeen hundred,' said Grace. 'Though I'll be adding a few more with some detours. And you?'

'My original plan was to drive to Paris. But I've been rethinking that over the last few hours. So I'm not entirely sure yet.'

'I was always too terrified to drive in Paris,' said Grace. 'I should have tried it first when I was younger, but I didn't, and now I doubt I ever will.'

'If you don't mind me saying so, you look like a woman who could do anything she put her mind to,' Deira said.

Grace smiled. 'Thank you.'

'I guess if you've done this trip nearly a dozen times, you're used to driving on the Continent,' said Deira.

'I've only driven there twice,' Grace told her. 'As a family, the furthest we travelled was to La Rochelle. My husband did most of the driving; he only trusted me behind the wheel every so often.'

Deira wasn't sure what to say in reply. There had been an undercurrent to Grace's tone that made her think the other woman might not always have appreciated being the passenger. She wondered where the husband was now, but she didn't ask.

The waiter arrived with Grace's main course (she'd also

opted for the tuna) and cleared away Deira's finished meal. Deira ordered coffee and then went back to the buffet to choose a dessert. Out of habit, she avoided the luscious chocolate tarts and selection of cheesecakes and instead went for a fruit salad and yoghurt.

Grace had returned to reading her book as she ate, and didn't look up when Deira sat down again. Deira supposed that the older woman would have liked a table for one just as much as she would. And yet it had been nice to speak to another person. Besides, there was something comforting in Grace's calm, melodic voice, something stabilising about her serenity. Somehow Deira could easily imagine her driving sedately the length of France and Spain. She had no idea how long such a journey would take, but it would certainly be a good deal more than the six or so hours from Roscoff to Paris. After Gavin had booked the ferry and Deira had looked at the route to the French capital, she'd wondered why he hadn't chosen a ferry to Calais instead. Paris was less than two hours from Calais by car. But he'd told her that he'd wanted to do the Cork to Roscoff journey again. That it had been lovely when he'd done it before and he wanted to share it with her. That had shut her up, because they never talked about his time before her. When he was married to Marilyn and part of a family with two children of his own.

Deira had never intended to become part of his life.

But she had.

And for a while, it had been the best thing that had ever happened to her.

Chapter 5

Dublin, Ireland: 53.3498°N 6.2603°W

She was twenty-five years old and had been working in Hagan's Fine Art Gallery and Auction Rooms for almost a year when Gavin Boyer walked in. She noticed him straight away, a tall, confident man with jet-black hair who ignored the carefully curated displays and strode up to the mahogany desk where she was seated. After introducing himself, he asked to see Kevin Hagan.

'Mr Hagan isn't here today.' Deira was polite despite the fact that Gavin had been abrupt. 'He's at an exhibition in London. Can I take a message?'

'He can't be in London. I have a meeting with him,' said Gavin.

'I'm sorry, Mr Boyer, but he's very definitely in London, and if you arranged a meeting with him, he's somehow mixed up the dates.' Deira knew she was right, but nevertheless she tapped on her keypad to check the online calendar. 'There's no meeting in his diary.'

'I should've texted him to confirm,' Gavin said irritably. 'He's hopeless.'

Deira kept quiet, but privately she agreed with the attractive man standing in front of her that Kevin *was* hopeless

34

when it came to meetings, especially if he set them up himself. Never knowingly missing a detail when it came to arts and antiquities, he was forgetful about everything else.

'The earliest I can schedule a meeting for you is Monday afternoon, if that helps,' she said.

'Monday it is, so.' He smiled suddenly, and looked less like a grumpy old man. Not that he was old in the first place, Deira thought as she logged the meeting. But he was older than her. Late thirties or early forties, she reckoned. She tapped the keyboard again.

'As you're here, would you like to browse the gallery?' she asked. 'We've got some great new work or, of course, you can look at our auction items.'

'I'll take a glance around,' said Gavin. 'Not that Kevin deserves it.'

Deira watched him from behind the computer as he walked around the gallery, pausing in front of some of the paintings and ignoring others. He was distinguished, she thought, and knowledgeable too, because he gave more time to the better artists, studying the paintings carefully. She smiled when she realised he was examining one of her favourites – a mother and child sharing a riverside bench, both holding bright orange umbrellas over their heads.

'Isn't it lovely?' She walked up to him with a brochure. 'It's a Thelma Roache. We've got more of her work here. It's very vibrant.' She turned and pointed to another painting, this time of a woman hurrying for a train, an emerald-green bag over her shoulder and her yellow coat flapping open.

'Yes, it is.' Gavin took the brochure from her, but continued to study the painting of the mother and child.

'I like how the brightness of their umbrellas contrasts with the surroundings,' said Deira. 'And how the river looks so dark and gloomy but the painting itself isn't.'

'Is that your critical analysis?' He sounded amused.

She glanced at him, embarrassed at her unvarnished praise for the painting, but he was looking at her with interest.

'Not so much a critical view, more a personal one,' she admitted. 'I like Thelma Roache and I think she should be better known. We've only recently started to show her work, but she's great. An older woman, which may be why she doesn't get the recognition. She's been painting since the seventies.'

'Oh.' Gavin looked surprised.

'But of course women don't get the same recognition as men anyway,' Deira said. 'No matter how good they are.'

'Women in general or women artists?'

'In general. But particularly as artists.'

'You're sure about that?'

'It was part of my thesis,' she said.

'You studied art?'

'Art history and modern literature,' she told him. 'My brother told me it was a useless degree, but it got me the job here.'

'You don't want to be an artist or a writer yourself?'

She shook her head. 'I can appreciate other people's work, but I know my limitations. What I like doing is matching people with paintings they love. Or helping out with exhibitions. Because it brings the beauty of art – whether it's paintings or sculpture or jewellery or books – to more people.'

'Have you organised many exhibitions?'

'Just one. But it was excellent. We sold all the paintings.' She beamed at him.

He said nothing in reply and she wondered if she'd over-stepped the mark with him. But he simply told her that he'd be back on Monday to meet with Kevin and that he hoped to see her too.

After he'd left, Deira couldn't help feeling that the gallery seemed very empty.

Kevin came back from his exhibition full of enthusiasm for some new names, and apologetic about having forgotten his meeting with Gavin Boyer.

'I didn't realise it was a definite thing,' he told Deira. 'But no harm done, we've been in touch and he's fine about it.'

He was in his office when Gavin called at exactly four o'clock on Monday afternoon. Deira brought coffee and biscuits to them and then went back to logging the items for their upcoming antique jewellery auction on the computer.

Afterwards, Kevin told her that Gavin was looking to exhibit some art himself.

'Huh? He's a rival?' Deira was taken aback.

'Not at all,' said Kevin. 'He's an executive with a life and pensions company. They're trying to reach out into the community a bit more and support cultural events.'

She grimaced. 'All these corporations trying to make nice when we know they'd rip the face off you if they could.'

'Perhaps.' Kevin grinned. 'But it's a worthwhile endeavour all the same. Solas Life has recently moved into a new building and they have a space they think could be used to display artwork. He's also thinking about historical retrospectives on aspects of the city, or great musicians or writers. Anyhow, his first idea is an art exhibition and he wants us to come up with some content.'

'That's exciting,' conceded Deira.

'Actually, you've already given him an idea he likes. He was very taken by Thelma Roache's work. He wants to exhibit some women painters.'

'Oh,' said Deira.

'He said that you were so aggrieved they don't get enough recognition that you based your thesis on it.'

'Gender inequality in the arts,' Deira said. 'Not only painting. You should know. You read it.'

'Well, you poked a sleeping beast with it anyhow.' Kevin didn't confirm or deny that he'd read the thesis he'd asked her to send him after he'd interviewed her for the job. Which made her wonder if he'd actually bothered. 'So, off you go. He's talking about twenty or so paintings, but you'll need to have a look at the space they have and see what you think.'

'You want me to do it?'

'Why not?' Kevin said cheerfully. 'You're the one with the big ideas around here.'

Deira had great fun curating the exhibition for Gavin Boyer, who was unexpectedly easy to work with. The space in the company's building on Dawson Street was ideal, and Gavin himself was supportive of the suggestions she made. On the night of the opening, he made a speech to the invited guests in which he thanked her profusely for all her help. Deira couldn't help being charmed by him and delighted by his compliments. It was good to be praised for doing a job that she'd loved, particularly as that praise was in front of the Minister for Arts and other important people in business and industry. Hopefully, she thought, as the glass of white wine she was holding grew too warm to drink, hopefully these people would remember that it was

38

Hagan's that had sourced the paintings and put everything together.

'Deira, isn't this lovely!' Thelma Roache, dazzling in a raspberry velvet dress, her normally loose silver hair pinned in a neat chignon, caught her by the arm. 'Thank you so much for suggesting my work. I want to have it seen by as many people as possible, and more people come into an insurance company building than an art gallery.'

'Gavin – Mr Boyer – has highlighted this new cultural space to all the company's customers,' said Deira. 'But it's not only for customers; it's open to everyone. I'm sure loads of people will want to come.'

'Obviously I want that to happen.' Thelma beamed at her in return. 'I'm not so much of an artist that I still dream of starving in my garret. Knowing that they'll be seen is a big thing.'

'I'm sure they'll sell,' Deira said. 'And I'm sure the other artists' will sell too.'

The exhibition had concentrated on four female artists. Deira had chosen them for the diversity of their work but also because their paintings were alive with colour and movement. Thelma, at almost seventy, was the oldest. Looking around the room now, Deira was delighted at how well all of the work was presented, and she couldn't help feeling another thrill of pride that she'd been involved.

'Great job, Deira.'

This time it was Gavin Boyer himself who was beside her. 'Hugely successful.'

'It is, isn't it.' She beamed at him. 'And you know what I like most?'

'What?'

'That it's going to be part of everyday life for people who come in and out of your building. That the art is just there. Not something they have to make an effort to go and see. I have to admit that I was a bit sceptical about your motives at first,' she added, 'but I'm really pleased to have been part of it.'

'I'm pleased you were too,' he said. 'I've never met anyone as enthusiastic as you about their work.'

'Oh, I'm sure everyone who works for Solas is equally enthusiastic,' she said.

Gavin laughed as her tone betrayed her doubt. 'You'd make a terrible liar,' he said. 'But whatever their enthusiasm for working in pensions, at least they'll all love the artworks.'

At that moment, a slender, dark-haired woman in a stylish blue shift dress joined them, accompanied by two teenage girls in jeans and T-shirts.

'My wife, Marilyn,' said Gavin. 'And my lovely daughters, Mae and Suzy.'

Deira knew now that Gavin was forty years old and that his wife had stopped working outside the home when his second daughter was born. They must have married very young, she thought, as she greeted his teenage daughters, neither of whom seemed overly thrilled to be there.

She spent a few minutes talking to Gavin's family before being approached by one of his colleagues who wanted to introduce her to the Minister himself. This is me now, she thought, with a jolt of pride, as she said goodbye to Marilyn Boyer. I'm the sort of person who gets introduced to the Minister.

I'm on the way up.

*

Two weeks later, Gavin came into the gallery and told her he was taking her to lunch.

'You can't,' she said. 'I have a heap of stuff to do.'

'I've already squared it with Kevin,' said Gavin. 'It's not a problem. I want to thank you properly for everything.'

'I was doing my job, that's all,' said Deira. 'I enjoyed it.'

'And now you can enjoy the fruits of it with me,' said Gavin. 'It's a business lunch.'

Deira had never been out for a business lunch before. Occasionally she and Kevin had eaten together in the small sandwich bar around the corner while they talked about an upcoming auction, but an actual sit-down lunch was an entirely different proposition.

'I'd better check with him first anyway,' she said, and ran up the stairs to Kevin's office.

Her boss had no problem with her going to lunch with Gavin and told her he'd keep an eye on things.

'Are you sure?'

'You think I can't manage my own gallery?' He raised an eyebrow.

'I don't entirely trust you not to knock a few hundred euros off a painting if you think someone really loves it,' she admitted, which made him laugh.

Gavin put his hand on the small of her back as he opened the gallery door and escorted her outside. 'I've booked the Saddle Room at the Shelbourne,' he told her.

Her eyes widened. The Saddle Room was a Dublin institution. She'd never eaten there. In fact she'd hardly ever gone into the Shelbourne, which was just as much of an institution. Her salary didn't stretch that far. She wished she was wearing something a little more elegant than her floral-sprigged

41

V-necked dress and ballet pumps. But this was her working look.

The maître d' nodded at Gavin in recognition when they arrived, and led them to a table for two in a quiet corner of the room. It was a table from which one could observe without being observed, and Deira was impressed to see Eamon Dunphy, the sports pundit, at another table, while Bono, easily recognisable in his yellow-tinted sunglasses, was seated at a third.

'It's a kind of who's who,' she murmured to Gavin, who laughed and said that it was one of his favourite places to eat.

Deira knew it was far too expensive to become one of hers, but she was happy to allow him to lead her through the menu and choose a bottle of wine to accompany the lamb she'd selected. She was only going to drink a glass. She didn't want to arrive back at work half-cut.

'So tell me more about yourself,' he asked when the waiter had left them alone together.

'You know everything there is to know,' she replied. 'We've talked a lot over the last few weeks.'

'We've talked about the exhibition,' agreed Gavin. 'But not that much about you. Where are you from? That accent isn't entirely Dublin.'

'Galway,' said Deira. 'But I've been here since college.'

'Would you like to go back?' asked Gavin.

'To Galway? No.' Deira was vehement.

'Have you family in Dublin?'

'No.' This time Deira's tone was more relaxed. 'But I'm happy here. I see my life here.'

'With Kevin Hagan?'

'For the time being, at any rate.'

She looked up as the waiter returned with her grilled prawn starter.

'Gosh, this looks great,' she said. 'I didn't realise I was hungry, but seeing it has made my mouth water.'

'Good.' Gavin smiled. 'So, getting back to what I was saying – where do you see yourself in five years from now? Still at Hagan's? Or is that a stepping-off point for you? Do you have other plans?'

'Jeepers, you sound like you're interviewing me!' Deira squeezed lemon over her prawns, then, when Gavin didn't say anything, looked up at him. '*Are* you interviewing me?'

'Maybe,' he admitted.

'I don't want to work in pensions,' said Deira. 'I don't know how you could possibly think I would.'

'I'm totally aware that you wouldn't want to work in pensions,' acknowledged Gavin. 'That's not what I had in mind at all.'

What he was thinking about turned out to be a position in Solas Life and Pensions as a corporate responsibility executive. Deira would look out for projects that suited their brand and ethos, he told her, as well as being responsible for the cultural space in their Dawson Street building. Obviously their next exhibition would have to be something very different to the four women painters, but he was sure she could come up with an idea. Solas wanted to be seen as promoting Irish heritage. He could think of no one better than Deira to do that for them.

'I'm not sure I'm qualified,' she said.

'You're supremely qualified,' he told her.

'All the same . . .'

'You're a ray of light in a dull, dull business,' he said. 'We'd love to have you on board.'

Then he mentioned the salary, which was double what she was earning at Hagan's, and she knew her decision was already made.

It was the job she'd been born for.

By the end of the year, she'd arranged a second exhibition, this time of photographs of Irish cities. The photos were a mixture of black-and-white and colour, and although some were of iconic features, like Christ Church Cathedral or Galway's Spanish Arch, others simply reflected a slice of city life. Deira's personal favourite was a photograph of a woman coming out of a café, a takeaway cup in one hand, a sandwich in the other, her hair blowing in the wind.

Both the art and photographic exhibitions had been given good write-ups in the press, and Deira herself had even been interviewed with the caption 'The Young Woman Who's Bringing Business and Heritage Together'. Gillian had sent her a congratulatory text when the feature had been published, and Deira had saved it, because Gill's praise of her younger sister was seldom and therefore doubly important.

At the Christmas party that year, Gavin told her that the company was more than delighted with the good work she was doing and the excellent publicity it had brought them. 'We're all about making a difference,' he said, 'and you've shown us how.'

Deira was too experienced in the way of business by now to believe every word he was saying. But she liked to think that she really had made a difference, and said so.

'You totally have,' Gavin assured her. 'You've made a difference to the company and you've made a difference to me too.'

'How have I made a difference to you?' Deira took a sip from her glass of wine. Solas had provided a free bar for its employees, and she was aware that she had, perhaps, taken advantage of it a little more than she'd meant to. But what the hell, it was Christmas.

'You've made me think differently,' replied Gavin. 'About how I approach my work. My life, too.'

'Your life?'

'Having you around with your positive attitude to everything has changed me,' he said. 'I used to look for reasons why things couldn't work. Now I look for reasons to make them work.'

She laughed. 'I'm glad you think I'm a positive person.'

'I think you're a lovely person,' said Gavin.

It was the free alcohol talking, Deira knew that. And it was the free alcohol that made her lean her head against his shoulder and tell him that he was a lovely person too, and that the day he'd come into Hagan's had changed her life completely and she was thankful to him for that.

'We're thankful for each other.' He put his arm around her and hugged her.

'Hey, lovebirds!' Derek Coogan from Internal Audit joined them. 'Don't worry. What happens at the party stays at the party.'

Deira sat up straight. 'Nothing's happening at the party,' she said. 'We were having a moment.'

'Says who!' Derek, who'd also clearly enjoyed the free bar, started to laugh.

Deira got up and walked away. It was late, and she reck-oned this would be a good time to leave. She collected her coat and walked outside the hotel where the party was taking place.

The rain was thundering down.

'I've ordered a taxi.' Gavin was standing behind her. 'Want to share?'

She turned in surprise.

'No party is worth staying at if you're going,' he said as a car rolled to a stop in front of them.

She wasn't sure how good an idea this was. But the taxi was waiting and she didn't know how long it would take to get another one. So she climbed in.

He'd kissed her before they even reached the main road.

Chapter 6

Celtic Sea: 51.5499°N 7.9756°W

The waiter, returning with the coffee she'd ordered, brought Deira back to the present. Opposite her, Grace had left her book on the table while she selected a dessert from the buffet. Deira could see that she was about halfway through it, although it was clear that it had been read many times before. She wondered if it was Grace's go-to book, the one she read when she needed comfort. If so, Grace's tastes were far more literary than her own. Deira's go-to book wasn't any of the great classics she'd studied at college, but a romantic thriller that had belonged to her mother, and which she'd read in her teens. Set in the late 1950s, *Nine Coaches Waiting* was the story of a governess who goes to France to look after the nephew of a count and then finds herself in mortal danger. Deira had been captivated by the glamour and intrigue when she'd started to read it one rainy afternoon, and had been totally caught up in both the predicament and the romantic entanglements of the governess. Even when she read it again now, she still felt a knot of tension in her stomach over the outcome. She'd never understood why people were so sniffy about romance in books when so much of real life was taken up with the

47

effect relationships had on everyone. But she'd never mentioned it to her tutor, who would have been appalled at the idea of one of his students reading what he insisted was inferior trash.

She sighed. She'd been caught up in the excitement of her forbidden (and secret) romance with Gavin for a long time too. Maybe she'd felt a little like a heroine in her own personal novel. Despite her guilt at their affair, she'd told herself that she was helping him through a bad time in his life. He'd spent a lot of time saying how difficult Marilyn was. How she undermined him in front of the girls. Deira hadn't intended to fall in love with him, but it had been inevitable. Moving in with him had been inevitable too, even though Gillian had been horrified and had come to Dublin to try to knock some sense into her. But Deira had told her sister that her days of interfering in her life were over and that she was old enough to make her own choices now. They couldn't be any worse than the ones Gillian had forced upon her.

Old enough but not necessarily wise enough, she thought as she got up from the table and nearly bumped into Grace, who was returning with the large slice of Pavlova she'd chosen as her dessert.

'Sorry,' gasped Deira as she sidestepped quickly.

'Well dodged.' Grace smiled. 'Enjoy the rest of your holiday.'

'You too,' said Deira. 'Safe travels.'

She walked out of the dining room and paused at the small bar area nearby. Despite her earlier decision to have only water, she suddenly felt the urge for a glass of wine. But the bar was crowded and there wasn't an available seat, so instead she went to the promenade deck, stepping out of the air-conditioned warmth into the chill wind. She shivered, and zipped her jacket up to the collar before glancing at the sky. It was almost dark overhead, but the horizon was a spectacular canvas of pinks and golds as the sun slid out of view.

She leaned over the rail, mesmerised by the rhythmic ploughing of the ferry through the water, and wondered what Gavin was doing now. She wanted to think that deep down, at least, he regretted what had happened. She wanted to think that he was ashamed. But she doubted it. He'd left Marilyn and Mae and Suzy to live with her, after all. And that hadn't bothered him in the slightest.

'Of course I'm sorry it didn't work out with Marilyn,' he told her the day they moved in together. 'But Deira, darling, the marriage had been on the rocks for years.'

She believed him about that. From the first moment she'd met Marilyn at the exhibition, she'd wondered about the two of them. Gavin's then wife had seemed remote and uninterested in the success of the night. She'd insisted on leaving early and taking the girls with her. Gavin had been disappointed to see her go.

I might have been the catalyst but not the cause, Deira often told herself. The relationship was already splintered when I met him. She reckoned that the thirteen years they'd been together since then proved it. Thirteen years wasn't a casual romance. It was a proper relationship.

Marilyn and Gavin had been together for twenty. She'd been right about him marrying young.

She leaned further over the rail.

'Are you all right?'

The male voice behind her sounded so concerned that she straightened up immediately.

'Of course,' she said as she turned around.

If he hadn't spoken with an Irish accent, Deira would have assumed the man standing in front of her was French. There was a studied nonchalance to the way he wore his old leather jacket, distressed jeans and scuffed trainers. His dark wavy hair was loose and a little too long, but it suited him.

Could he be the one? The question flashed into her head almost as soon as the words were out of her mouth. Could it be him? Was it fate meeting him here, now? What would Tillie think? What would she say?

Deira already knew, because even though Tillie hadn't said it earlier, she'd said it more than once when she'd learned of Deira's plans. 'Don't do anything crazy. Don't make a rash decision.'

She squeezed her eyes closed. Part of the reason she'd decided to come away was to stop asking the same question every time she saw someone new. To put herself in a different place mentally and physically. And yet here she was, same old, sad old Deira. Gavin would laugh at her if he knew what was going through her head.

'I'm sorry,' said the stranger. 'I thought you were feeling ill.'

'I'm fine. Thank you.'

'I didn't mean to disturb you.'

'It was kind of you to ask, though.'

'It's a bit choppy this evening,' he said. 'Sometimes it gets to people. But this wouldn't be the best side to vomit from. The wind is coming from the west.'

'Ugh.' She smiled involuntarily at the image. 'Do you do this crossing often?'

'I used to do it more than I do now,' he replied. 'Always enjoy it. And you?'

'It's my first time,' she said.

'Are you driving far afterwards?'

She supposed this was a standard question on a ferry crossing.

'I haven't decided yet,' she replied.

'Flying by the seat of your pants.' He grinned and pushed his hair out of his eyes. 'I like that. Have fun.'

The door to the interior of the ferry opened and a family clattered out, the younger children shrieking in delight, their parents watching them closely as they ran along the deck.

'I'd better get back in,' said Deira. 'Nice to meet you.'

'You too,' said the man.

He took up her place at the rail.

She stepped inside again.

He was a random stranger.

He wasn't the one.

It was considerably quieter now. Walking around the ferry again, Deira realised that many of the passengers had gone to the forward lounge, where there was music and entertainment, leaving other areas of the ship deserted. After buying some chocolate in the shop, for no reason other than something to do, she returned to the bar outside the restaurant, where she ordered the glass of wine she'd promised herself. She found a seat beside the window, then opened her iPad and selected maps.

If she stuck with her plan to go to Paris, the drive would

take five and a half hours, excluding breaks, travelling via the motorway and main routes. It would be an hour longer if she chose to avoid motorways, but she reckoned it might be better to stick to the major routes for her first few hours on Continental soil. The last thing she wanted to do was wander around the back roads of Brittany without any clear idea of where she was. Obviously the satnav would eventually get her to her destination, but she and Gavin had once had a dodgy experience in Italy where the satnav in their rented car had chosen to bring them down some almost impassable local roads to reach their hotel when there was a perfectly good main-road alternative. (Afterwards she'd worked out it was because they'd selected 'shortest route' in the preferences. The local roads had certainly been shorter, but in Deira's opinion, 'avoid terrifying routes' should have been an option too.)

She double-clicked on the map and brought up hotel suggestions for Paris. She didn't want her journey around the French capital to be a hair-raising attempt to find a central hotel, so she looked at possibilities on the outskirts. If her dinner companion, the seemingly imperturbable Grace, was too terrified to drive through the city, Deira reckoned she'd struggle herself. In any event, it wasn't as though she was a first-time visitor and needed to be in the centre. She'd been to Paris twice before with Gavin. On those occasions they'd taken the Métro from the airport to their chic boutique hotel. Staying outside the Périphérique would mean she could take the Métro again at first, and get her bearings before throwing herself at the mercy of the traffic.

Am I utterly bonkers to want to drive around one of the most chaotic cities in the world just because of a forty-year-old song? she asked herself. When I know there are plenty of things I can do no matter what age I am? What the hell is wrong with me?

But of course there was still one thing it was likely she'd never get the opportunity to do. And it was the most important thing in the world.

Out of nowhere, the tears came again.

Chapter 7

Dublin to New York: 5,112 km

Like Deira, Grace Garvey also had a cabin on Deck 8, which meant that she too had an outside balcony and a small seating area. After dinner, she'd spent some time on the balcony, but the chilly wind had driven her back inside, and now she was sitting at the low table, Ken's laptop open in front of her.

She was looking at the eight documents again, clicking on them one by one and shaking her head each time they asked for a password. She was torn between her desire to work it out and a quite separate desire to completely ignore Ken and his stupid documents and head straight for their apartment in the south of Spain without any palaver. It was about half an hour's drive from Cartagena, the name on the last folder.

But he'd got inside her head, that was the problem. He'd always been good at getting inside her head.

So she stayed looking at the computer screen and eventually turned her attention to the folder titled *Nantes*. Her initial guess at a password had been the date of their wedding anniversary, thinking it was the most likely answer, but no matter which way she entered it – numerically, with text, or a combination of both – she continued to get a 'password

54

incorrect' message. She felt her irritation with her late husband increase at every failed attempt to unlock the document, and imagined Ken's exasperation at her failure. He would have told her to think, she knew. He was always telling her to think. Use your head, not your heart, he'd say. Stop making mad, emotionally charged decisions.

She'd tried desperately hard, particularly over the last couple of years, not to make emotionally charged decisions, although his assessment of her approach was flawed. It was never as emotionally charged as he believed. But it wasn't based on pure logic either. She often told him that a man like him, who read so much, should be more in tune with feelings than he was. And he would say that it was precisely because he'd read so widely that he understood the disastrous effects of unfettered feelings. That was why he liked his life to be determined by reason. But not all the time, he'd add with a smile, because I married you, didn't I, Hippolyta, which was definitely emotion not logic.

Had he regretted that? And had his final decision been emotional or logical? She wished she knew.

She turned back to the documents. There had to be *something* she hadn't tried yet.

'You idiot,' she muttered as she got another 'password incorrect' message. She wasn't sure if she was talking to herself or to her husband. 'If you wanted me to solve this, if it's as important as you want me to believe, then why did you make it so bloody hard?'

Because he'd loved mysteries, she supposed. And riddles. And codes. After he'd cut back on his academic workload, he'd taken up setting crossword puzzles for the professional journal he subscribed to. He liked to make them as difficult as possible. After all, he told her, his peers were clever people. He had to pose a worthwhile challenge to them.

'But not annoy them too much, surely,' she'd said. 'You want them to be able to finish it, don't you?'

'Eventually,' he'd replied. 'But not immediately. I don't believe in instant gratification.'

She'd never been able to finish one of his crosswords. In fact she was triumphant if she solved more than a couple of the clues correctly. Now she had eight to work out and no idea how she was going to go about it.

Were we completely incompatible? she wondered, as she continued to enter a variety of dates into the password bar. Was our entire marriage based on him being super-intelligent and me being super-thick?

She thumped the keyboard, to no effect. She knew she wasn't stupid. But there was a difference between her intelligence and Ken's. She was life-clever. Competent at resolving issues and conflicts. Competent at getting things done. He was – had been – intellectually clever. Which was very different.

She'd known that from the start.

Grace Garvey had met Ken Harrington on her first transatlantic flight from Dublin to New York. Transatlantic was a promotion for her and she'd worked hard not to show her nervousness as she greeted the passengers with a confident 'good morning' and a pleasant smile so that they felt personally welcomed on board.

She'd noticed him initially because he didn't have his boarding card ready when he arrived at the door to the plane. If there was anything that was guaranteed to put a passenger in Grace's bad books it was not having their boarding card ready and consequently holding everyone else up as they searched through everything they possessed to find it.

As he tried his inside jacket pockets and then the battered leather satchel that was slung over his shoulder, she reminded herself that he could be one of the many people who were heading to the States in search of work that simply wasn't there in Ireland, and that he might be distracted and upset, the boarding card the least of his worries. She had sympathy for the emigrants, who she normally identified straight away – young men and women with resigned expressions on their faces. But Ken didn't have their broken air of despair. He was quietly confident, if somewhat distracted over the disappearance of the boarding card, and he frowned and rubbed his beard in frustration while he wondered aloud where it could be. Unlike his hair, which was dark brown, the beard was liberally sprinkled with fiery red.

'Perhaps in the pocket of your jeans?' she suggested.

'Oh God, yes. Sorry.' He found and handed her the boarding card. 'I'm not good on details,' he added.

She bit back her riposte that the boarding card wasn't a detail and directed him to his seat before turning her attention to the queue of passengers behind him.

When everyone was finally boarded and the plane was being pushed back from the stand, she did her walk through the cabin to make sure that seat belts were fastened and table trays up. She generally divided the passengers into two categories. Those who buckled up as soon as they took their seats and who watched the safety demonstration intently before checking out their nearest escape route; and those who rebelled by not bothering to do either and who sighed theatrically when she asked them to fasten their belt and secure the tray in the seat-back in front of them.

Ken Harrington, seated in 35D, was a rebel, having neither fastened his belt nor put up his table tray, on which he'd propped a large bound manuscript that he was studying intently from behind his black-rimmed glasses. He didn't respond when she first spoke to him, and she had to tap him on the shoulder to get his attention.

He looked up at her with big brown eyes that in other circumstances might have melted her heart. But she needed to complete the cabin check and she didn't have the time or the patience for rebellious passengers.

'Seat belt,' she said. 'Table tray.'

'Huh?'

'Seat belt. Table tray.'

'Oh. Right. Sorry.'

'Thank you, sir.'

'I suppose I should be grateful to have Hippolyta looking after me so assiduously.' He put the manuscript into the seat pocket in front of him and winked.

She glanced at her name badge, even though she knew it said 'Grace Garvey'.

'Hippolyta was an Amazon queen,' he said. 'You remind me of her.'

A smart-arse as well as everything else, she thought.

The broad smile he suddenly flashed at her was genuine, and this time her heart did melt a little. 'I really am sorry,' he said. 'I get caught up in stuff, you see.'

'I understand,' she told him. 'But you have to listen to the instructions of the cabin crew. It's for your own safety.'

'Of course, Hippolyta,' he said.

'My name is Grace.' She touched her badge. 'If there's anything I can do to make your flight more comfortable, don't hesitate to ask.' And then she continued down the cabin.

She'd half expected him to be one of those demanding passengers who spent their time pressing the call bell, but he stayed engrossed in the manuscript for most of the seven hours it took to get to New York. It was only when she came around to check the cabin for landing that he stopped her and asked if she'd like to meet him for a coffee while he was in the city.

She looked at him in astonishment.

'If you've nothing better to do,' he added.

'Thank you for the invitation,' she replied when she'd recovered her composure. 'But I'll be overnighting with the crew and heading back tomorrow.'

'I'd like to see you again,' he said. 'Perhaps after your next flight?'

'I'm not an Amazon queen,' she told him. 'And I doubt I'm your type.'

'I'd like to think you were my type, but I accept I might be punching above my weight.' He reached into his pocket and took out a dog-eared business card, which he handed to her. 'Still, I'd be grateful if you'd consider it.'

She looked at the card and knew that she was very definitely not a woman that Kenneth Harrington BA, MA, MPhil (Dublin) would be interested in. And that she'd be far too intimidated by his educational qualifications to want to spend time in his company either.

'I hope you have a great stay in New York,' she said, giving him her professional smile and putting his card in her jacket pocket before turning to the next passenger.

Naturally she didn't call him. She wasn't entirely convinced that he hadn't been teasing her the whole time. And she hadn't been brought up to phone men she didn't really know. So before she went to bed that night, she threw the card in the trash and forgot about him.

She sometimes wondered if it was fate that put him on her flight again four months later. At first she didn't recognise him, because the red-flecked beard had gone and his previously unruly mop of brown hair had been tapered at both sides while left curly on top, giving him a younger, more up-to-date appearance.

'Hippolyta,' he said as he showed her the boarding card already in his hand. 'You never called.'

'Welcome on board, Mr Harrington,' she said. 'It's good to see you again.'

'Your silence broke my heart,' he told her.

'Seat 37C,' she told him. 'Have a nice flight.'

The return from New York to Dublin was overnight. Ken pressed the call bell once the cabin lights had been dimmed and the passengers were trying to sleep.

'I was pretty sure you wouldn't get in touch,' he said when she asked what she could do for him. 'Although I'd kind of hoped you would. I was going to try to find you but I was too nervous. You're so beautiful, you see. You have all the power.'

'I find it hard to believe that I could possibly make you nervous,' said Grace.

'A particularly beautiful woman is a source of terror,' said Ken.

She smiled involuntarily.

'I could pretend I said that first, but it was Jung,' he told

60

her. 'He also said that as a rule, a beautiful woman is a terrible disappointment.'

'I'm sorry if I've terrorised you or disappointed you,' said Grace.

'Your beauty terrorises me. The only disappointment is that you didn't call. And I really would like to have coffee with you.'

'I don't know that I'd be interesting enough to have coffee with,' she said.

'You totally would be.'

'We'll see.'

Before he left, she gave him her number.

Two days later, he called her.

He wasn't as intimidating as she'd expected, but he was very sure of himself.

He'd gone to the States, he said, as part of an exchange programme with an American professor. In New York, he'd shared his thoughts about the influences of Greek mythology on modern literature, while his counterpart discussed European influences on American novelists.

Grace told him that her favourite novelists were Maeve Binchy and Rosamunde Pilcher and she couldn't honestly think there was much Greek influence there for him to talk about. He said that he'd never heard of either of them but that she should read the great American novelists. Everything you needed to know about life, he said, could be learned from Fitzgerald, Hemingway and Steinbeck.

'I read *The Great Gatsby* in school,' she said. 'I hated it and all the characters in it. But Maeve and Rosamunde write about life and love, so I think I have the bases covered.'

'Oh, Hippolyta.' Ken took her hand in his. 'I have so much to teach you.'

The weird thing, she thought now, was that he did teach her to appreciate things that she didn't necessarily like, and she did fall in love with him too, even though he was her polar opposite in so many ways. Because beneath the arrogant intellect, Ken was a good man. Even if he hadn't always put his family before his career, he was still a thoughtful father and a faithful husband. Perhaps he'd pushed the children a little too much, and perhaps he hadn't always taken Grace as seriously as she would have liked, but they'd made it work, and she missed him.

She particularly missed him because she needed him to unlock this stupid folder.

It was almost eleven thirty, and she knew that disembarkation would start at around seven in the morning. She needed to get some sleep. But first she had a task to complete, one that could only be done under cover of darkness.

She opened her carry-on bag and took out the cylindrical cardboard tube. The pattern on it was of the moon and the stars over a midnight-blue sea. It had been the most appropriate available. She opened the door to the patio and stepped outside. The air was significantly cooler now and she felt goose bumps along her arms.

She shivered and leaned over the rail, looking in both directions to see if anyone else seemed to be outside. But no one was daft enough to be standing out in the cold. She held the tube in her right hand and raised her arm as high as she could. It was important that she get a bit of distance. Then she took a deep breath and threw it.

There were notices all over the ship telling passengers not

to throw anything into the sea. But the tube was biodegradable. And so were its contents. So she didn't feel too badly about it. It might not have been exactly what he'd had in mind, but it was the best she could do.

She stayed outside for another minute.

She didn't cry.

Chapter 8

Roscoff, France: 53.8006°N 4.0694°W

Deira had expected the movement of the ship to lull her to sleep, but the constant rocking had the opposite effect and she was awake at five thirty when the ship-wide announcement that they would shortly be arriving at Roscoff was made. She'd just finished dressing after a quick shower when a steward arrived with her Continental breakfast, and she gave thanks that booking the most expensive cabin meant that it had been brought to her and she didn't have to face the excited holidaymakers in the restaurant again.

As she sipped the strong, aromatic coffee, her phone beeped with three alerts in quick succession. She froze, the cup halfway to her mouth, then replaced it carefully on the saucer and checked the messages.

They were all from her Irish service provider, detailing roaming and data charges outside her package. She exhaled slowly. There was nobody who should be trying to contact her at this hour on a Sunday morning, but the beeps had reminded her that there would still be a reckoning for what she'd done.

She didn't care.

She finished her coffee, but she was no longer hungry, so

she wrapped one of the buttery croissants in a paper napkin and put it in her bag. She planned to stop at motorway services on her journey, but she wasn't sure how long it would be before her first break and reckoned it might be useful to have something to snack on until then.

Another announcement informed passengers that they would shortly be able to access their cars. Once again, Deira chose the stairs rather than the lifts to get to the car deck, where many people were already standing beside their vehicles. They were mostly young families with slightly harassed mothers keeping an eye on their children, and fathers engrossed in making sure that the containers on the car roofs and bicycles attached to the backs were securely fastened.

A pregnant woman with a toddler in her arms walked to the SUV in the lane beside Deira. She strapped the toddler into his seat and rubbed her back before getting into the car herself. A couple of minutes later her husband arrived with a bottle of water, which he handed to her before kissing her lightly on the forehead.

That could have been me, Deira thought, as she looked at the woman.

It should have been me.

It should have been us.

But it was far too late for that.

It was about twenty minutes after the huge doors at the stern of the ship had been opened and disembarkation had commenced before the lane of cars that Grace was in began to move. Even though it took time, and patience with the process was necessary, she'd always liked the efficiency of how it was done. She slid the gear lever in the Lexus to the drive position and moved slowly forward.

The hazy clouds had begun to dissipate while the passengers had been waiting below deck, and the weak rays of sunshine were becoming stronger. Grace took her sunglasses out of the glove compartment and put them on, knowing that for the first part of the drive at least, she would be travelling eastwards into the glare.

She continued to follow the cars ahead of her out of the port and onto the local road that cut through countryside dotted with brick houses and slate roofs. Although it was a few years since she'd last done the trip, the same hoardings urging arriving visitors to check out the supermarkets with their cut-price wine and cheese offerings lined the route. She recalled going to one of them on their return from a holiday in Saint-Malo, loading up the back of their estate car with boxes of Merlot (for Ken), Chablis (for her) and a selection of cheeses (for both of them).

A wave of nostalgia almost overcame her and she gripped the steering wheel more tightly. She was suddenly uncertain about the trip and her reasons for doing it. She was unsure if she could manage it on her own after all. She'd told herself that her cabin-crew days had accustomed her to travelling on her own, but of course she hadn't been on her own back then. She'd been with the team. And hundreds of passengers. This was entirely different.

After about half an hour, the procession of cars, camper vans and caravans from the ferry began to string out, while the sun had risen enough to reflect brightly off the nearby River Penzé. The sight of the cheerfully painted boats anchored along its length banished Grace's self-doubt, and she recalled the times in the past when she and Ken had hired one. She'd never felt a hundred per cent comfortable on the water, but Ken and the children enjoyed sailing, and he'd been competent, if not accomplished, in a boat. He used to tease her about her dislike of them, saying that planes were a far more dangerous mode of travel, something she always refuted with an army of statistics. If he were beside her now, she thought, he'd start talking about hiring a boat. She could almost hear his voice in her ear.

'It'll be fun, Hippo. The children love it. You'll love it too if you give it a chance.'

She leaned forward and switched on the audio system. Classical music filled the car.

She breathed out.

Relaxed.

Deira was wondering at what point she could drop the roof of the Audi. She glanced at the temperature gauge and saw that despite the fact that the sky ahead was now cloudless and the sun was shining brightly, it was still only 17 degrees outside, so she decided to wait until she spotted a good service station. Or perhaps when the gauge reached 20 degrees. Whichever happened first.

She'd left the extra breakfast croissant, still wrapped in the paper napkin, on the seat beside her, and she nibbled on it as she drove, loving the sounds of the unfamiliar towns as she read them on the signposts. Henvic, Saint-Brieuc, Montauban-de-Bretagne . . . As she passed each one she felt freer and more light-hearted, even though everything that had weighed her down for the last couple of months was still there. Nothing had really changed. But right now, at nine o'clock on a bright Sunday morning, she felt as though it had.

Her phone rang, startling her so much that she dropped the remains of the croissant and allowed the car to veer towards the outside lane. An enormous camper van, with the brand name Vengeance, gave her a long blast of its horn as it sped by. There were three pink children's bicycles on the back.

'Asshole,' she muttered as her heartbeat returned to normal.

She pushed the button on the steering wheel to answer the phone, but she was too late; the caller had already disconnected. It couldn't be anything important, she told herself, because she hadn't recognised the number when it had flashed up on the screen in front of her. So she had nothing to worry about. Nothing at all. Not yet.

She increased her speed by another ten kilometres an hour and set the cruise control.

Grace had relaxed into the drive from Roscoff, the memories of previous journeys still crystal clear in her mind. In the early days she'd been in charge of the map-reading, something she was good at, even if Ken occasionally ignored her instructions because he thought there was a better route. In the later years, they'd used the satnav, but Ken still sometimes ignored its advice and took roads he thought might be quicker. (He never had found better or quicker routes, but he used to claim that whichever way he'd chosen was an easier drive, even when it wasn't.)

She dropped her speed a little so that she stayed at a comfortable distance from the Range Rover in front. She was happy to drive at a steady 100 kph, even though the limit was 130 and there was a constant stream of other cars over-taking her on the left. She wasn't in a hurry. She didn't want to arrive at her hotel too early. She wouldn't be able to check in before two, so she might as well take her time and savour the beauty of Brittany's rolling hills and green meadows, which reminded her so much of Cork and Ireland.

Ken had always liked Brittany. He'd liked the coastal scenery with its deep inlets forming natural harbours that made sailing and related activities so popular. He liked the Breton culture and art, and invariably brought copies of Jules Verne to read when they were on holiday there because the famous writer had been born in the region.

'Quite the genius, Verne,' he used to say when they'd reached whatever campsite they were staying in and had got themselves settled. 'Sadly, none of those sci-fi writers of the past realised that technology would become miniaturised. Their robots were enormous metal devices with wires and valves rather than microchips. But what imagination all the same!'

Ken had started writing his own novel on one of their holidays. He told her it was a reflection on family life, which worried her slightly, but she became less concerned the more time he spent on it, because she doubted it would ever get finished, let alone published. She asked to read it a number of times, but he always shook his head, telling her that the only people qualified to pass judgement on his work were professionals. She bit back the comment that the most impor-tant people who'd pass judgement would be his readers. In the end, she simply left him to it, not interrupting him when he retreated into his study to write or when he brought foolscap notebooks on subsequent holidays and covered them in his scrawling script.

It took him five years to complete. And it was another five years before it was published.

'Excellent reviews,' he told her after the first month, although sales were low and, from her perspective, when she'd finally been allowed to read the novel, the female characters highly improbable.

Nevertheless, he'd achieved a lifetime dream, and it allowed him to update his online biography to say 'critically acclaimed author'. Whenever Grace spoke about him, she called him a critically acclaimed author too. Their marriage might not have been perfect, but she had always supported him. And it had endured.

That wasn't something many people could say these days.

Sometimes enduring was just as important as loving.

Maybe more.

Chapter 9

Loire-Atlantique, France: 48.1173°N 1.6778°W

After almost two hours of driving, and with the signposts showing that she wasn't far from Rennes, Deira pulled into a big service station off the N12. The almost sleepless night and early-morning start had caught up with her, and as well as wanting to drop the roof of the convertible, she needed a bathroom break. She could do with another coffee too, she thought, even though she'd finished the pot on the ship earlier.

She filled the petrol tank before going to the café. Many of the customers were other passengers who'd made the crossing; she recognised the family who'd been beside her on the car deck, as well as an older couple dressed in identical yellow cagoules. And there were plenty of Irish accents ordering coffee and pastries. After using the bathroom, Deira got a tray and selected an individual tarte tatin before asking for a large Americano. She took her purchases to the counter that ran along the wall of the café, where she sat on a high stool.

The coffee was strong and the pastry delicate. Deira felt herself relax again as she began to tune in and out of the conversations around her.

'We're nearly there,' a father was assuring his young son, who'd been demanding to know how much further they had to go. 'You're really going to love it.'

'I'm sick of the car,' said the boy. 'We've been in it forever.'

'We'll soon be at the campsite,' his mother promised.

'I hate this holiday.'

'You'll have a great time,' his dad assured him. 'Do you want to get something from the machine?'

'OK.' The boy's expression brightened.

'I'm sorry.' The father turned to his wife. 'You can ban all sweets once we get there. But in the meantime, it's the only way of keeping sane.'

How would she and Gavin have coped with a small boy who was bored? Deira wondered. She would have been well prepared in advance with books and games to keep him amused, but would she have caved in on sweets or biscuits or other rubbish to keep him quiet? She accepted that children got fed up in a car. So there might have been tears and fretfulness and arguments. All the same, she was sure she would have managed.

But there were no children to take into account, and Gavin had planned a series of exclusive hotels for this holiday. Chateaux and country houses, no campsites. Yes, I want to do Brittany again, he'd said, but no, I don't want to rough it. I did the camping thing once and that was enough. Nothing but the best this time. Leave it all to me. So she had. But then he'd dropped his bombshell, and there was no more talk of spending idyllic nights in French chateaux.

He'd said he was sorry.

And that, pretty much, was that.

Her fingers tightened around the waxed cup and the coffee

72

almost sloshed over the side with the pressure. She willed herself to relax once more. But the rage still balled inside her, hard and unforgiving.

She took her phone from her bag. The missed-call notification was still on the screen, and even as she looked at it, the phone rang again with the same caller ID that she hadn't recognised earlier.

'Yes?' Her tone was cautious.

'*Bonjour!* It's me.'

'Tillie!' She sighed with relief. 'What number are you ringing from?'

'Long, boring story about smashing my phone last night and having to borrow one,' said her friend. 'I thought I'd call and see how you were doing. I missed you earlier.'

'That was you ringing me at the crack of dawn?' exclaimed Deira. 'You scared the life out of me; I'd no idea who it was.'

'I went for an early-morning jog,' explained Tillie. 'Sorry if I startled you.'

'I thought it might be . . . Well, I'd no idea who it might be,' said Deira. 'But it's lovely to hear from you.'

'So . . . how are you? Are you OK to talk while you're driving?'

'I'm grand. The weather is gorgeous. And you've caught me while I'm having a coffee at a service station, so it's fine to talk.'

'How much longer to Paris?' asked Tillie. 'Have you decided where you're going to stay?'

'Not yet,' replied Deira. She watched some more passengers from the ferry walk to another enormous camper van. She'd never considered a camper van holiday. She still wouldn't.

73

But at least their owners had ready-made accommodation. 'I was looking at TripAdvisor last night. You know me, hopeless at choosing anywhere.'

'Pick the first place that doesn't look like the Bates Motel,' advised her friend. 'You can always change after the first night. Any word from you-know-who?'

'No,' said Deira. 'And hopefully I won't hear from him until he realises the car is gone.'

'Maybe not even then,' said Tillie.

'He'll figure it out eventually. But feck it, Tillie, we were going to come here in this car together. Why shouldn't I take it?"'

'No reason at all.' Tillie gave the same assurance she'd given from the moment Deira had told her about her plan. 'I was wondering, though – he doesn't have some kind of webcam alarm on it, does he?'

'Is there such a thing?' Deira thought of Gavin tracking her and felt sick.

'I dunno,' replied Tillie. 'The world is full of so many gadgets, it's not impossible, but you would've seen it, I'm sure. Anyhow, I sent you my most positive vibes this morning, so I promise everything is going to be fine. I went to my favourite spot in the woods behind my house and drenched you in sunlight and good thoughts.'

'Thanks.' Even though Deira didn't believe that Tillie's positivity would have the slightest effect on her life, she was grateful for her friend's unconditional support.

'I sent thoughts that you'd be happy and maybe meet someone but not do anything mad.'

And there it was, thought Deira. Tillie's inevitable warning.

'If there's an opportunity, I'll take it,' she said. 'I don't have that many, after all. I'm thirty-fecking-nine, Tillie. I'm positively geriatric.'

'You're not, you know you're not. You're a strong, confident woman—'

'Ha!' Deira's snort interrupted her.

'You are. So have a great holiday,' Tillie added. 'Just . . . you know . . . take care.'

'I might check out Airbnbs around here instead of hotels in Paris.' Deira changed the subject.

'Where were you meant to be staying originally?' asked Tillie.

'There was a lot of talk about gorgeous country houses and chateaux,' said Deira. 'But he hadn't got around to making any bookings. Which has turned out to be a good thing, because it gives me freedom.'

'In that case, why don't you forget about Paris and go somewhere more relaxing,' suggested her friend. 'After all, France is a huge country, with lots of nice places you probably wouldn't get to if you didn't have a car. So take advantage of it.'

'I should have thought about it before I left,' said Deira. 'It was all a bit chaotic on my part.'

'I went to Marseilles once,' Tillie said. 'That was lovely. Or how about Lyons, maybe? Or Toulouse?'

'Marseille is on the south coast, you klutz,' said Deira. 'It'd take me a full day to get there. Maybe more.'

'You have all the time in the world,' Tillie pointed out. 'No reason why you couldn't go. Or drive anywhere else, for that matter. You could do a grand tour.'

'A grand tour?' Deira laughed.

'You've nearly three weeks,' said Tillie. 'One way or another, you wouldn't have spent it all in Paris, would you? I know you earn a decent wedge, Deira, but you'd be bankrupt by the end of it. All those chic shops!'

Deira laughed. 'I guess so.'

'There's always Cannes,' added Tillie. 'That's not far from Marseilles. You could disport yourself with the movie and yachting set.'

'Gosh, yes, the film festival is around now, isn't it?' said Deira. 'Although that'd probably mean everywhere is booked up or out-of-my-league expensive. Still, I might give it a look.'

'Make the most of your time. Stay positive,' said Tillie. 'And go with the flow.'

'Until the police come looking for me thanks to Gavin's secret webcam.'

'I wish I hadn't mentioned it. I'm sure it's fine. You'll be fine.'

'You're a good friend,' said Deira. 'And I'm sorry I've been a bit . . . well, distant lately.'

'I don't blame you for that one little bit,' said Tillie. 'You needed space. Now you've got it, so make the most of it.'

'I'll do my best.' Deira glanced around. Most of the people she'd identified as being from the ferry had left now, and the newer arrivals were French families.

'Anyway, keep in touch and drive safely,' Tillie said.

'I will. Thanks again.'

Her coffee had gone cold. Deira ordered another and brought it back to the counter, where she opened her iPad and began looking at her maps again. She had two initial choices, she thought as she studied it. Head east to Paris as she'd originally intended. Or turn south towards Bordeaux, from where she could think about Tillie's suggestions of Toulouse, Marseille and Cannes. Her friend was right – it didn't matter how far away they were; she had plenty of time.

Looking at the map more closely, she saw that Toulouse, Lyons and Marseilles formed a large triangle, and Toulouse was on the same road as Bordeaux. So she could stop at Bordeaux and then continue on. In fact there were a few other towns on that southern road that might be nice to visit. La Rochelle, for example. Or Biarritz. Hadn't Biarritz been a jet-set kind of place in the sixties? Perhaps it still had a touch of glamour. Perhaps she might find what she was looking for there.

Right, she thought. Change of plan. South it is.

She got up from the counter, picked up her bag and the takeaway cup and walked towards the exit, still harnessing the power of positive thinking.

The power of positive thinking didn't last very long.

A couple of seconds later, she was face down on the floor of the café, her coffee cup spiralling across the tiles. She'd no idea what had happened. One moment she was walking towards the automatic door, the next the ground was rushing up to meet her.

'Are you OK?'

She was glad that it was an Irish accent she could hear as she tried, and failed, to turn herself over.

'Take it easy.' The owner of the voice was kneeling beside her. 'You took a terrible tumble there.'

She recognised him. He was the man she'd spoken to on the deck of the ferry the night before.

Did meeting him again mean something?

Was it a sign?

She began to struggle upright, but a sharp pain in her side made her stop.

'Take it easy,' he repeated.

'What happened?'

'You tripped,' he said. 'It was like it happened in slow motion. You seemed to go up into the air and then come back down with a terrific thump. And you didn't manage to put your hands out to stop yourself in time. You're lucky you didn't smack right down on your face.'

'I guess so.' Deira winced and gently rubbed her side as she finally succeeded in sitting up. The man had been joined by some of the café's staff, including a young woman whose badge said 'Chantelle' and who asked her, in English, if she needed medical assistance.

'No,' said Deira. 'Thank you. I'm OK.' But she winced again.

'It was an awful fall,' said the man.

'There was nothing on the floor for you to fall over.' Chantelle, who seemed to be the manager, looked anxious.

The man shrugged. 'There could have been a small spillage.'

'We are very careful,' said Chantelle. 'We clean all the time.'

'Don't worry,' Deira said to the younger woman. 'I'm not going to sue you. It was an accident.'

'Can I get you another coffee?' Chantelle asked.

'No thanks,' replied Deira.

'You should have something,' the man told her. 'Give yourself a few minutes before you get back into your car.'

Deira thought for a moment, then nodded. 'A tea, please,' she said.

'Black?'

'Um . . . do you have peppermint?'

'Of course.'

'That would be perfect. Thank you.'

She made an effort to get to her feet, assisted by the man, who supported her as he led her to a table. The knot of people who'd been watching dispersed. Deira released a slow breath and then allowed herself to sit on one of the plastic chairs.

'Are you sure you're all right?' the man asked.

'I'll be fine,' said Deira.

'Would these help?' He reached into the back pocket of his jeans and handed her a strip of foil-wrapped Nurofen.

Deira was about to say that she didn't need them when another sharp pain in her side made her realise that she probably did. After Chantelle had left her with the peppermint tea and a strawberry macaron 'on the house', she swallowed two of the tablets.

'There must have been something on the floor no matter what she says.' The man looked sceptical.

'I didn't see anything,' said Deira. 'And the fact that I went face down makes me think I simply tripped over my own clumsy feet.'

He laughed. 'You don't look clumsy.'

'I can be.' She took a sip of the tea and felt her shoulders relax.

'Have you decided where you're going yet?' he asked.

'Bordeaux,' she replied.

He looked concerned. 'That's another five hours. It's a long drive, especially if you're in pain.'

'Do you know the route?' she asked.

'I've driven it a few times,' he replied. 'It's pleasant enough, but do remember that the French will drive up behind you and expect you to get out of the way if you're in any of the outside lanes. They take no prisoners on the motorways, you know.'

Deira smiled. 'I'll be careful. Are you going that way yourself?'

He shook his head. 'I'm off to Paris.'

If falling had been a sign, perhaps she should abandon her decision to go to Bordeaux and revert to her original plan of driving to Paris instead, thought Deira. And perhaps she could meet up with her knight in shining armour for a drink later. Because bumping into him again had to mean something. Didn't it?

He stood up.

'If you're sure you're all right, I'll be off.'

'I'm much better now,' she told him. 'Honestly. And thanks for looking after me.'

'No problem,' he said. '*Au revoir.*'

'*Au revoir,*' she repeated as he walked away.

Her eyes followed him out of the café and across the car park. He unlocked a medium-sized red van and got in.

It hadn't been a sign.

He still wasn't the one.

It was another fifteen minutes before she returned to her own car. Alone again in the café, her hands had begun to tremble and she'd suddenly felt a lot shakier than she'd done when she'd been insisting she was fine. She told herself it was the coffee that was making her shake, not the shock. But she took her time before leaving.

She grimaced as she slid gingerly into the driver's seat. For someone who'd once prided herself on her insights and competence, she'd turned out to be pretty shit at both. If Gavin were here, he'd laugh at her. But he wasn't.

She blinked back the ever-ready tears as she started the car and flicked to the satnav menu, entering Bordeaux as her destination. It was nearly five hundred kilometres away, and the (still nameless) man from the services was right: the journey would take about five hours. Hopefully, she thought, the Nurofen would keep her pain-free till then.

She rejoined the main road and was so lost in her thoughts as she drove that she was startled when the satnav told her to take the exit towards Nantes and the Atlantic coast route. The sudden command threw her into another spasm of indecision. Paris or Bordeaux. Bordeaux or Paris. Maybe the man she'd met on the boat and in the café *did* matter. Maybe he was important to her future. Maybe she was making another massive mistake. Paris or Bordeaux. Bordeaux or Paris.

At the last minute, she veered to the right and took the off ramp, much to the annoyance of the ancient Renault behind her, whose driver blasted her with a long hoot of the car's horn.

There are no signs, and no man is important to my future, she told herself. I'm going to Bordeaux.

Besides, maybe the man I need is there.

There were fewer Irish-registered cars on her new route, and Deira supposed that most of them had stayed in the more northern parts of Brittany. Staying in Brittany would have been the most sensible choice of all, she thought. But now she was committed to the west coast. In normal circumstances, a five-hour road trip wouldn't have bothered her – she'd often driven to Galway and back, which took about the same amount of time as the journey to Bordeaux – but despite the painkillers, the ache in her side was persistent and tiring.

About forty minutes after leaving Rennes, she pulled into a service station for another break. The heat from the sun, after the air-conditioned comfort of the car, surprised her. She stood with her back to it, allowing the warmth to penetrate her bones, and hoped it was benefiting her poor bruised ribs.

After walking around to stretch her legs, she sat at one of the wooden trestle tables in the grassy area behind the services. Sitting was fine. Nothing hurt when she was sitting.

She took out her phone.

She'd missed a call from Gillian, and realised that her sister had phoned at around the same time as she'd made her previous stop. She hadn't noticed that the slider button on the phone had moved to 'mute'. It must have happened when she fell, she thought, because she hadn't muted it herself. Gill had left a voice message, despite the fact that Deira always told her never to bother, and that sending a text was far more efficient. She hesitated before accessing it, not really wanting to hear anything her sister had to say.

'Hi,' said Gillian. 'There's a slight change of plan about Bex and Dublin. I was going to run it by you, but since I can't get hold of you, I hope it's OK. I'm driving her up myself. She got a call after I talked to you to ask if she could come to the interview tomorrow morning. I have your house key, so I hope you don't mind us staying there tonight. Enjoy your holiday. Bye.'

Deira tapped her fingers on the table, then hit Gill's number.

'Hello,' said Gillian. 'My call went straight to voicemail, so I thought you didn't have a signal.'

'I've stopped for a break. I got your message.'

'Oh, great.'

There was a moment's silence, and Deira suddenly realised that her sister hadn't expected to be called back quite so quickly.

'I was a bit surprised,' she said.

'I had to make a spur-of-the-moment decision,' Gill told her. 'Bex badly wants this job. She's absolutely peppering about the interview. I checked out some B&Bs and hotels, but Dublin prices are extortionate and it seemed ridiculous to shell out all that money when your place was lying idle.'

'And what about her friend?' asked Deira.

'Lydia was able to come today too,' said Gillian.

'So all three of you are planning to stay?'

'It makes so much more sense than a B&B,' said Gill.

Does my sister really think it's perfectly fine to make herself at home in my house? wondered Deira. Or am I the unreasonable one?

'Look, I know it's not ideal from your point of view,' conceded Gillian when Deira stayed silent. 'But this job is important to Bex – and she *is* your god-daughter after all.'

'It's just for tonight?'

'Well, Bex and Lydia had hoped to stay in Dublin for a few days,' said Gillian. 'They wanted to meet up with some friends, do some shopping, you know yourself. I'll probably do a bit of shopping too.'

'In that case, you'll be going back when?'

'A day or two,' said Gillian. 'But don't worry. I'll make sure everything is left in pristine condition.'

'I only have two bedrooms,' Deira said. 'I'm sure you don't want to share with two nineteen-year-olds.'

'Oh, look, I'll use yours,' said Gill. 'I don't mind. We're sisters after all.'

The throb in Deira's ribs turned into a stabbing pain as she inhaled sharply.

'Yes, but—'

'It's good security for you too, having people going in and out.'

Deira knew she wasn't going to win the argument. She never did with Gill.

'OK, but in future you've got to ask me first,' she told her. 'I could have made other arrangements for the house while I'm away.'

'But you didn't.'

'No, but . . .' Deira's voice trailed off. She knew there was no point in continuing the conversation.

'We'll be grand,' Gillian said. 'Have a good time yourself. Drive safely.'

Deira ended the call without saying another word. Her ribs were aching more than ever.

Chapter 10

Loire-Atlantique, France: 47.1987°N 1.6537°W

Despite sticking to a steady 100 kph, Grace arrived far too early at her hotel to check in. The Atlantique, with views over the Loire, was small but friendly – she and Ken had stayed there before, and she presumed that was why he'd booked it again. There were two elements to the building: an old house that contained the reception, dining and bar areas as well as the de luxe suites, plus a small modern wing where most of the bedrooms were located. Ken, extravagant for the first time in his life, had booked her into one of the suites.

Grace parked the Lexus, then strolled to reception, pulling her overnight case behind her. The young receptionist told her she was welcome to leave the case with them and avail herself of any of the hotel services until her room was ready. There was a pool, she told her, and a café if she would like some refreshment. And of course she was welcome to relax in any of the public areas.

Grace thanked her and went to the café, where she ordered tea and a pastry. One of the drawbacks of doing a road trip, she thought, was the amount of snacking it entailed. When she'd been with the airline, she'd felt the pressure to be slim and attractive, and she rarely ate between meals. The old habit of not grazing had stuck with her. Except when she was driving. She was sure that was why she always put on weight during the holidays.

She took an appreciative sip of the tea and then opened Ken's computer. The documents were still neatly arranged on the desktop. Still looking for their passwords. Still urging her to do what Ken wanted. And still making her feel even more stupid than usual.

She closed her eyes and pinched the bridge of her nose. Her late husband was still pulling her strings, even though most of his ashes were now scattered, as he'd wished, in the Celtic Sea. The rest were in the boot of the Lexus, waiting for her arrival in Spain. It seemed somewhat disrespectful to leave them in the car, but she hadn't wanted to pack them in her luggage. All the same, fulfilling Ken's wishes was how she'd persuaded her children that she needed to do this trip.

'You could fly to Murcia with the ashes and hire a car,' Regan told her when she'd said this to her. 'Honestly, Mum, Dad wouldn't have expected you to take the ferry and drive. Not on your own.'

'You're in Argentina on your own,' Grace pointed out.

'Well, yes. That's different, though.'

'Not really,' said Grace. 'Anyhow, I'll be fine.'

'I don't doubt you'll be fine,' Regan said. 'But will you enjoy it?'

Which was an entirely different question. And one to which Grace still didn't know the answer. Along with the passwords.

Before she'd left the previous stop, still riled up about Gill and Bex commandeering her house, Deira had put down the roof so that, Paris or not, she could enjoy the freedom of open-top driving. And if it hadn't been for her aching side, she would have enjoyed it immensely; the sun was high in the sky and it was glorious to speed along the road without feeling insulated from the world around her.

But every bump in what had looked like a very smooth carriageway was now sending a knifing pain through her, and she wasn't sure how much more of it she could take. She wished she'd stopped at the motorway services she'd passed ten minutes earlier, but she'd told herself to keep going. Now she knew she'd have to rest again and reconsider her options.

The next sign on the motorway was for an *aire*, which she'd worked out was a lay-by or camping site. She indicated and pulled into it, parking in one of the spaces beneath the trees. The rustling green leaves provided shelter from the direct sunlight as she sat at the only unoccupied picnic table. Families were eating at the others, while further away, a group of children were playing, chasing each other around a couple of camper vans and an SUV with a large roof box.

Deira remembered her own days of chasing with her best friend, Cecily, who lived two doors down from their home in Galway. Deira had tried to spend as much time as she could in Cecily's house, which always smelled of home baking, and where Mrs Donnelly was ever present. She would sometimes create scenarios in her head that resulted in Mrs Donnelly having to adopt her. She felt that living with her best friend and visiting her dad at weekends would be a much better way to manage things than being constantly ordered around by Gillian, or ignored by Peter. She knew her Dad did his best, but he worked long hours as a sales rep and often left the house early in the mornings, not returning until after seven in the evening. And although Deira was sure Dom O'Brien loved his children, he hadn't been a hands-on father before her mum had passed away, and that didn't change afterwards. His relationship with them had always been remote, and even now, retired and living in a small bungalow in Spiddal, he didn't engage with them very much. He didn't know about her and Gavin. She hadn't told him. He wouldn't have had anything useful to offer on the situation anyhow.

She made a determined effort to push the complications of her life to the back of her mind and opened Google Maps on her phone. Her search for hotels nearby showed there was nothing within a thirty-minute drive, but that wasn't all that surprising. Even though she could hear the sound of cars speeding along the motorway, she was in rural France. So she tapped on the first hotel on the list, which was on the outskirts of Nantes, saw that it had availability and booked a room there and then. It didn't much matter to her what it was like, given that all she wanted was to lie on a bed for a few hours. Hopefully the worst of her pain would be over by the morning and she could resume her journey to Bordeaux.

If, of course, she wasn't arrested for stealing her own car before then.

Grace had abandoned the password-protected documents in favour of finishing *The Sun Also Rises*, although the only reason she was reading it was because it seemed appropriate to bring one of Ken's favourite books on the journey. She'd started it on one of their camping trips years earlier, but had abandoned it saying that she couldn't warm to any of the characters.

'You're obsessed with wanting to like the characters in the books you read,' Ken told her.

'What's wrong with that?' demanded Grace.

'Great literature isn't always about likeability,' Ken said. 'And Hemingway won a Nobel Prize.'

'Maybe because his was the best book around back then,' retorted Grace. 'But there's a lot more to choose from now. Besides,' she added, 'I've read all about him and he doesn't seem to have been a particularly nice character himself.'

'You have to make allowances for his genius,' said Ken.

'Why is it only male geniuses we make allowances for?' she demanded. 'Why can men behave appallingly and we give them a free pass but a woman has to be calm and composed in order not to be dismissed as hysterical no matter how brilliant she might be?'

'I never make those judgements.'

'Not knowingly,' she muttered.

'What's that supposed to mean?'

Grace said nothing. She didn't want to start an argument with Ken because she never won arguments with him. He always managed to tie her into linguistic knots so that by the end she was agreeing with him even though she didn't really. It was hard work, she often thought, being married to a college professor who could turn everything she said into the opposite of what she meant.

But now, even though she was still finding the book more hard work than pleasure, one line had struck home and made her think that maybe Ken had had a point, and old Ernest wasn't quite as bad as she'd first thought.

You can't get away from yourself by moving from one place to another.

Was getting away from herself what she was trying to do? wondered Grace. Or was she trying to get away from Ken? Not that she could, of course, with his open laptop on the table in front of her and his ashes in the boot. Dammit, he'd planned all this. More of it than she'd ever expected. And he'd betrayed her. Other people could say what they liked, but Grace saw it for what it was. A massive betrayal of everything they'd had together. He'd freed himself from her yet somehow she wasn't able to let go because she was here doing what he'd wanted just like she always had.

Men were bastards.

Even the ones you loved.

Especially the ones you loved.

Chapter 11

Nantes, France: 47.2184°N 1.5536°W

The satnav directed Deira to her chosen hotel on the outskirts of the city. The view over the river was the only exceptional thing about it, she thought, but that didn't matter. It was nothing more than a pit stop for the night. A pit stop that many others seemed to have chosen too, as there were no available spaces in front of the main building and she had to park under a wooden pergola a little further away.

She winced as she hauled her large suitcase as well as her overnight bag out of the boot. She might only be staying for one night, but she needed a change of clothes, and as the temperature was rising the further south she travelled, she wanted to wear something lighter the following day.

'*Oui, madame*, you booked online,' said the receptionist when Deira arrived at the desk. 'I am sorry, but you are early.'

'That's OK,' said Deira. 'I'll hang around till the room is ready.'

She left her cases with the concierge and sat down cautiously on a sofa near the window. Looking around, she reckoned she'd been lucky to get a room at short notice, because the hotel was busy. Most of the guests seemed to be French families and businesspeople. She didn't know if the area was popular with holidaymakers; she didn't know anything about it. She could be anywhere. Maybe it would be a good idea to look at her exact location on a map.

She'd just taken out her iPad and was accessing the Wi-Fi when she heard someone say her name. Her heart did a triple somersault and she felt it pound in her ears. But it was a woman's voice. Gavin hadn't somehow turned up, spitting fury at her, thanks to Tillie's mythical webcam tracker.

'How nice to see you again.' Grace Garvey stood in front of her, smiling yet with an expression of surprise. 'I thought you were going to Paris.'

It was nice to see Grace too, thought Deira, although she'd assumed the older woman would've wanted to make better progress in her journey through France and Spain. But then perhaps, like her, she wasn't in too much of a hurry.

'Change of plan,' she said. 'And then I was sort of forced into stopping here.'

'Really?' Grace looked at her enquiringly.

'Yes.' As Deira gave her a brief summary of her mishap in the service station, Grace's expression changed to one of sympathy and she sat down opposite her.

'Oh, how horrible for you,' she said. 'Hurting your ribs is always so painful. Are you badly bruised?'

'Not that I could see,' replied Deira. 'It's usually internal, though, isn't it?'

Grace nodded. 'Have you taken anything?'

'Painkillers.'

'I have arnica,' Grace said. 'I'm not sure how well it'll work on bruised ribs, but it won't do you any harm.'

'Oh, I couldn't—'

'Of course you could!' Grace opened the wheelie case she

had with her and took out a large cosmetic bag containing a selection of painkillers, an antiseptic spray, plasters, stomach tablets, antihistamines and eye drops as well as half a dozen small tubes of cream.

'This one,' she said, handing one of the tubes to Deira, who was looking at Grace's pharmaceutical supplies with a mixture of bafflement and admiration.

'I'm not a complete hypochondriac, but I always pack for every eventuality,' explained Grace. 'Comes from having travelled a lot with children. If something can go wrong, it does, but at least with the kids there's very little that can't be cured by a sticking plaster and some ice cream.'

Deira laughed and then held her side.

'Keep the arnica,' said Grace. 'I rarely use it these days, but it became a staple after my son was born and I can't help including it. Fionn was an absolute devil as a child, into everything. If there was a tree he could climb and fall out of, he did. If there was a stone he could bump into, he found it. He was a walking disaster. Probably still is, but he's not my problem any more.'

'I'm sure there's a pharmacy nearby and I can get some myself,' said Deira.

'Probably,' agreed Grace. 'But why put yourself through looking for one? Though if you do want to go into the town centre, it's about five kilometres.'

'Maybe later,' said Deira. 'At the moment, lying down is my priority.'

Grace nodded. 'Have a snooze as soon as your room is ready.'

'I'm not usually good at sleeping in the middle of the day,' admitted Deira.

'A nap is good for you,' Grace said. 'It restores your brain power.'

'I'm not sure I have any brain power to restore. If I'd been watching what I was doing, I wouldn't have slipped in the first place.'

'Accidents can happen.'

'I know. I seem to be prone to them lately, though.' Which was true, Deira thought. Ever since she'd split with Gavin, she'd been uncharacteristically clumsy. And stupid. And forgetful. It was as though when he walked out on her he'd taken part of her with him. And he was holding on to it so that she wasn't functioning properly any more.

'Are you having problems sleeping generally?' asked Grace.

'God, no, I'm fine.' Deira was suddenly afraid she was talking to a doctor or nurse who was feeling forced into giving her a free diagnosis. 'My life's been a bit up and down lately, that's all. Resulting in me being all over the place.'

At that moment the receptionist walked over to them and said that Grace's room in the old house was available and that Deira's, in the new wing, would be ready in five minutes.

The two women looked at each other hesitantly, but it was Grace who spoke first, surprising Deira by asking if she'd like to have dinner with her later. Almost immediately she added that it was merely a suggestion and that Deira should feel free to ignore it. Deira then surprised herself by saying that she didn't have plans and it would be fun to meet up.

'Shall I see you back here around six thirty?' asked Grace. 'We can decide then what we'd like to do.'

'Perfect.'

Deira watched Grace walk across the reception area. Tall. Beautiful. Confident. Married with children. Possibly even grandchildren.

She wanted to be her.

Grace had been taken aback to see her table companion of the night before at the hotel reception, but she was even more taken aback at herself for saying hello rather than hurrying away so that she wouldn't be noticed. As for suggesting dinner that evening – she didn't know what had come over her. She wasn't one for suggesting things. She normally waited for them to be suggested to her. Besides, the road trip wasn't a journey on which she'd expected, or wanted, to meet new people. And Deira, with her dark, haunting looks and permanently worried expression, hardly promised an evening of light-hearted conversation.

What mad impulse made me do that? she asked herself. Now I'm stuck with something I can't get out of.

She didn't normally act on impulse. Over the years of her marriage to Ken, she'd lost her youthful spontaneity and become a more measured person, weighing courses of action carefully before making decisions and then implementing them. She'd learned to build on the skills she'd gained in dealing with people at the airline company. Like the many passengers who seemed to go into a brain freeze as soon as they stepped on board, Ken had assumed that someone else would sort things out for him. And she always did.

But she hadn't been able to sort out the most important thing, in the end.

She'd let him down.

She could never forgive herself for that.

She couldn't forgive him either.

As soon as she was alone in her room, she took out the laptop again. She worked her way through a selection of memorable dates, names and numbers, but none of them opened the first document. Finally she tried random keys, banging hard on them in her fury.

Password incorrect.

Password incorrect.

Password incorrect.

'Damn you!' she cried. 'Damn you to hell and back! I'm not doing this any more. I'm not!'

She snapped the laptop closed and walked out of the room, slamming the door behind her.

Deira had fallen asleep almost as soon as she lay down, and she was disorientated when she opened her eyes again. Looking at her phone, she saw that it was late afternoon, and although her side still ached, she felt considerably better. She took a long shower, which eased the pain in her ribs, and felt herself relax even more. Afterwards she changed into a pair of cotton trousers and a light T-shirt from her case, swallowed a couple of paracetamol and went downstairs.

The sun was still shining and she took a short stroll around the hotel grounds. But beyond the river in the distance, there was very little to see, so she sat at one of the outdoor tables and scrolled through her phone. There were no further missed calls or messages from Gillian, although Deira's home alarm app had sent a notification that showed the alarm being disarmed a couple of hours earlier, so she knew they'd arrived. Once again she felt a spurt of irritation that Gillian had put her in this position, as well as unease at the idea of her sister sleeping in her bed. She told herself that Gill was right and that as sisters it was perfectly reasonable for her to sleep in Deira's room. But the point was, Deira thought, it wasn't really just her room; it was still hers and Gavin's, no matter what had happened. And Gill staying there was weird. Also – the thought made her shudder – she was pretty sure that even if Gill didn't make a forensic examination of all her possessions, she'd still pull open the drawers in the chest against the bedroom wall, and examine the clothes in her wardrobe, and investigate the contents of the bathroom cabinet. She wouldn't be able to help herself.

I should have been more forceful, thought Deira. I should have said no.

In her professional life she never had the slightest problem saying no, or telling people why an idea wouldn't work. But as soon as Gill opened her mouth, Deira reverted to younger-sister mode, unable to stand up for herself in the face of Gill's strength of personality.

'Nothing I can do now,' she muttered. No point in thinking about it.

She opened her phone and began to scroll through photographs of the French countryside on Instagram, but she couldn't help running over her sister's actions in her head. She rehearsed what she'd say to Gill the next time she saw her, while knowing that she'd forget all of it as soon as they actually met. Irritatingly, she only ever thought of the right words when it was too late.

A shadow fell across the screen and Deira looked up. When

she saw it was Grace, she checked the time on her phone and was horrified to realise it was almost six thirty.

'It's unbelievable how much time you can waste doing nothing useful with your mobile,' she said. 'I didn't realise it was so late.'

'My stomach told me it was time to eat.' Grace smiled at her. 'But if you're busy . . .'

'Like I said, just wasting time.' Deira put the phone, and her thoughts of Gillian, away. 'Have you got a plan for this evening? Did you want to eat here or in town?'

'It's a few years since I was last in Nantes,' said Grace. 'My husband and I went to a nice restaurant near the river that time. It's about ten minutes by car.'

'I don't mind driving,' said Deira. 'I was in agony when I arrived, but I feel a lot better now and I'd like to test how my side feels.'

'If you're sure,' said Grace. 'Because I'm quite happy to drive too.'

'Absolutely.'

The two women walked across to the parked car.

'Nice wheels,' said Grace as she looked at the Audi.

'I know,' said Deira in a brittle tone that startled Grace. But then she smiled and said it was a joy to drive, before asking Grace if she had an address for the restaurant so she could put it in the satnav.

'I looked it up on Google Maps,' Grace replied. 'I'll direct you.'

It was nice to have someone in the passenger seat beside her, thought Deira. It wasn't that she couldn't cope on her own, but it was good to be able to chat. And Grace was chatty without being overpowering, telling her about the last time she'd stayed at the Hotel Atlantique with her husband on their way back from their apartment.

'You used to drive from Dublin to Spain as well as doing your camping holidays?' Deira said. 'You must love being on the road.'

'I quite enjoy the trip,' agreed Grace. 'But neither of us was crazy about taking the car into strange cities. That's why we usually stayed in out-of-town hotels. Actually, it's not the driving through the cities I mind – if you exclude Paris, that is,' she added. 'It's the parking. Most of the city hotels have frighteningly small underground car parks that must have been built in the 1950s and designed for those tiny little Citroëns the French loved so much. I remember once taking about twenty minutes to get out of a car park in Bordeaux. My nerves were in shreds.'

'I'm planning to stay in Bordeaux,' said Deira. 'You'd better tell me where that car park is so that I can avoid it.'

They arrived on the outskirts of Nantes and Grace turned up the volume on her phone so that Deira could hear the directions. A few minutes later, she pulled up outside a narrow building with a blue and white striped canopy over the window. The old-fashioned sign outside proclaimed it to be La Belle Mer.

'This is convenient,' remarked Deira as she parked a few metres past it. 'You'd be lucky to get street parking near a restaurant in Dublin.'

'Oh, well, Nantes isn't a capital city. The population is only a few hundred thousand.' Grace glanced at her. 'Are you going to put the roof up?'

'Sure.' Deira pressed the button.

'So cool,' said Grace. 'Maybe I should trade in the SUV.'

The two of them got out of the car and walked into the restaurant. It was as chic as Grace remembered, with pale blue walls hung with charcoal drawings of boats and ships and a dozen dark-wood tables beautifully laid with polished cutlery and sparkling glasses. About half were occupied, and there was already a quiet hum of conversation. A young waitress led them to a free table in the corner and brought them a basket of bread accompanied by a selection of olive oils.

'Oh, it's lovely.' Deira looked around her with real pleasure. For the first time since she'd left Dublin, she felt as though she might be on a holiday instead of – well, whatever she was on. And for the first time in the last couple of months, she felt hungry too. She took a piece of bread and dipped it in the oil. 'Thanks for asking me to eat with you,' she said to Grace. 'This is so much better than having hotel food.'

'Thank you for saying yes,' said Grace. 'I prefer to eat out rather than in hotels too.'

She faltered on the last words and for the first time her air of serene confidence seemed to desert her. Deira didn't say anything, though, as at that moment the waitress returned with a blackboard chalked with the day's menu, and asked if they'd like anything to drink.

Deira declined wine as she was driving, but Grace ordered a glass of Chablis to go with the duck they both decided on. When she'd taken a sip, she looked at Deira and asked her if she enjoyed travelling alone.

Deira dipped her bread in the olive oil again and took a bite. For a moment Grace thought she wasn't going to answer and wished she hadn't asked the question. But then Deira spoke.

'I wasn't meant to be alone, but I've broken up with my . . . my . . . partner.' She busied herself with the bread so that Grace wouldn't see the tears that had filled her eyes once more.

'I'm sorry to hear that.'

'Oh, it's in the past now,' said Deira, although from her point of view it wasn't. 'But I needed some time out to get myself back together, and we were going to come to France anyway, so . . .'

'At least you're going to have a great time driving through some fabulous countryside. Bordeaux you mentioned already. Have you decided on anywhere else?' Grace spoke as if she were unaware that Deira was doing her best not to cry.

'Not yet,' said Deira as steadily as she could. 'I might plan out a route tonight. But given that I abandoned my plan to start there, I'm finishing up with Paris. And you?'

'My entire trip is mapped out for me already,' said Grace. 'I have no control over it.'

'Really?' Deira looked at her in surprise. From the moment she'd first seen Grace, she'd thought of her as completely in control. She was cool and calm and collected in a way Deira knew she could only aspire to. And yet the sudden undercurrent in her voice made her think that the unflappable woman might have issues of her own.

Deira watched as this time Grace was the one who busied herself with the bread, slicing a portion into narrow slivers and arranging them on her side plate. The control was there, for sure. But emotions were definitely bubbling under the surface.

'I suppose I could change it if I wanted to.' When Grace looked up, her blue eyes were as serene as before, and it was as though the tremor in her voice had been a figment of Deira's imagination. 'It's just that in theory I need to do this trip in a certain way. Even though I'm not sure I can work out exactly what it is I'm meant to be doing.'

Deira couldn't immediately ask her what she was talking about as the waitress returned to place their meal in front of them. But when she did, Grace took her time before replying.

'It's a bit mad,' she said. 'You'll think I'm off my trolley if I tell you.'

'No I won't.' Deira knew that she could see Grace's madness and raise her own. 'Do you want to talk about it? You don't have to. We can change the topic if you prefer.'

Grace never talked about her personal life to strangers. She didn't want to be judged. But did it matter if Deira judged her? She was never going to see her again, after all.

'It's not like you're going to see me again.' Deira echoed her thoughts. 'But I don't want to make you uncomfortable, so let's think of something else.'

'My daughter is always on at me to talk,' said Grace. 'She thinks it's good to share.'

'Sometimes it is,' agreed Deira. 'But there can be too much sharing too – think about some of the posts people put on social media.'

Grace smiled. 'I don't do social media. Not really.'

'Me neither.' Deira refilled her water glass.

'I'll tell you,' said Grace. 'If you don't mind.'

'Of course not.'

'So . . . I'll start at the beginning.'

'I was twenty years old when I married my husband,' she said. 'I was airline cabin crew and I met him on a flight. Back then, of course, we were called air hostesses – trolley dollies was the less flattering phrase. I didn't mind,' she added. 'Being an air hostess was seen as a glamour job. A good job too; we were paid well and had fantastic perks. I stayed working for a few years after we got married, but both of us wanted to start a family and that would've been tricky if I was flitting around the world serving drinks at thirty thousand feet.

'So I left, and I got pregnant nearly straight away. We had three children, and even though I missed work, I was happy at home. Ken was doing well in his career and it was good for me to be able to support him.'

She broke off and took another sip of wine while Deira wondered if it had been a difficult decision for Grace to give up a job she seemed to have loved.

'Anyhow, we rattled along quite happily,' continued Grace. 'Ken moved up the ladder of success. The children grew into well-adjusted individuals – at least, I like to think so. They've had their moments, of course, but they're generally OK. Aline, my eldest, is married with a little boy. Fionn is an engineer with a technology company in China, and Regan is currently living her dream and working on a polo ranch in Argentina.'

'It sounds like they've done well,' said Deira.

'They're happy, at any rate,' Grace said. 'Which is the most important thing. When Regan was fifteen, I decided it was time for me to work outside the home again, and I returned to the airline because they were looking for experienced staff. A few years later, Ken had a heart attack.'

'Oh Grace. I'm sorry.' Having already heard Grace refer to her husband in the past tense, Deira assumed it had been fatal.

'He recovered.' Grace's words were coming more quickly

now, and her voice was considerably less serene than before. 'He bounced back from it and afterwards became a bit of a fitness freak. Our holidays after his attack were always active ones – boating, skiing, hill-walking . . . we even did a few stages of the Camino. He got into organic food, wouldn't eat anything processed, drank litres of water every day. He looked great on it, to be honest. Everything was fine until last year, when he had an unexpected fall. And then, not that long afterwards, another one, totally out of the blue. Eventually he agreed to see a doctor. He was diagnosed with motor neurone disease.'

'Oh no,' said Deira, with even more sympathy. 'That's what Stephen Hawking had, isn't it? I saw the movie about his life. It was amazing.'

'He had a form of motor neurone, yes,' said Grace. 'Ken and I saw that movie too, and when they told us of Ken's diagnosis I thought . . . well . . . Everyone was surprised at how much Professor Hawking achieved despite his illness. I knew it would be different with Ken, but I thought it might help, both of them being academics. Both professors. It was stupid. He laughed at me.'

'I'm sure it was very difficult,' said Deira.

'You know how it is.' Grace sighed. 'You want to be positive. You talk about all the good things you can do together. You try very hard.'

Deira nodded.

'But Ken didn't want to be positive. He was furious with life. Furious with his body. Furious with himself. And furious with me.'

'Why with you?'

'Because suddenly, in his eyes, I was more valuable than

104

him,' she said. 'He'd always been the driving force in the family. Everything we did revolved around his schedule, his work, his publications, his brilliance. I was his support. Even when I went back to the airline, my hours had to fit in with his.'

'*Was* he brilliant?' asked Deira.

'He was a brilliant intellectual, that's for sure,' said Grace. 'I often think he married me because I would never be able to challenge him. I was pretty and looked good beside him, but I hadn't read the books he'd read or done the studying he'd done. So I was his . . . his accessory.'

'All the same, I'm sure he loved you.'

I love you, Hippolyta. Grace remembered him saying that on their wedding day. She remembered him telling her how lucky he was that someone like her could love someone like him. But he'd rarely said it afterwards. And there was a part of her that always thought he'd considered her a prize to be captured from the moment he'd seen her on the flight to New York. He may have loved her, but *how* had he loved her? As Grace Garvey? Or as the person he'd chosen? She'd asked herself the same question on more than one occasion. She'd never really known the answer.

'We were married for nearly forty years, so I guess he must have done,' she told Deira. 'Though I'm not sure we were so bothered back then about men loving their wives as much as their wives were supposed to love them. You met someone, you got on well, you wanted sex, you tied the knot.'

'Seriously?' Deira looked at her sceptically.

'OK, not just to have sex,' conceded Grace. 'But it was important to be married. It really was. And I was punching above my weight with Ken, that's for sure.'

'Maybe he was punching above his weight with you.'

Grace smiled. 'That's exactly what he once said, but no. He was the brains. I was the—'

'Brains too,' said Deira. 'As well as the beauty. I can see that.'

'Well preserved is the term I've heard,' Grace said. 'But I suppose I was attractive enough when I was younger. Back then, being pretty was part of the job description when you worked as cabin crew. Anyhow,' she continued, 'Ken and I were a good partnership for a very long time. But once he was diagnosed, it was difficult to make it work.'

'Did you split up?' Deira couldn't imagine how awful it would be to break up a marriage when one person had a terminal diagnosis.

'Of course not,' said Grace. 'I would never have done that. I told Ken that if he only had a certain amount of time left – the prognosis was two to five years – we should spend it in the best ways we could. I suggested this trip. He'd always organised our holidays before and I thought if we did it again it would be great quality time together as well as giving him a project to focus on. It seemed like it was a good suggestion, because he got very animated about it. He said he'd put it together, plan everything, book our berths, our accommodation in France and Spain, everything. There were more stops than we'd normally make, of course, because otherwise it would have been too difficult for him. It would have been our wedding anniversary next month, so he called it the Great Anniversary Road Trip. I thought it really mattered to him.'

She paused and took another sip of wine.

'Then his condition deteriorated. Not tremendously, but noticeably. Ken said we'd never be able to do the trip, that he'd be in a wheelchair before long. I told him that even if he was, he'd still be well enough to make it, and he didn't have to worry about a thing because I could do all the driving. I guess that was a mistake. He said that I was enjoying being the one in charge a bit too much, that it was clear I was only putting up with him and that the sooner he was dead, the better.'

'That must have been awful for both of you.'

'He was frustrated and I couldn't blame him. I asked him how far he'd got with the planning, because he'd spent so much time on it. He'd said it was all sorted. Everything was booked. He'd put all the information on his computer. I said I'd been looking forward to it for ages and that there was no way I wasn't going to go. I thought it would spur him on, make him feel more positive about it himself.'

She drained her glass of Chablis and for a moment Deira thought she was going to order another. But instead she filled her water tumbler from the jug on the table.

'People who are well spend a lot of time telling people who are ill to be positive. To fight and never give up. It's arrogant of us really. Anyone living with a long-term condition is entitled to be negative if they want. But they're bombarded by stories about others who've done great things despite living with illness. Their role models are supposed to be anyone who's trekked the Himalayas or organised massive fund-raisers for research or had a glittering career like Stephen Hawking, and it's hard to live up to that. It's like saying you're not allowed to feel bad because you're sick. It's pressure you can do without.'

Deira nodded slowly.

'All the same, Ken eventually came around to the idea that we could do the trip together,' continued Grace. 'He became quite animated about it, spent more time on the computer – he told me he was streamlining everything – and he even said he hoped he'd be able to drive a bit of the way. I said I hoped so too, although to be honest, I wouldn't have dreamt of allowing him behind the wheel. But I wasn't going to upset him by saying otherwise. He seemed so gung-ho all of a sudden. I was delighted. And relieved. And then, the following week, when I was out at night for the first time in months, he took our car and drove it off Howth pier.'

Deira looked at her in complete shock. Even though she'd heard what Grace had said, it was taking her time to process the reality of it.

'He drowned, of course.' Grace's voice was calm and steady once again as she continued speaking without waiting for a response from Deira. 'There wasn't a chance that he could be saved. If I'd been more alert, I might have guessed what he'd planned. I might have been able to stop him.'

'Maybe it was an accident,' said Deira.

'That's what everyone wanted to think,' said Grace. 'It's what I want to think too. But Ken wouldn't have done something like that by accident. I know he wouldn't. He did it because . . . because he couldn't live with me any more and he didn't trust me to . . .' She broke off. 'I was his wife and I wasn't enough to stop him.'

'You shouldn't blame yourself,' said Deira.

Grace couldn't count the number of times people had said that to her.

'There are times when I feel he *wanted* me to blame myself,' she told Deira.

'Oh no, Grace, I'm sure he didn't. He probably wasn't thinking straight.'

'Ken prided himself on the clarity of his thinking,' said Grace. 'He didn't have time for people who, as he put it, emoted.'

When Deira spoke again, her words were slow and thoughtful.

'You said he was an academic, like Professor Hawking. A physicist?'

'No,' said Grace. 'He lectured in English literature.'

'Your name is Grace Garvey. But was he Professor Garvey?'

Grace shook her head. 'He was Kenneth Harrington. I didn't change my name when I got married because it was too much faff at work. And then . . . well, I was always Harrington with the children but Garvey on my own.'

'Professor Harrington was one of my English lit tutors at college,' said Deira. 'I majored in art history, but English was one of my subjects too. Your story sounded familiar because I remember seeing it on the news at the time and being really shocked. I'm so sorry, Grace, I should've realised earlier, but . . . well, I thought back then his drowning had been a terrible accident. I didn't know . . .'

'They called it misadventure in the end,' said Grace. 'He hadn't been going very fast and it was dark, so they said he could have made an error of judgement. Ken didn't make errors of judgement.' She shook her head. 'I never for a moment expected to meet one of his former students on this trip. And I definitely didn't expect she'd turn out to be you!'

'We met once before,' Deira told her. 'Only for a few seconds. It was at a college reception. I can't recall what for. But he introduced you to me.'

'I don't remember.' Grace shook her head. 'I'm sorry.'

'Why should you?' asked Deira. 'I don't properly remember

109

you either. I'd had a few drinks by then. Thinking about it, it's probably a good thing you don't remember me. I was pretty bolshie as a student, and if I was drunk, I might have been horribly rude to you.'

'Ken liked bolshie students. And I'm sure I'd remember if you'd been rude.'

'He talked about you sometimes,' said Deira. 'He called you Amazing Grace.'

'What?' In speaking just that one word, Grace's voice was shakier than ever before.

'I'm sorry,' said Deira again. 'I didn't mean to upset you.'

'I'm not upset.' Grace took another sip of water, then replaced the glass carefully on the table. 'He never called me Amazing Grace, not to my face anyhow.'

'He used to say that you were sharp in your assessment of the written word,' Deira told her. 'He said that you didn't like self-indulgent nonsense.'

'He said that?' Grace looked at her in disbelief. 'He used to laugh at me because I liked Maeve Binchy.'

'He never laughed at you when he mentioned your name to us,' said Deira. 'Never.'

Grace shook her head slowly. 'I wish he'd said that to me.'

'Maybe people never say what they really think to the person closest to them,' said Deira. 'Even when it's complimentary.'

'Especially when it's complimentary, in Ken's case. He was more likely to . . . Oh, it doesn't matter now, does it. He's gone.'

'Did he . . . did he leave a note?' asked Deira.

'Not that sort of note,' replied Grace. 'That's why they were able to call it misadventure. But he'd sent me an email instructing me that if anything should ever happen to him, I was to take the holiday we'd planned, enjoy the treats in store, do what he asked and scatter some of his ashes in the sea and some near the apartment.'

'So you're doing this trip to fulfil his last wishes,' said Deira.

'To be perfectly honest, I'm not sure why I'm doing it,' Grace said. 'I hate the idea of him trying to orchestrate my life from the grave. It was bad enough when he was alive.' She grimaced. 'Sorry, that sounds really disrespectful, but he left us. Deliberately. So he should have left us – me – in peace.'

'And yet you're here making the trip. *Did* you scatter his ashes in the sea?'

Grace told her about throwing the tube overboard. 'I wasn't going to. I was terrified someone would see me. But I can't . . . I can't simply ignore him. As far as the trip goes, he put so much effort into it. He . . . well, he's given me other things to do. Left clues to puzzles for me to solve. Which is typical bloody Ken when it comes down to it.'

'I'm sure he didn't mean to upset you,' said Deira. 'He was obviously trying to make it a great trip.'

'I was a damn sight more upset when the police called to my house and told me what had happened. They knew it wasn't an accident, no matter what the coroner said. The garda who broke the news was lovely, but I couldn't help feeling she was judging me. Thinking that I'd allowed it to happen. But I'd no idea what he was planning. I suppose that's even worse. I know it would have got harder and harder for him, and I understand how awful it was. But I still thought we had a lot more time together. I felt that I needed it, to get my head around everything. The kids certainly did. Fionn and Regan didn't come home when he was first diagnosed. He didn't want them to race back and we agreed that the summer was the best time. So although they FaceTimed and everything, they didn't see him properly before he died, and that hurt them tremendously. If he'd said something, given me some indication . . . If he'd wanted to end his life, perhaps we could have . . . well, you know. I would have investigated that with him. I would have helped. Not to end his life,' she added hastily. 'But . . . I'd have been there for him. The way he did it was awful for all of us.'

'Like I said, he probably wasn't thinking straight,' said Deira. 'Maybe he thought it was all for the best. I'm not saying he was right to think that way, of course. But under the circumstances . . .'

'The circumstances caused all sorts of problems,' said Grace. 'Practical problems for me. Emotional problems for everyone. I should be mourning him, but the truth is, I'm finding it very hard to forgive him, and I'm finding it hard to forgive myself too.'

'You've nothing to forgive yourself for,' said Deira. 'You did everything you could.'

Grace said nothing.

'If you're angry about him arranging this trip, will doing it actually help?'

'I don't bloody know.' Grace looked uncertain. 'Throwing the tube of his ashes overboard was cathartic. But I still have more in the boot, along with my suitcase and the hazard warning sign. Which makes me an unfeeling monster, doesn't it, leaving my husband in the back of the car.'

'Of course not,' said Deira. She leaned across the table

and squeezed Grace's hand. 'I liked Professor Harrington, you know. He was a very understanding sort of man, at least towards his students. I'm sure he wouldn't have expected you to carry him around in your handbag.'

The two women's eyes met and Grace choked back a sudden desire to laugh.

'I couldn't believe it when I saw the news about his death,' continued Deira. 'And if there's anything I can do to help, please let me know. We're old acquaintances, even if neither of us remembers it.'

'Talking to you today has been a help,' said Grace. 'It's the first time . . . Well, I haven't really . . . It's hard, you see. People don't know what to say to you. Friends don't know how to behave. They came to the funeral, they said the standard words and then they disappeared. They don't want to have to think about his illness, but even more they don't want to think about how his life ended. They don't know what to say outside of the funeral setting, so they say nothing at all. These last months, I've felt cut off from everyone.'

'How are your children now?' asked Deira.

'Fionn and Regan went back to China and Argentina a month after the funeral,' said Grace. 'We speak every few days and they seem to be doing OK, but how can I be sure? Aline had called around to see Ken with her little boy Declan the afternoon it happened. Ken loved Declan, and of course a two-year-old wouldn't know there was anything wrong so he didn't treat his grandfather any differently. Truth is, we *all* tried not to treat him any differently, but the fact that we knew was enough as far as he was concerned. Aline tried to shoulder the blame for not realising something was wrong.

I told her if she blamed herself she had to blame me even more, because I was living with him. She had a closure ceremony for him after the funeral, but I'm sure she's still hurting.'

'It must be very hard.' Deira understood how people found it difficult to talk to Grace about what had happened. Beyond platitudes, she didn't know what to say either.

'It is what it is.' Grace sat up straighter. 'Anyhow, I've very uncharacteristically dumped all that on you and made our meal a lot less cheerful than it could have been, so I can only apologise.'

'You were right to tell me, said Deira. 'And you're right to talk about it to someone you hardly know. Because sometimes it's harder to share stuff with people you're close to than with a complete stranger. And maybe me having been your husband's student helps a little too. I realise that what happened was really hard on you and your family, but I remember him as a good man. Perhaps he thought he was making it easier on you, even though it wasn't.'

'You're very kind,' said Grace. 'Is there anything you'd like to tell me? You know, quid pro quo?'

Deira smiled. There were things she could have told her. But as hers was a far more selfish story than Grace's, she wasn't going to say a word.

Chapter 12

Loire-Atlantique, France: 47.1987°N 1.6537°W

After they'd finished their meal, Deira drove them back to the Hotel Atlantique, where she popped another couple of painkillers. She decided to remain in the garden, but Grace went back to her room and sat at the window, shocked that she'd spilled her story to a complete stranger. She'd never been the sort of person to confide in others, preferring to keep her own counsel. She'd never spoken about her life with Ken to anyone; never confessed that he sometimes made her feel inadequate or asked aloud if enduring really was as good as loving. Because in the end, her marriage had worked for her. They'd been a good partnership. People had envied them. And she'd liked that.

Yet she'd blurted out everything to Deira O'Brien and she couldn't understand why. It wasn't as though Deira was the type of warm, open person who invited confidences. If anything, she was a little distant. Was that it? Grace wondered. Had she been able to share with Deira precisely because she wasn't the sort of woman who'd wrap her arms around her and encourage her to have a good cry? Grace was uncomfortable around people who believed you should wear your heart on your sleeve the whole time. She preferred to keep her heart hidden, like it was supposed to be.

It had been a big surprise to learn that Deira had once been her husband's student, but even more surprising to hear what she'd said about him. And the things he'd said about Grace. Because Ken hadn't been a heart-on-his-sleeve kind of person either. The phrase 'Amazing Grace' repeated over and over in her mind, both soothing and annoying her. If her late husband had really believed she was all that amazing – if he'd believed it enough to actually say it to his students – then surely he could have said it to her face at least once. Had he meant it when he'd told his students that she didn't like self-indulgent nonsense? And had he really spoken of her in public as warmly as Deira had implied? She would have loved to have heard those words from him. Over the years of their marriage, Grace had convinced herself that Ken put up with her more than loved her, that she was the lesser of the two in the relationship. She had always been intimidated by his intellect, and horribly aware that while he had a string of qualifications, she hadn't even made it to college. Part of the reason she'd kept her own feelings in check was because she didn't want to appear foolish in front of him. Now she wondered if it had bothered her more than it had bothered him.

She wished he'd confided in her more. She wished they'd been closer in those last few months. She wished he was here so she could say all this to him now.

She looked at the list of documents on the laptop screen and entered another random selection of letters and numbers. *Password incorrect.*

A sudden thought occurred to her, and she tried 'Amazing Grace' as a password, but that was incorrect too. Then, more out of hope than any belief, she entered 'Maeve Binchy'. For one glorious moment she thought she'd cracked it, because the little coloured ball on the screen started to spin, but then the 'password incorrect' message came up again.

She stared at the screen for a moment, then closed the laptop and brought it downstairs with her.

Deira was sitting at the outside table, a glass of soda water in front of her. She looked up in surprise at Grace's return.

'You said you'd help me in any way you can,' Grace said as she sat down beside her. 'So can you help me now?'

'Of course. How?' asked Deira.

'I mentioned earlier he'd left me some puzzles to solve,' said Grace, who went on to explain about the locked documents and her unsuccessful attempts to open them, while Deira listened in amazement.

'You were his student,' she concluded. 'Maybe you have some insights I don't.'

'He didn't leave you any hints?' asked Deira, who couldn't quite get her head around the fact that the professor had left some kind of macabre treasure trail for his wife to follow after his death. 'Like that they were numbers or phrases or . . . anything at all?'

'No.' Grace detailed her hopeless attempts and told Deira that she'd tried 'Amazing Grace' without success too. 'I wondered if there was anything he'd ever said to you that would make you think of a possible clue?'

'I left college over fifteen years ago!' exclaimed Deira. 'I couldn't possibly have a sensible idea.'

'But can you remember anything he said, any particular likes or dislikes . . .'

'Grace, it's you he wanted to be able to open the documents,'

Deira pointed out. 'He'd be thinking of something special to you, not to me.'

'You're right, of course.' Grace sounded defeated. 'I don't know what I was thinking.'

'Well . . . let's put our heads together anyhow.' Deira pushed the glass of soda water to one side and leaned over to look at the laptop's screen. 'Do you have any idea how long the password is? Because obviously a four-symbol one would be a lot easier to crack than anything as long as "Amazing Grace".'

Grace shook her head.

'Let me try.' Deira tapped the keyboard, then turned to look at her. 'I don't think it *can* be more than four characters,' she said. 'The cursor doesn't appear to go any further than that anyhow.'

'Oh, but . . .' Grace made a face. 'I thought it might seem that way but still be longer. Sometimes sites don't show exactly how many characters you need.'

'Possibly, but this is an internal document password and I honestly don't think it's massively encrypted. So that narrows it down at least.'

'There must still be an enormous number of four-character passwords, though,' said Grace. 'Otherwise it'd be easy to crack a mobile phone.'

'True,' Deira conceded. 'But let's think about this clearly. The professor *wanted* you to work this out. He couldn't have made it too difficult.'

'I've tried every combination of memorable dates I can think of,' Grace said. 'Birthdays, anniversaries . . . Oh God!' Her face paled and she pulled the laptop back towards her. She typed in a combination, then sighed with relief when she got the 'password incorrect' message. 'I thought for a second he might have put in the day he died.' She covered her face with her hands.

Deira said nothing. It was the first time she'd seen the other woman anything but composed – even in the restaurant, as she'd recounted her story, she'd been totally self-possessed.

After a moment, Grace took a deep breath and looked at her again. 'Sorry,' she said. 'I'm fine.'

'Grace . . .'

'Really.' Her voice was firm and steady. 'Carry on. Any more thoughts?'

'Do you think it could be anything to do with the places you're visiting?' asked Deira, who wondered if Grace's apparent calmness in the face of a terrible tragedy was simply a coping mechanism, or if she truly was one of the least emotional people she'd ever met. 'Nantes. La Rochelle. Bordeaux . . .' she continued, 'is there anything special about them?'

Grace shook her head. 'Other than the fact that we've been to them all before, no,' she said. 'As for the rest, I haven't been to Pamplona, Toledo or this place called Alcalá de Henares. Ken did a literary lecture tour in Spain just before he was taken ill, and although I can't remember exactly where he was, I'm assuming he went to those places. He's certainly been to Pamplona a few times. *The Sun Also Rises* is . . . was one of his favourite books, and he went there for the running of the bulls. He didn't run himself,' she added, 'but he sat in the cafés around the square and drank wine and channelled his inner Ernest.'

'You were reading that on the boat,' recalled Deira.

'As I said, it was Ken's favourite. I thought it would mean something to read it on this trip. I'd have preferred to reread Rosamunde Pilcher, to tell you the truth.'

Deira smiled slightly, remembering her own run-in with Professor Harrington over her critique of Hemingway's best-known novel. Then she turned her attention back to the computer screen.

'Cervantes was born in Alcalá de Henares,' she remarked.

'Cervantes?'

'The guy who wrote *Don Quixote*,' said Deira.

'Yes, sorry, I know who he is. Ken had an old copy of the book in his study.' Grace nodded. 'He thought it was brilliant.'

'I know,' Deira told her. 'I remember one of his lectures on Cervantes in college. It was riveting.' She twirled one of her curls around her finger and looked thoughtfully at Grace. 'He loved Cervantes and he loved Ernest Hemingway and both of the towns they're associated with are on your list.' She continued to stare at the screen in front of her. 'He liked classic science fiction too,' she said slowly. 'Ray Bradbury. Arthur C. Clarke, Philip K. Dick . . . and Jules Verne.' She looked up at Grace. 'Jules Verne was born here, in Nantes.'

'Oh!' Grace looked at her with excitement. 'He always brought a Jules Verne when we came to France. The first password must have something to do with him, don't you think?'

She used her phone to google Jules Verne.

'The twenty-fourth of March 1905 is his birthday,' she said. 'Worth a try?'

Deira entered 2403 in the document labelled Nantes and got the 'password incorrect' message.

Then she typed in the year.

'Oh my God,' she said. 'Bingo!'

'Seriously?' Grace looked at the screen and started to smile. 'We did it,' she said. '*You* did it! Thank you.' She read through

120

the document, then looked up at Deira. 'But what the hell does any of this mean?'

'It's a clue to another password,' replied Deira. 'But as for what it means, I haven't the faintest idea.'

Chapter 13

Congratulations, Hippo! they read. *You're on your way. You're not journeying to the centre of the earth for the next password but you're heading down into the deep. How deep did he go – you only need the first number here. You'll also need the number of portholes on the Atlantic (or should that be Atlantique); if you keep an eye out when you're relaxing, you'll find it. Finally, you have to take a photo of the door of his very own space and upload it to the link at the end. If you've got it right, you'll be given the last number for the clue, as well as a letter to keep till the end. Think logically and you'll find the answer. Don't forget from here on your guesses are limited before you're locked out. You have ten for this clue. Tread carefully.*

'Actually, I've only seven,' said Grace. 'I made some random guesses earlier and I got a message saying seven remaining. So I stopped.'

'Right.' Deira looked at the screen thoughtfully.

'But what the hell is he on about?' asked Grace. 'Deep down where? Is the *Atlantique* a famous ship? Should I know how many portholes it has? And what space is he talking about? None of it makes sense.'

'I'm sure it will if we think about it for long enough,' said Deira. 'Back when I was at college, Professor Harrington used to run literary treasure hunts for the students with clues like this. D'you remember them?'

'I've no idea what he used to do, to be honest,' said Grace. 'We didn't really talk about his work much. I only ever went to occasional events with him, and certainly nothing like a treasure hunt.'

'They were like the literary pub crawls that tourists in Dublin do,' said Deira. 'Except we didn't call in to a number of pubs; we'd just meet up in one at the end. We had to find clues along the way. All the clues together would give another clue to a book or an author or something on the literary scene. Any student who worked it out went into a draw for a signed copy of a book the professor liked. It was more social than serious, and it was good fun.'

'Well, he's certainly done the same thing here,' agreed Grace. 'But I don't know how I'm supposed to work out any of the clues. Or if it matters in which order. I'm thinking it does because it's the route I'm supposed to be taking. He pre-booked my hotels, which means I have to be in La Rochelle tomorrow night, so I only have tonight and tomorrow morning to find the door I'm supposed to be taking a photo of. It's not a lot of time.'

'In the treasure hunts he set for us you definitely had to do it in order, unless you made some very lucky guesses,' said Deira. 'When you solved one clue it gave you the password to the next one and so on. All of the clues together at the end will make some kind of sense.'

'For crying out loud.' Grace slumped back in her chair. 'How on earth did he expect me to solve this? He was the literary genius in our house, not me. He might have called me Amazing Grace to his students, but he used to tell me I was an Amazon. That's why he called me Hippo – it's short for Hippolyta. She was an Amazon queen.'

'Oh, good. I thought it might be an extra clue.' Deira grinned. 'I should've guessed. The professor often gave students nicknames from Greek mythology. All the same, it's a travesty calling you Hippo. You're a sylph.'

'He abbreviated Hippolyta when I got pregnant and absolutely ballooned,' said Grace. 'It sort of stuck.'

'That wasn't very kind.' The words were out of Deira's mouth before she could stop them.

'Kindness wasn't Ken's forte,' said Grace. Then she shrugged. 'Oh look, I'm being unfair. He didn't mean to be unkind. It simply never occurred to him that his words could hurt. Not that I *was* hurt by it,' she added. 'When I was expecting the children, I put hippos to shame.'

Deira tried and failed to imagine Grace as anyone other than the slender woman in front of her.

'Anyhow,' said Grace, after they'd lapsed into a slightly awkward silence, 'we still have to figure out what he's trying to say here.'

'The first part is almost self-explanatory,' said Deira slowly. 'It's the rest that's stumping me.'

'Self-explanatory?' Grace looked at her in astonishment. 'You're way ahead of me in that case, because I haven't a clue what it means.'

'Well, I'm pretty sure the first element is still about Jules Verne,' Deira said. 'Verne wrote *Journey to the Centre of the*

124

Earth as well as *Twenty Thousand Leagues Under the Sea*. I'm guessing 2 is the answer to how deep did he go, as it's the first number in twenty thousand.'

'OK.' Grace nodded. 'That makes sense. So what about the portholes? Was the ship in *Twenty Thousand Leagues* called the *Atlantique*?'

'Strictly speaking, it was a submarine,' said Deira. She closed her eyes for a moment while she thought. 'Not the *Atlantique*. The *Nautilus*. He could have written a book about a ship called the *Atlantique* but I don't know it if he did.'

'I haven't a notion,' said Grace. 'I never read any of them. I'm not a sci-fi buff.'

'Hardly sci-fi now,' said Deira. 'I think his first book was published in the 1860s. Let's forget about the book for a moment.' She frowned as she studied the document. 'The next part of the clue is the door of his very own space. I'm wondering if it's his house – it might have a plaque or some-thing outside the door. What d'you think?'

'It must be!' Grace's eyes lit up. 'You're good at this, Deira.'

Deira opened the laptop's browser. 'Good but wrong,' she said after she'd googled it. 'Verne's house is in Amiens, near Paris. But . . .' her fingers flew over the keyboard, 'there's a museum in Nantes. The Musée Jules Verne.' She clicked on Google Maps and entered the museum's address. 'Gosh, it's not far from where we ate last night.'

'Really?' Grace moved closer to have a look.

'Street View,' said Deira as she dragged the icon onto the map.

The view of the street was perfect. Deira used the cursor

to rotate the picture until a small whitewashed building with red brick around the windows filled the screen.

'Musée Jules Verne.' Grace read the sign on the wall beside the door 'Oh my God, Deira, you've cracked it.'

'Fingers crossed,' said Deira. 'So basically you have to take a photo of the door and upload it. Probably include the sign, too. I guess it's some kind of program that compares it with one the professor uploaded before.'

'But how would he . . .' Grace's voice faltered. 'The last time he was here, he was well. He couldn't have known then that he'd be setting this up.'

'Maybe he took a photo when he was there and it gave him the idea later,' said Deira. 'I'm surprised at him being so tech-savvy as to put all this together. Back in the day, he used a massive Filofax and used to wander around the college with piles of folders covered in Post-it notes.'

'Oh, he totally embraced technology,' said Grace. 'He said it was a great tool for researchers, although I didn't realise he'd gone so far as setting up a program to compare uploaded photos. Or adding passwords to documents. I didn't know he'd been to the Jules Verne museum either, though I suppose on one of our trips he could've gone without telling me. I thought he spent a lot of his time in his last months reading the old college stuff he'd saved on his laptop,' she added. 'Being nostalgic, you know, not devising treasure hunts. I guess I didn't really know him at all.'

Deira gave her a sympathetic smile but remained silent.

'That bit about the Atlantique.' Grace gathered herself and spoke more firmly. 'Maybe there's a boat called *Atlantique* inside the museum?'

'Maybe,' said Deira. 'Let's think about it a bit more. We'll work it out eventually, I know we will.'

Grace admired her confidence. And she hoped she was right.

She FaceTimed Aline before going to bed that evening, telling her that the crossing had been smooth and her journey to Nantes uneventful. She added that she'd had dinner with Deira O'Brien, whom she described as a friendly woman she'd met on the ferry.

'I'm glad you've had some company at least,' said Aline, who was sitting on the sofa in her pyjamas, her legs tucked beneath her. 'Is this Deira woman going in the same direction as you?'

'She's driving to Bordeaux tomorrow,' said Grace. 'She hadn't planned on staying in Nantes at all but she had a minor accident and needed to break her journey. Which was lucky for me, otherwise—' She broke off. Although Aline knew that she'd been bringing Ken's ashes with her, Grace hadn't said anything about the treasure hunt. Because on the surface it might have been a fun game devised by her late husband to keep her amused on the trip to Cartagena (albeit with some kind of reward at the end), but Grace couldn't be entirely sure that there hadn't been some other kind of motivation behind it. And that wasn't something she wanted to share with her daughter. Although, she thought suddenly, perhaps Aline would have some ideas about future clues. After all, Deira wouldn't be around for the next one.

'Otherwise what?' asked Aline.

'Otherwise I would've probably eaten in the hotel on my

127

own and it was nice to go out.' Grace decided to keep the treasure hunt to herself for the time being.

'You *will* take care on the road, won't you, Mum?' Aline said. 'I know you've broken your journey into short stages, but even so, it's a lot to do on your own.'

'I'll be grand,' said Grace. 'It's good for me.'

'All the same, I wish I could have come with you.'

'You're busy with your husband, your child and your job,' said Grace. 'You couldn't possibly have given me the time.'

'Nevertheless . . .'

'Please don't worry about me, Aline,' said Grace. 'I'll call you tomorrow from La Rochelle.'

'I remember when we went there. It was lovely.'

It had been their last complete family holiday together, and although Aline, at seventeen, hadn't been all that enthusiastic and insisted she'd be just as happy staying home by herself, it had ended up being one of their most enjoyable visits to France.

'Yes, it was,' said Grace. 'Anyhow, I had an early start this morning and I'm pretty much whacked now. So I'm off to bed and I'll talk to you tomorrow.'

'Goodnight, Mum,' Aline said. 'Love you.'

'Love you too,' said Grace.

She put the phone on the nightstand, got into bed and, for the first time in months, was asleep within minutes.

Chapter 14

Loire-Atlantique, France: 47.1987°N 1.6537°W

She was in a deep sleep when a loud, insistent alarm startled her into wakefulness again. It took her a moment to realise that it wasn't her phone but the hotel's fire alarm. She slid her feet into the soft shoes she'd left beside her bed, opened the door and went into the corridor. Other guests were already there and heading for the fire escape. She sniffed the air but couldn't smell any smoke and was already thinking that this was a false alarm when there was a loud bang from outside the building, followed by a terrified shriek.

Grace's heart began to beat faster, but she stayed calm even as the woman behind her tried to push past.

'We won't get out any more quickly if you do that,' she said, in the controlled voice she'd used during her years of cabin-crew experience. 'Don't rush, there's plenty of time for everyone.'

The woman looked at her in surprise, but in reaction to Grace's quiet authority she stopped pushing and followed her down the stairs and through the reception area to the garden beyond.

That was when they saw the flames rushing along the wooden pergola that covered one of the parking areas and fanning across the gap to the ivy-covered hotel building. As Grace watched, the flames took hold and began burning the green foliage, sending more smoke and flames billowing into the night air.

'*Putain de merde!*' cried a man behind her.

Grace didn't understand the words, but their meaning was obvious. Although the immediate danger was currently confined to the newer wing of the hotel, the fire could easily spread. She thought about Ken's laptop, still in the bedroom, and wished she'd had the presence of mind to grab it. But, as she'd been trained to do, she'd abandoned everything.

A sudden siren heralded the arrival of the fire brigade, to shouts of encouragement from the guests, most of whom were now watching the ever-growing fire with a mixture of apprehension and ghoulish interest. Meantime, a hotel employee was trying in vain to count them, a difficult task when everyone was intent on the unfolding drama. The firefighters were focusing jets of water on the flames to further cries of encouragement and approval. The smoke turned blacker. Ash rose into the air and then fell on the onlookers, some of whom started to cough. Grace's eyes began to sting.

A woman beside her was screaming for her husband, while at the same time a man was yelling out for 'Amélie!' A moment later the two reunited, amid applause from the crowd. Grace couldn't help thinking that everyone was being rather overdramatic. Yes, the hotel had been in some danger, but the firefighters seemed to have things under control, and although there was still a lot of smoke, the flames themselves had been quenched. As far as she could see, the building wasn't damaged, although the wooden pergola was almost destroyed and the cars parked beneath it had taken hits from the burning wood as well as the deluge of water. She was thankful she'd found a parking space in front of the main building, then suddenly thought of Deira's convertible. And then she thought of Deira herself and looked for her. But people were still milling around and it was hard to identify individuals.

The firefighters continued to keep a cordon around the area even when it was clear that the fire itself had been extinguished, but after a time, the guests were allowed to enter the main building, where the management shepherded them into the public rooms, saying that all of the bedrooms needed to be checked before they could return to them.

'Deira!' Grace finally saw her, in a tracksuit and fleece, standing barefoot at the window overlooking the garden. 'Are you OK?' When Deira didn't say anything, she went over to her and repeated the question.

'My car,' said Deira. 'I need to get to my car.'

'I don't think they'll let anyone into that space for a while,' said Grace. 'Anyhow, the car is the least of your worries. The most important thing is that you're all right yourself.'

'The car is the most of my worries.' Deira's face was white, her green eyes clouded with anxiety. 'It has to be all right.'

'I'm sure it is,' lied Grace. 'Come and get a coffee. Or hot chocolate. Or whatever it is they're handing out.'

Deira followed her wordlessly. There was nowhere to sit in the café, so Grace continued walking through it towards the hotel bar, where, although the seats were taken, there were deep window sills suitable for perching on.

'I'll get you something,' said Grace, who had decided that Deira was in shock. 'Don't move.'

131

A few minutes later, she returned with brandies for both of them.

'The queue for hot chocolate was longer,' she said. 'So I thought we should make the most of what we could get.'

'I don't usually drink—'

'Nor do I,' interrupted Grace. 'But take a sip anyhow. It's a pretty decent cognac.'

Deira did as she was told, then made a face. 'Decent or not, the only time I drink brandy is hot with lemon and honey when I have a cold.' But her voice was stronger and Grace thought she looked less fragile than before.

'I'm not a big fan either,' she admitted. 'But hey ho. Needs must.'

Deira smiled faintly and took another sip.

'Feeling better?' asked Grace.

'What happened?' Deira responded with a question of her own.

'I haven't a clue,' said Grace. 'I was asleep when the alarm went off.'

'The car will be ruined.' Deira's teeth began to chatter. 'I'm so fucked.'

'Your insurance will cover it,' Grace said.

'Even if it does, he'll kill me,' said Deira.

'Who?' asked Grace.

'My partner – my ex-partner,' said Deira. 'Everyone thought it was mine. But he took out the loan.'

Grace looked at her in confusion.

'I was the one with the mortgage, you see,' said Deira. 'He did the car. But I paid the insurance. It's comprehensive, so it covers fire. But does that only mean the car itself going on fire? What about damage in another fire? Does that count?

132

And if it's a write-off because of fire damage, will they pay out? How much will they pay? I don't know that either. Gavin will freak, I do know that.'

'Gavin's your ex?' Grace grasped at the most fundamental part of Deira's incoherent monologue.

'Yes.' Deira buried her face in her hands. 'I knew it was a mistake. I was looking for a sign. But there wasn't one.'

Grace hadn't entirely got to grips with what the younger woman was saying, but she did know that she was very distressed. So despite her natural inclination not to get involved in anyone else's emotional issues, she put her arm around her shoulders and hugged her gently, as she used to do when any of the children was upset. They stayed like that for what to Grace seemed like an age, as her arm had gone numb by the time Deira sat up straight again.

'I'm so sorry,' she said, her voice suddenly steadier and calmer. 'I don't know what happened to me there. I'm fine now.'

'I doubt that,' said Grace. 'Obviously you've had a lot going on and tonight's escapade has added—' She broke off and gave Deira a wry smile, 'I was going to say fuel to the fire, but I guess that's horribly inappropriate.'

Deira laughed. A shaky laugh, but a laugh nonetheless.

'What's done is done,' she said. 'I can't change it, I just have to find a way to deal with it.' She took another sip of brandy. 'Though I'm not sure I can deal with it if I drink much more of this. It's terrible.'

'I'll go and see if I can rustle up a hot chocolate this time,' said Grace. 'Stay there.'

Deira did as she was told, sitting deeper into the window alcove and pulling her knees up against her body so that she could rest her chin on them. No matter which way she looked at it, this was a monumental cock-up. Of course Gavin was always going to find out she'd taken the car, but she'd expected to have a few days before having to properly worry about him. And even then, when he ultimately realised that it hadn't been actually stolen and that she was the one who'd taken it, all that would have happened was that he'd have lost his temper with her, which wouldn't have been anything new. Not these days. Admittedly she'd been concerned that by some weird cosmic process he would have immediately sensed the car had been taken from its parking bay beneath the apartment and suspected her, but despite her earlier worries about him setting the police and/or the gendarmerie after her, that hadn't happened. Besides she'd been mentally prepared for that situation. She'd rehearsed the conversation. But she certainly hadn't rehearsed telling Gavin she'd taken the car and allowed it to become a burnt-out wreck.

'Here.' Grace returned with a large cup of steaming hot chocolate. 'Get this inside you. And take another couple of sips of the brandy too.'

'Thanks,' said Deira. 'You're good in a crisis.'

A member of staff walked into the bar and announced that the fire services had now declared all the bedrooms safe.

'So you may return,' he said. 'And we apologise for the inconvenience.'

'A bit more than an inconvenience,' said Deira as she warmed her hands on the cup.

'Well, nobody was injured and that's the main thing,' said Grace. 'Stuff can be replaced.'

'You're right.' Deira's words got caught in her throat. 'But people . . . nothing can replace people.' She winced as she caught Grace's expression. 'I'm sorry. I'm sorry. I'm so bloody insensitive. I didn't mean . . . the professor . . .'

'You're right,' said Grace. 'People can't be replaced. I know that. I accept that. I've accepted it since the day he died. As for your situation, if you want to tell me what's wrong, I'm happy to listen. I bent your ear earlier today, remember. It was surprisingly good for me. Maybe talking would be good for you.'

Deira shook her head. 'Another time.'

'OK,' said Grace.

She continued to sit with Deira, but eventually she felt her eyes start to close.

'I have to go to bed,' she said. 'Will you be all right?'

'Sure I will.' Deira gave her a weak smile. 'Don't worry about me, Grace. I'm fine.'

But she didn't feel fine. She felt terrible.

She stayed sitting in the alcove, not in the slightest bit tired, staring ahead of her, allowing the last few months to replay in her mind, as she'd done so often before. She thought of the things she should have said and done, but the bottom line was that the result was always the same.

Gavin had left her.

And before that, he'd lied to her.

She would never forgive him.

She would never forgive herself.

It was almost four in the morning and the sky outside was beginning to lighten by the time Deira decided she was tired enough to go to bed. She deliberately didn't look out of the window at the damage the fire had caused. It would still be there when she woke up again. Grace was right. It was only stuff. There was no point in stressing. Tomorrow (or more accurately, later today) was time enough to worry about it.

The bartender had closed the bar and most of the other guests had gone back to their rooms, although a few continued to wander around the public areas, which still smelled faintly of smoke. Nevertheless, after the pandemonium of earlier, it was quiet and peaceful.

Deira left her empty cup and half-empty glass of brandy on the bar counter before turning to head upstairs. And then she turned back again. She couldn't understand how she hadn't noticed before. The hotel bar, like the restaurant she'd eaten in with Grace, had a nautical theme. A net hung from its ceiling, supporting some green and red glass buoys. Semaphore flags decorated the wall. And on a long shelf was a wooden boat, with a chrome plaque beneath it that said *Atlantic Lady*. Set into the hull of the boat were five portholes.

Surely, thought Deira, this was the answer to the professor's clue? A ship called *Atlantic Lady*. Behind the bar. A place where he might have expected Grace to relax. In a hotel called the Atlantique.

The first clue had given them the number 2. The uploaded photo would give them another number. Along with 5 for the portholes, Grace would be on her way to unlocking the next folder and continuing on her way to whatever prize her late husband had left for her. But that left them a number short if the password was four digits again. Maybe the uploaded photo would give a two-digit number. Or perhaps the first clue was 20 and not 2. The title of the novel was *Twenty Thousand Leagues* after all. She'd talk about it with Grace later. But right now, she needed to sleep.

*

She woke up at nine o'clock, her eyes snapping open, instantly alert. She showered as quickly as she could, pulled on jeans and a T-shirt and hurried downstairs. The smell of smoke hung in the air and she had to steel herself to walk outside and survey the possible damage to her car.

She wasn't the only one. Although the fire zone was still cordoned off, a small group of people clustered nearby. Most of them were either taking photos or talking animatedly into their mobiles. Deira edged past them to have a look. And groaned.

Even if the convertible wasn't the burnt-out wreck of her worst imaginings, it certainly didn't resemble anything that would be drivable in the near future. The paintwork was bubbled and scorched from the heat of the flames, and a plank of wood from the pergola had burned its way through the fabric top, falling onto the passenger seat and setting it alight too. Only the prompt arrival of the fire brigade had stopped further damage, but it was clear to Deira that the interior would have been ruined by the water from their hoses. As for the mechanical parts, she couldn't imagine that a few thousand litres at high pressure would've done them much good either.

She stayed where she was for a few minutes, but as there was nothing she could usefully do, she abandoned the depressing sight and went into the hotel. Breakfast was being served in the café, and she helped herself to some pastries and a large coffee from the buffet.

'Deira.' Grace Garvey, sitting at a window table with a cup of coffee in front of her, waved at her. Despite the drama of the night before, she looked wide awake and refreshed, dressed today in a plain white T-shirt and cornflower-blue capri pants. She'd substituted a blue pendant for the turquoise necklace.

'Hi.' Deira plonked her tray on the table. 'How are you?'

'I'm fine. What about you?'

'Apart from the fact that my car is probably a total write-off, I'm grand,' said Deira.

'Oh dear.' Grace looked at her sympathetically. 'What are you going to do?'

'Have some coffee,' Deira said. 'After that, I might be able to put my mind to it.'

'Good thinking.'

'But . . .' Deira added milk to the coffee and smiled suddenly, 'on the other hand, I might have solved our clue.'

'You might? Really?'

'Yes.' Deira explained about the boat and the portholes, as well as her idea that the first number was 20 and not 2 as she'd previously thought.

'So that means that all I have left to do is take a photo of the door to the museum,' said Grace.

'If I'm right.'

'I bet you are.' Grace beamed at her. 'I'll do it this morning. Do you want to come?'

'I have to hang around while they sort out what's going to happen to the car,' Deira said. 'And I really need to talk to the insurance company. Otherwise I'd love to.'

'I'll leave in about an hour,' sat Grace. 'If you've heard before that, let me know. Otherwise I'll go on my own. I'll give you my number.' She took out her phone and they exchanged contact information. Then she headed back to her room, leaving Deira to her breakfast.

Chapter 15

Loire-Atlantique, France: 47.1987°N 1.6537°W

Deira was pouring herself another cup of coffee when her mobile buzzed and caused her to splash a good deal more than she'd intended into her cup. Once again she worried that by some process of osmosis, Gavin had discovered what had happened to the car. But when she took the phone from her bag, she saw a message from Gillian.

Just to let you know that all is well in your house. It's a good thing we came because you left milk in the fridge! Also, I've watered your plants. And I've folded your bed linen and put it away along with your smalls. Will do the laundry before we go. Lovely day here.

Deira sighed.

She'd forgotten that she'd left her washed bed linen as well as a selection of her undies drying in the tiny utility room off the kitchen. Naturally Gillian had found them. Even though there'd been no need for her to go into the utility room at all. As for the fact that her sister had put away her underwear . . . Deira was trying hard not to think about the fact that Gill had probably poked through her chest of drawers and seen, along with the lacy lingerie she liked to wear, the sex toys that she and Gavin had often used together in bed.

She shuddered but didn't bother responding. Instead she finished her coffee and got up from the table.

Although she dreaded having to deal with the issue of the car, she knew she had to stay on top of the situation, so she went out into the bright sunlight of a day that was getting more glorious by the minute. The early-morning clouds had parted and the sky was a bright blue. The sun was warm and only the hint of a breeze disturbed the air.

The police had lifted the cordon around the parking area and were now allowing people to inspect their vehicles. The convertible had come off the worst of all of them. When she opened the door, water sloshed from the side panel and soaked her feet. The service manuals in the glove compartment were soaked too. But she was able to find the number for the global assistance package that had come with the car, and when she called it, the person she spoke to was sympathetic, although he pointed out that as her issue wasn't a mechanical fault, the company wasn't responsible.

'But we can get it towed to the nearest authorised dealer if you want,' he told her. 'It will be at your expense. Hopefully your insurance will cover it.'

She thanked him and rang the insurance company. After spending an age following the instructions of the automated answering system, she eventually got to speak to a human being. The insurance agent was perfectly pleasant, but Deira felt he didn't quite believe her story about a burning pergola raining fire down on the convertible.

'You can fill out a form online,' he said. 'But we'll need a mechanic's report before we can assess the claim. However, it sounds to me as if the hotel is responsible.'

That was the trouble with insurance companies, she

thought. Always trying to shift the responsibility to someone else.

'What about a replacement car?' she asked.

'We can't supply you with a replacement car in France.' He sounded horrified at the very idea.

She'd expected that, of course. But without a car, she was stuck in Nantes. Which, while a perfectly nice town, was hardly the number one attraction for a tourist. Why hadn't she listened to the inner voice telling her that coming away was a bad idea? And why hadn't she taken heed of any possible sign that would've pointed to it? Why hadn't she gone to Paris?

And what the hell was she going to say to Gavin?

Deira sat down at one of tables outside the Atlantique to wait for the tow truck, and texted Grace. When the other woman joined her a short time later, Deira gave her a résumé of her earlier conversation.

'How long will you have to wait?'

'I don't know.' Deira's shoulders slumped. 'I should've known this trip would be a disaster.'

'Oh, but why?' asked Grace. 'The fire wasn't your fault.'

'Something was always going to happen,' said Deira.

'Why?' repeated Grace.

'It . . . it doesn't matter.' Deira shook her head. 'Are you leaving for La Rochelle soon?'

'I haven't taken the photo at the museum yet,' Grace reminded her. 'Are you sure you don't want to come?'

'I've no idea how long it will take them to arrive and tow away my car. So I'll have to wait here. But let me know when you've uploaded the photo. I'd love to know if it works.'

'OK,' said Grace. 'See you later.'

She waved to Deira as she drove past, a little guilty at the relief that it was the younger woman's car that had been ruined in the fire and not the Lexus. Because that would have thrown her entire trip into disarray. Given that Ken had set the timetable by booking the hotels in advance, and that he'd restricted the number of guesses for each clue, she wouldn't have put it past him to have some kind of time limit on the treasure hunt itself. In fact she had images of the documents on the laptop simply disappearing if she didn't work out the answers in time, like a scene from *Mission: Impossible*. She still didn't really know why Ken had devised this expedition. Or when. She hoped that in solving it, she'd understand her late husband a little more.

But she wasn't betting on it.

When she returned a couple of hours later, Deira was still waiting for the tow truck. Grace had enjoyed her trip to the museum, which contained displays of manuscripts and books as well as models of some of the machines in Verne's novels.

'There was a small boat there too,' she told Deira. 'But I didn't see a name on it. Just in case, I counted the portholes. There were eighteen. So maybe that's the extra digit, not the 20 from *Twenty Thousand Leagues*, although that would mean *Atlantic Lady* was wrong, and it feels right to me.'

'Too many options and two few guesses.' Deira frowned.

'I know.'

'Did you take the photo?'

Grace nodded and took out her phone to show her. 'I'll get the laptop and upload it now,' she said.

Deira felt she should say that Grace didn't need to try to

unlock the document in front of her, but she was aching to know if they'd solved the clues, so she stayed silent.

'Oh, look!' As Grace stood up, she pointed towards the driveway of the hotel. 'Your tow truck has arrived.'

'I hope so,' said Deira. 'I'm beginning to think they've forgotten me.'

But Grace was right. The driver of the truck attached the convertible and told Deira that someone from the dealership would be in touch. She watched as it lumbered back towards the main road, and then returned to the table, where Grace was now sitting with the laptop open in front of her.

'Well?' she demanded. 'Did it work?'

'I was waiting for you,' said Grace.

'Gosh, you're patient. I wouldn't have been able to contain myself.'

The two women waited while the photo uploaded to the site. Grace tapped her fingers against the side of the table as she watched the progress bar move slowly across the screen.

You have successfully uploaded your photo, said the onscreen message. *Please wait.*

'What now?' wondered Grace. 'Should I—'

She broke off as another message appeared.

Congratulations. Your photo is a match. Your final number is 3.

'So will we go with 2 for the novel, 18 for the portholes in the museum's boat and the 3?' asked Deira. 'Or 20 for the novel, 5 for the portholes in the bar and 3?'

'I'm not a hundred per cent convinced about the museum boat,' admitted Grace. 'I counted eighteen portholes but maybe I missed one. And, like I said, there wasn't a name on it.'

'How many guesses do you have?'

'Seven,' said Grace.

'Plenty.' Deira gave her an encouraging nod. 'Go for it.'

Grace tapped in the numbers 2183.

Password incorrect.

She made a face at Deira. 'In that case it must be 2053.'

She entered the numbers.

Password incorrect.

'What have we got wrong?' asked Grace.

Deira shook her head slowly. 'I don't understand. I was sure this had to be it. Was there anything at all on the boat you saw that might point us in the right direction?'

Grace closed her eyes and called up the image. 'It had three little cubes along the top with two portholes on each side of them,' she said, her eyes still closed. 'The third cube – the one I thought was the bridge – had another cube on top of it with one porthole each side and two on another . . . or two on both – maybe that's it! Maybe the three cubes had other portholes that I missed. They were very close together. What if they were like the bridge and had an additional one each on either side?'

'So twenty-four altogether,' said Deira.

'Will I give it a try?' asked Grace.

Deira nodded and Grace entered 2243.

Password incorrect.

'For crying out loud!' Grace was exasperated. 'What's wrong with this?'

'I don't know,' said Deira.

'Maybe I should reverse the numbers,' said Grace. 'Start off with the 3?'

'We'll run out of guesses,' said Deira. 'But it might be worth a try.'

144

'Let's do it on the first set we put in,' said Grace. 'After all, we were the most confident with that. I'm not sure about all these extra portholes.'

She tapped in 3812, and when she got the inevitable 'password incorrect' message, she tried 3502.

Password incorrect.

'Shit,' said Deira.

'What now?' Grace looked at her anxiously. 'We have two guesses left.'

'I don't know,' said Deira. 'I'm sorry. Maybe I've pulled us down a rabbit hole with all my talk of portholes. Maybe it's something else entirely.'

'It can't be,' said Grace. 'It really can't. And I think it's much more likely you're right with the ship in the bar. Is there a chance you counted the portholes incorrectly?'

'No,' said Deira. 'I was staring at it for quite some time. There were five. Oh!'

'Oh?'

'That's it!' exclaimed Deira. 'That's the mistake.'

'What is?'

'Try 2103,' said Deira.

Grace stared at her. 'Why?'

'The second number is 10,' said Deira. 'I know it is.'

'Good enough,' said Grace.

Both women held their breath as she entered the numbers.

Password correct.

'Oh!' She turned to Deira. 'You clever, clever thing.'

'Ten portholes,' said Deira. 'Five on each side. I suddenly realised I'd only counted one side of the *Atlantic Lady*. And you can actually see them reflected in the bar mirror. It was stupid of me not to think of that straight away.'

'I think you were brilliant to think of it at all,' said Grace as she looked at the computer. 'And we need that brilliance again. Because I haven't a notion what this is all about. Do you?'

Deira looked at the unlocked document, which was headed 'La Rochelle'.

'No,' she said.

Grace read the clue aloud.

Well done, Hippo. You did it! Your reward is the letter I. You need to keep that letter safe until the end, along with the others you'll get if you solve the rest of the clues. And now for the next one. It's no mystery that Georges spent some time here. Why wouldn't he when it's so beautiful, even if he did sometimes show the seedy side. You'll need to upload a picture of his favourite café for your first number. You'll also need the number of the place where the crime took place. Then tell me the day Brigitte arrived at your hotel. Only nine guesses this time, to keep you on your toes. Good luck!

'Crikey,' said Deira. 'I've no idea. George. Brigitte. A crime. A café. Where it took place maybe? Did someone write about an unsolved crime in La Rochelle? Did anything happen when you were there with the professor?'

Before Grace had time to reply, Deira's mobile vibrated and took her attention completely away from the treasure hunt, because the call was from the garage, saying that they'd be in touch as soon as possible with a report about the car. Almost as soon as she hung up, the hotel manager came to ask her to sign some documents for the Atlantique's own insurance report. She followed him inside and signed the sheaf of papers he put in front of her, even as she wondered if she should have asked for a translator to tell her exactly what she was agreeing to.

'I might have absolved them of all responsibility,' she told Grace after she'd finished with them. 'Though he did assure me it was all about the hotel's potential liability.'

'Be positive,' urged Grace. 'What will be will be. Are you going to stay here for a few days?'

'I don't have much choice,' Deira replied. 'It's not like I have any means of getting away.'

'It's such a pity to have your holiday messed up,' said Grace.

'I seem to be managing to make a mess of my entire life right now, so what's one more thing.' Deira's words were light, but her face told a different story.

'Surely not,' said Grace. 'But if there's anything I can do to help . . .'

'I'm fine, really,' said Deira, although she suddenly felt close to tears. She cleared her throat and smiled brightly. 'I guess I could spend some time thinking about your new clue to keep my mind occupied. I could text you my ideas. Not that I have any right now.'

As she spoke, she asked herself if it was Grace's seemingly perpetual positivity that helped her stay so calm and composed despite the tragedy that had befallen her. She wished she had some of it too, but the truth was that Gavin had sapped every drop from her.

'That would be great,' Grace said in response. 'But I'm not in a rush to leave, so we could spend a little time brainstorming together if you like. How about some coffee to help?'

'Coffee would be lovely.'

'We thought the links were writers that Ken admired,' said Grace when the drinks arrived. 'So perhaps if we google "La Rochelle writers" it might set us on the right track.'

The top hit on her search was a writer named Pierre Drieu La Rochelle, who seemed to have spent all his life in Paris.

'The professor said Georges, not Pierre,' Deira pointed out.

Grace changed her search to 'Georges writer La Rochelle'.

'Oh, of course,' she exclaimed. 'It's Georges Simenon. Ken was a fan of his too. I should've remembered.'

Deira nodded. As with Jules Verne, she'd read a number of Simenon's books, but not since her college days.

'He wrote the Maigret detective novels,' she said. 'I've seen them as a TV series too. The crime must be something to do with one of his books, don't you think? Maybe the café is fictional or maybe it's in the town. D'you recall the professor mentioning one when you were there? Or could it be in the hotel he's booked for you?'

'It'd be a bit odd of Ken to book me into a crime scene, even a fictional one,' said Grace. 'The hotel is called the Fleur d'Île. We've never stayed there before, but it certainly doesn't say anything on its website about it being the setting for a crime. Or a crime novel, for that matter.'

'I don't suppose it would,' said Deira. 'It wouldn't want to advertise that its guests might get murdered over their breakfast.'

Grace laughed. 'It actually seems like a very nice hotel. Better than the ones we stayed in when we had the kids with us, that's for sure. In fact most of the hotels he's booked me into are nice.'

'You're on a very exact itinerary,' commented Deira. 'Every night accounted for. No room for diversions.'

'You think it's weird, don't you?' said Grace.

'A bit,' admitted Deira. 'He's not really allowing you to do your own thing, is he?'

Oh for heaven's sake, Hippo. Leave it to me. You need organising, you know you do.

Deira was right, Grace thought, as she heard her late husband's voice in her head. But the thing was, she'd never minded letting him set the agenda. She was OK with being told what to do. It made sense that he'd be the one to take charge. Deira was being judgemental without knowing what their lives had been like. So many people were these days. Grace and Ken had met in simpler times.

'I like having it planned out for me,' she told Deira. 'One less thing to worry about.'

Deira nodded, even though she couldn't help thinking that Professor Harrington had been a total dinosaur where his treatment of his wife had been concerned. She hadn't given his attitude much thought in college. But that was because she'd considered him an old-fashioned man even then. His enthusiasm for male writers and his very male points of view had seemed endearing at the time. But she reckoned they would be wearing to live with.

She turned the laptop towards her and typed in 'Simenon café'.

'*Voilà!*' she exclaimed as she angled it so that Grace could see the page. 'Café de la Paix,' she read aloud. 'Simenon was an *habitué.*'

'So basically you've solved two parts of it already,' said Grace. 'The crime scene has to be one of his novels, and you've found the café too. You're far more in tune with Ken's thinking than I could ever be. I knew about Simenon. One of his books was on the curriculum when I was at school. I realise that was over forty years ago, but I should have made the connection.'

'You would've worked it out.'

'Ken set out this entire treasure hunt for me,' said Grace. 'But if you weren't here, I'd be heading to La Rochelle with no idea of what I was looking for. As it is, I now know I've to go to the Café de la Paix and take a photo – I'm presuming that's the one Ken means. And I know I've to read one of his books, although which one, I've no idea.'

'He could hardly expect you to read them at all,' remarked Deira. 'Certainly not in one night! And in French, too. It has to be something more obvious.'

'A title?' suggested Grace.

Deira clicked on a link to Simenon's books and began to scroll through them. Then she stopped.

'*The Crime at Lock 14,*' she read.

'And once again she comes up with the goods.' Grace beamed at her.

'Teamwork,' said Deira. 'We've solved most of the La Rochelle clue before you even get there. The photo of the café will give you the first number, then 14 from the book. Presumably there'll be something in your hotel about Brigitte, whoever she is.'

'It must be Bardot,' said Grace. 'She has to have stayed there.'

'You'll have time to enjoy yourself there now instead of fretting about clues,' said Deira. 'Is it a nice town?'

'It's very pretty, especially at night. Lovely to walk around. Lively and fun.'

'Not quite Maigret territory, so.'

'Was he part of your English lit course too?' asked Grace.

Deira shook her head. 'But Professor Harrington urged us to read widely. He liked Simenon's style. It was quite pared-back.'

'Like Hemingway?'

'A bit, I suppose.' Deira nodded. 'The professor did seem to favour men who wrote in an almost journalistic way. And of course most were from, or writing about, very different times.'

Grace nodded. 'For all that he thought he was a modern man, Ken had some pretty antiquated views.'

'Like?'

'Me working, for one. He hated it. Thought he should be able to provide for me and the family. Which was the prevailing view back then, I suppose. But later, after the children were a bit older, he still wasn't mad about me going back to work. And even though he was proud of Aline when she graduated, I don't think he ever considered her as someone who could get a serious job. Mind you, he was right about that. She faffed around after college and then went into something that was nothing to do with her degree. To be fair, I think her priority was always to be a mum, and even though she works part-time now, I know she'll give it up if she has another baby. Regan is an entirely different proposition. She loves what she does and she never really saw eye to eye with her dad.'

'He seemed old-fashioned to me when I was at college,' admitted Deira. 'Although in a nice kind of way. But then I suppose I seem old-fashioned to my niece and her friends, no matter how I feel inside.'

'You're a stripling in comparison to me.' Grace laughed.

'But I've still wasted the best years of my life.'

'Deira!' Grace stared at her. 'How can you possibly think that? The best years of your life are still to come.'

'No, they're not.' Deira leaned back in the wooden chair and rubbed her aching side gently. 'I know we like to say things like that. To believe there's always everything to live for. But I fucked it all up, Grace. And there's no coming back.'

'How?' asked Grace.

'I believed a man,' Deira said. 'And it was the stupidest thing I ever did.'

Chapter 16

Nantes to La Rochelle: 136 km

'Tell me,' said Grace. 'I told you my story. You have to tell me yours.'

Deira hesitated. 'It's not a story like yours. It's not something you can sympathise with me over.'

'Let me be the judge of that.'

'Seriously . . .'

'Oh for heaven's sake, Deira. Just tell me.'

Deira took a deep breath, then brought Grace up to speed with how she'd first met Gavin.

'I felt guilty about Marilyn and the girls, of course,' she said. 'Especially Mae and Suzy; I didn't want them to have a bad relationship with their father and I encouraged him to see them as much as possible, but I was absolutely a hundred per cent convinced that the marriage itself was over and that Gavin and I were forever. I'd never loved anyone the way I loved him.'

Grace nodded.

'We were blissfully happy,' Deira continued. 'It was a bit awkward initially at work, but eventually that evened itself out. Nobody else was bothered by it and our business relationship evolved over time anyhow. The company's corporate responsibility strategy expanded and I took control of that;

153

meantime he grew more involved in the pensions side of things. We were specialising in different areas so our work and private lives didn't clash. We both moved ahead and it was great.'

'A power couple,' observed Grace.

'Sometimes I thought that,' agreed Deira. 'We bought a mews house near the canal, we spent a lot of time out at functions, we lived a kind of glamour life.'

'You said before that *you* bought the house, not both of you,' Grace reminded her.

'Well, yes, I took out the mortgage. It would've been messy otherwise, especially as it took so long for him to get the divorce. We didn't want the house to get mixed up in it all. Afterwards, he said it was right that it should be my place. I thought it meant that he was a good person. I loved him.'

'You were happy,' said Grace. 'Why didn't you marry?'

'Mainly because of the girls,' said Deira. 'They hated the idea of their dad marrying again. If it had only been Marilyn, I'd have done it like a shot simply to annoy her. She was so bloody difficult about it all. I know it was hard for her, I do, truly, but she never let up.'

'You mean she wanted him back?'

'Actually, no,' said Deira. 'I don't think she did. But she didn't want to make it easy for him either. She was forever phoning up, complaining about things, asking for more money for either Mae or Suzy – for essentials, she'd say.'

'But surely the divorce settlement dealt with all that?'

'Eventually it did,' Deira conceded. 'But prior to it, she was relentless. Even afterwards she kept demanding things, and he wasn't willing to get into a battle with her because he didn't want to antagonise the girls.'

'You said you wanted him to have a good relationship with them. Does he?'

'On and off,' replied Deira. 'They're certainly in a better place now than they were at the start, but it's been tough. At first Marilyn wouldn't let them visit the house, but after a while Gavin managed to persuade her to allow them to come if I wasn't there. I used to stay with my friend Tillie those times. Sometimes for a few hours, sometimes for a weekend.'

'That must have been difficult.'

'I didn't mind initially, but afterwards I came to resent it,' said Deira. 'When I'd get home, I'd find things had been moved around or hidden away. Occasionally they'd have squeezed out the contents of my make-up into tissues that I'd find in the bathroom waste bin. Once they mashed up a brand-new Bobbi Brown palette I'd been silly enough to leave behind. They pulled the heels off a pair of Prada shoes too.'

'Oh Deira! That's awful.'

'They were angry,' said Deira. 'They blamed me. I understood.'

'Didn't Gavin say anything? Do anything?'

'I never told him,' said Deira. 'I didn't want them to have a row. I reckoned they'd grow out of it.'

'Did they?'

'Eventually. The visits became less fraught and we got on better, although we never really became close. That's partly why . . .' She broke off and closed her eyes.

Grace recognised the signs of someone trying to keep herself under control. She'd had to do it often enough over the last few months, not wanting to burst into tears in front of Aline or Fionn or Regan. She'd had to be strong for them.

Strong for herself, too. She'd refused to allow herself to cry; not when the police came, not when she identified Ken's body and not at his funeral. The anger helped, of course, while staying dry-eyed became something to hold on to, something to get her through the difficult days. And then it became an end in itself. *My husband drove his car off a pier and I didn't cry,* she'd think. And she'd feel proud of herself for that. She wondered if the young woman in front of her felt the same.

When Deira opened her eyes again, she saw that Grace was watching her, quiet and serene.

'Sorry,' she said. 'I got a bit . . .'

'That's OK,' said Grace. 'You don't have to tell me if you don't want to.'

'It's just that . . .' Deira rubbed the corners of her eyes. 'It's stupid really. Nothing special. Nothing I should be crying over.'

'If you need to cry, you need to cry,' said Grace. Seeing other people cry made her feel good about her own ability to remain dry-eyed. It reinforced her feelings of strength. Of being somewhere that Ken's actions couldn't reach her.

Deira used one of the paper napkins on the table in front of them to wipe her eyes.

'I loved him and we were happy; like you said, we were a power couple, and we were working through the problems with Marilyn and the girls. Everything was perfect until we talked about starting a family. Well, to be strictly accurate, I talked about it. He listened. He said no.'

'Straight out?'

'Straight out,' confirmed Deira. 'He said that he already had a family.'

156

'But you and Gavin were a family too,' protested Grace.

'I know. And when I reminded him of that, he agreed with me straight away. But he said he couldn't possibly upset the girls further by having children with someone else.'

'I can see where he was coming from,' said Grace. 'But he was bloody insensitive all the same.'

Deira picked at the paper napkin. 'After I talked about having a baby, he made an even bigger effort to get Mae and Suzy involved in our lives. He insisted that Marilyn allow them to come on holiday with us and have them over more often.'

'But that's not the same as you having a baby of your own!' exclaimed Grace. 'Surely he could see that?'

Deira shook her head. 'His children, our children. He seemed to think it was all the same.'

'Men are such fools.' Grace's tone was heartfelt.

'At least my relationship with the girls improved to the point that they stopped trashing my stuff,' said Deira. 'Gavin was pleased that we all seemed to be getting on.'

'But . . . but . . . didn't you tell him it wasn't enough?'

Deira shook her head. 'I knew the girls were enough for him. He hadn't left them just to do the same thing all over again. We were a different sort of family, he said. A family of two adults. He didn't want to upset it by bringing a baby into the mix. He reminded me that I didn't know anything about babies. That he was the one with experience. That they totally disrupted your life. That you never got to give them back.'

Grace raised an eyebrow.

'I know. Put like that, it sounds selfish. But he didn't mean it to be. He was pointing out how we were currently living compared with how we'd live if there was a baby.'

'Didn't you discuss it at the start? Before you moved in together?'

'We should have. But it never occurred to me. I was so in love and I guess I thought that over time the baby thing would happen. Besides, a lot of our emotional energy was taken up with his bloody divorce.'

'But in the end you agreed with him about the baby? Or did you?'

'I had to,' said Deira. 'He wasn't going to change his mind. And . . . well, children had never been a priority for me. It wasn't something I wanted to rush into. So deciding I wanted a baby was a bit left-field. Anyhow, Gavin was right about my lack of experience. My home life was disjointed. I would probably have been a hopeless mother.'

'Not at all,' said Grace. 'You're a kind person. You would have done just fine. You could still do just fine,' she added, 'if that's what you want.'

'I'm nearly forty and currently single,' said Deira. 'Besides, I believed that having a baby wasn't only for me. It was for both of us.'

'So you split up over it?' Grace's voice was full of sympathy.

'No,' replied Deira. 'I was in baby mode for the best part of a year, but in the end, I got over it. I decided Gavin was right, we didn't need a child. Even if deep down his daughters still regarded me as the Wicked Witch of the West, they were at least civil around me. Gavin and I were a strong unit. I was happy to live the life we were living. I made my peace with it. Besides,' she added, 'at that point Bex, my niece, was in her teens and wanting to come to Dublin all the time, so she spent quite a few weekends with us. Between her and Gavin's girls, we had plenty of young people around. They were exhausting, to be honest, and maybe they did put me off the idea a bit.'

Grace said nothing.

'Not entirely,' conceded Deira. 'But after they'd gone, Gavin would say to me that if we had a child of our own, they'd be there all week and never go home to someone else.'

'It's different with your own.' Grace thought of Aline, Fionn and Regan. She was happy that all her children were doing their own thing, and grateful that Aline dropped by regularly, while the other two FaceTimed her once a week (at least, since Ken's funeral; before that it had been less often), but even though she was glad to have time to herself, she sometimes missed the bustle of sharing the house with them. Although she hadn't raised the subject yet, she was thinking of putting it up for sale, because she didn't need a four-bed detached home with a long garden. She needed something like Deira had – an easy-to-maintain mews, or an apartment. Something a lot smaller, at any rate, so she wasn't rattling around like a lost soul.

'Oh, I know it would have been different if we'd had our own baby,' said Deira. 'But I put it out of my mind. I decided it wasn't for us and I was OK with it.'

'Did the subject ever come up again?' asked Grace.

'Never in the last five years,' said Deira. 'We were both very busy. Even if we'd wanted a baby, we didn't have time for one. That's what I thought, anyhow.'

'But?'

'I also thought Gavin and I were solid together. He was the one who planned this holiday, who wanted us to drive through France with the roof down. He made me think . . .'

Deira broke off again and used another napkin to dry her eyes.

'Sorry,' she said. 'I'm like the fecking Powerscourt Waterfall these days. Anyhow, I was totally confident that we were as happy as it was possible to be. Until six weeks ago, when Gavin came home and told me that he was leaving me.'

'What! Just like that?'

Deira nodded. 'He said things had been going wrong for a while. That this wasn't the life he wanted. I asked what *was* the life he wanted, seeing as he'd always told me he was living it with me. He said something warmer, more nurturing.'

'More nurturing!' exclaimed Grace. 'For heaven's sake! Surely he was getting all the nurturing he needed?'

'You'd think,' said Deira. 'Actually what he meant was that he wanted someone who put him first all the time. Someone who wasn't focused on her career, like me.'

'Seriously?'

'I'm obviously the most stupid woman on the planet, but I didn't even imagine that he was having an affair. Can you call it having an affair when you're not married to the person you're living with? Anyway, he was seeing someone else.'

'I'm so sorry,' said Grace. 'That must have been devastating.'

'What was devastating,' said Deira carefully, 'was the fact that she was pregnant with his child.'

Grace's expression was a mixture of shock and sympathy. Without even thinking, she reached across the table and took Deira's hand. Deira squeezed it, unable to speak. Other than with Tillie, this was the first time she'd told the entirety of the story to anyone. To Gillian, and all of her acquaintances, she'd merely said that she and Gavin had split up. Gill's response had been to ask if there was anyone else, and when Deira, unable to lie point blank, had said yes, that Gavin was now living with a new girlfriend, she'd come back with 'once a cheater always a cheater', a phrase that had been like a knife in Deira's guts. Because of course now she understood what it had been like for Marilyn when Gavin had left her. And though she'd always comforted herself by believing that his marriage to his former wife had been doomed from the start (we married too young, he'd told her; we didn't know what we were letting ourselves in for), there was nothing anyone could say to her now that made her feel anything other than a fool.

'That's awful,' said Grace.

'I believed him,' Deira told her. 'When he said he didn't want children because he didn't want to make Suzy and Mae feel unwanted, I believed it. When he said he wanted to live in an adult home, I believed it. When he said he was happy, I believed it. I let his words influence me and what I wanted because I believed, I really did, that I couldn't ask for more when I already had true love. How could I have been so damn stupid? I was there for him when he wanted me and then when he wanted something else he was quite prepared to get rid of me, the same as he did with Marilyn.'

She eased her hand from Grace's hold and took another napkin. 'And the thing is . . .' She sniffed and blew her nose, 'the thing is that I've wasted the best years of my life on him. The years when I could have had a child of my own. When it would have been possible. All that time he was saying no and my eggs were shrivelling up and dying, we could have had a baby. But he didn't want it. Not then. Not with me. And now, with Afton' – she almost spat out the name – 'he's "over the moon with excitement", at least according to his Insta-fucking-gram page. Instagram! He never bothered with it before. He called social media "a window into the narcissistic soul". But Afton is a PR woman, who frames her entire life in photographs, and of course he's now completely into posting pictures of his perfect life. There was one of both of their hands on her fucking bump!' At which point Deira started to cry again.

The sympathy Grace felt for her increased. It was so damn easy for people to tell you that you had plenty of time to start a family after doing the things you wanted to do, but life wasn't like that. It hurtled past when you weren't paying attention until suddenly you realised that policemen didn't only look younger, they *were* younger, and that you didn't recognise a single tune on the radio. And that somehow the exciting, energetic stuff you'd put off doing was now being done by other people while you rubbed Voltarol onto your aching back.

She could only imagine the depth of the hurt that Deira was feeling now that her ex-partner was doing what Deira herself had wanted, but with another woman.

'Not just another woman,' Deira said, when Grace made the comment. 'A twenty-five-year-old woman. She's the same age as I was the first time I met him, and younger than both his daughters!'

'How do they feel about it?' asked Grace.

'Mae sent me a text after he moved in with Afton. She said that now I knew what it felt like. But she also said she was sorry about what had happened and that her dad was a complete arse.'

'I can't imagine it's easy for them,' said Grace.

'No,' agreed Deira. 'I guess Marilyn will be OK – she's been in a relationship for the past few years – but I doubt the girls will get the opportunity to tell Afton what they think of her or ruin her clothes and make-up.'

'At least they can be a bit more mature about it, even if they hate it,' remarked Grace.

'Which is more than I'm being.' Deira sniffed. 'But it's so bloody demoralising. He swans out of my life with a gorgeous woman on his arm, and she gets the one thing I sacrificed for him. And not that I want a man in my life ever again, but I've given up my chances of having a child for nothing.'

'You're still a young woman,' protested Grace.

'No,' said Deira. 'I'm not. Not when it comes to my damn eggs, at any rate. Fertility-wise, I'm a shrivelled old crone.'

'I'm sorry it didn't work out,' said Grace. 'And I know it's more difficult to have a baby when you're older. But you never know, you could meet someone else – and there's always IVF.'

'I look at men,' Deira said. 'I look at them and I think, are you the one? Are you the man who could father a child for me? Are your little swimmers strong enough to find my diminished crop of eggs? Could you make a baby for me? It's another reason I came on this trip. I thought that away from Ireland I might meet someone and sleep with him and get pregnant and I'd have a baby.'

'Oh.' Grace was taken aback.

'I know it's crazy,' said Deira. 'Even as I ask those questions I know it's insane. Besides, being a mum, single or otherwise, is what *I* want, not what the baby deserves. How would I cope as a lone parent? Is it even right to want to? So I'm torn between wanting to shag every man I see and telling myself that I'm a selfish cow who's terrorised by her stupid biological clock. And IVF is practically useless for a woman my age. You wouldn't think that, would you, the way they talk about it so cheerily, but instead of all these pictures of older mothers with their cute babies, they might as well tell you to stop fantasising and get a dog or a cat. Or even a bloody hamster.'

Grace didn't know what to say. Her heart went out to Deira, who was in such distress, but she knew she didn't have any solution to the physical and moral dilemma that the younger woman was in. When she was younger, Grace had had rigid opinions about what constituted a family and how children should be raised. But over time her perspective had shifted and her views had mellowed.

'The worst of it is that when older men father kids, they're regarded as some kind of stud,' added Deira. 'Gavin is fifty-seven. But if a woman of fifty-seven was lucky enough to get pregnant thanks to IVF, she'd be looked at in horror and disgust.'

Grace nodded. Deira was definitely right about that. 'You're a long way from fifty-seven yet,' she pointed out.

'I've still wasted the best years of my life on him.'

'Oh no.' Grace shook her head. 'You can't say that. You've spent a small proportion of your life with him, and certainly not your best years. They're still to come.'

Deira gave her a watery smile. 'Thanks, but I don't think so. I'm washed up, Grace.'

'I don't want to say you're being ridiculous, but you are,' said Grace. 'You're thirty-nine, not ninety-nine. You've loads of good years ahead of you. And you know what, maybe you *will* meet someone lovely on this trip and it'll be great and—'

164

'Honestly, I don't need it to be great. I'm not interested in men. The sex is the only thing I care about,' Deira told her. 'But right now, I have a more pressing issue than getting pregnant.'

'What?'

'Gavin and Afton are away for a week,' Deira replied. 'A family wedding in Glasgow. I don't know how it happens that weddings take a week now, but there you go. Anyhow, they flew there on Friday evening. And I . . .'

Grace looked at her expectantly.

'I took the car.'

It took a moment for Grace to realise what she was saying.

'The Audi? The convertible? That's *his* car, not yours?'

'It was *our* car. But when he moved out, he took it. His view was that I was in the house so he'd have the car. He said his solicitor would eventually get in touch with me about everything. I don't think he deserves jack shit, to be honest. When I heard he was going away with Afton at the same time as we'd booked to come here, I thought – why not take it? The whole reason for planning this trip was to drive through France with the roof down. He said he wanted to do it before he was so old that people laughed at him. Driving sports cars is probably the only thing older men get laughed at for! I told him not to be silly, that he was still young . . .' She swallowed hard, unable to continue.

'Maybe he won't mind about the car,' said Grace. 'How are things between you now?'

Deira laughed mirthlessly. 'Pretty rubbish,' she answered. 'Though that's mostly my fault. I cracked up, you see, when he told me about Afton. I kept going into his office at work and arguing with him. I followed him back to the apartment he's sharing with her and demanded to be let in. I caused a scene in a café – he was having a breakfast meeting and I dumped his fry-up all over him.'

'You go, girl,' murmured Grace.

'He wanted to get a restraining order against me,' Deira said. 'In all honesty, I couldn't blame him. The HR manager at work persuaded him against it. Then she called me in, and although she was sympathetic to my situation, she suggested I take some leave. That's the other thing, isn't it? He cheats on me but he's given a pass. I'm the one who has to disappear for a while. Not that HR weren't right in some respects,' she acknowledged. 'It was toxic being in the same building as him. So it was a good idea for me to get away. And as the holiday was already booked . . .'

'Like mine,' said Grace.

'Gosh, yes.' Deira nodded. 'I didn't think – we're in a similar sort of boat, aren't we? Except that you're entitled to be driving your car and I'm basically a character from *Grand Theft Auto*.'

'Did you just rock up to his place and drive it away?' asked Grace. 'Did you have a key?'

Deira told her about sneaking into the apartment complex and taking the car. 'And yes, I had a key because I lost mine ages ago and had to get a new one. Then I found mine again and kept it as a spare. I was going to send him a text and let him know what I'd done before he got home. I knew he'd go ballistic, but there would be nothing he could do about it. Now . . . well, I've basically destroyed it.'

'Perhaps the dealership can repair it.' Grace tried to sound positive.

'The paintwork is burned, the seats are charred and the

interior is soaked. Even if it does dry out, it'll probably be mouldy. The roof needs to be replaced too – there's a massive hole in it. It's a disaster, Grace, and it's my fault. Gavin will go mental.'

'Tell him to eff off,' said Grace. 'He treated you disgracefully. Let him whistle for his car.'

Deira gave her a watery smile. 'I bet that's what you'd say in my position all right. You're so . . . so grown up. So together. Whereas I'm an idiot.'

'I'm not at all grown up,' said Grace, although she was pleased that Deira thought so. 'I'm someone trying to do her best.'

'God, yes. You've had a much worse trauma than me.' Deira was aghast at having pushed Grace's situation to the back of her mind. 'I'm sorry.'

'You listened to me offloading about Ken last night. It's only fair I should return the favour.'

'What are we like?' Deira blew her nose again. 'Well, what I really mean is – you're great. What happened with your husband was simply awful. A total tragedy. But you're . . . well, I'm not going to say coping, because I don't know you or anything and I'm sure it's still really difficult. But at least you're not a snivelling mess like me.'

'You're not a mess,' said Grace. 'You've gone through a shitty time. You deserve your break. And you should have it, despite the car.'

'I'm probably going to be stuck here for ages trying to work things out,' said Deira. 'So much for my French holiday idyll.'

'Why stay here?' asked Grace. 'There's nothing more you can do. The insurance companies can sort it out between

167

themselves. The dealership will either fix the car or not. What's the point in you hanging around while they decide?'

'What else can I do?' asked Deira. 'I've no car and no way of getting around.'

'But *I* have a car,' said Grace. 'And I have an itinerary. I also have more clues to be deciphered. We've already seen that two heads are better than one. Why don't you come with me?'

'On all your stops? Through France and Spain?' Deira looked at her in astonishment.

'Why not?' said Grace. 'To tell you the truth, you'd be doing me a favour. My elder daughter thinks I'm off my rocker doing this trip on my own. If I tell her I have company, she might stop worrying about me and asking me to share my location with her so she can check up on me without me even realising it.'

'I'm not sure . . .'

'We still haven't worked out the full La Rochelle clue,' said Grace. 'Besides, I'd love your company.'

'Really?'

'Why not?' repeated Grace.

Why not indeed, thought Deira. Why not do something even madder than her original plan and travel with a woman she hardly knew, following a treasure hunt set by a dead man? Because it's crazy, that's why, she told herself. Bonkers. But then you're crazy and bonkers too, aren't you?

'OK.' She smiled at Grace. 'I will.'

'Excellent,' said Grace. 'I think the best thing for you to do is contact your insurance company, tell them what you're doing and how to keep in touch, and then put it all out of your head.'

168

'I still have to tell Gavin,' Deira reminded her.

'He doesn't need to know yet,' said Grace.

'I guess you're right.'

'So, let's organise ourselves, do what we need to do, book you a room in La Rochelle, then head there and solve the clue.'

'Sounds like a plan.' Deira suddenly felt motivated. 'I'll get my stuff.'

She gathered up the tear-sodden napkins and threw them into the waste bin, then went back to her room to pack.

Chapter 17

La Rochelle, France: 46.1603°N 1.1511°W

Deira and Grace set off for La Rochelle at four o'clock. Deira was feeling more optimistic about the possible outcome for the car, having spoken again to her insurance company. Everyone seemed to want to resolve things quickly, and even though she knew from personal experience of the industry that a company's idea of a quick resolution wasn't always the same as a customer's, at least she'd been able to have reasonably intelligent conversations about her situation. Her conversation with Gavin, of course, whenever it might happen, wouldn't be intelligent. He would be incandescent with rage, and she couldn't blame him. But there were only so many things she could worry about at any one time, she told Grace as she put her bag into the boot of the Lexus, so she was going to try to forget about it for a couple of days.

'Absolutely,' agreed Grace. 'Let's just concentrate on having a good time.'

Now, despite everything, Deira felt herself adjust to the idea of enjoying herself. Enjoyment hadn't been the original idea behind her trip, but she was going to try. She resolutely refused to think about Gavin and the fact that his new partner was living the life she herself had given up for him. And she vowed not to look at every man she saw and wonder if he could be a potential father to a child she was never going to have.

The countryside on the two-hour drive from Nantes to La Rochelle was flatter and drier than the rolling hills and valleys of Brittany. The fields on either side of the road were carefully cultivated, and many had tall irrigation systems ready to water the growing crops when they needed it. Grace kept to a steady 100 kph, untroubled at being overtaken by ancient Peugeot and Citroën vans that seemed to be held together by string.

'It's always the same,' she told Deira after they'd been passed by another disreputable wreck. 'They see a foreign-registered car and their sense of pride means they have to overtake it, even if it's killing their own vehicle.'

'Gavin would've got into a pissing contest with them,' Deira remarked. 'He can't bear being behind anyone on the road. He certainly wouldn't have let a practically prehistoric van pass him.'

'I do understand that,' conceded Grace. 'Ken used to do all the driving for us, and he insisted that the journey was part of the holiday so there was no point in screeching along like a bat out of hell.' She laughed suddenly. 'Fionn, on the other hand, liked going fast. One year he brought a Meatloaf playlist and started off with "Bat Out of Hell" simply to annoy his dad. He succeeded.'

'Do you miss him?' asked Deira.

'Ken? Or Fionn?'

'I meant Ken.' Deira was sure Grace had deliberately mis-interpreted the question.

'You're always going to miss someone you've shared most of your life with,' Grace replied. 'But he's gone. He made a choice to go sooner than he had to. Like you with your Gavin, I'm angry and upset. But I still have to accept what he did.'

Deira noticed Grace's hands tighten on the steering wheel and dropped the subject. Then her phone pinged with a message from Tillie.

Hey, her friend had written, *hope all is going well on your trip. Was thinking of you when I saw the 88 bus. That's double good luck! Tx*

Tillie claimed that in some cultures the number 8 was considered to be lucky, and that she considered it to be lucky too. Given her fortune to date, Deira couldn't help thinking that the universe was simply mocking her.

'Everything OK?' asked Grace when Deira slid the phone back into her bag.

'Hope so.'

'I should have asked if you had a problem getting a room at the hotel.' She glanced at her. 'La Rochelle was always busy when we were there, and it's coming into the tourist season.'

'I booked a *remise* in the grounds. That's all they had available.'

'What's a *remise*?' asked Grace.

'A shed,' replied Deira, who'd clicked to translate.

'They're putting you in a shed!' Grace sounded horrified. 'How can they possibly get away with that?'

'I presume it's an upmarket shed, suitable for guests.' Deira grinned.

'I ask you to join me and you're forced to stay in a shed.' Grace chuckled. 'I'm so sorry.'

'I'm sure it'll be lovely,' said Deira.

172

'If you want to listen to music while we're on the road, feel free,' Grace said after they'd travelled in silence for a bit. 'I'm getting used to listening to playlists in the car. When the children were small, it was always nursery rhymes or kids' songs. Ken preferred listening to audio books, which I like myself, to be fair, but not all the time.'

'What sort of music do you like?'

'I'm easy,' Grace told her. 'I need to update my tastes, because I have a lot of old stuff on my phone. But I usually listen to female vocalists. Adele. Mariah Carey, that sort of stuff.'

'I have a mix you'll like,' said Deira. She paired her phone with the Lexus, and J.Lo's rich voice, full of pain and heartbreak, filled the car.

'Maybe not the most cheerful under the circumstances,' remarked Grace as Adele followed up with even more heartache. 'But like my mother used to say, they've got great lungs on them, those girls.'

Deira laughed.

'We're closer to the centre this time,' Grace said as they approached La Rochelle a while later. 'It's not such a big place, and even though there can be lots of traffic it's nothing like Paris.'

She followed the road through the flat landscape to the outskirts of the town, remembering the last time she'd been here with Ken and the children. She could hear them now, squabbling in the back seat of the car, and Ken telling them that if they weren't quiet, he'd stop and leave them on the side of the road. He might have done, thought Grace; he'd been a great believer in following words with actions. If he threatened to do something, he nearly always carried it

173

through, which meant that the children knew they could only go so far with him. She, on the other hand, had been a hopeless disciplinarian. She put it down to having to be strict in the aircraft cabin and not wanting to be the same at home.

She was still thinking of Ken as she drew up to the hotel. Unlike some of the newer, but somewhat soulless, hotels with sea views, the Fleur d'Île was a large old house with white-washed walls, a red-tiled roof and sky-blue shutters at the windows.

'This is lovely,' said Deira as they got out of the car. 'Even prettier than it looked on the website.'

'Let's hope the shed is equally lovely,' said Grace.

Deira felt sure it would be. The interior of the hotel was charming, casually decorated with a pastel blue and white seaside vibe. The walls were hung with art deco posters of beaches and railways, as well as old movie posters for films starring French actresses.

It was when she was handed the key to her hut and saw that instead of a number it had the name 'Brigitte Bardot' on the fob that she looked at Grace in excitement.

'She must have stayed here,' she said. 'That's definitely the answer to the professor's question.'

She turned immediately to the receptionist, a rather stern older man with a deeply furrowed brow and an enormous white moustache.

'I know nothing of Bardot and the hotel,' he said. 'Yes, we have named things for her. And for Madame Deneuve, and Madame Binoche. But they have not stayed here. Unfortunately.'

'Are you sure?' asked Grace. 'Because we thought Miss Bardot did.'

'I do not know why you would think such a thing.' The receptionist's moustache quivered above his lip. 'I am sorry if you got the wrong idea.'

'He has to be mistaken,' said Deira after they'd thanked him and Grace was accompanying her across the garden to the *remise*. 'It's too coincidental otherwise.'

'Absolutely,' agreed Grace. 'Maybe someone else in the hotel knows about it.'

Deira opened the door to the *remise* and stepped inside. It was decorated in a monochrome sixties style with white chairs and black rugs, while the walls were hung with black and white photographs of the iconic actress.

'She was stunning, wasn't she?' said Grace.

'A total babe,' agreed Deira.

'I'll leave you in peace to embrace your inner sex symbol. Will we meet up in an hour or so to talk about the clues?'

'Perfect.'

Grace nodded and walked back to the hotel alone.

Grace's own room was furnished in the style of an old country house, with dark wooden floors, luxurious furnishings and heavy drapes. She was surprised that Ken had chosen somewhere like this for her to stay. Over the years they'd travelled together, his choices had always been cheap and cheerful. He wasn't someone who needed creature comforts or even noticed his surroundings very much.

She opened the window and leaned out. The view from the top floor was breathtaking, looking out over the trees that surrounded the hotel to the vast expanse of ocean. Calm today, and azure blue, it lifted her spirits. It would have been nice to have stayed in this place with Ken, she thought. To have treated themselves, for once in their lives. She felt a lump in her throat and swallowed hard.

She was not going to cry.

She was never going to cry.

He didn't deserve her tears.

He'd probably spotted this place on one of his walks, she thought, as she turned away from the window and unpacked her cosmetics. He'd always enjoyed walking on his own, and on holidays invariably headed out before breakfast for an hour or so. So it was entirely possible he'd seen the hotel and wandered in to have a look. Yet he'd never said a word to her.

She'd gone on at him often enough about treating themselves when they went away for him to have known that this was the sort of hotel she would have liked to stay in. He'd ignored her when he was alive. But now, when it was all too late, she realised that he'd listened after all.

It was still gloriously warm when she walked into the garden to meet Deira, who told her she'd done some research on the Café de la Paix, which was a twenty-minute stroll from the hotel.

'Do you want to check it out now?' asked Grace. 'I guess we could get something to eat there too.'

Deira nodded, and the two women left the grounds, following the quiet street with its intermittent views of the sparkling sea. There were plenty of other people, tourists and locals alike, also out taking the evening air, and it was hard, Deira thought, as a couple of young women passed them in shorts and strappy tops, not to feel a little bit summery and carefree too. After a few minutes, the street widened into a pedestrianised zone, bordered by sandstone-coloured buildings. At street level they were mostly occupied by small artisan shops and cafés with chalkboard notices encouraging visitors inside with promises of souvenirs or delicate pastries.

Then they emerged into the cobbled area of the old port itself, where coloured lights were strung up around the busy stalls. There were more pavement cafés here, as well as bigger, busier restaurants vying for business.

'Ken always said it was the most picturesque French place he'd ever been,' said Grace when Deira remarked on how picture-postcard it looked. 'He loved it here.'

'I can see why,' said Deira as she consulted Google Maps. 'OK, Grace, the café we're looking for is further along, away from the port.'

They passed through a wide archway set with a large clock and continued walking until the street widened out into a plaza with a brightly coloured merry-go-round in the centre, where children, watched by their parents, squealed in excitement as they went round and round on painted unicorns. Almost directly opposite was the Café de la Paix.

'Here we are,' said Deira. 'Simenon's favourite watering hole.'

Grace looked at the building. As a family, they'd never come to this part of La Rochelle, which meant this was another place Ken had explored on his own. Until now, it had never bothered her that she hadn't been included in his daily walks or his academic pursuits. But there was something unsettling about the thought of him finding places that had ended up as clues in the treasure hunt he'd subsequently set for her. He couldn't have been thinking about treasure hunts all those years ago, she knew, but he'd remembered these places in far more detail than she ever could. Perhaps it was because he was interested in their history – or at least in the history of the writers who'd lived in them or visited them – that his memory was so sharp. He'd never shared that interest with her. He'd kept her in a different compartment of his life.

'OK?' Deira glanced at her.

'Yes, absolutely. Will we take the photo now?'

'Why not.' Deira nodded. 'Be sure and get the full name of the café.'

Grace pulled out her phone and took a couple of snaps. She showed them to Deira, who agreed that they were perfect for uploading.

'Would you mind taking one of me too?' asked Grace. 'It's another way to prove to my children that I'm doing fine on my own.'

'Why would they think otherwise?' asked Deira after she'd taken the photo and handed the phone back.

'We all struggled in the weeks immediately after Ken's death,' said Grace. 'It was very difficult for everyone. I think they expect me to keep on struggling. After all, we were married for a long time, and the children can't imagine me without him.'

If Professor Harrington really had been as controlling as sending his wife on the treasure hunt implied, Deira could understand their concerns. Yet it was clear that despite her husband's influence, Grace was a very independent woman. Had she simply hidden that aspect of her personality from her family? Or had it lain dormant all the years she was married? Did men change you in ways you didn't know? Had Gavin changed her?

'Let's go inside.' Grace broke into her thoughts. 'We can get some food and I'll forward the pic to the kids.'

The interior of the café was decorated in a belle époque style, with elaborate high ceilings, polished wood panelling, gold-coloured fittings and large mirrors. The lights were mellow white in large round shades. Some were wall-mounted, some were set into the marble-topped counter, and others hung from the ceiling.

'It's fabulous, isn't it?' said Grace. 'It's exactly the kind of place where writers should write! I can see Simenon coming in here, ordering a cognac and scribbling away in his note-book.'

'Me too,' agreed Deira.

'What would you like to eat?' asked Grace.

'I'm fine with a coffee. I'm not hungry.'

Grace raised an eyebrow, but ordered coffee for two and, for herself, a toasted sandwich that turned out to be larger than she'd expected. She offered Deira half.

'Half of half,' said Deira.

Grace grinned at her and cut the sandwich.

'So,' she said. 'Now that we've got the photo, let's think about the last part of the clue. Brigitte, who is possibly Bardot. You didn't find anything in your posh shed, by any chance?'

'Afraid not.' Deira shook her head. 'By the way, calling it a shed is a bit harsh. It's very comfortable. Isn't it weird how things turn out?' she added. 'I was expecting another night in Nantes stressing out about the car, yet here I am sitting in a lovely café with you and staying in a quirky hotel that puts guests in luxury sheds.'

'I'm sorry about your car, but I'm glad you're travelling with me,' said Grace. 'It's making it a lot more fun.'

'It *is* fun,' conceded Deira. 'At least until Gavin finds out about the Audi.'

'You might hear back from the insurance company ahead of him finding out,' said Grace. 'Don't worry about it until then.'

'I'm only worrying intermittently.'

Once they had finished eating, Deira suggested they should go back to the hotel and continue their investigations there.

The area around the port was busier now, with even more people gathered around the stalls. Deira and Grace could see that as well as selling bric-à-brac and local produce, there was an entire street of stalls devoted to second-hand books.

Deira liked second-hand book stalls, and second-hand book stores too. While she usually bought her books new, or downloaded them onto her iPad, she loved knowing that previously read books were getting the chance to be read again.

'Ken built up a library of old books,' said Grace as they approached the first stall. 'His parents were big readers. When they died, their collection was shared out among the family and he added to it over the years. I've never heard of half of the authors myself, but I presume they're well known.'

'Did he have many brothers and sisters?' Deira picked up a translated edition of an Agatha Christie mystery.

'Two brothers,' replied Grace. 'Paul was a good bit older and he passed away before Ken was diagnosed. Dessie is older by a couple of years; he took early retirement a while back and lives in Spain with his partner. It was partly because of him that we bought the apartment near Cartagena. He was always going on about the great lifestyle he and Margaret had. But Ken would never have dreamt of retiring there. He liked his life at home.'

While Grace was speaking, Deira picked up another book. 'Here you go,' she said. 'It's a Maigret case.'

The cover was dark green, with the title *Maigret et le Corps sans tête* written in green print on the front, and Simenon's name underneath.

'*Maigret and the Headless Corpse*,' translated Grace. 'Yuck.'

'There's a complete collection of them,' Deira said as she investigated the books on the stall.

'Are they all in French?' Grace leafed through the one she was holding. She could translate fragments but she knew she'd never be able to read it.

'Afraid so,' said Deira. 'They're great, though, aren't they?'

'Is the Lock 14 one there?' asked Grace.

'Not that I can see. But maybe the title is different in French.' Deira took out her phone and did a search of Maigret titles while Grace returned the book and moved to the next stall, where the novels were rather more literary.

Deira joined her as Grace was flicking through an even older edition of *The Sun Also Rises* than the one she'd brought with her.

'More Hemingway?' Deira grinned. 'You're a glutton for punishment.'

Grace made a face. 'I'm trying to be cultural. Any luck on the Maigret?'

'Yes.' Deira waved a slim paperback under her nose. '*The Crime at Lock 14* was originally called *Le Charretier de la Providence*, whatever that means.' She handed the book to Grace. '*Et voilà*. Here you go.'

'You found it! Did you buy it? How much do I owe you?'

'It was cheap as chips, so don't even think about it,' said Deira. 'Just add it to your collection.'

'My collection of books I won't read.' Grace laughed. 'This would be beyond me.'

'You know, Grace, I don't think anything is beyond you,' said Deira.

The older woman smiled, then shook her head.

They walked back to the hotel in companionable silence.

On their return, they went to reception to pick up the keys to their rooms. The white-moustached receptionist had gone, replaced by a young woman who gave them a bright smile and wished them a good evening.

'I like proper keys instead of cards,' remarked Grace. 'They're more— Oops.'

The key, which she'd been swinging from its wooden fob, slid out of her grasp and clattered onto the floor. There was a flurry of caramel fur as a large Labrador dog that had been asleep on a beanbag beside the desk leapt up and ran after it. He collected it in his mouth and returned it to Grace, even as the young female receptionist was calling to him. '*Non, non, Brigitte!*'

The dog ignored her, but Grace and Deira exchanged glances.

'Brigitte?' said Deira, while Grace took the key from the dog's mouth, patting her gently on the head and thanking her first in English and then with a couple of *merci*s. She glanced at the red leather collar around the dog's neck.

'Her name *is* Brigitte,' she told Deira.

'Wow. The dog . . .' Deira turned to the receptionist, who was clearly relieved that the guests weren't upset by the sudden game of fetch and were still petting Brigitte, who was looking pleased with herself. 'When did you get her?'

'She came here before me,' replied the receptionist. 'She belongs to the owner. She has her own photo, look.'

And there, on the wall behind reception, was a small wooden plaque: *Bienvenue Brigitte. 8 Août 2015.*

'That's the answer.' Grace turned to Deira, her eyes shining. 'The eighth of August: 8!'

'Hopefully we would've got there eventually, but we've caught a lucky break,' said Deira. 'Do you want to get the laptop?'

'Of course I do,' said Grace. 'Wait here.'

Deira took over the petting of Brigitte while Grace went to fetch the computer. The dog accompanied them to the large, squashy sofa in the reception area and rested her head on Deira's legs while Grace called up the files.

'OK,' she said. 'Here we go.'

She began by uploading the photograph of the café. Once again there was a nerve-racking wait while the progress bar moved slowly across the screen, and another nervous moment before the message that the photo was a match appeared. This time the number for the password was 7.

Grace closed the screen and clicked on the document file. '7148,' she said. 'We're in agreement?'

'Go for it,' said Deira.

Grace took a deep breath, then entered the numbers.

'Password correct' appeared on the screen, followed by Ken's message.

Well done, Hippo. I'm very impressed that you're ploughing ahead. I always knew you had it in you. Your reward is the letter R. I'm going to give you a break now. There's no clue for Bordeaux in the folder, just the details of your hotel. We didn't ever spend enough time there for me to come up with anything useful. But I wanted to talk to you a little before you head to Pamplona. So follow this link to the video I've made. When it's finished, you'll get the clue. Bonne chance. *Or* buena suerte. *Whichever you like! By the way, isn't Brigitte a beauty? I bumped into her when I was out walking in La Rochelle the last time we were here. She reminded me of Brett and I followed her home. I had a lovely talk with the owner of the hotel; that's why I booked it for you. Anyway, talk soon!*

Grace glanced at Deira, who'd also been reading the document. 'Brett was our dog,' she said. 'We had her for years. He never bloody walked her. None of them did.' She looked back at the screen. 'Oh well, I guess I should click on the link.'

'In private,' Deira told her. 'I'll go to the *remise* and you can give me a shout when you're ready.'

'OK.' Grace nodded. 'But I doubt he has anything to say that you couldn't hear.'

'Nevertheless,' said Deira as she got up from the sofa, 'his message is for you. We're not in a rush, so take your time. I'll see you later.'

Grace nodded again, then, after patting Brigitte on the head once more, walked to her room. Deira watched her as she went.

She hoped that the late professor had something nice to say to his widow. But she wasn't entirely confident about that.

Chapter 18

La Rochelle, France: 46.1603°N 1.1511°W

Back in her room, Grace sat in the small armchair with the laptop open on her knees. She hadn't yet looked at Ken's video. She wasn't sure she wanted to.

There were, of course, plenty of other video clips of her husband over the years. Aline had played a lot of them on the night they'd had the closure dinner, streaming them to the TV so that they could watch themselves on family holidays, birthdays, Christmases and other family occasions. There were videos in which he'd appeared fleetingly or unknowingly as he'd walked into shot when someone had been recording something else. And there were excerpts of lectures he'd given at seminars he'd attended, where his love for his subject shone through his occasionally dry presentations.

So Grace had plenty of means whereby she could see and hear her husband at any time she chose; but those videos were of the Ken she'd known all her life. This clip was something new. And she didn't know if she was prepared to see and hear her late husband saying something new. She wasn't sure how she felt about watching a recording he'd made without telling her. She was afraid that the entire clip might

185

be a justification for his actions – Ken explaining why he was going to do what he'd done, rationalising his decision, telling her why he was in the right. It would be unbearable to hear him talk like that when she'd gone through agonies of guilt and self-recrimination and wondering if she could have made a difference. She'd replayed those last months again and again in her head, asking herself if she'd said anything that could have caused him to think she'd be better off without him. She'd wondered if, deep in her heart, she'd even thought that herself. Because of course looking after Ken had been hard. He'd fought against the limitations of his illness and he'd fought against her efforts to help him. At the same time, when he needed her, he expected her to be there straight away. There had been days when she'd been hurt by his dismissal of her offers to do things for him or frustrated by his insistence in pushing her away, and others when she'd been exhausted by his demands. There were times, which she now bitterly regretted, when he'd called for her and she'd pretended not to hear, because she didn't have the strength to cope. The truth was that Ken had always been a demanding sort of person, and she'd often pretended not to hear him when he was in the fullness of his health too. He'd always expected her to fit her life around his. He hadn't behaved any differently when he was ill. She'd tried not to behave differently either.

Perhaps that was the problem.

She stared out of the window, across the hotel gardens toward the sea. Had she been a bad wife? The fact that she was even asking herself the question made her think the answer was probably yes. And that knowledge shattered her, because being a wife and mother had been the most important part of her existence. She'd given up her career for it, after all. She might not have ever changed her name, but she'd stopped being Grace Garvey and become Grace Harrington in every other way.

She took a deep breath, hesitated once more, then finally tapped on the link.

It was disconcerting to see him there, sitting in his office chair. The window blinds behind him were tilted almost closed, but the lamp on the desk was lit and threw shadows across his face. He didn't look ill. But that was the thing – a lot of the time he'd actually looked perfectly fine. It was only when he moved, and sometimes when he spoke, that it was evident he wasn't a well man.

'So, Hippolyta, *cherie*,' he said. 'You've got as far as my video. I said in my note that I was impressed, and I am. Although, to be fair, the clues weren't that difficult and you had plenty of guesses. I didn't want to make it impossibly hard for you. Did Aline come with you? I half thought she might, and of course that would have made it all a bit too easy, because despite her innate laziness, she has a quick brain. So do you, Grace, but you don't always use it.'

Grace pressed pause. If all he was going to do was damn her with faint praise, she wasn't going to listen to him. He'd done it a lot over their lives together, telling her that she was clever but that she never took advantage of it. And then he'd say that she didn't really have to, because her beauty was her passport to whatever she wanted anyway. And that he didn't really like women who were too clever. Not that women shouldn't be clever, he'd add, just that the clever ones tried to show off too much. They were too loud about it. Too shrill. Too strident.

I was never strident, thought Grace. I had nothing to be strident about. She took another breath, then pressed play again.

'If you're watching this, it's because I'm no longer around,' said Ken. 'It's a weird kind of thing making a recording that you know people will only see after you're dead. It should be liberating, but being honest, it's not. On the other hand, if I am still around and I'm on the trip with you, you'll never get to see it. And now I've said something silly, because I'm talking to you about something that may or may not have happened. I'm sorry for such a clumsy sentence, Hippo. If I were writing you a note, I'd be far more eloquent. But it's easier for me to talk than write now.

'So, if I'm talking to you, it has happened: I'm very definitely dead and we'll have to get on with it, won't we? I hope you're enjoying the treasure hunt and that it's making the trip more fun for you. However, as well as being fun, it could be important to your future. The letters are the key. Once you have them all, you'll understand, and you'll be able to unlock the treasure. Have fun in Bordeaux – I'm sorry we never got to explore it. The next clue is for Pamplona, and if you click the link at the end of this video, you'll see it. Don't let me down, Hippo. Don't let yourself down. Good luck.'

The video ended.

Grace stared at the blank screen.

Seeing him, hearing him speaking to her in the way that he always had, feeling as though, despite his words, he wasn't really dead at all but could at any moment walk into the room had been disconcerting.

She'd been in love with him when she'd married him.

188

They'd endured for nearly forty years.

She missed him.

Yet despite those forty years she wondered if she'd ever truly understood him.

Even though she knew that Grace had to see the video on her own, Deira was worried about how the older woman would react to whatever it was the professor had to say. Despite Grace's outward calmness and self-assurance, Deira knew she'd been jolted by the realisation that her late husband had left her a video message, and she hoped that whatever he had to say was warm and loving and would allow Grace to move on with her life.

We're like two injured soldiers, Deira thought. Limping along and telling each other that we're OK, but feeling deep down we're probably not. She rubbed her bruised ribs, then cradled her arms across her stomach and closed her eyes, thinking of Gavin and Afton and of the baby they were going to have together. Once again she was almost overwhelmed by the unfairness of it all.

What had happened to Grace was unfair too, she thought, but at least she hadn't had a wasted life. However things had turned out for her husband, she'd still created a family for herself. She had three children and a grandson. She'd built a legacy. Deira had built nothing. And now she had nobody.

Her phone beeped and she picked it up. Well, not nobody, she thought as she saw that a call from Gillian had gone straight to her voicemail. Gill was a part of her life. A part she couldn't get rid of. She hit return call.

'Oh!' Gillian answered almost straight away. 'I left you a message.'

'I didn't get it,' said Deira. 'I rang you back straight away.'
Like an obedient child, she thought. Because she always rang
Gillian back.

'I was updating you on the Bex situation,' Gillian said.

'There's a situation?'

'You know what I mean.' Gillian sounded irritated. 'With
her interview.'

'How did it go?' asked Deira.

'They've given her a callback to come to another one on
Thursday.'

'What day is it today?' As a result of the travelling and the
fire and the treasure hunting, Deira had completely lost track
of time.

'Monday, you idiot,' said Gillian.

'So . . . you're basically saying that you're staying in my
house till the end of the week?'

'Well, the girls are,' Gillian told her. 'I have to go back to
Galway tomorrow. I have other children to look after, you
know.'

Deira remained silent in the face of her sister's implicit
suggestion that she would never understand the kind of
responsibilities that being a mother entailed. Whenever Gill
commented on Deira's childless state (and she did, quite
often), she'd remark that it must be lovely to live the kind
of life where you never had to think of anyone else, where
you could do whatever you wanted, whenever you wanted.
A bit selfish, mind you, she'd add. And of course you'd
never know the sheer joy and love that being a mother
brought. You'd always miss out on that. But still, if being
able to do your own thing was what you wanted, Deira
certainly had it made. And then she'd smile the smile of

190

someone who believed that they had reached a level of fulfilment that Deira never would. And who basked in that fact.

Deira had never told Gill about wanting to have a child. She'd once said that it was something she and Gavin were considering, but when it hadn't happened, she allowed Gill to assume that they'd dismissed the idea. Deira had been unable to tell her that it was Gavin who'd dismissed it and that she'd acquiesced. She didn't want her sister to pity her.

That was why she hadn't been able to say anything about his new girlfriend's pregnancy. She felt bad enough about it without having to take on the weight of Gill's inevitable rush to judgement. And, perhaps, her belief that Deira was only getting what she deserved.

Because when Deira had first told her that she was moving in with Gavin Boyer, Gill had been horrified.

'He's a married man!' she'd exclaimed. 'With a young family. *And* he's seventeen years older than you. What the hell were you thinking getting involved with him in the first place?'

'I didn't plan it,' said Deira. 'But when we started working together, we . . . we clicked. He's my soulmate. He's everything I ever wanted.'

'He's married!' repeated Gill. 'Is that what you want?'

'His relationship with his wife has been on the rocks for years.' Deira supposed that this was what most married men embarking on an affair said, but in Gavin's case it was true. He'd moved out of the family home before their own relationship had become really serious.

'Oh Deira. This won't end well,' said Gill. 'Let him get his divorce; you can move in with him after that.'

191

'You know quite well it still takes four years to finalise,' Deira said. 'Hopefully that'll change in the future, but I'm not going to sit around for four years. Neither is he. We're moving in together and that's that.'

'It's really not the divorce thing,' Gill said, 'although I don't trust men who're divorced. *And* I'd hate to be someone's second choice. It's the age difference.'

Deira had said nothing about being second choice. She wasn't. She hadn't even known him when he was first getting married. He hadn't had the option to choose her. But if a marriage hadn't worked out, it was surely better to admit it and move on than to live in misery. She'd gritted her teeth and told Gill that age was just a number and didn't mean a thing. Gill had snorted derisively at that.

But Gill was right: age *did* matter, she thought now. It meant everything. At least when you were a woman.

'Deira?' Gillian's voice down the line jolted her back to the present. 'Are you still there?'

'Yes.'

'So it's OK for Bex and Lydia to stay till Friday?'

Deira sighed. 'Fine.'

'You could sound slightly more welcoming about it.'

'What can I say?' asked Deira. 'They're going to stay anyway.'

'You're impossible,' snapped Gillian. 'You don't care about anyone but yourself. You never bloody have.'

I cared about Gavin, Deira said to herself. I did the things he wanted me to do. I lived the life he wanted me to lead. I cared about him and his children, and because of that I put them first and I stopped thinking about me. Yet people seem prepared to believe I *only* think about me because I didn't get married, because I have a career and because I don't have children.

'They're perfectly welcome to stay,' she told her sister. 'Of course they are. It's unexpected, that's all.'

'So is you flitting off to France without a word,' said Gill. 'And that's what I mean about thinking about yourself.'

'There was no one else to think of,' Deira said. 'It's not like I have to ask your permission.'

'It would be nice if you'd let me know,' said Gillian.

Only because you still want to manage my life, thought Deira. To interfere like you did before.

'Listen, I've got to go,' she said. 'I'm meeting someone later.'

'Someone? Who? A man? Have you got back in the saddle already? The stuff in the drawers isn't enough for you?'

Deira felt her cheeks flame with embarrassment at the knowledge that her sister had seen her sex toys, even as she told herself it was perfectly normal to have them. She was tempted to hang up, but that would have allowed Gill to feel as though she'd scored a point. So instead she kept her voice as casual as possible.

'You should try them sometime,' she said. 'They're a bit of fun, especially when you've got someone to share. But no, I'm not back in the saddle, as you so eloquently put it. I'm travelling with a woman I met on the boat.'

'Travelling where?'

'Around France, obviously,' replied Deira. 'I'll be in touch, OK?'

This time she didn't wait for Gill's response, but ended the call. A couple of seconds later, her phone buzzed. She looked at the message.

*Hey, Deira, thanks for letting me stay on. You're really good.
B xx*

Best of luck with the interview, Deira messaged in return, even as she wondered if the job was based in Dublin, and if so, whether Bex would be looking to extend her stay in the house.

It wasn't true that she didn't have family, she told herself as she put the phone back in her bag. She did. It was simply that she didn't have the family she'd wanted.

It was much later that night before Deira and Grace met for a drink on the outdoor terrace that overlooked the sea. Brigitte was already stretched out on the warm tiles, and she padded over to them as soon as they arrived, putting her head on Grace's knees and drooling happily over her pristine capri pants. Grace rubbed the Labrador's ears and Deira tentatively asked her about the video.

'I'll show you.' Grace gave Brigitte a final rub, then opened the laptop that she'd brought downstairs with her and played the clip.

Although Grace hadn't thought that Ken looked ill, Deira was shocked at the appearance of her old tutor, who was much thinner and greyer than she remembered. But then, she reminded herself, it was a long time since she'd been at college, so she had to expect that he would have changed even without his illness. What hadn't changed, though, was his self-confidence, his unerring belief in his own superiority. Deira could see how that attitude might be hurtful to Grace now. Whatever he might have been feeling himself, Ken Harrington came across in the video as being unconcerned about his wife's emotions.

194

'Are you OK?' she asked. 'I'm sure that was difficult to watch.'

Grace shrugged. 'It's typical Ken.'

'Do you still want to go ahead with the treasure hunt?' asked Deira. 'I totally understand if you don't.'

'He says it could be important to my future.'

'In what way?' asked Deira. 'And does it really matter? If you don't want to do it and if you're fine the way things are, then you don't have to.'

'I know.'

'Could it be money?' Deira wondered. 'Is it possible he has a . . . oh, I dunno, a bank account you don't know about?'

'A secret stash?' Grace shook her head. 'I can't see how. He was an academic, not a high-rolling businessman. There was no way for him to make extra money or siphon off expenses or anything like that. Besides, he wasn't a money-motivated sort of person. We argued about that sometimes,' she added a little ruefully. 'I thought he could put himself about more, but for Ken it was always about the knowledge and the learning, not the promotions and the pay grade.'

'What else could be important?' wondered Deira.

'I don't know. And of course, important to Ken might not be important to me,' said Grace. 'Our priorities were often quite different. All the same, I feel . . . obliged, I guess, to figure it out, even though he's just jerking me around. He was always good at playing on my emotions, making me feel . . .' She broke off and gazed out over the Bay of Biscay, where the sun was dipping towards the horizon and turning the water into liquid gold.

'You should do whatever your heart tells you,' Deira

said. 'If this is too difficult for you, you can let it go, Grace.'

'What's difficult is that he keeps setting these silly clues.' Grace turned towards her again. 'If there really was something important he had to tell me, why didn't he say so like a normal person?'

'Maybe he left another message for you somewhere in case you didn't work it out,' said Deira.

'I've spoken with his solicitor. He doesn't have any envelopes marked "not to be opened until my daft wife returns from her trip empty-handed".' Grace snorted.

'But if it's so important, surely he'd want you to get the message regardless,' said Deira.

'You'd think. Which is why I don't really believe it's important at all. And yet . . .'

Deira gave her a sympathetic look. 'If you want to abandon it, that's absolutely your choice,' she said. 'He's not here, Grace. You have to live the life you want to live now.'

'You're very wise,' said Grace, a comment that made Deira stifle a snort herself because it was so far from the truth. 'But you know what, I want to solve them for *me*. Because I want to believe I can do it. Besides,' she continued, 'every hotel on the route is already booked and paid for. I'm not the sort of person who can walk away from something that's paid for. He probably knew that.'

'I'm sure you could get the money back, either from the hotel or from your insurer,' said Deira.

'Perhaps,' conceded Grace. 'But I bet it's a lot of faff for not a huge amount. Not like your car. Any news about that, by the way?'

'Not yet. I'll call tomorrow afternoon if I haven't heard before then.'

'I'm sure it'll all work out,' said Grace.

Deira smiled at her. 'You want things to work out for me and I want them to work out for you. Maybe we should want things to work out for ourselves.'

'One thing I've learned about life is that no matter how shitty a time you're having, it does pass,' said Grace. 'And then you look back and say, that was a terrible week, or month, or year. But you've got to remember that it's only a tiny amount of your whole life. It's important to put it in perspective. Right now, I'm going to have to put Ken in perspective.'

Deira could see a certain sense in Grace's words, but she suspected that putting her husband's actions into perspective was easier to say than to do. Deciding to cope with pretty much everything difficult was easier to say than to do. Looking at her own situation, and leaving aside the particular trauma of the fire and its outcome, there were thirteen years with Gavin for her to come to grips with. And no matter what Grace said, those thirteen years were a massive chunk of her life that she'd never get back.

Her hand moved involuntarily towards her stomach again as she felt her womb positively twang with raw longing. The intensity of it shocked her every single time.

'Do you want to look at the clue for Pamplona?' Grace asked. 'I haven't clicked on it yet.'

Deira ignored her womb and pushed all thoughts of babies from her mind. She nodded, and Grace double-clicked the link.

Hi, Hippo – you've made it to another clue, and this time it's really easy. What's the number of the Old Man's room? Upload Hemingway himself for the final number – the sign you want is near a place he loved. Your reward letter is P. And that's it for Pamplona. I couldn't have made it any easier if I'd tried. Eight guesses this time! Good luck.

'He's giving me fewer guesses with each clue,' said Grace. 'I'll be lucky to get to the end.'

'We didn't need them all the last time, and he's right that this one has to be relatively easy,' observed Deira. 'The Old Man is definitely Hemingway.'

'Yes, I got that.'

'And the room must be where he stayed whenever he was there,' said Deira. 'I have a vague memory of him being associated with a specific hotel, but I can't remember the name of it. It'll be easy to look up, though. And places he loved – well, I remember there was a bar or café . . .' She smiled suddenly. 'What is it with grizzled old male writers and their bars and cafés? I wonder did they hold court there, talk about their brilliance, big themselves up?'

'Probably,' agreed Grace. 'But it doesn't matter who or where they are, I reckon men always like to make themselves feel important.' She looked up from the laptop. 'Are you sure you're happy to keep solving clues and trekking along with me, Deira?'

'Absolutely,' Deira replied. 'This treasure hunt – well, it's keeping my mind off other things.'

'OK then,' said Grace. 'Anyhow, I know the hotel already. It's the Gran Hotel La Perla. That's where I'm staying. I looked it up before I came, and the website mentions Hemingway as well as other famous people who've stayed there.'

Deira nodded. 'If we're going to keep doing this together, I should book myself into hotels on the route too. I'm a great one for leaving things till the last minute, but it would be better to know where I'm going.'

'You're right,' said Grace. 'The next shed mightn't be as attractive as your *remise*! Book the same ones as me if you can. In Bordeaux it's an Ibis.' She clicked on the computer a couple of times and found the website. 'Here.' She pushed the laptop over to Deira, who booked a room at the Ibis for the following night. But when she continued on to the Gran Perla's website, the hotel was fully booked.

'It's probably very popular, given its history,' she said. 'I'll see if I can get something else nearby.' She amended her search and found a small, reasonably priced alternative a few streets away. From the photos on the site and the comments of guests, it seemed a pleasant place to stay, so she made a reservation. Then she looked at hotels in Alcalá de Henares, where Ken had reserved Grace a room in a boutique hotel near the university.

'I know it's an Ibis tomorrow, but I can't believe he's gone for expensive boutique-style places everywhere else,' Grace said while Deira looked through the available rooms. 'The Gran Perla is very pricey. It's so unlike him.'

'He wanted to look after you,' said Deira.

'Yes, well . . .'

Deira busied herself with the reservation while Grace stared out over the dark sea.

'OK,' she said finally. 'I'm all set.'

'Great,' said Grace. 'Let's not think about treasure hunts or anything else until tomorrow night. Would you like a glass of wine?'

'Yes, I would. But you stay there. I'll get it.'

And Deira went inside the hotel, leaving Grace alone with Brigitte.

Chapter 19

La Rochelle to Bordeaux: 190 km

They were halfway through their two-hour drive to Bordeaux the following day when Deira's phone rang. It was her insurance company, informing her that the Audi had been considered a write-off. They were agreeing a settlement, the agent told her, and would be emailing her some more forms to complete.

'The valuation as a write-off won't be as much as it was worth,' she told Grace, 'but it's better than nothing.'

'Are you going to call your ex and tell him?'

'When I get the forms,' replied Deira. 'I'd better look through them first.'

Grace nodded, and they continued the journey without much more conversation. Deira found herself feeling almost cheerful as they drove past swathes of fields bursting with the bright purple and yellow of lavender and sunflowers while Kylie Minogue's greatest hits played in the background. As they approached the Dordogne, the river more grey than blue under the bright sun, the landscape began to flatten out, and the colourful fields gave way to more and more buildings. Grace continued towards the city, and the wide bridge that crossed the equally grey Garonne.

'Given that there's no clue to solve, I could have kept

going till Pamplona,' remarked Grace as she followed the satnav's instructions.

'It would've been a long drive,' Deira pointed out. 'Extra tiring on your own.'

'I guess.' Grace slowed down and allowed a van to overtake her. 'I still wonder if Ken really expected me to do all this by myself.'

'You *were* doing it by yourself until I latched on,' Deira pointed out.

'True.' Grace turned and smiled at her. 'I've got so used to your company already that I'd kind of forgotten that.'

The two women grinned and then Grace shrieked and stamped on the brakes as another van cut in front of her. 'Honestly,' she said, 'you can't afford to let your concentration lapse for a second.'

The hotel that Ken had booked was in a built-up area but had an easily accessible car park, which, said Grace, must have been why he'd selected it. 'Like I said before, he rarely drove into cities.'

'Maybe he thought you'd be better at it than him,' Deira said as Grace parked the Lexus in the first available space. 'You're an excellent driver.'

'Thanks.' Grace switched off the engine, and they took their bags from the boot and went to reception, where they checked in.

'Would you mind if we went our separate ways tonight?' she asked after they'd been given their keys.

'No problem,' Deira told her. 'I'm sure you need a bit of down time without me hassling you.'

'You're not hassling me at all,' Grace assured her. 'All I want to do this evening is call the children, then chill out.'

'I want to make some calls myself,' Deira said. 'So that's fine. We can meet up after breakfast. Have a good evening, Grace.'

'You too.'

The first person Grace FaceTimed was Aline, who picked crumbs out of her son's hair as she talked to her mother. She said that she was delighted that Grace seemed to be enjoying herself, but expressed some anxiety about her hooking up with Deira.

'You're a very trusting woman, Mum, and I don't want anyone taking advantage,' she warned.

I trusted your father to take care of us, thought Grace. I trusted him not to break our hearts. I'll never trust anyone again. She didn't say the words out loud. Instead she told Aline that Deira was a good travelling companion but she'd watch out for any attempts by the younger woman to hit her over the head and make off with the Lexus.

'You know that's not what I meant,' said Aline.

'I do. I'm just teasing you.'

Aline's face disappeared from the screen for a moment as she chased after Declan, who'd wriggled out of her hold. 'Sorry,' she said. 'He was climbing up the back of the sofa.'

'You've got your hands full,' said Grace. 'I'll leave you to it.'

'Have a good time, Mum,' said Aline. 'Take care of yourself. Stay safe.'

'I will,' said Grace. 'Love you.'

'Love you too.' And Aline disappeared to deal with her son again.

*

It was almost midnight in Beijing but the ideal time to catch Fionn, who was watching YouTube videos in the apartment he shared with two of his colleagues.

'You look well,' he told her. 'This trip is obviously good for you.'

'I'm enjoying it,' said Grace, suddenly realising that she was speaking the truth and not having to pretend for the sake of her son. 'The weather is great and the driving has been easy enough. La Rochelle was lovely.'

They spent a pleasant couple of minutes reminiscing about the times they'd been there as a family, and she told him about buying old copies of classic books, which made him smile and comment that she was more like his father than she knew. Unlike Aline, he wasn't bothered by the fact that she was travelling with a woman she'd met for the first time on the ferry, although he did ask her to be careful when she was driving and to keep in touch.

'Of course,' said Grace. 'I'll send you a message every day.'

As she ended the conversation by telling him that she loved him, she vowed she would never stop telling her children how much they meant to her.

And how lucky she was to have them.

Her final call was to Regan, who was eating a roll at one of the big wooden tables on the tiled terrace of the ranch. Regan was the most happy-go-lucky of the three, thought Grace, as her younger daughter brought her up to date on life in Argentina; she was the sunniest in outlook too.

'I hope you're not overdoing it,' said Grace when her daughter had finished.

'I'm always overdoing it.' Regan's wide smile filled the screen. 'But I love it. How about you?'

Grace told her the same things she'd told both Aline and Fionn and, like her brother, Regan couldn't help reminiscing about their childhood holidays. She asked a bit more about Deira too, and said that she was pleased her mother had someone to keep her company.

'It must be odd visiting places you've been with someone else.' Her voice faltered a little.

'It's different,' said Grace. 'But we'll be heading to other places shortly, so I won't have those memories at the back of my mind. Of course it's not the same without you guys with me. Still, I'm glad you have those memories and that you've all become independent people.'

'And you?' asked Regan. 'How are you doing?'

'It's a struggle sometimes.' Grace had always found it easier to confide in her youngest child than in either Aline or Fionn. 'But don't worry about me. I'll be fine. How about you?'

'The horses help,' said Regan. 'All the same, I wish it had been different. And I want you to be all right, Mum.'

'I'll be fine,' said Grace again. 'And I'm always here for you, Regan, you know that.'

'I know. I love you, Mum.'

'I love you too.'

When she ended the call, Grace stretched out on the bed and closed her eyes.

If nothing else, she thought, she had three great children. A precious gift from Ken. And she was very grateful for that.

Deira had changed her mind about phoning anybody. Initially she'd thought about calling Tillie for a chat, and then had been filled with a sudden urge to confess everything to Gavin, but in the end she hadn't felt like doing either. She felt disconnected from Ireland and her life there, even though she'd only been away for a few days. And she felt disconnected from what had happened to the Audi too, as if the fire and its aftermath had nothing to do with her at all. In fact there was a part of her that was in denial about everything to do with taking the car and driving it to France, as though it had all happened to a different Deira, someone else entirely.

So instead of making phone calls or sending texts, she changed into a pair of shorts, pulled on her trainers and headed outside. Twenty minutes later, she'd reached the embankment of the Garonne, where many of the town's inhabitants were strolling in the afternoon sunshine or eating ice creams at one of the small cafés. She continued to walk at a steady pace along the river. Walking along the Grand Canal on Saturday mornings had been a thing for her over the past few years as she tried to make her target of ten thousand steps a day (she never succeeded, though she did feel better after the walks). But ever since Gavin's bombshell, she hadn't wanted to walk anywhere. She hadn't wanted to leave the house.

Now, as she headed along the Quai Richelieu, she felt her energy levels increase and found her rhythm again. She'd missed this, she thought. She'd missed feeling like herself. Deira O'Brien. A woman who knew who she was and what she wanted from life. A woman comfortable in her choices.

And then she saw the man walking towards her, holding the hand of a small boy, and she felt the visceral stab of longing that had pierced her every day since Gavin had left her. The man was tall and well built, his skin mocha brown, dark hair neatly buzzed to his scalp. His arms bulged beneath the short sleeves of his grey T-shirt, and his legs – visible because he was wearing shorts – were muscled and strong. Could he be the one? Deira wondered as she pictured herself in bed with him, imagining him moving inside her, slowly at first and then faster and faster. Could he give her what she needed? She could already see the baby that would grow inside her, a beautiful girl, perhaps, in contrast to the boy beside him now.

Then the man waved and let go of the little boy's hand. The child immediately ran towards a tall, slender woman holding three ice creams.

'*Merci, Maman!*' Deira heard as the man kissed the woman and the boy took an ice cream cone.

She released the breath she'd been holding and wrapped her arms around her body, as though by physically holding herself together she could do so mentally as well. She walked over to one of the wooden benches facing the water and sat down. The man, the woman and the boy disappeared from view.

She leaned forward so that her head was almost touching her legs. The pain was raw and physical, like an open wound exposed to the elements. Every single day was a battle with a body that screamed at her that it wanted a child. And it was relentless. Until Gavin had left her – and except for the couple of weeks when she'd felt broody and desperate – she'd barely given pregnancy a thought. Now it was ever present. Back then, her choice to stay childless had been more than simply acquiescing; she'd agreed with Gavin that adding a baby of their own to the volatile mix that was his relationship with Marilyn and the girls would have been a mistake.

But a mistake for whom? Her or him?

She reminded herself, as she so often did, that she'd accepted it. That she'd thrived as a career-focused woman. She'd done well in her chosen field. She'd succeeded. She'd been happy.

Until he'd told her about Afton.

And now all she felt was anger and bitterness and jealousy. And she simply couldn't let it go.

Chapter 20

Bordeaux to Pamplona: 289 km

Grace and Deira met up at breakfast the following morning. Over fruit and pastries they gave each other upbeat accounts of their activities the night before, neither admitting to any moments of melancholy or doubt. Then Deira took out her phone and googled the route from Bordeaux to Pamplona.

'It's a little over three hours,' she said.

'I've never driven this way before,' said Grace as she studied it. 'But it looks straightforward.'

'We could share the driving if you like,' offered Deira. 'My ribs are a lot better now and I think I'd be OK for an hour or so behind the wheel.'

'Are you sure?' asked Grace.

Deira nodded. 'I've been sitting in the passenger seat like the Queen of Sheba while you do all the work,' she said. 'I'd like to earn my keep.'

'You already have,' Grace said. 'You've pointed me in the right direction on the clues. I'd never have got this far without you.'

'I bet you would.'

'Perhaps,' conceded Grace. 'Still, you've been invaluable.'

'And I can be even more useful if I drive,' said Deira. 'What time do you want to set off?'

'It's ten thirty now,' said Grace. 'Half an hour or so?'

'Perfect.' Deira finished her coffee. 'I'll get myself organised.'

She took the lift to her room, where she brushed her teeth and her hair, then packed her toiletries into her bag. After that, she took out her phone.

Nobody had been looking for her. A few months ago, she'd have been horrified not to have any calls or messages. Now all she felt was relief. But Gavin was due home the following day, and she knew she couldn't let him arrive back to an empty parking space. She might have done if she was safely driving the Audi around France. But not when she was with Grace in Spain and it was a charred mess somewhere in Nantes.

She took a deep breath and started typing.

Grace also did her packing, and then took out her own phone. She didn't have any messages either, although she sent one to Aline telling her that she'd call her from Pamplona later that evening. It was daft, she thought, to think that her children might be worrying about her. She was the one who was supposed to be doing the worrying. But Ken had changed all that, had shifted the responsibility from her to them. It was another thing she found hard to forgive. Aline, Fionn and Regan had their own lives to lead. She didn't want them fretting about hers. Especially when the only thing she had to be concerned about right now was getting to Pamplona.

Pamplona.

There was something about the name that resonated with

her far more than Bordeaux or La Rochelle had done. Perhaps it was that she'd been reading Hemingway and could already feel the heat of the Navarre sun and taste the richness of the red wine. Truth was, red wine made her sneeze, so she hardly ever drank it. But the novel had been so full of heat and wine that she couldn't help feeling as though she was already there. She was looking forward to her visit and to working out the complete solution to the clue. She was totally involved in the treasure hunt now, even if it did mean that Ken was still controlling her life. At least for a little while longer.

Deira was enjoying driving the Lexus, although the scenery in this part of France was dull and unchanging – almost an hour of straight road through a pine forest that formed part of a natural park. But by the time they were close to the border with Spain and the foothills of the Pyrenees, the landscape had become a more vibrant green, and pretty chalets with shuttered windows and gently sloping roofs dotted the sweeping mountains ahead.

'Do you want to change over?' asked Grace when she spotted a sign for services.

Deira hadn't been going to say anything, because she felt she owed it to Grace to drive for as long as possible, but her side was starting to ache again and she welcomed the idea of a rest.

'I feel so hopeless,' she said as they got out of the car and stretched their legs. 'Driving for a couple of hours wouldn't normally bother me at all.'

'Bruised ribs are the worst,' Grace told her. 'I did mine on one of our holidays years ago. I was wiped out for the entire fortnight.' Fionn had accidentally hit her with an oar in a boat they'd hired on the first day. The bruises she'd sustained were the stuff of family legend.

She slid into the driver's seat and continued along the route through the mountains, occasionally hitting patches of low-level cloud that engulfed the car and transported them to a different, less hospitable world. But these moments were fleeting, and by the time they reached the outskirts of Pamplona, the sun was blazing high in a cobalt sky.

'This is the tricky bit,' murmured Grace as she followed the satnav's instructions. 'I hope my maps are up to date.'

Deira was hoping the same thing, as they seemed to be driving through a mainly pedestrian zone of narrow streets that clearly formed part of the old town. She was worried that the local police would suddenly appear and stop them. But then the satnav announced that they were arriving at their destination, and they saw a wide plaza ahead of them.

Both women were surprised at the modernity of Pamplona's main square. Deira had imagined it as a sepia-tinted image from Hemingway's books – small and dusty, surrounded by dark and equally dusty bars. The reality was different. The bars were there, along with cafés and restaurants. But they were bright and welcoming, and the centre was filled with young people in shorts and T-shirts, backpacks beside them as they took the obligatory selfies.

'Maybe it's because Hemingway isn't exactly cheery himself that I thought it would be more drab,' she remarked to Grace as they got out of the car. 'This is lovely.'

Grace nodded and busied herself with her bag. 'You'd better take yours too,' she told Deira. 'There's valet parking, and heaven knows where the car will end up.'

'Living the life.' Deira grinned.

They walked into the cool marble interior of the hotel, where Grace checked in and gave the car keys to the concierge.

'I feel bad that you're not staying here too,' she said to Deira. 'As though I'm leaving you to find your own way in an unfamiliar place.'

'My hotel isn't far,' Deira assured her. 'Don't worry.'

'Will we meet up later and talk through the clues?' asked Grace.

'Of course,' agreed Deira. 'Text me when you're ready.'

Once in her room – or, to be more accurate, the suite named for Ernest Hemingway that Ken had reserved for her – Grace called Aline to let her know she'd arrived. She held the phone at a distance so that her daughter could see the elegance of her surroundings as well as the Hemingway memorabilia. Aline was impressed, and said that booking Grace into such a beautiful hotel showed how much Ken had loved her.

Did it? wondered Grace as she recalled the loveliness of the Fleur d'Île. Had Ken thought that she, on her own, deserved better than they'd shared together? Or was it because he'd stayed in this same room himself when he'd done his lecture tour five years earlier – in which case he'd been treated very well indeed by his hosts. He hadn't said anything to her about his accommodation in either Pamplona or Alcalá de Henares, where he'd also lectured as part of the series he'd given on Hemingway's influence on modern literature. The success of his talks had led to him being asked to fulfil additional engagements in Toledo and Granada, both also part of her treasure hunt itinerary. Maybe all the hotels he'd stayed in were equally upmarket and had triggered an interest in the better things in life even if they'd never shared them together.

Grace looked around the room again. She'd clearly under-valued Ken's work and the esteem with which his colleagues had regarded him. She'd let him down.

She tuned back in to Aline, who was suggesting that the two of them should take a girlie break together sometime.

'Why don't you join me in the apartment later in the summer?' said Grace. 'September, perhaps?'

'Are you planning to be there till September?' Aline was shocked.

'Of course not. I've a return berth on the boat in five weeks. But I may go back later. By plane, though.'

'Could be a plan,' said Aline.

When she'd ended the conversation, Grace took a couple of paracetamol to combat the tension headache that was starting to form at the base of her skull, mainly as a result of the unwelcome thought that she might have underestimated Ken and his lecture tours. She wondered how he'd spent his time after his talks. She'd never asked. She'd assumed it had all been academic stuff that would be above her head. But had it mattered to him that she hadn't been bothered enough to want to know? Was this why he'd wanted her to come here now? To show her how well regarded he'd been? To prove a point?

She thought about the clues for Pamplona. Ken had said they were easy, and they were. She hadn't needed Deira to tell her that the Old Man was Hemingway. That was obvious. And given that Ken had actually booked her into his room, she knew the answer to the clue already. The number was 201. All she needed now was to take a photo of Hemingway near a place he had loved. She'd agreed with Deira it was probably the café that had featured in *The Sun Also Rises*. The Café Iruña. It was nearby. There were even information leaflets about it in the room. So it would be no trouble to find it, upload a photo and solve the clue before dinner.

Deira had been right when she'd told Grace not to worry about her, because it took her less than five minutes to find her own hotel. It was smaller than the photos on the website had made it appear, but it was clean and well maintained. A tiny lift brought her up to the top floor, where her room looked out over the old town. She left her case against a wall and took her phone out of her bag.

There was one message.

From Gavin.

Her heart pounded in her chest as she opened it.

I can't believe you had the nerve to contact me. This is bordering on harassment. And you have form in harassing me. For your own sake, Deira, you have to stop. I'm not getting in touch with you again. Please don't even think of responding.

She exhaled slowly. The text she'd sent him before setting out on the drive had simply asked him to call her. She'd said it was urgent. She hadn't said anything about the car.

Maybe that had been a mistake. Maybe he'd been thinking about the last time she'd asked to talk to him urgently.

So she couldn't really blame him for his response.

It had been at the office. She'd been sitting at her desk, staring at her computer screen without seeing the images of the vintage clothes that were to be a part of her next exhibition for the insurance company. *Ireland – Fashion*

Through the Ages was the title, and she'd been thrilled by the response she was getting from the people she'd contacted to help. She'd shared her excitement every day with Gavin, who'd been enthusiastic too. And then he'd dropped his bombshell about Afton, and the bottom had fallen out of her world.

After that, she'd simply gone through the motions. Although Gavin had moved out, she knew that every single day he was sitting at his desk two floors above her. She sometimes saw him in the communal breakout areas, or at the coffee dock, laughing and talking with colleagues as though he hadn't a care in the world. She couldn't understand how he could be getting on with his life while her heart was broken. But not because he'd left her, she decided that day as she gazed blankly at the photo of a tartan miniskirt, circa 1967, which she was sure had scandalised rural Ireland; her heart was broken because he'd left her without giving her the chance to have what Afton was going to have.

A child of her own.

It had come to her then in a wave of grief and fury, and she'd hit the sleep button on the computer, grabbed a couple of files and got up from her desk. She'd walked the length of the open-plan office, ignoring the furtive glances of her colleagues. They all knew about her and Gavin. The entire company knew. And they felt sorry for her, because people always felt sorry for the woman when a relationship went sour. She was almost invariably seen as the loser. No matter how or why things ended.

People turned to look at her when she arrived at the quieter setting of the fourth floor. She could feel a ripple of tension follow her as she strode towards the corner office with the glass windows, where Gavin's attention was focused on the screen in front of him.

She heard an intake of breath from his assistant, Kamala, as she pushed open the door and stepped inside.

'What the hell do you want?' demanded Gavin as he looked up from the report he'd been studying.

'To talk to you.' Deira pressed the button that turned the glass walls opaque. 'In private. It's urgent.'

'We've nothing to talk about,' said Gavin.

'Yes, we do,' she told him as she sat opposite him. She moved the tall glass trophy he'd received at the industry awards the previous year to one side so that there was nothing in their line of sight.

He exhaled slowly and pushed his chair back from the desk. But he didn't get up. 'I'm all ears,' he said.

'You slept with Afton even though you didn't love her,' said Deira.

'Look—'

She held up her hand to stop him talking. 'You can't have been in love with her that first time. It was just a thing.'

'I don't know what it was,' said Gavin.

'A thing,' Deira repeated. 'Let's face it, you were still coming home to me. And still sleeping with me too. So you were sleeping with her for the sex and yet you were telling me you loved me. You do remember saying that, don't you?'

'I don't see—'

'But maybe I'm wrong and you were in love with her even though you were sleeping with me. So maybe you were having sex with me and in love with her?'

'We can't help who we fall in love with,' said Gavin. 'And I don't have time for this conversation.'

'Yes, we can,' said Deira. 'And you do. It's all about choices, Gavin. You chose to walk away from me. Same as you chose to walk away from Marilyn. Were you sleeping with her too, when you were telling me it was over?'

'It's completely different.'

'It's not. But what I'm getting at is that you're perfectly capable of sleeping with someone you don't love. You have form.'

'Look, I'm sorry I hurt you. I'm sorry it's happened this way. But you're embarrassing yourself here, Deira. You've got to get over it.'

'Oh, I'm over you,' she said. 'I absolutely am. No need to worry at all about that. I was angry and, yes, embarrassed that I'd made such a stupid mistake, but I'm over you.'

'So what's all this about?' He picked up his mobile from the desk and glanced at it. Deira sat silently in front of him until he put it down again.

'I want something from you,' she said.

'What?' His tone was wary.

'I want you to get me pregnant.'

'Huh?' He looked at her in astonishment. 'What are you talking about?'

'We've established that you're perfectly capable of sleeping with someone without loving them,' said Deira. 'We've also established that you're packing healthy swimmers. You've managed to get two separate women up the duff, after all. So that's what I want from you, Gavin. A baby. I realise . . .' She held her hand up again as he tried to interrupt. 'I realise that you wouldn't want anything to do with me or the child. That's fine. But I want a baby, and the least you can do after all our time together is give me one.'

218

'You're off your head,' said Gavin. 'I'm not sleeping with you to get you pregnant.'

'Why not?'

'Because it's a ridiculous idea.'

'I wanted a baby before and you said no. You were totally into our power-couple lifestyle, and because I loved you more than I loved the idea of having a family, I went along with it. But I wanted a baby all those years ago, Gavin, and that's when I should have had one. The ridiculous thing was me giving in. I'm running out of time. So I need you to do this for me now.'

'No,' he said.

'Don't make me beg.' Deira's voice cracked. 'I don't want to have to beg.'

'Listen to me,' said Gavin. 'You're asking the impossible. I can't sleep with you now. I'm in another relationship.'

'You slept with *her* when you were in another relationship,' said Deira. 'You slept with *me* when you were in another relationship. I don't see what the problem is.'

'I'm not a performing seal!' cried Gavin. 'I can't just—'

'Oh, I bet you can,' said Deira.

'Even if I slept with you, I wouldn't want you to get pregnant,' said Gavin.

'It'd be none of your business.'

'It would be my child,' said Gavin. 'And no matter what you think of me, I've never walked away from my responsibility to my children.'

He was right about that, thought Deira. Even when they had been so angry with him they didn't want to speak to him, Gavin had kept in touch with Mae and Suzy. She'd always had to take their feelings into account. He hadn't been a bad father to them. He wouldn't be a bad father to any child.

'You could be as involved as much or as little as you like,' she said.

'No, I couldn't,' he told her. 'Because it's not going to happen. Afton is pregnant now and we're going to make a life together. I'm not about to jeopardise that for a whim of yours.'

'It's not a whim!'

'If you want to have a baby, feel free to find another father,' said Gavin. 'But it's not going to be me.'

Deira sat in silence. She'd been sure he'd say yes. Sure she could have persuaded him. And yet he'd refused her the only thing she'd ever really asked of him. The one thing he'd given to the woman before her and the woman after her. Why? What was wrong with her?

She wanted to ask, but the question she put to him was entirely different.

'Are you happy?'

'Huh?'

'In your life? With Afton? Are you happy?'

'Mostly,' he replied.

His answer caught her like a blow to the solar plexus. If he'd said yes, she might not have believed him. But his reply had been honest, because the truth was that nobody was happy all of the time. He'd always been honest. Except when he'd been cheating on her.

She got up abruptly from the chair and turned towards the door.

'Oh, Deira!'

She turned back towards him, thinking that maybe he'd

suddenly changed his mind, that he would sleep with her after all.

'The house,' he said. 'I know it's in your name. But it's still our family home. I don't mind you living there. But you have to buy your half from me. It's the only fair thing to do.'

She felt herself trembling with rage. He was right, of course; he'd put money into the house and he was entitled to his share. But how dare he call it a family home when they weren't a family? They'd never been a family. And they never would be.

She picked up the glass award and threw it to the floor, where the slender, tapered spire snapped in two.

'Fuck you, Gavin Boyer,' she said, and walked out, slamming the door behind her.

Chapter 21

Pamplona, Spain: 42.8125°N 1.6458°W

Grace had fallen asleep after talking to Aline and didn't wake up until almost six thirty in the evening. She was shocked at having slept for so long but pleased that she was feeling refreshed and alert, with no trace of her earlier headache. She picked up her phone and saw that Deira had sent a message half an hour earlier asking if she wanted to join her on a walk around the town.

She responded by telling Deira about her unexpectedly deep sleep and asking what time she'd like to meet to chat about the clue. And have something to eat, she added.

Café Iruña at 7.30? replied Deira after a few minutes.

Grace sent a thumbs-up emoji in reply before heading for the shower and then changing into a pretty floral dress and a pair of flat sandals with multicoloured jewels on the straps. She tidied her hair and hung the blue pendant around her neck again. Then she took a map of the town from the information folder on the bureau and went outside.

The plaza was busy, with plenty of tourists sitting in the many cafés that surrounded it. Grace walked towards the famed Café Iruña, not because she expected to see Deira there, as it was far too early, but because she hoped to find a statue or plaque relating to Hemingway outside. Once the photograph was taken, she'd have all the elements of the clue. However, even though she walked the length of the small block, she didn't see anything referring to the great writer.

She completed a circuit of the plaza, looking out for whatever might seem obvious, though given that the clue said 'near a place he loved', she was sure it was the café. Perhaps, she thought, the tribute was inside.

As it was still far too early for Deira to show up, and Grace didn't want to sit there alone, she decided to continue her stroll by walking along the narrow street that ran alongside the hotel. At ground level, the shops were a mixture of old and new; above them were old apartments with wooden shutters and wrought-iron balconies. Grace liked how people on the Continent still lived in old buildings in the centre of the city, something that had become increasingly rare in Ireland. She'd grown too accustomed to her own house and garden to ever want to live in an apartment in the centre of town herself, but there was a part of her that loved the sheer vibrancy of city living. However, even though it made sense for her to downsize to a smaller home with a smaller garden, it was easier said than done. Homes weren't only physical structures. They were everything that structure represented.

She thought of the kitchen wall where she'd carefully marked off the heights of the children on their birthdays, and the way the afternoon sun slanted through the Velux window in the kitchen, which always lifted her spirits. She thought of the garden that she'd tended so lovingly, and the organised chaos that was still Ken's office because she hadn't felt able yet to sort it.

When I get back, she promised herself. I'll deal with everything when I get back.

She turned onto a street that she assumed would take her back to the Plaza del Castillo and her hotel, but realised she'd somehow lost her sense of direction and hadn't a clue where she was. The plaza at the end, which she'd assumed was the main square, was actually much smaller, shaded with a few trees and with a water fountain in the centre. There was a bench near the fountain, where she sat down and consulted the tourist map, although as it only showed the main streets, it wasn't much help. Nevertheless, the dappled sun, slanting through the leaves of the trees, was warm on her shoulders, and a soft breeze cooled the hot air. She folded the map again and closed her eyes, filled with a sense of tranquillity, a peace in both mind and body, that she hadn't experienced since Ken's diagnosis. She realised too that the burden of guilt, which had never left her, had eased a little too. She was in the moment, and the moment was perfect.

She released her breath in a long, heartfelt sigh and wished it could last forever.

Not having had an immediate response to her text, Deira had opted to go for her walk by herself. Her own ramble had taken in many of the same streets as Grace, although she'd also found time to explore the area around the city walls, which included a large park where tourists and locals alike were relaxing in the shade of the spreading trees.

She pulled out her phone to take a photo of the city walls, and at that exact moment, it buzzed. As always, her heart skipped a beat, but it was only Gillian.

Just to let you know I'm home. You might like to text a good luck message to Bex.

Deira made a face at the screen. Once again Gill was telling her what she should do, and it irked her, especially as she'd sent a message to her niece.

It gave her a certain satisfaction to reply, *Already done* to Gill.

It was ridiculous to think that at this stage of their lives, their relationship was still more or less the same as it had been in their teens, a regular series of meaningless battles for one-upmanship. Somehow neither of them had got past Gill's self-promotion to mother status; Deira hadn't stopped resenting it, and Gill had never stopped flaunting it. 'Or meddling in my life,' muttered Deira as she closed the cover on the phone.

Of course if Gill had left well enough alone when they were younger, things might have turned out very differently and their relationship might be less fractious than it was. But she had meddled, and Deira had never quite forgiven her. It didn't matter that it had been (at least in Gillian's eyes) for Deira's own good. It didn't matter that Deira had forged a successful career doing what she loved afterwards. Gillian had interfered and changed everything when she should have minded her own damn business.

Deira never really knew if it was Gill's innate snobbishness or simply her distrust of Thomas Kinsella and his family that had made her get involved. Not that her motives mattered; the result was still the same.

Thomas had been Deira's boyfriend back when she was in her final year at school, and she'd been head over heels in love with him. At first Gillian hadn't said anything, but over time she began to make offhand remarks about the unsuitability of a boy who hadn't gone to college and was working full-time at a petrol service station on the Oughterard road for a girl who was smart and pretty and could do better for herself.

When Deira protested that they loved each other, Gill snorted and asked if she really thought he was what her mother would have wanted for her.

'She would have wanted me to be happy,' Deira replied. 'Thomas makes me happy.'

And he did. He was a kind, uncomplicated person, lacking the nagging sense of injustice that both Gill and her father always seemed to carry with them. (Peter didn't count; her brother did his own thing, untroubled by Gillian's efforts to boss him around.)

'You're too young to know about love and happiness,' Gill said. 'The problem with you, Deira O'Brien, is that you think you know it all, but you don't.'

Maybe Gill had a point now, Deira conceded, but she hadn't back then. And yet she'd managed to split them up, though at the time Deira had had no idea about her inter-ference. She didn't know that Thomas stopped calling because Gill had gone to the service station and told him that Deira was going to college when she left school and that Thomas would hold her back by stopping her forming new friendships and making new connections. She didn't know that Gill had told him that ending their relationship quickly and cleanly would be better for everyone, especially Deira. She didn't know that Thomas, thoughtful, gentle Thomas, had taken Gill's words to heart. Had believed them. And had broken up with her the next day without ever saying why.

Of course they'd been young and of course things might have ended of their own accord when Deira started college.

But when, at her graduation, her sister casually mentioned that the day wouldn't have happened without her, and said, with a certain sense of pride, that she'd been responsible for Thomas splitting up with her, Deira had felt herself go white with rage. And even though it was four years later and she was going out with someone else at the time, she could neither forgive Gill for interfering nor for souring her graduation day.

She'd eventually put it behind her and found happiness (at least until the moment Gavin had come home and told her about Afton), but any time she'd heard Thomas Kinsella's name, she'd taken a sharp breath and wondered if they would still have been together if it wasn't for Gillian. Because she heard quite a lot about Thomas Kinsella, one way or another. His father, who'd worked as a bricklayer, had moved into construction and development just as Ireland's economy started to boom. Over the years, Danny Kinsella had bought up small plots of land, which had suddenly become valuable as they were rezoned. Kinsella and Son became one of the leading developers in the county. And Thomas and his wife Sinead became well known on the social scene. They even appeared in the pages of the celebrity magazine *RSVP*, posing in their huge country house with their three adorable children. Deira didn't begrudge Thomas one bit of his success. But in the last few weeks, she hadn't been able to help thinking about him and his family, asking herself if it could have been hers, and resenting the fact once again that her older sister hadn't minded her own business.

She shook her head and got up from the bench where she'd been sitting. Young couples were strolling hand in hand through the park, and as she made her way through the exit in the city walls, she wished them all happiness and joy in the world. But she wondered if she'd ever experience those emotions herself any time in the future.

It was shortly after seven when Grace returned to the Café Iruña. All the outdoor tables were occupied, and there seemed to be some kind of party going on inside, but she was quite happy to lose herself in the anonymity of the crowd.

The place reminded her of the Café de la Paix in La Rochelle, with its high ceilings, gold fittings and dark wood. She imagined Simenon at his marble table five hundred kilometres away, and remembered Deira's comment about grizzled old men holding court in their bars and cafés. Hemingway, by all accounts, had enjoyed downing bottles of wine and mixing with wealthy expats while he wrote. Simenon had probably had a good time too. No matter what era you talked about, she decided, men generally seemed to allow themselves less responsibility and more fun than women. Or was it simply that women took it all too seriously? That they didn't allow themselves to have fun?

As she walked through the café, she saw a life-sized bronze statue of the famous writer propped up at a bar counter. Thinking of Ken's clue, she took a few photos and then walked back towards the entrance, where she sat at a high table beside the doors that opened onto the plaza. She ordered a sparkling water and waited for Deira to show up.

She could imagine Ken here with his academic friends, knocking back glasses of wine and discussing the literary greats. He'd have topped every comment they made with an observation of his own, always trying to be smarter and cleverer than everyone else. Ken had been a man who considered himself educated and cultured, who knew what he was talking about and whose judgements were valuable. And indeed other people must have seen him the same way, otherwise he never would have been invited here for his lecture tour.

Why did he marry me? wondered Grace for at least the thousandth time since he'd died, and probably the millionth time in their entire relationship. Why, when I'm so shallow by comparison? He would have been better off with someone like Deira. Someone who understood the things he understood. Who liked the same books. Who was knowledgeable about art – Ken had maintained a keen interest in art as well as literature. He'd enjoyed opera too. The only piece of opera that Grace liked was the chorus 'O Fortuna', which had been used in a beer commercial.

'Oops, sorry!'

The exclamation caused her to turn at the same time as a man with a glass of beer in his hand narrowly avoided a large group of people entering the café. His manoeuvre had caused him to bump into Grace's table, sending her water sliding towards the edge. She put out a hand to stop it falling.

'Good save,' said the man. 'Sorry again.'

'No harm done,' said Grace.

He looked at her and smiled. 'Irish?'

She nodded. 'We get everywhere.'

'Indeed we do. Would you mind if I shared your table for a short while? I'm meeting someone later so I popped in for a drink beforehand. I didn't realise it would be so busy this evening. It's not usually crowded at this hour.' He glanced around at the café, which was now almost full, and shook his head in puzzlement.

'You're welcome,' said Grace. 'Are you on holiday, or do you live here?'

'I don't live here, replied the man. 'But I visit from time to time. My ex-wife is from Navarre.'

'Oh.' Grace gave him a polite smile, then took out her phone so that they didn't need to share life stories. When she glanced up again, he'd done the same. She was suddenly aware that with his dark hair and five o'clock shadow, he was an attractive man. And then, as she put his age somewhere in his late thirties or early forties, she realised he could easily be her son.

Why do I have these random and probably inappropriate thoughts about perfect strangers? she asked herself as she switched her attention back to her phone and hoped that Deira would show up early. Is there something wrong with me?

Her prayers were answered five minutes later when she looked up again and saw Deira walk into the café. She raised her arm in greeting and Deira spotted her straight away.

'Am I late?' she asked.

'I'm early.' Grace was about to say something more when she realised that Deira was staring at the man sharing the table. Her expression was one of both surprise and recognition.

'Hello again,' said the man, who had looked up from his phone when Deira had arrived at the table. 'We'll have to stop meeting like this.'

'You know each other?' Grace was astonished.

'Not exactly,' said Deira. 'We met on the ferry. And he . . . I'm sorry, I never asked your name,' she said to him before turning back to Grace. 'He was my knight in shining armour when I fell and bruised my ribs.'

'It was nothing,' said the man. 'I hope you're feeling better now.'

'Much,' replied Deira. 'Thanks to Grace, really. She gave me the most brilliant gel. It seems I only meet the best people while travelling. But you two . . .' She glanced from one to the other. 'Are you old friends?'

The man shook his head and smiled. 'Perhaps we should introduce ourselves properly. I'm Charlie Mulholland.'

The two women introduced themselves too, then Charlie asked if he could get them a drink.

'I'll get these,' said Deira.

'No, no. It's my shout,' he insisted.

'Seriously, I owe you one,' said Deira. 'Grace too. What will you have?'

Charlie asked for another beer, while Grace stuck with sparkling water.

Deira went to the bar and ordered the drinks, choosing a wine for herself and also accepting the small dish of mixed nuts and olives the barman gave her.

'So,' she said when she'd settled at the table. 'How come you're here in Pamplona? I thought you were going to Paris.'

'I did,' said Charlie. 'But my plans were thrown into a bit of a muddle, so I came here sooner than planned. I'm a documentary maker,' he added when both women looked at him enquiringly. 'My most recent was a series about EU citizens living and working in Ireland.'

'Oh, I think I saw that!' exclaimed Grace. 'Was it the one where the Lithuanian woman bought a farm in Tipperary?'

'Yes.' He looked pleased.

'I loved that episode,' said Grace. 'And the one with the Polish guy who set up his own business. Very inspiring.'

231

'Thanks,' said Charlie.

Deira gave him an apologetic look and said that she didn't watch much TV but she'd look for the series on catch-up later.

'Don't feel obliged,' said Charlie.

'No, I'm interested,' Deira assured him. 'So what are you doing now?'

'That programme in reverse,' replied Charlie. 'Irish people living and working in the EU. I know the Irish abroad has been done a million times,' he added quickly, 'but I'm concentrating on people who've become an integral part of the life and culture. The reason for the Paris trip was to interview a woman with an intriguing personal life story who's working for a prestigious publishing firm. Unfortunately she had to head to the Basque country for a family funeral and won't be able to do it till later. However, I'd also set up an interview with an Irishman in Bordeaux, so I did that instead and then came on here to meet Amaya. She's my ex-wife,' he added. 'I always visit when I'm here. I've a couple of interviews to do in Spain, so I'll head back to Paris again after that.'

'That sounds exhausting,' said Grace. 'We were in Bordeaux yesterday. We could just as easily have bumped into you there.'

'Are you doing it all on your own?' Deira asked. 'Don't you have a crew?'

He nodded. 'My sound and film people have gone on ahead.'

'I can't believe you're driving everywhere,' said Grace.

'Makes it easy for the more out-of-the-way locations,' Charlie said. 'Not everyone is living in a big city.'

'Was the team on the ferry with you?' asked Deira.

'No. Dave and Lou flew to Paris and I picked them up

there,' replied Charlie. 'They went straight to Madrid after the Bordeaux interview.'

'It all sounds very glam,' Deira said.

'Not really.' Charlie grinned. 'But it beats being in an office.'

Everyone agreed that a job that included travelling beat being in an office. Grace told a couple of anecdotes about her airline days, while Deira said that although she was office-based, her job involved getting out a lot. When Charlie asked what she did and she told him, he looked surprised and told her that Amaya ran an art gallery.

'Part of the reason I drove was to bring some paintings for her,' he said. 'She's running an exhibition of painters from other countries. So I brought some she wanted from Ireland.'

'Isn't that amazing?' Grace looked from Charlie to Deira. 'Two Irish people with a common interest in art meet in a bar in Pamplona.'

Charlie smiled. 'To be honest, I'm not much of an art buff,' he confessed. 'I only brought what Amaya wanted. Two artists – a man named Bernard Boyne and a woman called Jennifer Roache.'

'Oh!' Deira couldn't help the exclamation. 'I know Jennifer Roache. My very first exhibition included her aunt's paintings. Thelma passed away a few years ago, but Jennifer is a great painter too, and her art was part of one of our later exhibitions.'

'That's unbelievable,' said Grace. 'Although maybe not really, because it doesn't matter where you go, you'll find an Irish person and they'll always know someone you do.'

Charlie nodded. 'Researching the documentary was like that,' he said. 'I don't think there's anyone we're interviewing who doesn't have at least a passing acquaintance with someone we already knew.'

'You should visit the gallery, Deira,' said Grace. 'Check on your Irish artist's work.'

'I might.'

'It's not far from here,' said Charlie. 'Calle Cortez.' He reached into his pocket and took out a business card, which he handed to her.

'Amaya Saez Zubiri,' she read. 'Galería de Arte.'

'The gallery is open until ten o'clock,' said Charlie. 'I'm sure you'd enjoy a visit.'

'Your divorce must have been very amicable if you're promoting your ex-wife and transporting paintings for her,' remarked Deira.

'Tough at first,' Charlie said. 'Amicable enough in the end. It's partly what interested me in the whole thing about people living and working in different countries. Amaya was in Ireland when we met, but she wanted to come back here when her parents grew more infirm. I was doing well in Ireland and I didn't want to move. When I did, I resented it. It's my fault really that it didn't work out. I didn't give it a chance.'

'Oh, but could you still?' asked Grace.

Charlie shook his head. 'Too much water under the bridge. She has a new man now anyhow.'

'It all sounds so civilised.' Deira picked up her phone as she spoke and checked for messages. There were none.

'I'm probably making it sound better than it was,' said Charlie.

'Sorry.' Deira put the phone down again. 'I didn't mean to make light of it. When did you divorce?'

'Three years ago. It doesn't seem that long, to be honest. Life goes by in a blur sometimes. And you miss things you didn't know you'd miss. Like conversations about painters I've never heard of.'

'Do you have children?' asked Deira.

'Amaya has a son from before we married,' said Charlie. 'Iñaki. He's great. We keep in touch with FaceTime and stuff, but it's not the same.'

Would you like a baby? A son of your own? Someone you could see all the time because you'd be in the same country? I could do that for you. You could do that for me. Deira didn't say the words out loud, but she was thinking them.

She'd wondered on the ship if he could be the one. And now here he was sitting in front of her talking about children in a very upfront way. He knew what having a child entailed. Perhaps meeting him was meant to be. A real, proper sign. Surely Tillie would think so. She'd text her later and ask her opinion.

Grace could see that Deira had gone into a dream world of her own, but she could also see that there was a connection between her and Charlie. Enough to make sure they were on the same page as each other. Meanwhile, Grace herself was invisible to him. It wasn't that she'd been thinking that anything could happen between her and Charlie, but she was aware that she'd been sidelined in the conversation, shunted out of the way, while he and Deira had almost naturally slid into an easy familiarity that excluded her.

'I think I overdid it earlier.' She drained her water. 'I'm really sorry, but I need to go and lie down.'

'Grace! Are you OK? Do you want me to go back to the hotel with you?' Deira looked at her with concern.

'No, I'm fine,' said Grace. 'I just need to be alone for a while.' She picked up her bag.

'Are you sure you don't—'

'I'm fine,' repeated Grace. 'I'll see you tomorrow sometime.'

'But what about the—'

She'd gone before Deira had time to finish the sentence.

Chapter 22

Back at the hotel, Grace curled up in the comfortable armchair in her room. She felt silly now at having rushed from the café simply because she'd been upset by the mutual attraction she'd sensed between Deira and Charlie. She didn't quite understand it. After all, she wasn't seriously attracted to him herself. But the idea that she was too old to be noticed by a man was depressing. She didn't want anyone new in her life, but nor did she want to think that she'd become the invisible woman. It was crushing to think that no matter how much care she took over her appearance, nobody – male or female – would take the slightest bit of notice, because she was now part of the army of older women who, at best, fell into the category of 'looking good for her age'.

She reached for the laptop, opening the link to upload her photograph of Hemingway. At least, she thought, as she watched the progress bar creep along the screen, she'd solved this clue herself without any input from Deira O'Brien. Grace was suddenly fed up with Deira and her ability to solve Ken's clues so easily. Acknowledging that she was being irrational didn't make her feel any better. She wished she hadn't made her impetuous invitation to the younger woman to come along on the trip with her. She hardly knew her, for heaven's sake. Why would she need her looking over her shoulder?

Photo is not a match.

She looked at the message in disbelief. How could it not be a match? It was Hemingway. And it was in a place he loved. It had to be right. Unless there was something wrong with that particular photo. She'd taken a few from different angles. Maybe a different one would work.

It was weird, she thought, her mind wandering back to the bar again as she browsed through the photos, that she should feel disconcerted in thinking Charlie Mulholland's attention towards her had evaporated the moment Deira had walked into the Café Iruña. In her entire married life she'd never so much as looked at another man or wondered if a complete stranger might fancy her. She'd been married to Ken and that was enough. Except when Matthew McConaughey was on TV, and surely any woman would be given a pass for him!

She closed her eyes and tried to imagine Ken beside her now. It was hard to see him as he had been before his illness. Hard not to remember him as a weaker version of himself. He'd always been her rock. And if not always there for her, he had, at least, always been part of her life.

And yet here she was, thinking about another man. Not fantasising about him, not thinking inappropriately about him, but thinking about him all the same. And jealous (really, Grace, she said to herself, really?) that he seemed to have a closer rapport with Deira than with her.

She chose another photo and uploaded it.

Photo is not a match.

For crying out loud! She looked at the screen in irritation. It had to be a match. She tried a third.

Photo is not a match.

She snapped the computer closed and flung herself on the bed.

Her headache had returned.

'I hope she's OK,' Deira said after Grace had hurried out of the bar. 'She's behaving oddly for her.'

'Do you want to go after her?'

Deira shook her head. 'She has her reasons for acting oddly from time to time. I should stay out of her space.'

'Oh?' Charlie looked at her enquiringly, but Deira had no intention of sharing personal information about Grace with a perfect stranger. Even if he was a perfect stranger whose baby she wanted. So she said it was nothing really, and that Grace would be fine.

'Would you like to have a peek at Amaya's gallery now?' Charlie glanced at his watch. 'I'm due to meet her in ten minutes and it's not far from here.'

'I . . . Well, yes, that'd be great.' She'd thought she might go to the gallery in the morning, but given that Grace had abandoned the treasure hunt and gone back to the hotel, this was as good a way of spending her time as any. Besides, she wanted to find out more about the possible future father of her child.

She drained her glass and slid off the high stool she'd been sitting on, then followed Charlie out of the café and across the plaza. She was acutely conscious of him alongside her, aware of the height of him, the bulk of him – the very maleness of him – so close to her that their arms were almost touching. Would he be good in bed? she wondered. Not that his technique would matter. The only important thing would be that he was strong and virile and could make her pregnant.

She glanced at him, but he was striding forward, not taking any notice of her. Which was a good thing. Sometimes she feared that people could read her thoughts. If Charlie could read hers, he'd think she was a crazy person. She supposed he wouldn't be the only one. But she wasn't crazy. Just desperate.

He continued to lead the way before turning onto a narrow pedestrianised street lined with artisan shops and stopping outside a building with a maroon awning, the words Galería de Arte stamped on it in gold. A large landscape painting in a vibrant mix of blues and greens was displayed in the window. Deira recognised Jennifer Roache's work immediately.

'Here we are,' said Charlie. 'Amaya's gallery.'

Deira took a deep breath and focused on the here and now rather than the thoughts that had been swirling around in her head.

A bell jingled as they stepped inside. In contrast to the shaded street, the room was carefully lit, and the high-gloss marble floor gave it an elegant air.

'Fabulous,' said Deira as she looked around. She smiled to see another of Jennifer's paintings, this one a seascape, prominently displayed.

'*Hola* – oh, Charlie, it's you. How are you?' A slight woman wearing jeans and a T-shirt, her dark hair tied up in a pony-tail, walked into the gallery.

'I'm good. Sorry if I'm a bit late. I've brought a visitor.' He introduced Deira and explained that she knew Jennifer.

'How lovely!' Amaya's brown eyes lit up. 'It's so nice to meet people who like the same things as you.' She spoke briefly about her delight in Jennifer's work and then showed Deira some of the other paintings, explaining her plan to exhibit artists from different countries. The two women continued to chat about art while Charlie leaned against Amaya's glass desk and scrolled through his phone. Then the doorbell jingled again and an older woman, accompanied by a young teenager, entered.

'How's my boy?' Charlie put away his phone and embraced the teenager, while the older woman kissed Amaya on both cheeks.

Charlie, his hand still on the boy's shoulder, introduced him to Deira as his son, Iñaki, and the older woman as Amaya's mother. She smiled at Deira before turning and speaking to Charlie in Spanish. He laughed and shook his head, while Amaya gave him an amused look

'She wanted to know if we were an item,' he explained to Deira. 'I told her that we're travellers who keep meeting on the road.'

'And it was lovely to meet you again, but I'd better be off.' Deira was feeling slightly uncomfortable under the speculative eye of Amaya's mother. 'It was great to meet you too, Amaya. Best of luck with the Jennifer Roache paintings. I can't wait to tell her I met you.'

'Keep in touch, especially if you see anything I might be interested in,' said Amaya. She took one of the business cards that Charlie had already given her, and scribbled on it before handing it to her. 'That's my personal mobile.'

'Thank you.' Deira slipped it into her bag.

'How long do you plan to stay in Pamplona?' asked Charlie as he walked to the door with her.

'Only till tomorrow,' replied Deira. 'We're actually driving to Cartagena and this was one of our designated stops along the way. I think Grace will want to head off sometime in the early afternoon.'

'Sounds fun,' Charlie said. 'Though it's a shame you're leaving so soon because you really need a couple of days to get the most from the city. Would you like to meet up in the morning before you leave? I could show you around.'

I could meet you for sex, thought Deira. We could spend the morning shagging each other senseless and I could end up pregnant at the end of it.

'I . . . I think Grace has plans,' she said. 'But thank you.'

'Here's my own card.' He handed her a slightly more battered one than Amaya's. 'Give me a shout if you need anything. Also, if you're looking for a nice place to stop . . .' He reached into his pocket and took out yet another card, 'can I recommend this? It's owned by an Irish couple. I'll be interviewing them for the documentary too. If you get the chance, you should definitely stay a night.'

Deira looked at the card, which was pale green with a sketch of an old-fashioned well and the words 'El Pozo de la Señora' written on it. Below that it said 'Retreat, Relax, Recharge' and 'Wellness Centre'.

'I'm not sure it fits in with Grace's itinerary,' said Deira. 'Or that we have time to retreat and relax. But thanks.'

'You never know,' said Charlie. 'We all need time to do those things.'

Ask me again about tomorrow morning, thought Deira. Ask me and this time I'll say yes. I don't know what held me back before.

But then his phone rang, and after a moment, Deira walked out of the shop, closing the door behind her.

She'd left without another word because she was afraid of embarrassing herself by saying out loud the things that were in her head. She walked rapidly, not caring what direction she was taking and not noticing what was around her, until suddenly she found herself on a wide street and saw the city's famous bullring directly in front of her. There were hordes of tourists outside the gates, but Deira had no interest in going inside, so she made an abrupt turn and walked back towards the old quarter of the city.

She was hungry now, so she stopped at a table outside one of the many bars and ordered a glass of wine and some tapas. She'd just finished eating when she got a message from Bex.

Hi, Deira. I don't want to freak you out or anything but I'm pretty sure I saw Gavin outside the house earlier today. He was standing on the far side of the street looking at it. I know you two have split up and it seemed really weird. It's probably me being silly, but if you dumped him and he doesn't know you're away, is he being a bit stalker-ish? B x

She read the text through a couple of times.

She'd thought Gavin wasn't due back until the following day, but clearly she'd been mistaken. Why had he come to the house? To see if the car was parked in front of it? Had he already decided she must have taken it? Had she been caught on CCTV at his apartment? She hadn't seen any cameras, but then again, she hadn't looked.

If he thought she'd had something to do with it, he could have called her. It would have been rational for him to phone rather than stand outside the house exactly, as Bex had said, like a stalker. So why hadn't he? Why had he gone to the home they'd shared and waited outside? To scare her? He had no need to do that. Maybe he'd wanted to check it out, to see if the convertible was there before he called to yell at her.

Don't worry, she texted to her niece. *I think I know what it's about. I'll get in touch with him.*

Even though he'd definitely yell at her then.

Much to Grace's surprise, after her earlier siesta, her night's sleep had been deep and refreshing, without the nightmares that still often plagued her. They'd been nightly immediately after Ken's death – dreams in which she was with him in the car, trying to save him but drowning alongside him as water poured through the open windows and seaweed entangled itself around their bodies. She would wake up gasping for breath, her heart and her head pounding. But this morning her eyes had flickered open gently and she'd had a few moments of complete restfulness before becoming fully awake.

When she got up and opened the curtains, she was cheered by the blue sky and the sound of people already going about the business of the day. As she showered and then dressed in her travelling clothes of T-shirt and capri pants, she thought of Deira and the feelings of jealousy she'd harboured towards her the previous evening. In the bright light of the morning, she found it hard to believe that she'd resented her for being younger and prettier and catching the attention of a man. Why should she care? Besides, Deira was going through a trauma of her own. And in Grace's opinion, she was a lot less well equipped to cope than Grace herself was. While not being part of the so-called snowflake generation, the younger woman hadn't had the tough-love upbringing of Grace, who'd been told from an early age that life wasn't fair, that she could never have everything she wanted and – one of her father's favourite sayings – that there were more important people in the world than her. Of course there were more important people, she acknowledged, but you were the most important person to yourself. The trick, she reckoned, was not always behaving as though that were the case.

She'd raised her three children with a lot more demonstrations of affection than her own parents had shown towards her and her siblings. She'd raised them as though they were the most important people in her life, because that was true. She hoped it had been a better way of doing things. She hoped that it meant they could cope with whatever life threw at them, and still feel loved and cherished. Somehow she got the impression that Deira didn't feel that way, which was sad.

It was shortly after nine when she went to the breakfast room. As she selected fruit, coffee and croissants, she allowed herself to think about the clue that she hadn't yet been able to solve, the clue Ken had said he couldn't make any easier if he tried. She knew the number of the room was right. But how could the statue of Hemingway be wrong?

She poured herself a second coffee and texted Deira. But there was no reply. She wondered if Deira was annoyed with her for rushing away the previous evening. But there was no reason for her to be annoyed. She didn't know the thoughts that had been going through Grace's head.

Going to see if I can find a photo of Hemingway to upload, she texted when she'd finished her breakfast. *It's not the one I took of him at the café yesterday. Let me know when you want to meet up. I thought we could leave about midday provided we manage to solve the clue. It's a four-hour drive to Alcalá de Henares.* She put her phone in her bag, took an information leaflet from the stand in the hotel's reception area and went outside.

There was a Hemingway route through the town that took in various locations relating to the writer's time in Pamplona, so she crossed the plaza and walked along the Paseo Sarasate – a wide street with a paved *rambla* where people could walk and sit. The apparent significance of the street was an old restaurant where Hemingway used to eat that was now a chocolate shop, but other than the fact that the chocolate looked amazing, there was nothing remarkable about it. Nor was there anything noteworthy about the next stop on the map either. She was beginning to think that every business in Pamplona had a tenuous Hemingway connection simply to draw business their way.

Five minutes later she was in front of the bullring. That was where she saw Deira, phone in hand, taking photos.

'Fancy meeting you here,' she said as she caught up with her.

'Grace.' Deira smiled. 'I've just seen your text. Are you feeling better?'

'Much,' said Grace. 'And Deira, listen, I'm sorry about last night.'

'What for?' asked Deira.

'I kind of left you in the lurch with Charlie,' said Grace. 'I—'

'You were feeling a bit frazzled. Don't worry about it. I went to the art gallery and it was lovely.'

Grace had been so sure that Deira would have picked up on her irrational jealousy about Charlie that she couldn't quite believe the other woman hadn't a notion what she was talking about. She exhaled in relief.

'What d'you think about the clue?' she asked. 'I'm completely gobsmacked that it wasn't the statue at the Iruña.'

'Let's recap,' said Deira. 'The Old Man's room—'

'The number of my room at the hotel – 201,' Grace interrupted her. 'So that's not a problem. It's as easy as Ken said. But I was convinced the upload of Hemingway was the bronze statue of him at the café. I keep getting a "photo doesn't match" message when I try. I can't understand it.'

'The statue is the most obvious answer, that's for sure,' agreed Deira, 'but you know how precise the professor was. If it's not right, I think we need to focus on the fact that he mentioned a sign.'

Grace nodded. 'I thought there might be a plaque somewhere with Hemingway's picture. That's more of a real sign, isn't it?'

'Near a place he loved,' Deira reminded her. 'Which is why I thought of here.'

'And is there a sign?' asked Grace.

'Not on the bullring itself,' said Deira. 'But just as you arrived, I saw this.'

She took Grace by the shoulder and rotated her so that she was looking at a large granite street sign. It said 'Paseo de Hemingway'.

'Oh for heaven's sake!' Grace shook her head. 'D'you think this is it?'

'It's his name on a sign near a place he loved,' said Deira. 'I hope it's right, because otherwise I'm out of ideas.'

'Did you take a photo?' asked Grace.

Deira shook her head. 'You go ahead.'

Grace took a few pictures of the sign, then put her phone back in her bag and looked towards the bullring.

'I can nearly smell it, you know,' she said. 'The sand and the sawdust and the blood and the sweat.'

'Me too,' agreed Deira. 'It's very atmospheric, but I wouldn't like to go to a bullfight.'

'Oh God, no.' Grace shuddered.

'You said the professor came for the bull run. Did he go to a fight?'

'I don't know,' confessed Grace.

'You didn't ask?'

'No.' Grace shook her head. 'We rarely talked about his trips; any conversations we did have were about the lectures and the people he met more than the things he did. Ken was all about the knowledge and the people. I'm sure experiences were part of that, but he didn't share them.'

'Maybe he knew you'd disapprove of bullfighting,' said Deira as they made their way back to the hotel.

'My disapproval wouldn't have mattered,' said Grace. 'He did what he liked.'

Deira stayed silent.

'Not in a bad way,' Grace added. 'Ken was Ken, that's all.'

When they arrived back at the hotel, Grace invited Deira to see the Hemingway suite.

'Wow, it's fabulous,' said Deira when she stepped inside.

'I also thought the photo might have been the bust on the shelf there,' Grace remarked as she opened the laptop. 'But given that the room number was a clue, I didn't think the bust could be as well.'

'If the street sign doesn't work, then we should try that,' suggested Deira. 'And at least we don't get locked out of uploading photos, so we can try as many as we like.'

'You're right that the clue is in the word "sign",' Grace said. 'I'm pretty confident.'

She began the upload, and both of them waited anxiously for the progress bar to complete.

The screen faded, and then, much to their relief, the message appeared: *Congratulations, your photo is a match. Your final number is 3.*

'Yay!' Deira waved her hands over her head in celebration. 'Well done us.'

Grace smiled and entered the numbers in the Alcalá de Henares document.

They both looked at the next clue.

And then at each other.

'Oh for God's sake,' said Grace. 'Now he's showing off!'

Chapter 23

Pamplona to Alcalá de Henares: 357 km

'Todos nuestras locuras proceden del estomago vacio y una cabeza llena de aire' – he was right and he was born here. Enhorabuena *(congratulations) on getting this far. Your reward letter is A. Now I want you to upload a photo of his most famous character – you'll find him near his house. Also, how old was Sister Iñez when she died? It's easier than you think. And what month was it when Sister Julia joined her? Seven guesses. Good luck, Hippo.*

'What on earth does all that mean?' asked Deira.

'I said he was showing off, and he is,' said Grace. 'It's from Cervantes and he used to quote it all the time. It means that all of our craziness comes from having an empty stomach and a head full of air.'

'He might be right.' Deira laughed. 'I always make my silliest decisions when I'm hungry. I'm glad you understood it. OK, there must be a statue – or a sign, like Hemingway's – around somewhere. But Sister Iñez and Sister Julia? Obviously they're nuns. Have you any idea what that's all about? Is there a convent in the city that's associated with Cervantes?'

'There's certainly a monastery,' said Grace. 'But I don't know if he's linked to it in any way. Or if it has anything to do with a convent.'

'Perhaps Iñez and Julia were done for hopping over the convent wall and fraternising with the monks.' Deira grinned.

Grace raised an eyebrow. 'I hope that wasn't what led to their demise.'

'I hope so too. Anyhow,' continued Deira, 'I know we have to figure out the nuns bit, but overall I think the clues are getting easier.'

'You do?' Grace looked doubtful. 'We nearly didn't get Pamplona, even though Ken said it was easy.'

'But we did,' said Deira. 'And we didn't need all those guesses. We're a good team.'

'I'm glad you think so.'

'No doubt about it.'

'Like I said before, it's about four hours to Alcalá de Henares, allowing for a stop.' Grace studied Google Maps. 'Pretty direct, though.'

'And after that, no more than an hour to Toledo,' observed Deira.

'And then about three and a half hours to Granada.' Grace added it as a destination and followed up with the address of her apartment, a further three and a half hours away.

'You know, we're doing so well on the clues, we could probably finish it all in a couple of days,' said Deira. 'Then you could get to your apartment quicker.'

'But we wouldn't get to explore the various cities,' said Grace. 'Ken and I talked a lot about travelling through Spain and staying in out-of-the-way places. I guess this is partly his way of making me do it.'

'To be fair, none of these places is particularly out of the way,' said Deira.

'Well, no,' agreed Grace.

'Though we could add a more secluded destination if you like.' The thought had been in her mind ever since Charlie had given her the business card.

'Where?'

Deira took the card out of her bag. 'It's somewhere between Granada and Cartagena,' she said. 'En route, so to speak.'

'How do you know it?' asked Grace.

Deira cleared her throat. 'That guy, Charlie, gave it to me. He said it was worth a visit.'

Grace's glance flickered from the card to Deira and back again.

'Will he be there?'

'He plans to interview the owners, though I don't know exactly when. Probably not for ages,' she added.

'Is there something going on between you two?' Grace put the card down. She didn't look at Deira as she typed the address into Google Maps. 'Did something happen last night?'

'No!' exclaimed Deira a little too forcefully. 'He was a nice, agreeable kind of man and this place sounded interesting. I thought it might be fun to visit.'

'And that's it?'

'Seriously, Grace. There's nothing between us,' said Deira, even as she clamped down on her visions of having sex with Charlie Mulholland. 'He seems to be very close to his ex-wife.'

'I'm sure that wouldn't stop him sleeping with you if that's what you wanted. Do you?'

'For heaven's sake!' Deira felt herself blush.

'It's not an unreasonable question given your circumstances. Given what you've already told me.'

Deira could hear disapproval in every word. 'I . . . It was an idea. That's all.'

'Ken's itinerary doesn't allow us time for heading off into the mountains, which is where this place is.' Grace turned the laptop towards her.

'I've no problem sticking with the itinerary.' Deira's glance at the map was fleeting as she stood up. 'We'd better get on our way, don't you think? I still have to check out of my hotel.'

'Deira—'

'It's fine. Everything's fine,' said Deira. 'I'll see you back here in half an hour or so.'

She left the room without waiting for a response.

When Deira returned nearly forty minutes later, Grace was standing by her car, which was parked outside the hotel. Grace opened the boot and Deira stowed her bag before getting into the passenger seat. Almost immediately, Grace started the engine and moved away.

'Did I delay you?' asked Deira.

'No,' replied Grace. 'It's just that they expect you to go as soon as they bring the car from the car park.'

'Sorry.'

'Not a problem.'

But there was a problem, thought Deira, because she could feel a tension in the air between them, an atmosphere in which it would be easy to say the wrong thing. Or, to be accurate, more of the wrong thing, because she'd started it by suggesting the additional stop, and Grace was perfectly correct in thinking that her only reason to go to the quaintly named El Pozo de la Señora was to see Charlie Mulholland again. Because if he'd suggested it, surely it meant he was interested in her and might want to sleep with her – and if that was the case . . . Well, why shouldn't she take advantage of it? And what business was it of Grace's anyhow? There was no need for her to get judgemental about it. Deira was fed up with people judging her. She was fed up with Grace too, and her serene way of going through life as though nothing, even the horrible circumstances of her husband's death, truly touched her.

She glanced across at the older woman, but Grace's eyes were fixed firmly on the road ahead. They were journeying together but they were very different people, thought Deira. And although they'd got along perfectly well until now, they might have reached the end of the road with each other. She wondered if she could abandon Grace in Alcalá de Henares. The town wasn't that far from Madrid, and there must be some kind of public transport to the capital. She could get a flight home from there and leave the other woman to her own devices. But that way she'd be passing on the opportunity to sleep with Charlie. Not that the opportunity actually existed, because, of course, Grace wasn't going to divert to the mountain village and she wasn't going to give Deira the chance of getting pregnant by a man she hardly knew. No matter what, Grace was a woman who'd been brought up in a different age to Deira. Her values were different too.

Deira nibbled the tip of her nail and wondered what her own values were right now. Was it right to want to sleep with someone – anyone – simply to get pregnant? She'd never have thought so before. But personal circumstances changed everything. Even your most deeply held beliefs.

She'd thought her life was sorted. That she had everything she wanted. Now she realised it had simply been a fantasy. And yet, she reminded herself, when I was with Gavin, I *did* have everything I wanted. I had a career and a nice home and a man I loved. As for the baby . . . well, maybe he was right that it wouldn't have worked for us as a couple. Maybe I was fooling myself in thinking that it would have been fine. Maybe the only way I was ever going to have a child was to meet someone else. Gavin was prepared to make it work with Afton. But not with me.

She glanced at Grace again and saw something in her set expression that reminded her of Gillian whenever her older sister was annoyed with her about something. Is it me? she asked herself. Am I the common denominator in everyone's problems? Am I the one who needs to take a long, hard look at herself?

She felt the vibration of her phone buzzing in her bag and took a deep breath. The buzz was a text and not a call. She dug the phone out of the bag and looked at the notification.

Gavin Boyer.

He'd texted her.

Finally.

She took a deep breath and opened the message.

What's the name of our car insurance company?

That was it. No 'hello', no 'please' or 'thanks'. Just a question. And he needed to ask it because she was the one who looked after all the domestic things. The car insurance. The house insurance. The property tax. The utility bills. The cleaner. She did it all, and he didn't know where any of the policies or paperwork was.

It only struck her now how confusing it could have been if

he *had* known the insurers' details and had called them to report the missing car while the company was processing a claim for it having been burnt out in France. They'd think it was some elaborate hoax or scam. She laughed to herself, although it wasn't really an amused laugh. It was more of a relief of the tension she'd been carrying around inside. More of a realisation that the chickens had finally come home to roost.

Call me, she replied.

Tell me the name of the company ffs.

She thought for a moment. Should she call him anyhow? Keep calling till he picked up? So that she could explain it to him properly. Texting was so impersonal. A text wouldn't make him understand what had motivated her to take the car in the first place. But, she thought, even if she spoke to him, he wouldn't understand. So what good would talking do? It hadn't worked before; why should it now? Anyhow, people didn't talk any more. Bex's generation hated the faff of actually speaking on the phone. All their communication was by text. Most of it consisted almost entirely of emojis.

Do you want to report the car stolen? she typed.

Why? The response was almost immediate.

Because it hasn't been.

And you know that because?

I had it.

Had? Have? Where is it now?

I took the ferry to France and brought it with me, she typed. *We were supposed to be on holiday now, remember?*

You had no right to do that.

Well, I did.

For fuck's sake, Deira. I need the car. There could be an emergency.

256

I'm sure lots of people have emergencies but don't have cars.
Don't get smart with me.
Just saying.
When were we supposed to be back?
The trip was for three weeks.
You're some piece of work, you know that.
Indeed. But you'll need to make alternative arrangements
for the next few weeks anyhow.
Why?
I don't have the car any more.
Was it stolen!!!!!!!!

Deira laughed out loud at the exclamation marks. Grace
glanced at her and broke the almost hour-long silence.

'Everything OK?'

'It's Gavin,' said Deira. 'And it's getting to the crunch
moment. My next message will tell all.'

'Oh.'

Deira's fingers flew over the keypad as she explained what
had happened. A minute later, the phone rang.

He'd called her. He was the one who'd cracked.

'Hi,' she said, ignoring the fact that her heart was beating
faster.

'What are you talking about?' he demanded. 'A fire? What
sort of fire?'

She told him.

'You allowed my car – mine, Deira, the only thing I took
with me – you allowed it to burn? Or did you set fire to it
yourself?' His voice was shaking with rage.

'Of course I didn't set fire to it,' she said. 'It was an accident. I've dealt with it. I've spoken to the insurance company.
There'll be a payout. I have to send back some forms.'

'I don't believe it. I don't believe you,' he said.

'What part?'

'Oh, I believe that the car is destroyed.' His voice was still shaking. 'I believe that all right. What I find hard to believe is that you had nothing to do with it. And that you had the bare-faced cheek to steal the car in the first place. You know it's important to me.'

'Yeah, well, things that were important to me haven't worried you too much over the last few months, have they?'

'Is that what this is about? Some kind of revenge fantasy?'

'If I wanted my revenge on you, I'd think of something better than torching the car,' she said. Although she wondered what better scheme she could have come up with. And then she asked herself if he was right anyway. She'd seen coming to France with the car as some kind of therapy for her, but had it really been a kind of revenge on him?

'I'm reporting you to the Gardaí,' he said. 'The car is registered in my name. You're nothing more than a common thief.'

She'd thought the same herself when she'd first taken it. But not now.

'The car was a shared asset,' she said. 'And it was sitting in the car park even though it was booked to go to France.'

'The car didn't know it was going to France!' cried Gavin.

'Perhaps, perhaps not. You always referred to it as "her",' she reminded him. 'You used to call it Lucy, after the song.'

'I never thought . . . For God's sake, I can't believe you've lured me into this deranged conversation,' said Gavin. 'Bottom line, I'm calling the police.'

'Good luck with that,' she said. 'If you do, I'll tell them you were loitering outside the house.'

'What?!'

'You were seen. Yesterday. Outside the house. Loitering.'

'I'm perfectly entitled to be outside my own house.'

'Well, I'm entitled to take my own car.'

'But it's not your car, it's mine.'

'In that case, it's not your house, it's mine.'

'How would you feel if I torched it?' demanded Gavin.

'The house? You wouldn't. That'd be arson. And you'd go to prison for it. How would the lovely Afton manage then?'

'You're a crazy bitch, Deira O'Brien. My mates told me to watch out for you, that you'd try to get back at me. I didn't believe them. Now I know they were right. You haven't heard the last of this.'

He ended the call.

Deira exhaled slowly and dropped the phone back into her bag.

Grace indicated and took the slip road to the service station half a kilometre ahead. She pulled into a parking space, shaded from the sun.

'You OK?' Her voice was warmer than before.

Deira nodded, and then started to cry. She didn't know why she was crying, but she buried her face in her hands while she sobbed. Grace watched her for a minute, then put her arm around her shoulders and suggested they get a coffee.

'Probably not a good idea.' Deira sniffed a couple of times. 'I don't need to be caffeined up right now.'

'Fair enough,' said Grace. But she opened the car door and stepped outside.

Deira did the same. A blast of warm air hit her and she felt herself relax slightly.

'I'm guessing he's not too thrilled about the car,' said Grace as they walked to a wooden bench beneath a tall tree.

'I don't blame him,' said Deira.

'So what's going to happen?'

'Oh, he wants to report me to the police. I was worried about that when I first took it,' Deira added, 'but it's not like they can do much about it now. And I'll forward him the insurance money when it comes through. So he's pretty much wasting his time.'

'I'm glad you're seeing it in a practical way,' said Grace.

'I'm not practical at all,' said Deira.

'Of course you are,' said Grace. 'You've been practical all along. You took the car when he wasn't there. You came away. You found me. I realise that was accidental,' she added, 'but I was a practical solution for you. You've been practical about helping me solve the clues. And you're practical about the next moves you want to take. You saw that guy, Charlie, you assessed him, you want to make a diversion on our journey so that you can see him again—'

'That's not why,' lied Deira again. 'I thought it would be a nice thing to do.'

'Oh, please,' said Grace. 'Give me credit.'

'He might not even be there.'

'But if he is?'

'Look, we're not going,' Deira said. 'I'm not making you do something you're not comfortable with. I was thinking about all this, Grace. I can leave you after Alcalá de Henares. I can get a flight home.'

'Is that what you'd like to do?'

'It might be best.'

'Whatever you want,' said Grace.

260

They sat in silence for a moment. Then Deira said that she needed to use the bathroom.

'I'll wait for you in the car,' said Grace.

Grace got back into the Lexus while Deira went into the service station.

She was sorry that she'd annoyed the younger woman again, but in all honesty, she hadn't been able to help herself. Even though she felt acutely sorry for her, she also thought that Deira's attitude was completely wrong. Yes, her boyfriend had treated her appallingly, but that didn't give her the right to treat other people equally badly. Which, as far as Grace could see, was how Deira was thinking about Charlie Mulholland. She wanted to use him, and that wasn't right, but she simply didn't care.

Maybe realising that someone you thought had loved you had betrayed you did that to a person, mused Grace. She leaned her head against the window and wondered how Ken's actions had changed her. If they had. Because even though she'd come away on her own, which was certainly a change, she didn't feel very different inside. She was still angry with him. And yet she was also still proud of the life they'd had. Of the marriage they'd worked at. She was proud that they'd stayed together through all the ups and downs. But had that simply been inertia? she asked herself now. A desire not to rock the boat? Because they were happy enough together? Not setting the world alight, but getting along OK. Giving a secure family life to the children.

If there hadn't been children, would they have stayed together?

The question lodged itself in her mind and wouldn't go

261

away. Had Ken stayed with her because of Aline, Fionn and Regan? Or because he loved her for herself?

The day of his death came back to her, clearer than she'd ever recalled it before. The police car waiting outside her house when she arrived home. The two Garda officers stepping out to meet her, one male, one female, their faces composed into expressions of sympathy, so that she'd known, before they even spoke a word, that something terrible had happened.

And the guilt that she'd carried with her since that day, because she might have provoked it. Because she'd gone out without him even though he'd asked her not to. But she'd wanted to meet Melissa for dinner and a catch-up. Melissa, who'd been one of her best friends in her cabin-crew days. Who'd married an American hedge-fund manager and moved to the States. Melissa, whom she hadn't seen in over five years, had come to Dublin and asked to meet and Grace had wanted to go, even though Ken had asked her to stay home that night.

'It's the only time I can meet Mel,' she told him.

'It's not like you have that much time left with me,' he said.

'I'll give you all my time later,' she promised as she dropped a kiss on his head before going out.

But there hadn't been any later.

And she was to blame for that.

When Deira returned from the restroom, she could see that Grace's eyes were closed. She didn't want to get into the car and disturb her, so she sat on one of the wooden benches set in the grassy patch outside the services building.

A young woman in a brightly coloured hijab sat at another bench, a few metres away. She was joined by a couple of other women, and the sound of their laughter carried on the still air. Deira envied them, thinking that her own laughter over the last few months had been joyless and cynical. She wished she could rediscover the fun in life, the things that would make her laugh without inhibition.

Was it a consequence of getting older? she wondered. Or was it simply that she'd lost the capacity to find joy in anything?

The door of the Lexus opened and she saw Grace walking over to her.

'Are you all right?' asked the older woman.

'Yes.'

'I'm sorry,' said Grace. 'I might have been a bit out of order.'

'It's fine,' Deira said. 'I'm not at my best right now.'

'Are you coming with me?'

'I certainly don't want to be abandoned at a service station.'

'Let's go, so,' said Grace.

Deira got up and followed her.

They continued the journey in silence.

Chapter 24

An hour later, Grace drove them into Alcalá de Henares, an old town of such stunning architectural beauty that both women were awestruck.

'Clearly all these buildings have been renovated.' Deira broke the silence as they followed the signs to the underground car park a few minutes' walk from their hotel. 'But they're spectacular.'

They were even more spectacular close up. The two women pulled their cases along a narrow street of old buildings with iron-grilled windows and enormous wooden doors. The pavement was lined on either side with tall cypress trees and pretty flowers.

'That's the university.' Grace observed the brick sign on one of the buildings. 'Our hotel is a couple of metres past it.'

And it was – another old building with a renovated facade and a glass door that said 'Hotel Santa Ana'.

'I wonder if Santa Ana knew the two nuns in the professor's clue,' said Deira. 'Maybe they were all mates, but she was the one who behaved herself and was made a saint.'

'Let's not rule it out.' Grace pushed the door open.

It took a moment for their eyes to adjust to the dimly lit interior after the brightness of the street, but both of them immediately felt the pleasant coolness from the fountain in the centre of the octagonal reception area, which was two storeys high. An internal walkway ran around the irregular brick walls, with small corridors leading in various directions at ground level. There was a staircase close to one of the corridors, along with a small desk.

A door opened and a man in a dark suit asked if he could help them. Grace told him that she and Deira had reservations for the night. After checking the computer, the receptionist told them, in a tone of regret, that he hadn't been able to allocate them rooms beside each other as Grace's had been reserved earlier than Deira's, and the hotel was full that night.

He asked Deira to wait at the desk while he led Grace along a long corridor into another internal courtyard set with flagstones and gravel. He opened an old-fashioned wooden door and turned on the lights as they went into the room, because it faced directly onto the courtyard, which was its only source of natural light. It was small but beautifully decorated with dark-wood furnishings and an elegant four-poster bed. In contrast to the old-world look of the room itself, the bathroom was modern, sleek and elegantly functional.

When he was sure that Grace had everything she needed, the receptionist returned to the reception area to bring Deira to her room on the first floor. This was smaller but equally well furnished, although unlike Grace's, the window overlooked a narrow street behind the hotel.

Deira pottered around the room for a short while before

texting Grace to ask if she wanted to meet up and search for the Cervantes statue. She wasn't sure what the relationship between them was like right now. Grace had been kind at the service station, but Deira knew she still disapproved of the suggestion to stop off at El Pozo de la Señora. Deira hadn't made up her mind if she wanted to try to get there herself, stay on the treasure hunt with Grace, or leave her here in Alcalá de Henares and go to Madrid for a flight home. She was going to have to face up to Gavin sooner or later. Perhaps sooner was the better option.

Her phone pinged. Grace's reply was that she was going to have a short siesta and she'd text Deira again later.

Deira was far too restless to even think of a siesta herself, so she went downstairs and walked outside, blinking in the bright sunshine. She strolled along the cypress-lined road without any real destination in mind and eventually ended up in a large park filled with flowering shrubs and trees.

Sitting once again in the shade of a tree, she suddenly had the feeling of being outside of her own body, of looking down at herself and wondering how on earth she'd ended up here, in a place she didn't know with a person she didn't know when she should have been in Brittany with the love of her life. How was it that in the space of a few weeks, everything had changed so utterly? And how was it that, having loved and been loved by Gavin Boyer, she now felt nothing but rage towards him, as, she supposed, he also felt towards her?

She took a few photos and sent them to Tillie. Her friend had texted every day asking how things were going, and even when she'd had to tell her about the car, Deira's replies had been uniformly upbeat. But right now, despite the heat of the sun and the beauty of the park and the fact that she should be feeling fine, her sense of disconnection was huge.

Out-of-the-world place, she added to one of the pictures. *I feel as though I'm lucky to be here.*

Tillie's message came back immediately.

Live in the moment. Be in touch with yourself.

Easy to say, thought Deira. Not quite so easy to do.

Her phone buzzed again. This time it was a message from Bex.

Hi, Deira. There's a bit of an issue at your house. I've been out since early this morning but I've come back now and Gavin is here.

Have you talked to him?

Yeah. I asked what he was doing and he said he's taking his stuff.

Is he still there?

Yes.

Are you there too?

I'm outside. I didn't want to annoy him. Lydia is with me.

I'll call him. Don't worry.

Deira took a deep breath, then scrolled to Gavin's number.

Grace felt remarkably refreshed when she woke from her siesta. She'd fallen asleep almost as soon as she'd stretched out on the bed, and that sleep had again been deep and undisturbed. She appreciated it very much, as so many of her nights had been broken by images of being trapped in the car with Ken as it sank beneath the water. Even when she was awake she still imagined what it had been like for him; if, as the water had poured into the car, he'd changed his mind and been unable to do anything about it. Had he been scared? Or resigned? Had he been thinking about her and what would happen next? Or had he simply been relieved that it was nothing to do with him any more?

Grace had been grateful for the verdict of misadventure when it came. It made her feel better that other people would believe it.

But she had her husband's laptop and his final email.

And she knew that it wasn't the truth.

There was no immediate reply to the text she sent Deira asking where they should meet, so Grace wandered towards the Cervantes plaza. As she approached, she saw the younger woman standing in the shade of a tree, engrossed in a phone conversation. She stopped a short distance away to give her some privacy but Deira's words were carried to her by the soft breeze.

'I know we haven't come to any formal arrangement yet,' she was saying. 'I understand that. But it's not right that you should simply walk into the house when—'

There was a long silence, and then Deira spoke again.

'Yes, I also know that my bloody family taking up residence there at the drop of a hat is a problem. You told me that often enough. But you can't blame what you did on Bex and Gillian!'

A further pause.

'Take what you like. I don't care. I'll deduct it from the insurance money.'

And with that, Deira ended the call and shoved her phone in her bag. By the time Grace got to her, it was ringing again.

'Sorry,' she said. 'I'll have to answer it.'

'Of course.'

Deira stepped away slightly and took the call. 'What?' she said.

'Don't hang up on me when I'm speaking to you,' said Gavin. 'God Almighty, Deira, you've turned into the worst sort of bitchy woman. The sort of woman we always despised.'

'That you despised, for sure,' she retorted. 'And if *I* did, then I regret it. Because if a woman is being bitchy, she usually has a reason. In my case, it's you.'

'You have to be reasonable,' he said. 'I'm entitled—'

'I don't give a toss about your entitlements,' she said. 'Take what you want from the house – but not my coffee machine. And don't upset Bex and her friend either.'

'You can't keep the money from the car insurance,' said Gavin. 'I need a car. Afton could go into labour at any minute.'

'You've forgotten everything you ever knew about pregnancy,' said Deira. 'She's nowhere near due yet. Unless you lied to me about that too.'

'No. I didn't. But the stress—'

'Give me a break!' Deira snorted. 'She's not under any stress.'

'Of course she is. It's her first baby.'

Deira gritted her teeth. 'Take your stuff, go, and don't come back,' she said. 'I'll send you the name of my solicitor. It's time to put this on a more formal footing.'

'We don't need solicitors,' said Gavin. 'We need to be mature.'

'Oh, please.' She snorted again. 'I'll text you the details.'

And she hung up again.

'Things a bit fraught?' asked Grace when Deira walked back to her.

'He's taking bits and pieces from the house while my niece is there,' Deira said. 'I feel bad about that. I don't want her caught in the middle of my domestic dispute.'

Her phone buzzed again as she and Grace began to walk through the plaza, this time with a message from Bex saying that Gavin was gone and asking if she could go back into the house.

Of course, replied Deira. *I'm sorry he caused you problems.* She added a couple of sad-faced emojis. Bex replied with some of her own, telling her that Gavin appeared to have taken the elegant slimline kettle, the Victorinox kitchen knives, the Bose wireless speakers, the flat-screen TV in the bedroom and the abstract painting that had hung in the living room. *Other small things too*, she added. *But they're the big bits.*

'It's not too bad,' remarked Deira. 'At least he did as I asked and left me the coffee machine! I'm not impressed with him taking the painting; it was by an artist I exhibited years ago, and I'm sure he took it out of spite. But the rest can be easily replaced. Besides,' she continued, 'I never used those knives. I'm not a great cook. All in all, I'm happy that particular drama is over.'

'I wonder if there are people who never have any dramas or worries in their lives,' mused Grace.

'Realistically not,' replied Deira. 'Although Tillie does seem to float through hers, only fleetingly having anything to worry about. It might be a state of mind, but I can't help thinking that she was born under a lucky star.'

'My mum told me I was,' said Grace. 'Born under a lucky star, I mean. After all, I got into the airline when it was a well-paid, glamorous job. I met a guy who provided well for me. I have three great children.'

'But then your husband became ill and died.'

'We all die,' said Grace.

Deira was startled.

'I was thinking about him earlier,' Grace said. 'I don't want to now. Will we look for the statue?'

'We don't have to look far.' Deira pointed to the centre of the plaza. 'The man himself.'

'Except it's not a photo of Cervantes we want,' said Grace.

'Huh?'

'I read the clue again before I came out,' she said. 'Ken wants us to upload a picture of his most famous character. That's what it says.'

'You're right.' Deira gave her head an annoyed shake. 'I was rushing into things. There must be a statue of Don Quixote somewhere in the town.'

'In that case, let's find it,' said Grace.

They walked to the end of the plaza, where they turned onto a pedestrianised street of traditional family-owned shops. Despite Grace's desire to solve the clue as quickly as possible, she was distracted by displays of organic soaps and skincare, home-made ice cream and artisan jewellery, as well as tourist shops with any number of T-shirts, caps and bags emblazoned with images of either Cervantes or Don Quixote. Much to their bemusement, there were also lots of items embossed with images of storks, as well as figures of the birds themselves in a variety of materials.

'Storks weren't a big part of *Don Quixote*, were they?' asked Grace as she replaced a pewter version on a shelf and instead decided to buy a Cervantes snow globe for her grandson, to go along with the soap and pretty necklace she'd already bought for Aline.

'Not that I remember,' replied Deira. 'Then again, I read it in my second year of college and I might have forgotten a stork incident.'

They continued weaving in and out of shops until they reached the end of the street, where clusters of people were gathered outside a restored house. It had the same light-red and cream brickwork as all the other buildings in the town, with the same terracotta roof, and there was a small flowered garden in front. More importantly, from their point of view, a sign informed them that it was the Cervantes Museum, and outside was a bronze bench where the tourists were snapping photos of themselves sitting between sculptures of Don Quixote and his sidekick, Sancho Panza.

'Bingo.' Deira's mood lifted. 'I'm glad you read the clue properly, Grace. It would've been infuriating to have missed this.'

'Now all we have to do is wait till we can get a photo of him without a million other people,' said Grace.

It was a long wait. But eventually she managed to take a picture of Quixote. Then she asked Deira to take one of her sitting beside him, to send to her children.

'Do you want one of both of you?' asked an English tourist, waiting for her own opportunity to take a snap.

'Do we?' Grace looked at Deira.

Deira nodded, and they sat together on the bronze bench.

'Another one for the children,' said Grace.

'You're in touch with them every single day?'

'They worry about me,' Grace said. 'Sending the photos

keeps them happy. All this concern will pass in time, but they honestly don't need to fret, because I'm absolutely fine.'

'Makes two of us,' said Deira as she stood up and brushed dust off the denim skirt she was wearing.

Although she only half believed it.

Chapter 25

Alcalá de Henares, Spain: 40.4820°N 3.3635°W

Even though her annoyance with Grace hadn't completely dissipated, and she was still furious with Gavin, there was something about the atmosphere of Alcalá de Henares that soothed Deira in a way that Pamplona hadn't. The beautifully restored buildings – the monasteries, convents, churches and universities – seemed to reconnect her to the old books and paintings she'd always loved, evoking a different, slower way of life. And a way of life in which you didn't automatically think you were entitled to everything you wanted. The thought came to her as she and Grace strolled silently through the streets. Back in the time of Cervantes, there was little talk about your entitlement to happiness. It was all about surviving. Surviving life, surviving unhappy arranged marriages, surviving multiple pregnancies, surviving being a husband's possession. She wouldn't have had a choice not to get married or have children, she thought. The only way of avoiding it would have been to become a nun. And that wouldn't have been the sort of life that would have led to personal fulfilment.

She remembered a book she'd read back in her college days (and college was something else that wouldn't have been a choice for her in the sixteenth century, she reminded

274

herself). It had been about a woman who'd become a nun and gone mad. Many of the nuns in the convent had practised 'self-mortification', which meant beating themselves with ropes and chains. Their wounds had turned septic and the women themselves – all younger than Deira was now – had suffered terribly. Some had claimed to see angels and saints around their beds; many had attested to visitations by God or the Virgin Mary. As Deira had read the book, she'd realised that the nuns were hallucinating – either from the pain of their injuries or from the special 'draughts' they were given to drink. She couldn't help thinking of those women now, many of whom had been sent away for a variety of family reasons, including not having husbands. She realised that however difficult life was for her, it was a million times better than either being married off or being shut up in a convent.

She had no reason to complain. She said so out loud.

Grace looked at her in surprise.

'I'm lucky,' said Deira. 'Despite everything. I have options. Choices. Maybe not the ones I want, but I have them all the same.'

'Just because we have choices doesn't mean we should make bad ones,' observed Grace.

'I know,' said Deira. 'And you were right about El Pozo de la Señora and Charlie Mulholland. I guess I was thinking with some primal part of my consciousness and not my actual brain.'

'I do understand,' said Grace. 'I honestly do. I just don't think it's fair to . . . well . . .'

Deira nodded. 'I feel so . . . so pushed for time,' she said. 'Like I'm crumbling in front of my own eyes.'

'Which is sort of how I've felt myself these last few months,' admitted Grace.

'We're a right pair, aren't we,' said Deira. 'Wounded birds.'

Grace glanced upwards. 'Storks?' she suggested, nodding towards the high steeple of a nearby church, where two enormous birds were sitting in a nest.

'Goodness!' Deira looked surprised. 'They're actually real. I saw a couple earlier and thought it was some kind of art installation.'

Grace laughed. 'Not everything is art. Sometimes it's real life.'

Deira took out her phone and snapped a couple of pictures. Then she checked her photo stream and made a sound of disgust.

'What?' asked Grace.

'My flipping hair!' Deira ran her fingers through her curls. 'It's a mess. And look at all those bloody greys.'

'Embrace them,' said Grace. 'I have.'

'With all due respect, Grace, you have the loveliest unicorn-silver hair. My greys are all dingy pepper. And to be perfectly honest,' Deira made a face, 'I'm not ready to embrace it. In my head I'm still brunette.'

'In that case, get it done,' said Grace.

'Here?'

'Why not?'

Deira looked at her watch. 'It's a bit late for the hairdresser, surely.'

'You're in Spain,' Grace reminded her. 'Most of them will still be open. And if you don't mind me saying, you'd look great with it cut a bit shorter. Maybe straight across the ends.' She smiled. 'Back in my air-hostessing days, when we were all told how to look, we got lots of advice on hair and beauty. I've remembered it.'

'And you think I'd look good with short hair?'

'Shorter,' said Grace. 'More styled.'

Deira shrugged. 'OK,' she said. 'If we see a hairdresser's, I'll do it.'

Less than ten minutes later, they stopped in front of a salon. Deira pushed the door open and a young woman, her own hair a vivid orange, smiled at her.

'Cut?' asked Deira, miming the action. 'And colour?'

The girl nodded and waved her to a seat.

'It'll take about an hour, I guess,' Deira said to Grace.

'Excellent,' Grace said. 'That might be enough time for me to solve the clue of Sister Iñez and Sister Julia.'

'OK,' said Deira. 'Will we meet back at the hotel? Or at a bar? If I have my hair done, we have to go out,' she added.

'Text me when you're finished,' said Grace. 'I'll meet you wherever you like.'

'Will do,' said Deira as the hairdresser put a gown around her.

Grace was quite happy to have some time alone to solve the clue. She had a very good idea of how to find the answer, although she wasn't a hundred per cent sure of where it lay. Nevertheless, she felt confident as she walked back to the hotel.

She went up to her room immediately and took out the hotel information pack.

The Convent of Santa Ana was founded in 1652 as a Dominican convent dedicated to the devotion of St Anne, mother of Mary. She is the patron of unmarried women, women who want to be pregnant, grandmothers and teachers. The convent offered refuge to women in difficult circumstances. It flourished until the late nineteenth century, when the nuns moved to another location closer to Madrid. The building fell into disrepair but has been restored under the UNESCO heritage plans for the city of Alcalá de Henares and is now an intimate boutique hotel.

Given that Ken had booked her to stay in a convent, Grace was pretty sure that Sister Iñez and Sister Julia had been members of it. There must be more information about them somewhere in the building. All she had to do was find it.

She closed the folder and walked along the corridor, not towards reception but following a sign to the restaurant. This led to yet another courtyard, this time surprisingly large, surrounded by a cloister. One side was taken up by the restaurant, and another led to a lounge. Tables and chairs were placed along the third. Like the two smaller courtyards, this one also had a fountain in the centre, with paving stones leading from it, dividing the area into quarters made up of flagstones. There were stone slabs set into the flagstones.

Grace looked at them more closely.

They were tombstones. Old tombstones, some dating back to shortly after the convent had been opened. And although she couldn't understand every word, it was obvious that they were the tombstones of nuns who had lived here. It should have been eerie, and yet it wasn't.

She walked slowly, looking at them individually. There were Marias and Isadoras and Teresas and Anas . . . And then she saw the one she wanted. Sister Iñez, who'd died at a mere twenty-three years old. Grace swallowed the lump that had suddenly appeared in her throat. She wondered if Iñez had had a vocation, or if her family had sent her to the convent because she was a burden. Perhaps she wouldn't marry the man they'd chosen. Or maybe, for some reason, her parents were ashamed of her. She wondered what life had been like at the convent for a young woman of twenty-three; if there had been any fun, any joy in it. If Iñez had ever run along the cloisters or sat here on a chair, shaded from the sun. She hoped so. And she also hoped that whatever illness had taken the young woman's life, she hadn't suffered too much.

It took another minute to find Julia's tombstone. The nun had died in June of the following year, at the age of twenty-five. Had she and Iñez been friends? wondered Grace. Had they laughed together? Joked together? Shared stories with each other? And were they, as the inscription on Julia's tombstone seemed to suggest, at peace in heaven?

Grace didn't believe in an afterlife, certainly not the one of angels and saints she'd been taught about as a child. It didn't make sense to her. But here, in the quiet of the courtyard and the shade of the cloisters, she wondered if it might not be possible. And if it was, and she saw Ken there, what would she say to him? What would he say to her?

That was the thing, wasn't it? People talked about reuniting with their loved ones, but what if their loved ones had done awful things during their lives? And what if you'd found someone else after they'd gone? What sort of set-up was that for all eternity?

Heaven and all its conundrums could wait, she decided; meantime, she'd solved the clue and all she had to do was upload the photo of Don Quixote to get the last number.

She could do it now, she supposed, but Deira had been there for every other clue reveal, and even if things between them had been a bit strained lately, she'd feel bad about continuing without her.

She sat at one of the tables and ordered a water from the waiter who'd been hovering around since she'd arrived. Then she texted Deira to say she'd solved the clue and asked if she wanted to come back to the hotel to unlock it when she was finished at the hairdresser's, or would she prefer to meet in town.

It was about fifteen minutes later when Deira replied, congratulating her on solving the clue and suggesting they meet at the Plaza Cervantes again.

Grace was suddenly quite happy to get away from the silence of the cloisters.

Reading the next clue could wait.

When she got to the plaza, she looked around for Deira, but it took a moment before she saw her, standing near the statue and waving at her.

'You look amazing!' she exclaimed. 'It's fabulous.'

'I'm glad you think so.' Deira looked pleased. 'I thought about what you said and I reckoned that you always look great, so I followed your advice.'

Her curls, which had fallen to her shoulders before, had been chopped to just below the nape of her neck. The cut was more even than previously, but not harsh, and it gave her an edgier appearance.

'You need bright-red lipstick and some cool sunglasses for a bit of Parisian chic,' declared Grace, which made Deira laugh and remind her that she hadn't made it to Paris yet.

'Seriously,' Grace said. 'Red lipstick would look great on you.'

'I'm not really a lipstick person,' said Deira. 'I'm not a make-up person at all, to be honest. I try, but I never really get it right.'

'When I worked for the airline, you wouldn't have been allowed to fly without a full face of slap,' said Grace. 'But the lessons I learned have been really useful, especially now, when I need to spend twice the time to look half as good. You're naturally pretty, Deira, and you've got great skin. You wouldn't need much. Maybe a little bit of a tint and some eyeshadow and mascara to bring out your eyes. They're such an amazing shade of green.'

'I either do too much or too little,' confessed Deira.

'You can't go wrong with lipstick.'

'Red, though. I'm not sure about red.'

'Nothing ventured.'

Deira laughed. 'OK. If we see somewhere, I'll have a look.'

'There was a beauty shop in that street we walked down earlier,' Grace said.

'Was there?' Deira looked surprised. 'I didn't notice.'

'Beauty shops and pharmacies are my thing,' confessed Grace. 'I love them. I spent hours in the duty-free on the ferry.'

'Did you?' Deira frowned. 'There wasn't much there.'

'Five different serums,' said Grace. 'Hours of fun for me.'

Deira laughed again. 'In that case, let's go and have fun!'

They linked arms as they walked to the shop, which, though it looked small from the outside, was considerably more spacious within. Grace led Deira through the displays of L'Oréal and Rimmel and Bourjois to the Chanel counter.

'This is the best,' she said as she selected a shade called Pirate. 'It looks good on everyone and it'll be spectacular on you.'

'Fingers crossed,' said Deira.

'Like I said.' Grace nodded approvingly after she'd used a cotton bud from the display area to apply it to Deira's lips. 'Spectacular.'

'You like it?' An assistant who'd been watching them asked the question in English. 'There is also a good foundation,' she added. 'With sun protection. Although I always say you should wear extra sun protection and not depend on a cream or foundation. Save your skin, no?'

'I'm only here for lipstick,' said Deira, even as Grace picked up a dark eyeshadow.

'Try this,' she said.

'I usually go for nudes,' said Deira. 'They work with my eyes.'

'But not with scarlet lipstick.'

Deira gave a resigned shrug and allowed Grace to apply the product, as well as a swirl of blush to her cheeks.

'Oh,' she said when the older woman had finished. 'That's me . . . but not me.'

'A different version of you,' said Grace. 'We can do a nude one, though, if you prefer.'

She handed Deira a wipe and told her to remove the lipstick and eyeshadow. Then she selected another shade and applied it.

'That's more recognisably me,' said Deira when she looked at her reflection. 'But less . . . less wow.'

'You don't always have to go for wow,' said Grace. 'But there are times you definitely should.'

'OK.' Deira smiled. 'Can we wow me up again and go for a drink?'

'We absolutely can,' said Grace as she reached for the Pirate once more.

Deira groaned when she opened her eyes the following morning, because not only did they feel gummed together, but her head was aching. She tapped her phone to see the time and groaned again when she realised it was after nine.

It had been past two in the morning when they'd come back to the hotel. She remembered giggling as she'd taken off her shoes so that the heels didn't make too much noise on the tiled floors. And she remembered sitting in the cloister with Grace, gazing at the night sky, drinking water and talking about Sister Iñez and Sister Julia. They hadn't tried to look at the next clue. Grace had been afraid that because she'd had two glasses of wine and a very large gin and tonic, she'd accidentally input the wrong numbers and lock herself out.

Deira didn't remember how much she'd had to drink herself. She recalled going to a bar and sitting at a high table outside. She knew Grace had ordered the bottle of wine. But after that . . .

She pushed away the duvet and walked unsteadily to the bathroom. A glance in the mirror startled her – she'd forgotten about her shorter hairstyle and, despite clearly having drunk a lot, the scarlet lipstick still stained her lips.

She put on the disposable shower cap to protect her new hairdo and stood under the hot water, allowing it to massage the back of her neck. The sensation was soothing and she felt better afterwards, but she was still shaky when she walked downstairs.

Grace was already seated at one of the tables in the cloister, a cup of coffee in front of her. She looked up as Deira approached.

'Good morning,' she said. 'How are you?'

'Did I lose it completely?' Deira pulled out a chair and sat opposite her. 'Because I'm a delicate flower this morning. I can't believe I'm hung-over. I haven't been hung-over in months.'

'You were fine until the shots,' Grace told her.

'Shots!' Deira looked aghast. 'I don't drink shots.'

'You did last night,' said Grace. 'After the second bottle of wine.'

'Didn't we eat?' asked Deira. 'I don't usually get wasted if I eat.'

'The barman brought us some free tapas,' said Grace. 'We didn't bother about food after that.'

'Obviously I didn't eat enough of them. Weren't we talking to people, too?'

'A group of men,' said Grace. 'They heard us speaking English and they wanted to chat. They bought the second bottle because we'd finished ours, and then the shots afterwards. But they weren't trying to get us drunk or anything.'

'I didn't say or do anything awful, did I?' asked Deira as it started to come back to her. 'There was someone called Roberto, and . . . Leo, was it? They were lecturers at the university. Not literature.'

'Architecture,' supplied Grace.

'I can't remember the last time I did something like this,' said Deira.

'Me neither, to be honest.'

'But you're not hung-over.'

'Well, I didn't have the shots,' said Grace. 'But my secret non-hangover weapon comes with age. I know it's generally the case that the older you get, the worse your reaction to a late night is, but since the menopause, I don't get hangovers.'

'You're kidding.'

'Nope,' said Grace. 'It's a compensation for the hot flushes and memory loss. Mind you, I limit myself to a couple of glasses of wine any time I go out. And maybe a G&T afterwards. So I'm not exactly lashing it back. Doesn't affect me, though.'

'You should've saved me from myself,' said Deira.

'Why?' Grace smiled. 'You were having a good time. We both were.'

Deira got up from the table and helped herself to some fresh fruit from the buffet.

'I remember laughing a lot,' she said as she sat down again. 'So that was a good thing.'

'The guys knew Dublin,' Grace said. 'One of them had worked as a barman in the city when he was at college. They got the humour.'

'When he was at college!' Deira stared at her. 'Don't tell me we got drunk with a bunch of graduates.'

Grace took out her phone and scrolled to a photo. It showed the two of them raising glasses of wine to the four men behind them.

'Thank God,' said Deira. 'At least they don't look like kids.'

'In their thirties, I think,' said Grace. 'Which is young enough for them all to be my sons. Something I find hard to grasp even though I have a son who's thirty. And his sister is older!'

'We were talking a lot about Alcalá de Henares and its history.' Deira's memories were becoming clearer now. 'And the storks. We had a big discussion about storks!'

'That's because the bar was called La Cigüeña. Which means stork,' said Grace. 'They're one of the symbols of the city, apparently.'

'Right. Well, I'm sorry if it was my fault we ended up out half the night,' said Deira. 'Just because I wanted to flaunt my red lipstick and new hairdo.'

'I enjoyed myself mightily,' Grace told her. 'I haven't been out like that since long before Ken was diagnosed. I don't have many girlfriends. It's crazy really, but somehow I was never one for having groups of girls I was close to. There's a few, of course, but even then we wouldn't go out on the complete lash. I suppose it wouldn't be the done thing for women of a certain age to totter out of a pub.'

'It depends on the women,' said Deira. 'And the pub.'

Grace laughed. 'Are you feeling up to unlocking the clue?'

Deira nodded, and Grace took the laptop from the bag beside her.

'Hopefully we've got it all right,' she said.

She uploaded the photo and was rewarded with the message that it was a match, and that the number she needed was 5. So she typed in **5236** and waited.

Chapter 26

Alcalá de Henares to Toledo: 105 km

Good that you're still with me, Hippo. Your reward is the letter T. Did you like Alcalá de Henares? It's an amazing place, the history, the culture, the learning . . . I hope you had time to take a proper tour. Anyhow, moving on, you're going to have to find and upload a picture of our previous scribe in Toledo. Easy pickings, don't you think? It's not only about the literature, though; another creative artist did some of his best work here. How old was he when he died? And what month? Six guesses in case you need them, but I'm sure you won't. Easy-peasy!

'I wonder what these letters are going to spell out,' said Deira.

'Another place, perhaps?' suggested Grace. 'Somewhere else he wants me to visit.'

'Could be,' agreed Deira.

'Are you planning to continue the journey with me?' Grace asked the question casually.

Deira hesitated. She hadn't given much further thought to her idea of abandoning Grace in Alcalá de Henares. It had seemed the right thing to do when they'd argued, but now she didn't like the idea of walking away.

'I'd be happy if you stayed,' said Grace. 'But it's entirely up to you.'

'I was angry at you because you were reading my mind and I was being stupid,' said Deira. 'I'm sorry. If you don't mind having me with you, I'd really like to carry on.'

'We've come this far together. It would be a shame to break up a successful partnership,' Grace told her.

Deira smiled. 'True.'

'I'll leave you to have your breakfast in peace. There's no rush to leave. It's only an hour or so to Toledo. I'm going to go for a wander around the town again. Checkout is at eleven. D'you want to meet back here then?'

Deira nodded.

Grace walked out of the breakfast room.

And both of them sighed with relief.

While she lingered over the peppermint tea she'd decided would be better for her than coffee, Deira sent Bex a text asking if everything was OK at the house. Even though she'd initially been annoyed at her niece staying in her home, she felt terrible that she'd been caught in the crossfire between her and Gavin. But there was a part of her that was now happy to think that Bex was there and that Gavin and Afton couldn't try to move in. At the moment, the two of them were living in an apartment that, Deira had learned previously, actually belonged to Afton's parents. If she wasn't so angry with Gavin, she'd think there was something a little sad about a fifty-seven-year-old man living in an apartment owned by the parents of his twenty-something girlfriend, but she didn't have any room in her heart for sympathy.

There was no response from Bex, so she spent some time

checking social media, eventually turning, as she so often did these days, to Afton's Instagram. Normally Afton posted half a dozen times a day, but there had been nothing for the past week. Deira wondered if Gavin had asked her not to put anything up because he didn't want Deira to see their lives together. Whatever the reason for the other woman's social media silence, there were still no updates.

Having finished her tea, Deira filled her glass with more juice and sent a photo of the cloisters to Tillie. She was pleased to get a response straight away.

Looks super chilled and mindful.

Deira told her about the tombstones of the nuns.

Their spirits are watching over you, was Tillie's response.

Deira doubted that. And anyhow, she wondered if the spirits of two women who'd died young, probably from some contagious disease, could possibly watch over her in any way other than with disgust that she was so crap at coping with life at her advanced age. Back then, when life expectancy had been so much shorter, she'd have been considered an old woman. And now, despite her sharp new hairstyle and embracing of scarlet lipstick, her body still didn't think it was young. She thought of the statistics again. Even if by some miracle she did get pregnant, the chance of a miscarriage for a woman her age was 34 per cent; for a woman in her early twenties it could be as low as 9 per cent.

She thought of all the times in the past she'd worried about being pregnant: when she'd been at college and had a couple of drunken one-nighters; the relationships that hadn't gone anywhere but were important at the time; and a stupid encounter with one of her tutors that neither of them ever acknowledged again. She wondered if getting pregnant would have been the disaster she'd thought back then. Because if she'd had a baby when she was so much younger, that child would be an adult by now, and she'd have someone to call her own.

Yet if that had happened, she wouldn't be the person she was.

And she didn't know if that would be a good thing or not.

Deira had offered to drive to Toledo, saying that it was a short journey and her ribs were completely healed now, so it was she who brought them through a mostly uninspiring, flat landscape, with industrial estates close to the motorway and brown fields in the distance.

'We're driving around Madrid,' said Grace when Deira remarked on it. 'So I guess everything is geared towards the city.'

But as they approached Toledo, the road twisted upwards into the hills, so that when they reached the parador that Ken had booked for Grace (and where Deira had also managed to get a room), a spectacular view of the old city was spread out beneath them.

'I didn't realise we'd be outside the town, but it's worth it for the view,' said Grace after they'd checked in and were standing on the hotel's outdoor terrace. 'If this journey has proved one thing to me, it's that there are some really lovely places in Spain, and I truly regret that Ken and I never made these journeys together.'

'You should've done a blog of this trip,' said Deira.

'*We* should've, you mean,' Grace said. 'Women on tour.'

'We could've added Ken's treasure hunt to make it interesting.'

'Maybe the people following us would've worked out the answers to the clues quicker.'

'I dunno. We've solved them all in time so far.'

Grace smiled and started to take photos of the old town in the distance. Meanwhile, Deira checked her phone. There was still no reply from Bex.

Everything OK? she sent.

She wasn't worried about her niece because she knew that her generation didn't respond to messages straight away. But given the situation the previous day, she was surprised that Bex hadn't updated her.

'I was thinking of lying out by the pool for a while before going into town,' said Grace. 'I'm sure we'll find the Cervantes statue easily enough, and I'd rather trek around when it's a bit cooler.'

'Sounds good to me,' said Deira, who was still feeling tired and dehydrated. 'Besides, I know the answer to the second part, so we're not under any pressure.'

'You do?'

'You forget my artistic background.' Deira grinned. 'It's El Greco, the painter. He lived and worked in Toledo. I can't remember when he died, but that's a quick Google search.'

'Go, team!' said Grace. 'We're totally owning this. In fact, we're doing so well, Ken would've been disappointed. He'd have wanted me to struggle a bit more.'

'Surely he'd be thrilled,' said Deira. 'He wouldn't want you to miss out on the treasure, whatever it is.'

'No,' agreed Grace. 'But . . . I think he thought it would be more like the treasure hunts you say he did for the students back in your day. No mobiles, no googling, just pounding the pavements.'

'Perhaps,' agreed Deira. 'I guess it was hard for him to construct something like that when he was confined to the house.'

'Poor Ken.' Grace's face clouded over. 'Until the heart attack, he spent most of his time at his desk. Then he became addicted to action. And then he was diagnosed and he was stuck again.'

Deira thought there was more sympathy in Grace's voice than ever before. And it warmed her to think that her friend – because that was how she now considered Grace – was repairing her memories of her husband.

'Anyway, I'm heading to my room now. See you at the pool later,' said Grace.

'Later,' agreed Deira, and they went their separate ways again.

Grace had been amused at Deira's suggestion of a blog, as, although she hadn't done anything public, she'd started to email a synopsis of each day to Aline, Fionn and Regan, attaching some of the photos she'd taken. She'd started it in Bordeaux and all three of them had urged her to continue. So when she went back to her room, she composed an email about her night out in Alcalá de Henares with Deira. As well as attaching photographs of the beautifully restored buildings, and the interior of the hotel (including the tombstones), she added the one of her, Deira and the university lecturers they'd met at the bar.

It was a late night, she finished. *But we thoroughly enjoyed ourselves.*

And that was true, she realised as she hit send. For the first time since Ken's death, she hadn't felt the weight of guilt pressing on her shoulders. It had started to lift when she and Deira had gone into the beauty shop and she'd shown the younger woman how to use lipstick. Grace had always felt that there was nothing more uplifting than wearing a bright-red lipstick and swirling blusher on your cheeks, no matter how bad you were feeling. Shallow though she supposed other people might have found it, wearing Rouge Allure had helped her any time she left the house after Ken's funeral. But that had been a temporary lift. Now, it was different.

When they'd been at the bar talking to the lecturers, Grace had joined in the conversation without once thinking of Ken or worrying that he would have been embarrassed by her lack of knowledge of the town and its cultural heritage. The men had been quite happy to answer the questions she'd asked, without thinking them stupid. And they'd been equally happy to share the bottle of wine with her and Deira. It had been both cheering and liberating and she'd returned to the hotel in a haze of positivity.

She still felt positive.

So positive that she wasn't going to worry about baring her cellulite at the pool later.

Deira was about to go down to the pool herself when Bex FaceTimed her. Deira usually confined her phone calls to audio, but when her niece actually made an effort to speak rather than text, it was always FaceTime. Bex was sitting on the sofa, her feet up, propping the phone against her legs. She looked tired and less groomed than usual, her honey-blonde hair pulled back in a scrunchy. Too many late nights in the city, thought Deira.

'Is everything all right?' she asked. 'Gavin hasn't come back, has he?'

'No,' said Bex.

'Good. I'm sorry he bothered you.'

'He didn't. Not really.'

'It was wrong of him to come in all the same.'

'Maybe.'

Deira frowned. Her niece appeared distracted and worried, even though she'd said everything was OK. Although actually, she hadn't. She'd replied to the question about Gavin. Not about herself. 'Is everything all right with you?'

'Sort of.' Bex rubbed her eyes.

'Why sort of? Did you hear back about the internship? Didn't you get it?'

'I . . . I lied to you about that,' said Bex.

'In what way?'

'I didn't go to an interview.'

'Oh,' said Deira, although she was thinking that Bex had lied to her mother more than to her. She said so.

'I had to lie to her,' said Bex. 'She would've killed me otherwise.'

'Why?' asked Deira. 'Wouldn't she have let you stay in Dublin without her?'

Probably not, she thought as she spoke. Gill was the sort of woman who thought she was her daughter's best friend, who thought it was fun to do things together. But mothers weren't supposed to be best friends, not always. Sometimes they had to be mothers.

'I had a different reason for coming to Dublin,' Bex said.

A boy, thought Deira. It was nearly always a boy when you were lying to your mother.

'I couldn't tell her and I couldn't tell you,' continued Bex. 'But I'm here in your house and . . . and I have to talk to someone.'

'You can talk to me, of course,' said Deira, although Bex rarely confided in her, and she never expected her to.

'I came to Dublin for a . . . for a procedure.'

'What sort of procedure? A beauty job? Your nose? Your boobs?'

Like every young person Deira knew, Bex was obsessed with her appearance. It took her at least an hour to get ready to leave the house, thanks to a routine that involved the application of more products than Deira even knew existed, while her insistence on using at least half a dozen specialist concoctions meant that going to bed took almost as long. However, Bex reserved particular displeasure for her 34B chest, saying that her assets were paltry in comparison with those of her friends. The last time she'd stayed with Deira, she'd talked about surgery, and Deira, feeling old beyond her years for not thinking this was a good idea, had tried to persuade her otherwise.

'No,' said Bex in reply to her question. 'I stopped thinking about that ages ago. This was . . .'

'What?'

'Can't you guess?' Bex's frustration came through in the words. 'Can't you guess what sort of procedure I'd have and not tell my mother because she'd kill me?'

It took a moment before realisation hit Deira, then her hand tightened on her phone.

'An abortion?' She almost whispered the words. 'Was that it? Did you have an abortion, Bex?'

'I couldn't have a baby. I just couldn't.' Bex started to cry.

'It's the right decision for me, I know. I'm relieved I did it. I don't regret it. Not at all. But I keep thinking of going home and not saying anything to Mum and I'll want to. So I had to tell you instead.'

For the first time in her adult life, Deira was completely speechless. She concentrated on keeping her expression as neutral as she could, but she couldn't form the words to comfort her niece because she didn't have them. She didn't know how to tell Bex that she supported her one hundred per cent when all she wanted to do was yell at her and say that she could have had her baby and that she, Deira, would have taken care of it and that it would have been the best solution for everyone. She couldn't tell her that her heart was broken. That wasn't what Bex wanted to hear. But it was the only thing Deira wanted to say.

'It was . . . it was a one-off thing,' Bex continued into her silence. 'I didn't say no that night, but I wanted to. He wasn't . . . We're not . . . Well . . . it was easier to let it happen than to argue about it. But I'm not on the pill. I was going out with someone and we were fine, we used protection, but we split up and I went off with some friends and it was a party and we all had a bit too much to drink and . . . It was my own fault, really. I should've . . . I could've . . . I didn't say no.' The tears streamed down her face.

'It's not all your own fault.' Deira hardly recognised her own voice. 'It's not. You can't think like that, Bex.'

'I didn't believe I was pregnant. That it had happened to me,' said Bex. 'I mean, who truly thinks it'll happen the first time with someone? And it was only ever going to be the one time with him.'

'Did you tell him?'

296

'No!' Through her tears, Bex looked horrified. 'No. I couldn't. His parents are . . . they're well known in town. And he's . . . he's engaged to someone else.'

'Oh Bex.'

'He wouldn't believe me if I told him, I know he wouldn't. He'd say it wasn't his. And if I said anything different, they'd trash-talk me all around the town. I'd be the one who was in the wrong. I'd be called all sorts of names. It's always the girl who's in the wrong. It's always the girl gets called a slut. They'd say I was drunk and I didn't know who I was with. That it could've been anyone. They'd drag up all sorts of stuff about me even if it wasn't true.'

'Bex, you said it was your fault and it's not, it's really not. But I have to ask you – you said it was easier to go along with it. Did he rape you?'

'No. It was . . . it was a mistake. And I've fixed it. That's all.'

Deira closed her eyes. Her heart went out to her niece, who was hurting so badly but who was absolutely right about how she would be perceived by everyone around her. It would be all very well to say she'd been too drunk to consent, but many people would judge her for getting drunk in the first place. Deira understood exactly what had made Bex take the decision she had. She wanted to comfort her and to assure her that she loved her. Yet Bex had gone for a termination, when Deira herself would have given anything to have a baby of her own.

She had always vehemently believed in a woman's right to choose. She still did. It wasn't for her to make judgements about anybody else's choices. Nobody could understand the full circumstances except the woman making the choice herself. But she wished that Bex's had been different. She wished her niece had confided in her before she'd taken an irrevocable step.

'You won't tell Mum, will you?' asked Bex.

'Of course not.'

'You don't think I'm a whore, do you?'

'No! Bex, sweetheart, of course I don't. How could you even think that?'

'I had sex with someone I hardly knew who's going to marry someone else. And I got pregnant. So I'm . . . I'm . . .'

'*He* had sex with you when *he* was engaged to someone else. And he got you pregnant. He's as much a part of it as you, even though you're the one who had to make hard choices,' said Deira. 'Don't for one minute blame yourself.'

'Thank you.' Bex sniffed. 'Thank you for saying that. Thank you for understanding. I knew you would.'

'Bex, did you have this done yesterday?' asked Deira. 'Had you come home from the clinic when Gavin turned up?'

'Yes,' said Bex.

'I'm so sorry,' Deira said. 'You should have been able to stay there in peace and quiet, not have Gavin tramping around the place like some kind of wrecking ball.'

'Oh, it's OK,' said Bex. 'I went to bed when he left. I . . . Well, your sheets need cleaning. I put them in the wash today, but they're not—'

'Will you not worry about stuff like that!' cried Deira. 'I'm more concerned about you, Bex. Is your friend still with you?'

'Lydia? Yes, she's here. She's outside at the moment.'

'Good. I'm glad there's someone there for you. Do you want me to come home?'

'Oh God, no!' exclaimed Bex. 'I mean, please don't. I'm

fine. Lyds has been great. She organised everything. Of course we didn't expect Mum to want to come to Dublin too when we arranged it. We thought we'd fixed it to stay longer than her by planning a second interview, but we wanted to be sure she'd go home. So before we left I bought tickets for the new Disney movie and Lydia pretended to Lucia that she'd won them in a competition. Mum had to go back to bring her to it.'

Lucia was Bex's twelve-year-old sister, and a Disney fanatic.

'Lucky she agreed.'

'Oh, you know Mum,' said Bex. 'She's into her Disney too. I knew she'd want to go.'

'I applaud your ingenuity,' said Deira.

'I wasn't ingenious at all,' said Bex. 'I'm an idiot. I'm the girl no girl wants to be. But,' she added, 'I sorted it. I know there's lots of people who'd disapprove of me and say that I was selfish and that I should've had the baby, but I couldn't. I'm doing really well in college. I have plans. And I can't . . . I wasn't ready for this.'

She was right. There were plenty of people who opposed abortion on any grounds, at any time, for any woman. But they weren't the ones who were pregnant. And they weren't the ones who'd have to live with it for the rest of their lives. During the referendum to legalise abortion in Ireland, Deira had agreed with all of her friends and acquaintances who said this. She believed it herself. And yet even though she knew Bex had done what was right for her, her own heart was breaking.

She stayed on the phone to her niece for another twenty minutes, reassuring her that everything was fine, that she'd done what was best for her and that nobody else needed to know. And she told her that she could stay in the house for as long as she liked. By the time she ended the call, Bex was looking and sounding if not happier, at least a little less stressed.

It was Deira who lay on her bed and cried.

Chapter 27

Toledo, Spain: 39.8628°N 40.0273°W

Stretched out by the pool, which was set in a large lawn enclosed on two sides by the hotel building, Grace was suddenly aware that Deira hadn't come to join her. She wasn't bothered; she was perfectly content with enjoying the spectacular views towards the town, and dipping in and out of her book (having finally finished *The Sun Also Rises*, she'd moved on to a Joanna Trollope she'd bought on board the ferry and was enjoying it immensely). About a dozen other people were taking advantage of the warmth of the afternoon sun, including a dad and his two young children, who were racing each other up and down the pool. Every time they reached an end, he shouted encouragement at them and they turned to do another length.

It reminded her of the times that Ken would swim with the children on holidays, doing his best to tire them out so that they'd go to bed at a reasonable time and allow himself and Grace an hour or two of peace and quiet to unwind. Sometimes they'd sit together in silence, sometimes they'd talk. Their conversation was rarely idle; Ken didn't do chitchat. He enjoyed talking about politics, both national and the internal politics of the university, which was like a nation of its own. He liked to think of himself as a left-leaning liberal, but the older he got, the more conservative his views had become. Grace had always believed herself to be a conservative sort of woman – she'd given up her career to raise her family, after all – and yet she'd become more liberal with time. Her views were formed by her experiences, which mostly, she thought, revolved around the desire for people to be nicer to each other. To realise that life could be hard and outward smiles didn't always mean inner peace. Ken was impatient with anyone who struggled, and he found it diffi-cult not to hark back to the greater difficulties of his own youth relative to modern times. And yet he had championed every single one of his students, helping them be the best they could be, and was always vociferous about cuts to education budgets and a lack of investment in arts and culture. Conversations with him had always been challenging. Grace missed them.

She debated texting Deira to check on her plans, but decided to leave her alone. They were travelling companions, not soulmates. Nevertheless, she was pleased that Deira was still with her on the journey and that they'd overcome the awkwardness of their different opinions regarding her desire to sleep with Charlie Mulholland. Grace still believed that Deira was wrong, but she also accepted that the younger woman was struggling to cope with the result of her ex-part-ner's behaviour and the challenge of her declining fertility.

There had been a time, shortly after Regan was born, when Grace had suspected Ken of seeing someone else, and her suspicions had taken over her very existence. But when she'd eventually confronted him, he'd been truly shocked by her accusation and told her that he'd never even looked at anyone else. 'Why would I rock the boat for a fleeting moment of pleasure?' he'd asked. 'You know me better than that, Grace.' It was because he'd called her Grace, and not Hippo, that she'd believed him.

She understood that it was hard for Deira to accept that Gavin was now going to be a father by two different women when he'd refused to have a baby with her. Grace couldn't imagine life without Aline, Fionn and Regan. They were the foundation of her existence and the greatest comfort she could have. It didn't matter that her two youngest were so far away from her. She felt their presence every single day. And Aline was always there, ready to call around if needed. Ken's death would have been a million times more difficult if the children hadn't been there to support her. And if she hadn't been there to support them. That was what family was, she thought. People you could depend on when you were at rock bottom. And yet Ken hadn't depended on her. He'd excluded her from the most important decision he'd ever made.

She closed her eyes and let the book slide from her hand as she drifted into sleep. In her dream, she was driving through France with Ken again, the children in the back seat, arguing loudly. He wasn't taking any nonsense from them, telling them that if they didn't keep quiet, they weren't going out on the boat that afternoon. But the children were arguing more and more, until Ken suddenly swerved to one side and drove the car off the bridge over the River Penzé.

'No!' gasped Grace as they hit the water with a thud and she felt the airbag explode against her chest. And then she gasped again as the car began to fill up. The children were screaming and she was sobbing and Ken was looking at her and telling her that he was sorry, it had been an accident, he'd never meant for it to happen . . .

'I'm so sorry.'

The words were clear and distinct, spoken in a Scottish accent. Grace's eyes snapped open, and she saw a grey-haired man wearing bright-blue shorts and a white T-shirt standing at the end of her sunbed. He picked up the yellow inflatable ball that had landed on her.

'They were told not to kick it about. Alejandro, Susanna – come here at once!'

The two children she'd seen racing in the pool earlier scampered across the grass to stand beside him.

'Well,' he said. 'Apologise to the lady.'

The boy began to speak in Spanish, and Grace waited until he'd finished before saying that her Spanish wasn't good enough to understand everything but thanking him for his apology all the same.

'English,' said the man, and Alejandro repeated his apology in a Scottish accent.

Grace laughed. She couldn't help it. It sounded so odd to hear the gentle burr coming from a boy who'd previously spoken in perfect Spanish.

'Can we go back to the pool now, Grandad?' asked the girl.

'Scoot,' he said, and threw the ball into the water. 'But no messing, mind,' he warned. 'I'll be watching you, and I'll tell your papa if you step out of line.'

'We'll be good,' said Susanna. 'Promise.' Then she jumped into the pool, followed by her brother.

'You're not hurt, are you?' asked their grandfather.

'Startled,' said Grace. 'Otherwise fine.'

'They're good kids really. But you know what they're like when they see a pool.'

Grace nodded.

The man, who, she thought, looked young to be a grand-father of children who were about seven or eight, stayed where he was.

'You're not actually English, are you?' he asked.

'Irish,' she replied.

'I knew when you started to speak.'

'And you're not from around here either.'

'No,' he said. 'Aberdeen originally, but I've lived in Spain for the past twenty years. My daughter married a man from the local town, and so I've proper roots here now.'

Grace nodded. There were plenty of people in similar situations in the area around the apartment.

'Anyway,' he said. 'Sorry again about the kids.'

'No bother.' She smiled. 'I was having a rather horrible dream and it was good to be woken up.'

'Nightmares on the sunbeds are usually to do with people reserving them with towels.'

She laughed.

'See you around,' said the man, and went back to supervise his grandchildren.

Grace stayed by the pool for another hour before returning to her room. This time she did text Deira, who responded by saying that she wasn't feeling great and would stay where she was. She then sent a follow-up text saying that she'd do some investigating on the Toledo clue later, but that obviously there was a statue of Cervantes somewhere in the town and Grace should take the photo of it herself.

Clearly Deira's hangover had been worse than she'd let

on, thought Grace, as she got into the car and headed down the steep hillside towards the town on the opposite side of the river. Shots were always a disaster.

She found a car park on the outskirts of Toledo and left the car there before walking into the medieval centre. The throngs of tourists couldn't take away from the fact that it was like walking through the pages of history; at every turn she was faced with ancient city walls, Roman ruins, Moorish arches, churches, mosques and synagogues. In the narrow streets of the old town, the shops were full of knives and swords. When she stopped to look at them, a shop assistant told her that the city was famed for its steel work and that the knives were the best in the world. She invested in a set of steak knives and matching forks to bring home, thinking that ferry travel had a lot going for it; she'd never have got them through a luggage check at the airport.

She'd googled Cervantes before she left the hotel, and followed her map to find the statue, rather oddly placed at the bottom of some steps leading from a narrow cobbled street through an archway to a plaza. She took a photo, then walked along a pedestrianised street, shaded from the sun by brightly coloured sailcloths stretched across it. There were more knife and sword shops here, and jewellery stores too, but Grace's legs were beginning to ache, and when she found a small bar on a corner, with tables outside, she sat down at one and looked at the menu tucked into the napkin holder.

She ordered a sparkling water and a mushroom and herb omelette, which was lighter, fluffier and infinitely more tasty than she'd expected. From her table she could watch other tourists taking photos of a nearby church with an enormous wooden door, everyone adopting the same pose of looking as if they were knocking on it.

Are we all utterly predictable? she wondered as she sipped her water. Do we all think we're unique but actually end up doing exactly the same things as everyone else?

Given that everyone around her was happily taking selfies, Grace took one too and sent it to her children. Aline responded straight away with a 'looking good' message, and a few minutes later, Regan sent a thumbs-up emoji. Grace didn't expect to hear from Fionn, given that it was the middle of the night in Beijing.

Her attention was suddenly caught by the sight of the man who'd been playing with Alejandro and Susanna in the pool earlier. He was walking across the small square, his arm around a young woman wearing a pretty pink sundress. The children were nowhere to be seen, so clearly their grandfather was still looking after them. He's probably on the trip to give the parents a break, thought Grace, as her eyes followed them. There was something quiet and intimate about the couple, and once again she was transported to the past, but this time to before her children were born, when she and Ken would walk together around cities. In those days, when she was still working as cabin crew, she'd been able to get him cheap travel with her. It had been before the advent of budget airlines, when flying anywhere had been prohibitively expensive and a rare occurrence for most people. But she and Ken had travelled to Amsterdam and Brussels and Paris and Rome together. Back then, he'd enjoyed the perks her job brought. It was only after Aline had been born and she'd given it up that he'd got sniffy about air travel with her.

Were we a good partnership? she wondered. Or did we

simply put up with each other? She'd always thought that the fact they'd stayed together through good times and bad was a good thing. But what if it hadn't been? What if she could have had a happier life with someone who respected her more?

The grass is always greener, she told herself.

Be glad that you endured.

It was a little after nine thirty by the time she got back to the hotel. She was feeling pleased with herself, because as well as having taken the picture of Cervantes to upload, she'd looked up the answers to the El Greco part of the clue. But it would have felt wrong to try and unlock it without Deira, who was nowhere to be seen.

The sun was beginning to set and the edges of the sky had turned a flaming orange behind a city that was a pincushion of light from the terrace of the hotel. Grace ordered another sparkling water from a passing waiter and found a comfortable chair from which to look at the view. She'd only been sitting there for a few minutes when she heard the distinctive accent of the man from the pool.

'Is this chair taken?' he asked, indicating the empty one close to her.

'No.' She shook her head and glanced around. The terrace had filled up in the last few minutes, and it was the only one available.

'Thanks.' He angled the chair away from her slightly and sat down. A waiter placed a glass of beer in front of him. He took a sip while Grace observed him casually. In a pale-blue shirt worn loose over jeans, he looked fit and attractive. That she even noticed this was a little disconcerting to Grace. But it was true.

The waiter returned with some peanuts, which he placed on the table between them. The man pushed the bowl closer to Grace and asked if she'd like one. She took a handful, which she put on a paper napkin.

'You can have the rest,' she said. 'I shouldn't have any at all; I stuffed myself with food earlier.'

'Easily done here.' He nodded. 'The cooking is superb.'

'Where do you live?' she asked.

'Near Cartagena,' he replied. 'A place called Playa Blanca. It's in the south-east.'

'You're joking!' Grace turned her chair to face him. 'I have an apartment there.'

'Really?' He laughed. 'Small world. Although not that small,' he added. 'So many people have bought second homes in Spain that it's probably more likely than not that you'll bump into someone. How long have you lived there?'

'I don't live there full-time,' said Grace. 'My husband and I bought our apartment about six years ago. The plan was to spend more time there, especially in the winter.'

He nodded. 'Snowbirds,' he said. 'Home for the summer, back for the winter.'

'Actually, we ended up spending early summer here and then coming back in the autumn for a couple of months,' said Grace. 'We never quite made it through the winter. Too many commitments at home, and then . . .' She stopped. What is happening to me, she asked herself, that I've started blurting out my personal life to perfect strangers? First Deira and now this man. Not that I'm going to share anything with him. I'm not that sort of person.

'Duncan,' he said into her sudden silence. 'Anderson.'

'Grace Garvey.'

'Are you on your own, Grace?' he asked.

'No, I've a friend with me.'

'Ah.'

'A girlfriend,' she clarified. 'At least, I mean, a friend who's a girl. A woman. God!' She looked at the glass of water. 'Have they put gin in this or something? I'm blathering.'

He laughed. 'You're fine,' he said.

'Down at the pool, you said you came here a long time ago. Do you work here?'

'Aye,' he replied. 'Myself and the wife opened a restaurant.'

'Have you always cooked?' asked Grace.

'D'you mean did I know what I was doing or am I one of those people who thought I'd give it a go and do breakfast fry-ups and roast dinners on Sundays?'

'I wouldn't knock a breakfast fry-up, or indeed a roast dinner, although perhaps not here,' said Grace.

'Sorry if I was taking it a bit personally,' said Duncan. 'It's just that . . . Yes, I am a chef. Not the kind of chef that would've worked with Gordon Ramsay, but not the kind that'd be caught on his *Kitchen Nightmares* either. Not the sort that says he cooks honest food or smothers everything in cream. Good food, I hope, though.'

'I do feel I might have hit a nerve,' admitted Grace.

'Ah, it's me. I can get defensive about it,' he said. 'You should come and eat, though. As my guest.' He opened his wallet and took out a card. 'This is us.'

'Flor de la Esquina,' she read. 'Flower on the Corner?'

He nodded. 'It's small, but I promise you it's good.'

'Do your family work there with you?' Grace put the card in her bag.

'No,' he said. 'It's just me.'

'Not even your wife?'

'No,' he said again. 'Turns out the dream wasn't her dream after all. We divorced after ten years and before I took over the Flor.'

'I'm sorry.'

'She met someone new.' He shrugged. 'It happens.'

But Grace heard the catch in his voice.

'The restaurant keeps me busy,' he said.

'Did you work as a chef in Scotland?'

'In a hotel,' he said. 'And before that on a cruise ship. But I always wanted my own place, and now I have it. I hadn't intended to lose the wife along the way, but I reckon I'll give it another five years and then retire.'

'Sounds like a plan.'

'Everyone has a plan till they're punched in the mouth, isn't that it?'

'My husband used to say that too.'

'Are you still together?'

'He passed away recently,' said Grace.

'I'm sorry for your loss.' His voice softened.

'And after you get punched in the mouth, you make new plans.' She stood up. 'It was really nice talking to you, Duncan, but I'm heading up for the night. I'll definitely come to your restaurant, though.'

'Yes?'

'Yes.'

He stood up too.

When she got to the door of the hotel, she turned around.

He was still standing, looking after her.

*

When Grace came down to breakfast the following morning, she was surprised to see Deira already seated at a table. She'd been there for some time, it seemed, because a waitress was clearing the used crockery while Deira sipped a coffee.

'Good morning.' Grace slid into the chair opposite her. 'OK if I join you?'

'Sure,' said Deira.

'You're up early.' Grace thought Deira looked tired, with dark circles under her red-rimmed eyes.

'I didn't sleep well,' said Deira. 'So I got up a couple of hours ago and went for a walk.'

'Are you feeling OK?' asked Grace.

'Fine,' replied Deira.

'Have you heard anything more about your insurance claim?'

'Not yet,' said Deira. 'But I'm sure they're working their way through it. And then I'll have to deal with all the fallout between Gavin and me.'

'Get yourself a good solicitor,' advised Grace. 'I did, after Ken . . . I worried about what would happen to his life assurance if they ruled his death a suicide. Not that I wanted to be mercenary about it or anything, but he'd paid a lot into that policy. As it turns out, he'd taken it out five years earlier, so there wasn't an exclusion clause. But I would never have been able to ask the questions the solicitor asked.'

'You never think about things like that, do you?' asked Deira.

Grace shook her head. 'It was all horrible, to be honest. In some ways, that's what made me more angry than anything else. That he'd left me to sort it all out.'

'You've done brilliantly.' Deira gave her a comforting smile.

'I admire you, Grace. A terrible thing happened in your life. Both with the professor getting sick and then how it all ended. And yet here you are, driving through France and Spain and being . . . oh, I don't know . . . so unflappable about it.'

'I'm not unflappable,' protested Grace. 'I was practically catatonic when I had to identify his body.'

Which was true. The sequence of events was blurred in her mind and the memory of her time both identifying Ken and staying with him later had jumbled together, but she could still clearly picture the moment when she saw him lying in front of her at the hospital mortuary. There was a large bruise on his forehead and she'd wondered if the airbag hadn't worked properly and if he'd slammed into the steering wheel, but she'd been afraid to ask. He'd looked older and thinner beneath the sheet that covered him, and although she'd heard many people say in the past that dead relatives looked as though they were sleeping, it was very clear to her that Ken wasn't. The muscles on his face had slackened and he was paler than she had ever seen him before. When she went to touch him, she was shocked at how cold he was. It was him being cold that made it seem real. And yet she'd struggled to take it in. That he'd been alive and talking to her that morning. That he was dead now. That he must have, might have, could have planned this. She didn't want to say anything in case she incriminated him, although she knew that suicide wasn't a crime any more.

She'd asked if there was anything she could do. But of course there wasn't. The truth was that she was in the way.

The next time she'd seen him was at the funeral home. She and Aline had selected a suit for him to wear, and the undertakers had toned down the bruise on his face. But even though she knew it was her husband in front of her, it was obvious to her that the living Ken was gone and had left nothing more than a shell behind.

She'd never said this to the children.

Fionn had said that his dad looked peaceful.

Aline and Regan agreed.

All of them assured each other that it was probably very fast and that he wouldn't have suffered.

Grace had wanted to say that he must have suffered, that he'd drowned, that his last moments couldn't have been easy. But then she thought that perhaps they'd been easier for him than many of his living moments since his diagnosis, and she felt horribly guilty for still being angry with him.

She wondered whether the guilt and the anger would ever leave her.

Deira watched Grace, seeing how her jaw tightened and how she was holding her breath. She felt guilty for having brought back memories that Grace clearly wanted to forget.

'Did you take the photo of Cervantes?' She knew she was changing the subject abruptly, but she couldn't think of anything else to say.

'I . . . Yes. Yes, I did,' said Grace. 'And I checked out the answers to El Greco.'

'Well done you! Did you upload them?'

'No,' said Grace. 'I was waiting to do it with you.'

'You waited for me last time too. But it's your treasure hunt, Grace. You can upload the answers whenever you want.'

'We've been in this together the whole time,' said Grace. 'I wasn't going to do it without you.'

'Do you have the laptop?'

314

Grace nodded and took it out of the tote bag slung over her shoulder.

'Let me nab some of the breakfast buffet first,' she said to Deira.

She returned to the table a few minutes later with a selection of fruit and pastries, and then opened the laptop and uploaded the photo of Cervantes. As always, there was a nervous moment before it was accepted and she was given the extra number, which this time was 3.

'There's an El Greco museum in the city, but by the time I'd walked to the Cervantes statue, I wasn't in the mood for a museum, especially when Google is around,' said Grace. 'So the answer is 3, and then 7 and 2 for his ripe old age, and then 4 for April, the month he died. Agreed?'

'Agreed,' said Deira.

Grace took a sip of her coffee and then punched in the numbers.

'Right,' she said when the clue came up. 'Here we go again.'

Chapter 28

Toledo to Sierra de Andujar: 230 km

Another one successfully completed, Hippo! You're blazing a trail through Spain. I hope you visited the El Greco museum, it's well worth the trip. Or did you hotfoot it to Cervantes and then nip off to the square for churros and chocolate? I know it's a weakness! Anyhow, your reward letter is E. Now here's your Granada clue. Their most famous poet? Probably. He's not sitting in his park, though, so you'll have to find him elsewhere to upload his photo. Then tell me how many Galician poems he wrote and how old he was when he died. Five attempts. Best of luck!

'He's nearly right about me,' said Grace. 'I'm always thinking of my stomach. I went straight for the Cervantes statue and then around the corner to a little bar. It didn't serve churros, but I had a lovely omelette.' She made a face and then picked up one of the dainty pastries and put it in her mouth.

Deira laughed. A genuine laugh. 'I don't know how you stay so skinny on all the food you pack away,' she said.

'I've always been slender,' said Grace. 'Which people think

is great, but sometimes it's not so good. Look at my scrawny arms.' She held one out for Deira's inspection. 'I'd give anything for plumper arms. And lips. I'd love Julia Roberts' lips. Or Angelina Jolie's. But I have thin lips, and although my beauty therapist suggested a bit of collagen, I'm too scared to try.'

'I've never had injectables,' said Deira. 'Though some of my friends swear by Botox.'

'You're far too young for that, surely!'

'I'm the absolute right age,' said Deira. 'I think even girls in their twenties are getting it.' She grimaced. 'Afton – my younger, prettier and more fertile replacement – promotes a brand of filler on her bloody Instagram account.' She opened her bag and took out a tissue, which she used to blow her nose. 'Sorry,' she said. 'I'm a bit weepy at the moment. Again.'

'That's OK,' said Grace.

'Family stuff,' Deira said. 'Nothing to do with me and Gavin.'

'Would you like to take a little time out?' asked Grace. 'Recharge the batteries.'

'Do you want to stay here a bit longer?' Deira looked at her in surprise.

'No. I was actually thinking about what you suggested before. About that place in the wilderness. The place where Charlie Mulholland may or may not be.'

'Grace, I know how you feel about—'

'How I feel isn't the point. It's your life, your choice, Deira.'

'Yes, but—'

'And you said he might not be there.'

317

'He didn't tell me when he was filming. It was a stupid idea on my part.'

'But the place itself sounded nice.'

'Yes.'

Grace exhaled slowly. 'I've been thinking about it,' she said. 'I've been throwing a lot of advice your way but not really thinking about my own attitude.'

'Your attitude is perfectly fine,' said Deira.

'I'm not talking about my attitude to you,' said Grace. 'I'm talking about me.'

'In what way?'

'Following Ken's itinerary. Doing what he wants me to do, when he wants me to do it.'

'That's because there might be a time limit on the treasure hunt,' said Deira. 'It's because you want to get it right. And because he's booked all the hotels in advance.'

'The time limit is only set by the fact that he booked the hotels,' said Grace. 'And that means he's chivvying me along like he always did. Visiting all these places has been lovely, but I want to do something for myself too. I want to see somewhere that hasn't been approved by him in advance.'

Deira nodded slowly.

'And this place sounds . . . well, nobody would go there unless they'd heard of it, would they?'

'I doubt it.'

'One place that he didn't plan on me going to,' said Grace. 'Just one.'

'What if Charlie is there?'

'What if he is?' said Grace. 'You can do your thing. I'll do mine.'

Although she'd wanted to visit El Pozo de la Señora before,

318

Deira was less sure that it was a good idea now. But if she said no, would she regret not taking the opportunity that Grace was offering?

'If you're OK about it, then let's do it,' she said.

'Right,' said Grace, and opened the web browser.

She managed to get two rooms at the wellness centre and rebook the Granada hotel for the following day, and so, after they checked out, Deira put the address of El Pozo de la Señora into the satnav of Grace's car. She offered to drive, and Grace was perfectly happy to let her.

'It means Lady's Well,' Deira said as they set off. 'They should twin it with Galway.'

'Is there a place called Lady's Well in Galway?' asked Grace.

'There's probably loads of Lady's Wells around Ireland,' Deira said. 'I can imagine a whole bunch of grottos where someone in the past thought they saw apparitions of the Virgin Mary. My grandmother used to take us to the Galway one to pray. Apparently it had healing powers.'

'You wouldn't remember the summer of the moving statues,' said Grace.

'What?' Deira glanced at her.

'Sometime in the eighties,' Grace told her. 'I can't recall where it started, but a group of children claimed that they saw a statue of the Virgin Mary move. The place was inundated with pilgrims. Then it happened again somewhere else. Same thing. And a group of girls thought they saw her appear in the sky.'

'Seriously?'

'Oh, it was a total phenomenon,' Grace assured her. 'I'm pretty sure the locals were raking it in with all the pilgrims that turned up, though most of the towns were small and couldn't cope with the numbers. It was tens of thousands.'

'Wow,' said Deira. 'So what happened in the end?'

'I don't really know,' said Grace. 'Maybe people saw sense when autumn set in and they couldn't spend long evenings staring at statues, waiting for them to leap around.'

'I suppose there are times when people want to believe in something more than what's around us,' said Deira. 'My friend Tillie is a bit like that. Looking for meaning in everything. I'm not sure she'd have much truck with moving statues, though.'

'I'm sure the Spanish spring is just a spring,' Grace said.

'Given that they're calling it a wellness centre, I'm assuming that at the very least the water is supposed to be pure,' said Deira.

'Either way, it actually looks quite nice and restful on the website.'

They continued in silence through the flat and featureless countryside of Castilla–La Mancha. After a while, the road suddenly curved and rose through the mountains that marked the border with Andalusia.

'Wow,' said Grace, as the satnav told them to leave the motorway and they climbed even higher along a much narrower road. 'The views are breathtaking.'

'I'm concentrating more on where we're going,' said Deira. 'This is steep.'

And it was. A lesser car than the Lexus might have struggled with the incline, but they forged onwards and upwards, further and further away from the motorway.

'I hope we don't get a puncture,' Grace murmured. 'We're in the middle of nowhere here. Are you sure we're on the right road, Deira?'

'I have faith in the satnav,' Deira said. 'And I did check it on Google Maps too.'

'I'm thinking that the miraculous thing about this Lady's Well is that people got here at all,' declared Grace. 'It must have been some trek before cars.'

'I guess they had donkeys.' Deira negotiated a hairpin bend.

'Or maybe getting up here was a kind of pilgrimage in itself,' said Grace.

'It would certainly have been a penance.'

It took another thirty minutes of driving through the isolated countryside before they saw a large wooden sign saying 'El Pozo de la Señora'.

'Whew,' said Grace. 'It exists.'

'I was feeling a bit anxious that it didn't,' admitted Deira as she turned at the sign and followed an even narrower road.

'I guess if you're going to do a wellness retreat, this defi-nitely gets you off the beaten— Oh!'

Grace gave a cry of pleasure as the road opened out and she saw the building ahead of them. It was whitewashed and single-storey, built in a squared-off U shape. Vivid pink and purple bougainvillea cascaded from the terracotta roof over the deep-set windows. Neatly rounded orange trees lined the way to a covered parking area containing half a dozen cars.

Deira parked the Lexus and the two women got out. The heat was fierce and the silence absolute.

They took their bags from the boot and walked along a flagstone path to the entrance of the building – an enormous wooden door with a smaller door set into it. The smaller door was open, and they stepped through.

Like at the converted convent in Alcalá de Henares, there

was a fountain in the centre of the reception area, the cascading water effectively cooling the interior space. The floor tiles were dark green marble, as was the reception desk.

'Hello, and welcome.' A woman in her thirties with a mop of curly red hair came to greet them. 'Deira and Grace?'

'Yes,' said Deira. 'You must be Muireann.'

The woman smiled. 'That's me. It's nice to hear another Irish accent.'

'It's the last thing I would've expected here,' said Grace. 'How on earth did you discover this place?'

'My dad is from Aljaha. It's a small town nearby,' said Muireann. 'I was brought up in Cork, but I always loved coming to Spain. And then the opportunity to open this place came up, and I jumped at it.'

'That was brave,' said Grace.

'Ah, not as brave as you think,' Muireann told her. 'I know the area.'

'But there's so little around,' Grace said. 'And it's hard to get to.'

'Hard if you're coming from the north,' agreed Muireann. 'But easier from the south. Anyhow, let's get you ladies sorted.'

She registered them and then handed them two large key fobs.

'We're as back-to-nature as we can be,' she said. 'There are no TVs and no Wi-Fi, except in the designated Wi-Fi room, which is only open for an hour a day. We want people to disconnect as much as possible, which is why we encourage you to have your phones locked away while you're here.'

Deira had read all this on the website and had had no intention of handing over her phone. Yet here, in the quiet serenity of El Pozo de la Señora, she was beginning to think that there was a certain merit in doing so.

'The signal is a bit patchy anyhow,' said Muireann.

'How do you manage?' asked Grace. 'I mean, you need technology to get bookings and call people and so on.'

'We have a satellite system,' explained Muireann. '*We* need to be connected, but guests don't.'

'I suppose . . .' Grace hesitated.

'What we usually suggest is that you hang on to your phone until you're settled in, take some photos – the views from the back of the house are amazing – book a treatment, and then give it to us,' said Muireann. 'You can have it back if you're walking any of the trails, though. Can I also say that as you're a bit last-minute, it would be good to know if you want a therapy treatment. Our time slots are limited. I hate to pressure you, because we're all about no pressure, but I wouldn't like you to want to have a massage or something and be disappointed.'

She handed them brochures. Deira elected to have a body scrub and Grace chose a head massage.

'Excellent,' said Muireann. 'You'll be at three thirty, Deira. And you're at four, Grace. Now, I'll show you to your rooms. As you'll see,' she added as she led them along a dimly lit corridor, 'there's water available everywhere. We encourage you to drink as much of it as you can. It's from our own well and flavoured with our oranges and lemons. And here we are. This room is yours, Deira. Grace, you're a little further on. Settle in, relax, and if there's anything you need, just let me know.'

Deira let herself into the room. It was simply furnished, but, despite not having a TV, there was a digital music system with a selection of restful playlists. Long drapes covered what turned out to be floor-to-ceiling windows that opened out to a Zen garden and spectacular views of the valley.

Even if it doesn't work out the way I hope, it'll have been worth it, she thought as she stepped out into the garden.

But her heart was beating faster as she thought of Charlie Mulholland.

As she lay on the treatment table and lost herself in the bliss of having someone massage her temples, Grace was also thinking that it had been a good decision to stop off at the wellness centre. She'd never been a great one for pampering, but she'd been seduced by the serenity of El Pozo de la Señora, and it seemed wrong not to take advantage of it.

While the therapist gently rubbed her neck, Grace's thoughts drifted to the treasure hunt. She wondered if Ken had truly expected her to be able to solve all the clues. She'd managed with Deira's help, but the answers weren't imme-diately obvious, and she was pretty sure that on her own, it might have taken longer, and that she'd have used up every single password guess that each clue allowed. By booking the hotels in advance, he had also added unnecessary pressure to the trip. Had he never thought that she might take some time out for herself? To simply enjoy being away?

He used to say that travelling was about the journey, not the destination, but he'd made this all about destinations. She wondered how he'd feel about her deviation from his plan. Surely he wouldn't begrudge her being looked after. He used to say that it was important to do the things you loved, and she was loving this.

To be fair to Ken, he'd loved his own life. He'd loved

being who he was. He'd relished every day. Perhaps that was why he hadn't been able to live it as someone with an illness. Perhaps that was why he'd done what he'd done.

It was a comfort to think that. A comfort to believe that he hadn't driven off the pier because he couldn't bear her to be more important than him. Or because he didn't love her, or the children, enough to live for them. Perhaps it had only ever been about him, not them. And that, thought Grace, was a kind of relief.

Chapter 29

Deira and Grace met later in the relaxation room, where they lounged on day beds and drank lemon-infused water while looking over the Zen garden towards the valley. They agreed that the treatments had been superb and that they felt totally rested and chilled.

'The original building was a small monastery,' said Grace, who'd read all the literature in her room. 'And you're right, Deira, apparently there's a spring in the garden that was supposed to have been a holy well.'

'Not that I believe in the power of holy wells or anything, but there's certainly a great sense of peace and tranquillity here,' said Deira. 'And even though Muireann told me there are about a dozen guests, you feel as though this place is yours alone.'

'I haven't seen another soul,' said Grace.

'Apparently they come for retreats,' Deira said.

'Religious retreats?' Grace looked surprised.

'No. No. Retreats from the world. From the pace of life. And from technology,' added Deira. 'They usually stay for a week.'

'That'd be pricey,' observed Grace.

'I suppose if you feel more centred at the end of it, it would be worth it,' said Deira. 'Apparently there's a town five kilometres away with its own train station. So it's not as isolated as you'd think. The visitors come for the food, too,' she continued. 'They have a vegan kitchen here.'

'I thought I saw beef on the menu,' said Grace.

'It's not all vegan,' Deira assured her. 'That's a bit extreme for me, but I might go veggie tonight. I'm happy not to eat meat if the alternative is appetising.'

They sat in silence again for a few minutes before Grace turned to Deira and asked if she'd seen any sign of Charlie Mulholland.

'Not so far,' replied Deira. 'I was going to ask Muireann if he was around, but I thought that would sound very pointed. If he's here, I guess dinner will be the time to see him.'

'Have you a plan if he is?' asked Grace.

'None of my plans have worked out very well,' Deira replied.

'Perhaps this will be different,' said Grace, and they lapsed into silence again.

There was no sign of Charlie at dinner. Deira didn't know if she felt relieved or disappointed. Afterwards, she and Grace decided to go for a walk along one of the trails.

'Maybe it's for the best,' said Grace.

'Probably,' Deira agreed. 'I've made such an eejit out of myself these last few months that I couldn't guarantee not to do it again.'

'Ah, Deira, you've been through a tough time,' said Grace. 'Cut yourself a little slack.'

'You're very comforting, you know that?'

'Life is hard enough without us being hard on each other,' said Grace. 'And I'm sorry I was harsh before.'

'I need harsh,' said Deira. 'I need to face up to the things I can't change.'

Grace gave her a sympathetic smile as they continued along the trail.

'Oh!' exclaimed Deira after they'd gone a few hundred metres in silence. 'How amazing.'

They gazed at the panoramic view of the valley in front of them, an unexpected oasis of green among the dustiness of the mountains.

'Regardless of your motives, I'm glad you suggested this stopover,' said Grace as they sat on a strategically placed wooden bench. 'I truly do feel recharged.'

Deira wasn't sure if recharged was the right word for how she was feeling herself. The massage had been relaxing, the dinner superb and the walk enjoyable, but she was conscious of a sense of anticlimax at the fact that Charlie Mulholland wasn't here. It wasn't that she could really have expected his work to coincide with the one night that she and Grace were staying at the wellness centre, but she'd had this feeling of fate about him. Meeting him on the boat, at the service station, in Pamplona – those things had seemed more than chance. But unlike Tillie, she didn't believe in fate.

'We should go back,' she said to Grace. 'It's getting late and I don't fancy following that trail in the dark.'

When they returned to the building, Grace said that she was going to have an early night and allow herself the full benefit of her massage. Deira was happy to chill out too. She'd given her phone to Muireann, but kept her iPad, and sat in her room scrolling through her photographs. She saw herself age alongside Gavin, and wondered at exactly what point he'd fallen out of love with her enough to want to sleep with somebody else.

In her own room, Grace was scrolling through photographs too, although hers went back a good deal further than Deira's. Fionn had digitised their old family snapshots when he was at college, and the result was nearly ten thousand photos detailing their family life. She stopped at the ones of their holidays in France, remembering the moment each one was taken, finding it hard to believe that some of them were from over twenty years ago. There were very few of herself and Ken together – in the days before selfies, one or other of them had always been taking the snap. But she paused at one that she remembered Aline taking, where they were sitting on the bonnet of the car at one of the service stations on the way to La Rochelle. She'd automatically stopped at that service station on this trip too. Even though he was gone, Ken was still with her. Still beside her every step of the way.

When Deira awoke with a jump, she had no idea what time it was. The blackout curtains on her windows didn't allow the slightest bit of light to enter, and it took almost a minute for her eyes to adjust to the darkness. It was still night-time, she realised, when she got out of bed and parted the heavy drapes. But although the sky was black, it was lit by more stars than she'd ever seen before.

The information package on El Pozo de la Señora that had been left in the room had promised spectacular night skies thanks to the lack of light pollution in the area, but Deira hadn't imagined it could be like this. Instead of the dozen or so isolated stars she could normally make out when she looked upwards, there were hundreds above her. Maybe even thousands. Or perhaps hundreds of thousands. They were bright enough for her to be able to check her watch and see that it was almost four thirty in the morning.

In Dublin, at this hour, dawn would be creeping over the horizon, but further south, as she was now, it was still a couple of hours away. She slipped the catch on the door and stepped outside. Despite the altitude, the air still retained some of the warmth of the previous day, and she didn't need any more than the light pyjamas she was wearing. She sat on a wicker chair and gazed into the distance. Apart from the stars, the only other light was a small cluster in the distance that she presumed was the village in the valley.

She felt small and insignificant in the grand scheme of the universe. In knowing that she was sitting on a rock hurtling through space. She'd watched several popular science programmes in the past and she knew that the distances were enormous. She also knew that many scientists believed that there had to be other life forms out there. And she wondered if somewhere in that vast expanse of space there was someone else like her, someone whose life had been ripped apart because the person they'd cared for most in the world had betrayed them. Not that I have to head out to space for that, she told herself. Don't humans betray each other every single day?

She got up from the chair and walked barefoot along the smooth stone paths of the Zen garden. She kept going until she reached the more uncultivated space beyond, treading gingerly on the dry grass. As she rounded a corner, she gave a muted exclamation, because ahead of her, someone was sitting on a boulder doing as she'd been doing earlier, staring up at the sky.

The figure turned towards her and her mouth formed an O of both surprise and satisfaction.

Because the man in front of her was Charlie Mulholland.

She exhaled slowly.

Fate was on her side after all.

Grace had woken up a few minutes before Deira. She too had been unsure of the time and had parted the heavy curtains to look outside. And she'd also opened the door and stepped into the stillness of the night. She'd seen Deira emerge from her own room and walk through the garden, but she hadn't called out to her because it seemed to her that Deira needed some time and space of her own. In other circumstances Grace might have followed her to make sure she was all right, but somehow here, in the wellness retreat, she was sure that Deira would be fine. There was an atmosphere of tranquillity and other-worldliness that wasn't only down to the fact that the sky was ablaze with usually unseen stars, or that the staff were almost invisible in their unobtrusiveness, or even that the guests were unhooked from the technology that normally tied them to the everyday world. It came from the place itself, and from how it made you feel. And right now, at four thirty in the morning, Grace was more at peace than she'd been in months.

Her personal peacefulness was for a different reason than she would have expected. It was because she was, for the first time since his death, in a place that wasn't associated with Ken. He'd never been here before, either with her or without her. He'd never driven along the narrow road that led to El

Pozo de la Señora. He'd never eaten in the restaurant, or walked the mountain trail, or sat here, as she was doing, looking out into the darkness. He couldn't make a comment about how she should be spending her time, or quote one of his favourite authors at her, or point at one of the stars and tell her what it was.

This wasn't his place.

This wasn't their place.

It was hers alone.

And right now, alone was exactly what she wanted to be.

'You've done something to your hair,' said Charlie as Deira approached him. 'It's nice.'

'Thank you.' Deira was flattered he'd noticed.

'And you decided to come here.'

'We were on the road,' Deira said. 'It seemed a shame not to stop. I'm glad we did, because it's beautiful.'

'I first came when Muireann and Alfie opened it,' Charlie said. 'I've kept an eye on them ever since. It was such a brave thing to do in such an out-of-the-way place.'

'Muireann told us that it isn't really out-of-the-way at all.'

'Regardless of how good the motorway is, or even if you get the train to the town, it's still a bit of a trek through the mountains to get here,' said Charlie. 'And I like that. I like having to make an effort.'

Deira nodded. 'I liked that too. And I'm sure your documentary will bring a lot more visitors. Have you started your interviews?'

'We're nearly finished,' Charlie replied. 'We arrived yesterday and did some filming, and then did the rest of the interviewing today.'

'It's a pity Grace and I didn't see you earlier. We could've been on TV.'

'I could still do a piece with you if you like.' He smiled. 'A guest chilling out beneath the stars. They do astronomy sessions, you know, though mostly in the winter months.'

'Maybe I'll come back for that sometime. Are you staying here long?'

'No. We're heading off in the morning. We've got to go back to France to do the interview we missed out on before.'

'It must be an interesting job.'

'It's like all jobs,' said Charlie. 'Sometimes it's great, sometimes not so much. Other people always think it's more glamorous than it is.' He grinned. 'Amaya says the same about the gallery. People think that working with artists is always a joy, but she says it can also be a pain. I'm sure you think so too.'

'I'm not trying to sell the art, so it's a bit different for me,' said Deira.

'Would you ever consider a gallery of your own?'

Deira shook her head. 'I like what I do now. It's changed over the years, of course, but I still enjoy it.' Which was true, even if working at Solas had become a good deal more difficult than it had been when she and Gavin were a couple.

'Maybe I should do a programme on women in business,' said Charlie. 'That way I could interview you.'

'Women in business are the same as men in business except we do it in high heels,' said Deira.

Charlie laughed.

'Seriously. We're not a special breed. We just have to work bloody hard.'

'I get that,' said Charlie.

'And then we get shafted by some guy who—' She broke off. 'It doesn't matter. That's not what I want to talk to you about.'

'Is there something you *do* want to talk about?' asked Charlie.

'Maybe.'

She paused before speaking again, because a shooting star streaked across the sky. Charlie told her to make a wish.

'Too late for that,' she told him.

'It's never too late to make a wish,' said Charlie.

'Did you ever wish you had a child of your own?' She put the question abruptly, and he raised his eyebrows in surprise. 'After all,' she continued, 'Amaya had . . . Iñaki, was it? But you and she didn't have a child. Was that difficult for you?'

'I loved Iñaki from the first moment I saw him,' said Charlie. 'I still do.'

'But a child of your own is different.'

'Not to me, really,' said Charlie.

'You never wanted one?'

Charlie hesitated. 'It's not—'

'I'm sorry,' Deira interrupted him. 'I realise I sound like I'm quizzing you. I don't mean to. At least, not that way. It's just that . . .'

'What?'

She took a deep breath before she spoke. 'I want a baby.'

She could see from Charlie's expression that he was uncomfortable with the conversation. She understood. She was uncomfortable too. But she had to speak and she had to do it now, before she changed her mind.

'I want a baby, but I've split up with my long-term partner,' she continued. 'I should have insisted while I had the chance. Unfortunately, I didn't realise it then.'

'I'm sorry,' said Charlie.

'Me too,' said Deira. 'And of course my options are more limited now. I should've frozen my eggs when I was younger. Given myself a better chance. Still, it's not impossible.'

Another shooting star crossed the sky. This time she made a wish.

'I wished to find a good man who'd be happy to have a baby with me,' she told Charlie.

'I hope you find him,' he said.

'I think I already have.'

'That's good.'

'Charlie . . .' She turned to him and spoke rapidly. 'It's you. I want to have a baby with you. You can be as involved or not as you like in its care. I don't mind. I'm not asking for anything. I can look after a child myself. I'm in a fairly decent place financially.'

He stared at her without speaking.

'So there'd be nothing for you to worry about at all,' she added.

'Except for the fact that I don't know you or anything about you and yet you want me to be your baby's father,' said Charlie.

'You know I'm a reasonably sensible person,' said Deira. 'That I have a well-paid job. That I'll take care of the baby, give it a good home and a good life.'

'I don't know any of those things,' said Charlie. 'What I do know is that based on our very casual acquaintance, you've pretty much asked me to be a sperm donor. Which actually doesn't sound like something a reasonably sensible person would do.'

'I . . .' Deira closed her eyes. When she opened them

335

again, she saw that Charlie had got up from the boulder and taken a few steps away from her. 'I'm sorry,' she said. 'I got a bit carried away. I didn't mean to imply that you were simply a donor.'

'You didn't imply it. You said it.' Charlie's words were clipped. 'Women go through life understandably demanding that they're not objectified, but that's what you've done to me. I enjoyed your company when we met before. I liked talking to you. And now I realise that all the time you were simply weighing up the quality of my sperm and the likelihood of your getting it.' He turned back to her. 'Did you come here deliberately to meet me again and ask me this question? Would you have asked me some other way if we hadn't met tonight?'

She shouldn't have been upfront with him. She should have tried seduction. Or something. She was an idiot.

'I'm sorry you feel like that. I only—'

'How do you expect me to feel? To you I'm nothing more than a walking sperm bank.'

'That's not true. You're kind and interesting and—'

'A sperm bank with good qualities, obviously.'

'I'm sorry,' said Deira. 'I really am. I thought . . .'

'What? That men are happy to have sex with a random stranger and not care about the consequences?'

'There seem to be a lot who are.'

'You have a very poor opinion of us, don't you?'

'Based on experience,' said Deira.

'Great. You hate men but you still need one to father a child for you. So you're prepared to put up with us to get what you want. You'll put up with me.'

'You're getting it all wrong,' said Deira.

'I'm not. What's all wrong is your mindset,' Charlie said. 'You think you're entitled to have a child, but it's a privilege, not a right. I'm truly sorry that your previous choices have left you where you are now. However, that's your issue to deal with.'

'Charlie . . .'

He turned away from her so that he was looking into the distance.

'I could lie and say it would be fine and I could sleep with you,' he said. 'I could have a moment's pleasure for no pain. And you could walk away and still not be pregnant.'

'I know. I'm prepared to take that chance.'

He said nothing.

Neither did she.

Another shooting star cut across the sky. She made her wish again.

Charlie turned to face her again.

'You'd be taking a chance with terrible odds,' he said. 'Amaya and I did try for a child. It didn't happen. Given that she'd had a baby before, it wasn't her fault. My sperm count is low. So of all the men in the world you could have chosen, you've picked the wrong one. I guess that's some kind of karma, isn't it.'

She looked wordlessly at him.

'Are you still interested?' he asked.

'Oh Charlie . . .'

'Thought not,' he said, and walked away.

Chapter 30

Sierra de Andujar to Granada: 165 km

Grace was worried. Although she hadn't seen Deira since she'd walked through the Zen garden earlier, the sound of her conversation had carried across the night air. She hadn't been able to make out the words, nor did she know who Deira was speaking to, but the tone was evident. Deira was upset, and the man was angry.

Grace knew it was possible that Deira had succeeded in meeting Charlie Mulholland, which would mean she'd achieved her objective in coming to El Pozo de la Señora. But the heated tone that had reached her made her feel that, if so, things hadn't worked out according to plan. It was equally possible that Deira had found someone else among the guests whom she thought could be a likely father to her child and had met him in the middle of the night. But whatever the situation, it wasn't going well.

Grace didn't want to interfere in the other woman's life, but she couldn't help being concerned about her. And so when Deira still hadn't returned thirty minutes after all sounds of conversation had ceased, she went to investigate.

Years of watching crime drama on TV had her nerves on end as she followed Deira's path through the garden and beyond. The total silence of her surroundings meant that her breath echoed in her own head, like a diver wearing an aqualung, and she was uncomfortably aware that even in the cosiest of Sunday-evening murder mysteries, people who investigated things without calling the police usually ended up dead. She told herself that she was being silly (Ken used to call her a catastrophist, always imagining the worst), but Deira was going through a hard time, and Grace couldn't help being anxious.

The area beyond the Zen garden was uncultivated, and in the light of the stars, Grace could see that it was composed mainly of sandy soil, scrub grass and olive trees that had obviously been there a very long time. As she looked around, she felt her anxiety levels soar. Was there a potential murderer hiding behind one of the trees, ready to pounce? Had the angry man already done away with Deira? Would she be better off going back to the hotel and raising the alarm?

When she heard the sound of footsteps approaching, she almost screamed.

'What are you doing here?' asked Deira as she emerged from the shadows. 'Are you *following* me?'

'No.' Grace's heart was still racing. 'I wanted to check that you were OK.'

'How did you know I was outside?'

'I was awake. I saw you walk through the garden. When you didn't come back, I was afraid something might have happened.'

'What could have happened to me out here in the middle of nowhere?' asked Deira.

'It's *because* it's the middle of nowhere that I was worried,' confessed Grace.

'There's no need to worry,' said Deira. 'I'm absolutely fine.'

And then, almost inevitably, she burst into tears.

Grace put her arm around her and led her back through the garden to her own room, where she put on the kettle and made Deira a cup of camomile tea.

'It's all they have, I'm afraid,' she said, handing it to her. 'But better than nothing. D'you want to sit outside? There's more space.'

Deira allowed herself to be led to the small patio area outside the room and sat in one of the comfortable chairs. Grace sat beside her. Fingers of light were appearing at the edges of the sky now, and the chirping of birds was added to the nocturnal sounds. Deira sat in silence and sipped her tea as she gazed at the horizon. Grace didn't speak.

Eventually Deira put the half-empty cup on the small mosaic table between them and looked at the older woman.

'I suppose you want to know what I was doing,' she said.

'I don't care what you were doing,' said Grace. 'You don't have to tell me. The only reason I was worried was because I thought I heard you arguing with someone. Then I heard nothing at all. And I know I was letting my imagination run away with me, but . . .'

'You're a really good person.' Deira smiled faintly at her. 'For all you knew I could have been bashed over the head, but you came looking anyhow.'

'I was very much afraid you might have been,' admitted Grace. 'I did think that maybe you'd had a clandestine meeting planned with Charlie, though as we hadn't seen him earlier, I couldn't be sure that was it. I also wondered if your ex might have turned up and was having a go at you about the car. I know that's ridiculous, because he doesn't know where you are, but even so, I was a bit worried.'

'There was no need. Not about my being bashed over the head by a stranger, or by Gavin either.' Deira rubbed her eyes, then took a sip of the tea. 'You were right about it being Charlie, although meeting him was by chance. I've made such a fool of myself.'

'How?'

Grace listened in silence as Deira told her about their conversation.

'Such a stupid, stupid plan,' said Deira when she'd finished. 'How could I have ever thought it was a good idea? Begging him to sleep with me to make me pregnant. As though it was a transaction. As though he was someone I'd picked off a shelf! Did I really expect him to jump into bed with me and hang the consequences?'

'You're not yourself at the moment,' said Grace. 'All this with your ex, with the car, it's affected you.'

'Truthfully, what affected me this time was Bex,' said Deira.

'Your niece? How?'

Deira explained about Bex's abortion and the despair she'd felt inside when she'd told her. 'It sort of unhinged me,' she said. 'It made me feel as though I had to do something quickly to have a baby of my own. To replace the one that Bex . . . I understand why she felt she had to do what she did. I really do. And I absolutely respect her right to make the decision. I just wish . . . I wish it could've been different.'

'I'm so, so sorry,' said Grace. 'It's been a tough time for you.'

'I think I'm going crazy.' Deira's hands were shaking as she replaced the cup on the table. 'I can't get my head around

341

my life right now. I feel . . . flayed. As though everything that touches me hurts and I hurt everyone and everything right back.'

'We all go a bit crazy at some point,' said Grace. 'You'll come out of this, Deira. I know you will.'

'I've humiliated myself in front of a really nice guy. And I've humiliated him too because I forced him into telling me something personal about himself that he otherwise wouldn't have said. I'm so ashamed.'

Grace was dying with curiosity to know what that was, but she didn't ask. Instead she told Deira that he'd move on from it and she was sure Deira would too.

'I hope so. He'll probably use me as some kind of warning story to his mates,' said Deira. 'Batshit-crazy baby lady. That's who I've become. God.' She buried her head in her hands.

'You made a mistake, but you'll never see him again so there's no point in worrying about it,' Grace said. 'Let it go.'

Deira looked up at her. 'So many things I should let go. So many things that seem to be mocking me. Why can't life work out like it does in the movies, where everyone ends up happy?'

'Movies don't always have happy endings,' observed Grace.

'I only watch ones that do,' said Deira. 'Life's crap enough.'

'I know.' Grace shrugged. 'But even happy endings don't go on forever.'

'I suppose I wanted to think . . . Well, Gavin left his wife for me, and his children hated me for it. I wanted to believe that they would respect me eventually for having such a great relationship with their dad. I wanted to believe we *did* have a happy ending together and that it was worth it. But we didn't. So what was it all for, in the end? All that pain and misery and everyone blaming us. Blaming me.' Deira reached for the cup again and finished the tea. 'Something Charlie said made me think again,' she added. 'About who I am and what I want and, well, everything.'

'What?'

'He said it was a privilege, not a right, to have a child. Yes, it's something that most of us want, but just because we want it doesn't mean we should have it.' She exhaled slowly. 'Maybe there's a reason I'm childless. After my mum died, I often wished I hadn't been born. I thought it was really selfish of her to have had children when she wasn't around to look after us – obviously that was nuts, because she wasn't expecting to die, but I still blamed her. Especially because I was lumbered with Gill looking after me, and Gill is, at heart, a tyrant.'

'Hardly a tyrant.' Grace raised an eyebrow. 'Surely?'

'OK, she's bossy,' amended Deira. 'She likes being in charge. She likes ordering people around. Anyway, that's neither here nor there; what's important is that I often felt that as far as my parents were concerned, I was a mistake.'

'Deira!'

'Not just me, all of us. She and Dad didn't have the best of marriages. We all knew things weren't great. Not that they intended their marriage to be crap, of course, but when they realised – when she realised – it was dodgy, why did she have more children? Why didn't she stop with Peter or Gill? It was selfish of them to have kids in those circumstances. I'd hate a child to feel that I'd had him or her for a selfish motive, but that's what they'd think, isn't it? I'd certainly love my child, just as I'm sure my mum loved us, but I might not give them the life they deserve. A happy life.'

'Love gives children a happy life,' said Grace. 'Losing your mum was a tragedy for you and clearly it had an effect on you. But it doesn't mean you can't and won't love your own child. Or that he or she won't love you.'

'You have a point,' agreed Deira. 'But no matter how much you love someone, you still have to have a plan. And I'm not sure how good my single-working-woman plan would be. Sometimes it has to be more than love.'

'Lots of people have children in difficult circumstances and things turn out fine,' said Grace. 'Being a parent isn't like an office job, Deira.'

'I realise that, of course,' Deira said. 'But I can't help thinking that me and my baby could be one of those times when it all goes to pot. Where the mum is perpetually exhausted and the child is miserable. I was perfectly fine without children when I was with Gavin because I was happy with our life. If he'd left me for someone else who wasn't pregnant, I don't think I'd have lost it the way I did. But . . .' She frowned. 'But it's like my body has taken me over. My womb has been positively pulsating with the need to have something in there. All I wanted to do was make it feel right. I didn't think about finding someone and building a relationship or any of that stuff. I just wanted to have a baby.'

'It's a very strong urge,' said Grace.

'Not one that I had before,' Deira said. 'I wasn't devastated when Gavin said no that first time. I was upset, but I got over it. It's only because of Afton that I've lost the plot now. I wanted to have what she had. And if it wasn't going to be the man I thought was the love of my life, it was definitely going to be a baby. So all of my reasons were the wrong ones.'

'Don't beat yourself up about it,' said Grace. 'Everyone

344

goes a bit nuts from time to time. And Deira, maybe the reasons you wanted a baby seem shallow to you now, but perhaps there was something more fundamental going on with you. Perhaps you did always want a child.'

'If I did, I've left it too late.'

'Not necessarily.'

'I think I have,' said Deira. 'And I need to face up to that. I need to face up to me. But I'm too bloody tired to do it now.'

She closed her eyes. And as dawn broke over the mountains, she fell asleep.

When Grace woke from her own fragmented sleep later that morning, Deira was still out for the count on the lounger, shaded from the sun by the wide canopy that extended over the patio. Grace had a shower and got dressed and then, as Deira was still sleeping, went to breakfast without her.

Charlie Mulholland was at a table with two other men when she walked into the breakfast room. He looked up and saw her, acknowledging her with an almost imperceptible nod of the head. She could see that he was looking past her too, obviously trying to work out if Deira was with her. She supposed he was relieved when he saw that she wasn't.

Grace selected an assortment of fruit and yoghurt and sat at a small table in the corner of the room. It occurred to her, as she peeled an orange, that the last few months of her life had been filled with the kind of drama that she'd never associated with a woman like her. A suburban mother and grandmother. Someone who always put other people first. Even though it had been a wrench to give up her job with the airline, she'd always assumed that being a wife and mother

345

was what she was supposed to be. And she'd been happy doing it, at least most of the time. But now she was a widow and her children were grown up, and her husband, the man who'd orchestrated the direction of their joint lives for so many years, had no say in matters any more. When the great anniversary treasure hunt was over, that would be the end of Ken telling her what to do. Was it wrong to feel a certain excitement about that future? Was it wrong to think that perhaps there were new opportunities ahead? A different kind of life for her?

'Hi.'

She looked up and saw Charlie standing in front of the table. She remembered how jealous she'd felt when he'd seemed interested in Deira and not her, even though Charlie was so much closer to Deira's age. She wondered if there was an age at which people didn't think silly thoughts, do silly things, want impossible outcomes from the situations they found themselves in. She was beginning to doubt it.

'Hi,' she said in return.

'Is Deira around?' he asked.

'She's still asleep,' said Grace. 'She had a late night.'

'Yes—'

'I heard.' Grace interrupted him. 'She's mortified about what she said to you.'

'So she should be.'

'She's been going through a rough time.'

'Even so.'

'Can I tell her that you're not thinking of her as the batshit-crazy baby lady?'

Charlie grimaced. 'It's a good description.'

'Her own,' said Grace.

'You can tell her what you like. We'll never see each other

346

again. I'm heading back to France now, but I didn't want to walk out of here without saying hello and goodbye to you.'

'That's nice of you,' said Grace. 'Good luck with France. I'll keep an eye out for the documentary, especially the bit you did here.'

'It'll be broadcast in November or December,' he said. 'Nice to bring some warmth and sunshine into people's homes in the dead of winter.'

'Absolutely.'

'Well, goodbye,' said Charlie.

'You got on well with her,' said Grace. 'Deira, I mean. Before she lost it.'

'I liked her,' admitted Charlie. 'But—'

'Don't judge her,' said Grace. 'Everyone's very quick to pass judgement these days, and we don't always know what's going on in each other's lives.'

'I'll try not to.' Charlie gave her a quick smile. 'But batshit crazy is a fair assessment.' Then he turned away and followed his two companions out of the breakfast room.

Grace poured herself another cup of tea and waited for Deira to appear.

She showed up seconds before the buffet was cleared, and grabbed a couple of pastries and a large mug of coffee.

'I probably would've still been there except a fly landed on my nose,' she told Grace. 'It should have been the most uncomfortable sleep ever, but it wasn't. Mainly because it was totally dreamless.'

'Ken once told me that we never have dreamless sleep,' said Grace. 'We just don't remember the dreams.'

'Either way, it was good,' said Deira. 'Thanks again for

coming after me in the middle of the night, Grace. I was fine, but I might not have been. So it was good to know you had my back.'

'Hey, we're on the road together. We have each other's backs. Are you feeling OK now?'

'Yes. I suppose I need to put things into perspective, but I'm . . . I'm fine.'

'Sure?'

'Well, maybe not exactly fine, but getting there.' She glanced around. 'Hopefully Charlie has already left and I won't have to see him again.'

Grace didn't say anything about having spoken to him.

'I'm keen to get us back on the treasure hunt,' continued Deira. 'Do you have your laptop?'

Grace shook her head. 'I'm taking the no-tech rule seriously. We'll look at it again before we leave. It was all about a poet, wasn't it?'

'Federico García Lorca,' said Deira. 'I checked him out before we had to hand over our stuff. Obviously there's a monument of some kind to him in Granada that we need to find. We can look up how many poems he wrote. The final clue was how old he was when he died.'

'So it's relatively straightforward again?'

'I think so.'

Deira drained her mug and stood up. 'Do you want to get going?'

'We've plenty of time,' said Grace. 'There was availability this morning, so I booked us a couple of extra treatments.'

'You did?' Deira looked at her in surprise.

'I thought after last night we needed them. A massage for me and whatever you like for yourself. My treat,' she added.

'Oh, but—'

'Seriously, Deira.'

'Well . . . OK. Thank you.'

'They're at eleven thirty. So you've time to chill before then,' said Grace. 'See you later.'

'I'm so glad I met you,' said Deira, and went back to her room.

They left at two p.m., both feeling refreshed after their massages and eager to be on the road. Grace had looked at the clue on her computer and memorised it, but, as she said to Deira while they were putting their bags in the boot of the Lexus, it was surely one of the easier ones to solve.

'And then we're done,' she said. 'Unless Ken has added another one to the Cartagena folder. Which I hope he hasn't.'

'Are you happy it's nearly over?' asked Deira.

'Yes.' Grace spoke without hesitation. 'It's true that it's made the journey more interesting – although maybe it's you that's done that, Deira – but I don't want to be dancing to his tune forever.'

Deira didn't reply. She was surprised at how suddenly Grace seemed to have moved from a woman grieving her husband, and in particular the way his life had ended, to someone who seemed to be looking to her future. It wasn't only in the things she was saying; it was also in her body language. Her movements, always serene and graceful, were now more direct, more authoritative. Previously, she'd looked in control of herself. Now she looked in control of everything around her too.

Grace got behind the wheel and eased them out of the car park while Deira inputted the address of the hotel in Granada into the satnav. Then, for the first time since she'd handed it over to Muireann the previous day, she switched on her mobile phone.

There was a clatter of messages: a couple from Tillie checking up on how she was getting on, three from one of her colleagues at Solas regarding the exhibition they were working on, one from Gavin asking about the car insurance, and a final one from Bex the previous evening saying that she'd be getting the train home in the morning. Deira replied to Bex's message straight away, saying that she'd been out of touch for a few hours but that Bex was to call or text any time she needed. Her niece responded almost immediately with a thumbs-up emoji and a message saying that she was feeling OK, though still a little shaky, but that she'd be fine at home now. *Thanks again for the use of your house*, she finished. *I'll appreciate it forever.* Deira couldn't help feeling a hypocrite, given how annoyed she'd been with Gill's appropriation of it, but she was glad that Bex had had somewhere safe and comfortable to stay. She replied with *Any time* and was surprised to realise that she meant it. Then she replied to Gavin saying that she'd let him know as soon as possible about the insurance, and answered Tillie's messages by saying that her friend would be pleased to hear that she'd gone to an out-of-the-way wellness centre to heal her spirit.

Did it work? asked Tillie.

Maybe not in the way I expected, responded Deira. *But it was worth it.*

She didn't bother with Karen at Solas. It was Saturday, after all.

The road south from El Pozo de la Señora was less hair-raising than the road up to it had been, although there were still plenty of twists and turns and spectacular views across the mountains and valleys.

'It would've been nice doing this in the convertible,' commented Deira. 'Though obviously if it hadn't burnt to a crisp I'd have ended up somewhere in France, so I wouldn't be here.'

Grace grinned at her and then turned on the audio. She selected a classical guitar playlist that Ken had compiled the first year they'd driven to their apartment. The route had been different, because they hadn't needed to come through the heart of Spain. But the music suited the dusty fields of olive trees as much as the gently sloping vineyards. Then, suddenly, they were on the outskirts of the city and she turned off the music so that she could listen to the satnav's instructions.

Their hotel was near the old quarter, which meant, like in Pamplona, they were driving through streets that were ill equipped for cars. But Grace kept her nerve and didn't panic even when driving down a road so narrow that there was barely an inch either side of the wing mirrors. Although when it widened into a plaza and they saw the hotel, both women were relieved.

'Well done,' said Deira.

'Thanks.' Grace turned off the engine and got out. A warm blast of air engulfed them. 'Let's check in and go treasure-hunting,' she said.

Chapter 31

Although their plan had been to go looking for Lorca's statue straight away, it was far too hot to be out in the afternoon sun. Instead they sat in the hotel's sheltered colonnade and sipped iced water beneath ceiling fans that turned languidly above them. Grace opened the laptop and did some research, discovering that Lorca had been part of an influential group of Spanish poets during the 1920s, and that he had been executed by nationalists at the start of the Spanish Civil War.

'Europe was a cauldron back then,' remarked Deira, as they scrolled through the information. 'Nationalists, socialists, Bolsheviks, fascists . . . and then, of course, the Nazis came along. Lorca was a year younger than me when he was shot. It's hard to take in.'

'I can't help feeling that the world is always on a knife edge,' said Grace. 'It's like whack-a-mole. War stops somewhere but it breaks out somewhere else. People's capacity to exploit each other, or hate each other, or refuse to negotiate with each other is endless. It's so crazy and yet there's a part of me that understands not being able to forgive and forget.'

'Who are you telling?' Deira made a note on a piece of

paper. 'Look at me, for heaven's sake. Forgiving and forgetting hasn't been high on my agenda. Gavin hurt me and all I wanted to do was hurt him back.'

'One of the hardest things about what Ken did was that he hurt us and we *couldn't* hurt him back,' said Grace. 'He might have thought he was sparing us the harder times to come with his illness, but we were ready for that. We weren't ready for what he did. And much as I've come to accept why he did it, I'm still struggling with my anger.'

'I'd be angry too,' Deira said. 'Whichever way you look at it, you've had a lot to deal with. And you know what – you're doing great!'

Grace smiled faintly. 'I'd like to think I'm understanding his decision more. Maybe by the time we finish the treasure hunt, I really will.'

Deira nodded and pushed the paper towards her. 'Look. Lorca wrote six Galician poems. So our last three numbers are 638. We need to find the statue and upload the photo to get the first number, and then we can be on our way.'

Grace continued to search Google Maps. It took a while, but eventually she gave a cry of satisfaction.

'Less than a kilometre away,' she said. 'I reckon we should go now. It seems to have cooled down a bit.'

Deira agreed, and Grace returned the laptop to her room before they set out. The intense heat had gone out of the sun, but it was still very warm and there weren't too many people about. They followed the map to the Avenida de la Constitución, a wide street with a pedestrian zone running through the centre, bordered by flower beds and trees. A few minutes after they turned onto it, they found the bronze sculpture of Lorca, sitting on a bench.

'Will I take one of you with him?' asked Deira, after Grace had captured a few snaps of the famous poet.

'D'you mind another selfie? The children are expecting them now.'

So they sat either side of the poet, copying his pose by crossing one leg over the other and trying, as Grace said, to look as serious and literary as possible. She sent the photo to Aline, and almost immediately received a reply back saying that they looked as if they were having a good time. 'And Deira is fabulous!' Grace read out. 'Such a strong-looking woman.'

Deira laughed. 'If only she knew.'

'But she's right,' said Grace. 'No matter what you might feel inside at the moment, you *are* strong, Deira. And you definitely look it in this photo.'

'It's the hairdo and the red lipstick,' said Deira, who was thinking, with a certain amount of pleasure, that she did in fact look rather like a young Katharine Hepburn in an early Hollywood movie.

Grace shook her head. 'That's just gilding the lily. It's your personality that shines out from the photo. I know that you're struggling with the whole fertility thing,' she continued. 'I understand how important it is to you. But it's not the defining thing about you. I admire that you're a woman who's done well in her career. You've taken some personal knocks, but you're still looking at ways to move on. And you'll find them. I know you will.'

'I'm touched by your faith in me.' Deira's words were light but there was a lump in her throat, and she was cheered by Grace's confidence in her.

'I mean it,' said Grace. 'Now come on, let's get something cool to drink. I'm positively melting here.'

They walked back towards their hotel, stopping on the way at a small bar with tables outside shaded by parasols, where the young barman suggested that they needed a couple of refreshing mojitos to cool them down.

'Why not,' said Grace, and soon they were sipping the mint-infused drinks and thinking that the barman had been absolutely right.

They had a second drink before going back to the hotel and uploading the photo. Once again, the wait was agonising until the 'photo is a match' message appeared and they were given the number 9 to unlock the next clue.

'Or the result of the whole thing,' said Grace. 'You know, Deira, I'm not ready to do this yet. How about we leave it till later?'

Deira looked at her speculatively. 'Are you afraid of coming to the end?' she asked. 'Of finding out what the professor thinks might be important in your future?'

'A little,' admitted Grace. 'He's been pulling the strings in the background all along. I don't know what the conclusion will be, but I don't want it to ruin my evening here.'

'Whatever you think,' said Deira. 'I was considering the Alhambra tour tomorrow morning. There's one at eight thirty and there are still tickets left. I checked online. Would you like to come with me?'

'Ken and I visited the Alhambra a few years ago,' Grace said. 'It's magnificent, but I won't go again. We're not in a rush tomorrow, so you take your time and enjoy it. The drive to our apartment is about three and a half hours, but it doesn't matter what time we arrive. Even if Ken has added a clue for there, I know the place well, so it's no big deal.'

'OK,' said Deira.

'We're the ideal travelling companions,' observed Grace. 'Happy to do stuff together and equally happy to do stuff alone.'

'And rescue each other from night-time encounters in the middle of nowhere,' said Deira with a smile.

'And solve each other's problems,' added Grace.

'And share the driving – I'll do it tomorrow,' said Deira.

'Excellent.' Grace smiled. 'Would you like to eat together tonight or go our separate ways?'

'Oh, together, I think,' said Deira. 'This is the kind of city where together is good.'

Granada would always have a place in her heart, thought Deira as she got ready to leave the following morning. She'd been enchanted by the bustling old quarter the previous night, the city's Moorish culture clearly evident in the shops that opened onto the narrow streets, with their displays of aromatic herbs and spices, and glass lamps of intricate design and colour that lured you inside to find even more treasures. She'd felt the fire of Andalusia too, in the flamenco dresses in other shop windows and the extravagant fans that the local women snapped open and shut as they ate with their families in outdoor restaurants, where children, even at ten in the evening, sat in front of plates piled with calamari and tortilla. It had got under her skin in a way no other city had ever done before, and she knew she'd come back.

But as much as the night life had been fun, her visit to the Alhambra that morning had touched her soul. She'd walked through the rooms of the palace, marvelling at the exquisite mosaic work, the elegance of the tapering pillars, and the serenity that even the large group of tourists couldn't dispel. She'd thought of the people who'd walked through those rooms before her, the people who'd lived in the palace, with their thoughts and dreams and hopes, some fulfilled, some not. We're all just passing through, she told herself as she left. We're nothing more than a whisper in the story of time. The thought was strangely liberating.

The sense of serenity and liberation had stayed with her afterwards when she messaged Bex to find out how she was.

Her niece FaceTimed her in return.

'I'm OK,' she said. 'A bit achy but otherwise fine. It was the right thing for me to do, Auntie Deira.'

It was a long time since Bex had put the word Auntie before her name. Deira smiled. 'You look good,' she said.

'I had my hair done before leaving Dublin,' Bex said. 'There's a salon near your house. The colourist did a great job with my highlights.' She ran her fingers through it.

'She did indeed,' agreed Deira, who knew both the salon and the colourist. 'Have you said anything to your mum?'

'No. And I'm not going to. Ever. You have to promise me that you won't say anything either.'

'Of course not,' said Deira. 'All I want is for you to be OK, Bex.'

'I am,' said Bex. 'Thanks again for everything.'

'You don't have to thank me. I did nothing to help.'

'You let me stay in the first place,' said Bex. 'I knew I had somewhere to come back to. And when I told you . . .' She let out a long, slow breath. 'I had to tell someone. I couldn't keep it in. But I knew you'd be OK about it. You always are. You're my role model.'

'I don't think I'm that much of a role model.'

'You are,' insisted Bex. 'You're living your best life. Maybe

357

it's gone a bit wrong with Gavin and everything, but you didn't collapse in a heap and stay indoors and sob your heart out like I would've done. You went off and drove through France on your own. That's so cool.'

Deira hadn't updated either Gill or Bex on the situation with the car, or the fact that she'd teamed up with Grace. Her niece was seeing the surface, not what was underneath.

'You got yourself into a difficult situation and you made hard choices and you didn't collapse in a heap either,' she said. 'So you're pretty cool yourself. And I'm not perfect, not even close.'

'That's the point,' said Bex. 'You're not perfect but you still know what you're doing. That's sort of why I thought it would be fine to come to your house.'

'I'm glad you did.' Deira wasn't going to shatter Bex's illusions about her. 'What are you going to say to your mum about the job?'

'Oh, I actually have one in Galway.' Bex smiled. 'I had it before I ever went to Dublin. It's at a local recording studio.'

'I see.'

'Getting pregnant was a horrible mistake,' said Bex. 'But I don't regret the abortion.'

'You made a decision only you could make,' said Deira. 'All I want is for you to achieve everything you want to achieve.'

'I'll do my best,' Bex promised. 'And by the way, you look amazing. The hair. The lips.'

Deira laughed. 'It's my Continental look.'

'Stick with it,' advised Bex.

'I will. Take care.'

'You too. Bye, Deira.' Bex ended the call.

Deira still felt regret for her niece's choice. But the regret was for herself and the fictional future she'd dreamed of for Bex's baby. A future that wouldn't have happened.

No, she murmured aloud as she put her phone back into her bag, my future is something I have to work on myself.

Later that evening, she and Grace unlocked the final document. This time the message was short.

And so you've finished the treasure hunt. I never doubted you, Hippo. Well, maybe I did a bit, but I'm glad you made it all the way through. Your reward letter is C. And now here's a link to a video that will explain the last steps to you.

'Another video?' Grace released a slow breath and turned to Deira. 'Why does he think . . .' She tailed off.

'You don't have to look at it,' said Deira, who was scribbling on a piece of paper. 'You can forget it if you want.'

'No, I can't,' said Grace. 'But I'll wait and watch it at the apartment.'

Deira gave her a sympathetic smile, then tapped her pen on the table.

'I-R-P-A-T-E-C,' she read from her scribbles. 'Which is C-E-T-A-P-I-R backwards. Does that mean anything to you?'

'Not a thing,' said Grace. 'Maybe the answer is in Cartagena.'

'Do you want me to come with you?' asked Deira.

Grace looked at her in surprise. 'I assumed you would,' she said. 'Were you planning to stay here instead?'

'I want to find out what this is all about,' admitted Deira.

'But I don't want to be in the way if . . . well, who knows what the professor has got in mind for you.'

'You've been with me every step of the way,' said Grace. 'I'd like you to come. And to stay in the apartment too,' she added, 'in case you were thinking of booking into a hotel or something.'

'I can't impose on you,' said Deira.

'It's not an imposition, and you can stay as long as you like.'

'If you're sure.'

'Of course I'm sure,' said Grace. She closed the laptop. 'Come on,' she said. 'Let's go.'

Chapter 32

Granada to Cartagena: 294 km

The Lexus made short work of the climb through the foothills of the Sierra Nevada as they left Granada behind. Ahead of them the mountains reflected multiple shades of green against the brightness of the clear blue sky. There were few cars on the road and the drive was easy and relaxed.

Exactly three and a half hours after setting out, Grace pulled the car to a halt outside a low-rise apartment block with a panoramic view towards the sea. The narrow residential street was lined with orange trees, while the traditionally whitewashed apartments all had large balconies brightened by hanging baskets of colourful flowers.

'Home, sweet home,' said Grace as she switched off the engine.

'It's lovely.' Deira got out of the car and looked around her. 'Very peaceful.'

'That's why Ken picked it,' said Grace. 'He wanted it to be a kind of retreat. We were very happy here.'

She opened the boot and took out both her overnight bag and her suitcase. Deira took her own bags and followed her into the building.

'We're on the second floor,' said Grace. 'Which is nice, because there's a sea view from our balcony.'

When Deira stepped into the apartment, she saw that it was more spacious than she'd expected, with a long galley kitchen that led to a square living area, and patio doors opening onto the balcony. The bright blue of the Mediterranean was visible beyond the tops of the gently waving palm trees.

'Two bedrooms,' Grace said. 'This is the guest one – it doesn't have an en suite, but the master bedroom does, so you'll have the main one to yourself.'

'It's perfect. Thanks.'

'It's entirely my pleasure,' said Grace. 'I've really enjoyed having you along on this trip, Deira. I know I shouldn't be pleased that you had a disaster with your car, but it worked out well for me.'

'It's been fun,' said Deira.

When they'd finished unpacking, Grace asked Deira if she'd like a cup of tea before looking at Ken's video.

'I'm fine,' Deira replied. 'I'll go out while you watch it.'

'There's not going to be anything important in it,' said Grace. 'You've been here for everything else. You should be here for this.'

'Seriously, Grace. This is probably his last message to you. You need time and space. I'll go for a stroll and have a coffee or a juice at one of the beach bars. When you're ready, you can text me and I'll come back.'

'If you're sure.'

'Of course I am,' said Deira. 'Give me a minute to freshen up and then I'll leave you to yourself.'

As soon as Deira left the apartment, Grace opened a bottle of red wine, poured herself a glass and sat down at the kitchen counter with Ken's laptop. She opened the email and looked at the link that would take her to his video. It wasn't until she'd drunk a third of the glass that she finally clicked on it.

It took some time for the video to load, but eventually it started to play. Once again, Ken looked at her from the laptop's screen. Although he was wearing the same shirt as before, Grace reckoned he'd recorded this at a different time. He looked even older. Less well. Less like the man she remembered. She took a large gulp from the glass and waited for him to speak.

'So,' he said, his voice stronger than his appearance had suggested. 'You did it, Hippolyta. You solved the treasure hunt, you got to the end and you're listening to me speak from beyond the grave. Sorry – I couldn't resist the "beyond the grave" comment. It's both macabre and humbling to think that I've gone and yet my words and my image live on. Not printed, like in books or letters or photos, but real, living images. Maybe that's what they mean by eternal life now. There's stuff about us that will never disappear. It's quite frightening really. You know I'm dead, yet here am I still talking to you.

'Anyway, to finish the treasure hunt there's one more thing you have to do. You've got all the mystery letters, obviously, and now you have to use that information to get a USB stick. The last piece of information is there. Given that you've got this far, I'm sure you'll work it out. Here's a little clue, though. You're not looking for the name of a place. Just a name.

'I really am impressed with you. In fact, I take my hat off to you. Well, I would if I had a hat. And if I was in a place I could take it off. Good luck. Over and out.'

The video faded, and Grace sat looking at the blank screen for a moment. Then she took out her phone.

Deira was walking along the seafront when she got a text from Grace to say that she'd finished watching Ken's video. It was nearly an hour since she'd left the apartment, and she'd worried that Grace was finding her husband's last words difficult to deal with. But when she got back, Grace was as calm and composed as ever.

'If it *was* his last message, it was typical Ken – short, sweet and to the point,' she said. 'No farewell words, no messages to say he loved me or telling me he was sorry for what he was doing. Just more instructions. I've to use the letters to get the final piece of information. But he gave me a clue. He said it's not a place, it's a name. Weirdly, though, all I can do is keep thinking of place names. Not that any of them actually fit with the letters in the clue.'

'Maybe it's a person's name.' Although she'd kept her voice as matter-of-fact as Grace's, Deira was sad that Professor Harrington hadn't been more loving to his wife in his last message. 'Or the name of a company, perhaps.' She took a pen and paper from her bag and started scribbling. 'EPIC ART. Would he have left you a painting, d'you think?'

'I suppose.' Grace looked doubtful. 'He knew about art, or at least he had books about it, but it wasn't his main thing. You're the arty person. Is there a gallery in Dublin called Epic Art?'

'Not that I know of.' Deira continued to rearrange the letters. 'But I suppose there could be. Or maybe there's one called Pic Rate.'

'A photography shop?' suggested Grace.

'Or a book!' exclaimed Deira. 'It must be a book. Though with these letters . . .' She rearranged them again. 'All I've come up with is RICE PAT, which actually sounds like a Chinese takeaway. D'you—'

'Oh.' Grace's eyes widened and she thumped the table gently. 'It's not Rice Pat. It's Pat Rice. How did I not get that before now? He's one of Ken's oldest friends. Ken must have confided in him and given him this USB thingy. But why on earth didn't Pat say something to me at the funeral, for heaven's sake?'

'Maybe he thought it was inappropriate. Or the professor told him not to.'

'For crying out loud!' There was a spark of real annoyance in Grace's voice. 'What are these old codgers like with their secrets and their codes and their plans. If someone had given me a USB for the husband or wife left behind, I wouldn't feck around with waiting for them to come to me muttering secret codes. I'd tell them and hand it over.'

'Me too,' said Deira. 'But, well. Men. Deep down they all want to be superheroes or super-spies or whatever.'

Grace laughed.

'So does this Pat Rice guy live in Spain too?' asked Deira.

'I don't think so.' Grace got the computer and opened Ken's contacts. 'Look, here he is. Professor Patrick J. Rice, 18 Lindendale Avenue, Blackrock.' There was a mobile number and an email attached to the contact information.

'Are you going to phone him?'

'I wouldn't know where to start the conversation,' said Grace. 'I'll send him a message and see what he has to say about it.'

'Maybe he knows what the professor has left you.'

'A USB,' said Grace. 'That's all Ken said.'

'It must have information about your treasure on it,' said Deira. 'I hope it's a lovely piece of jewellery.'

'I'm honestly not getting my hopes up.' Grace closed the laptop. 'Let's head out and find something to eat.'

After a leisurely meal at a nearby restaurant, they returned to the apartment, where Grace made them a couple of generous gin and tonics. They sat on the balcony and chatted idly about their journey through France and Spain.

'Knowing Ken, the treasure will be a subscription to some kind of online library,' remarked Grace when Deira brought up the subject again. 'Or the *Times Literary Supplement*.'

'Oh Grace.' Deira laughed. 'I bet you're wrong. It'll be something fabulous.'

A nice piece of jewellery would be great, Grace thought as she lay in bed later, but she knew that for Ken, the treasure at the end was significantly less important than the fun he'd had in devising the clues for the hunt. If he were here, he'd tell her that the real treasure was in solving it.

And yet she didn't really mind. She'd completed the task. Tomorrow she'd scatter the remainder of his ashes.

Then she'd have fulfilled his last wishes. And there'd be nothing more he could ask of her.

Chapter 33

Cartagena, Spain: 37.6257°N 0.9966°W

The following morning, the insurance company phoned Deira to remind her to sign and return the forms they'd sent her.

'I already did,' she told them. 'I emailed them back straight away.'

'Yes, with a digital signature, but we need hard copies,' the agent said.

'Can't you print them off?'

'I'm afraid not,' said the agent. 'We need original hard copies with your signature. But as soon as we have those, we can make the payment directly into your account.'

Deira argued that her digital signature was just as good, but the agent wouldn't be budged. It was hard copy or nothing.

'I have a printer,' Grace said when Deira explained the problem. 'You can sign them here and post them.'

'It's going to take a few days for them to arrive. And goodness knows how long to process,' said Deira. 'I think I'd better go home and deal with it.'

'That's such a faff!' exclaimed Grace. 'It'll be fine. Stay a bit longer.'

'I'd love to,' Deira said. 'But Gavin will have a coronary

if he thinks I'm deliberately delaying things, and I really don't want to make the situation worse. Besides . . . I need to go back and sort out my life. This trip has been like stepping out of it for a while. In fact, I feel like I've lived a hundred lifetimes since getting on the ferry. But I guess everything has to come to an end. Is there an airport near here?'

'Murcia,' said Grace. 'It has regular flights to Dublin.' She looked at Deira thoughtfully. 'We could fly back together,' she said.

'Why would you do that?' asked Deira. 'You've booked the return ferry with your car, and you can't abandon it here.'

'That's not for ages,' protested Grace. 'Plus I was going to email Pat Rice and tell him to send me the USB, but it might be better to get it from him in person. The treasure is probably in Dublin anyway. If you're going back, we could book a flight together. I can return in a week or so, then drive home when I planned.'

'Are you sure?'

Grace nodded, and the two of them looked up flights on the computer. The earliest available one was in a few days' time, so Deira booked a one-way ticket while Grace bought a return coming back a week later.

Then Deira texted Gavin to let him know what was happening. The amount agreed by the insurance company was less than her claim, as they refused to allow for the fact that the Audi had had a package of optional extras included. But Deira felt it was reasonable, which was why she'd accepted it without argument.

You think I'm going to be able to replace the car with that money? You owe me big-time, he texted in return.

If you want to get some legal advice, feel free, she replied.

368

But the settlement is the settlement and I'll forward it to you
as soon as I get it.

She waited for another text from him, but nothing came. She dropped her phone into her bag. A couple of minutes later, it rang with a number that wasn't in her contacts list.

'Hello,' she said.

'Deira O'Brien?' a woman's voice asked.

'Yes.'

'Hi, I'm Bethany Burke. I run Executive Placements.'

Executive Placements was a high-end recruitment firm that Solas Life and Pensions used from time to time. They'd recruited Deira's last assistant for her.

'One of our clients is a big-name tech company,' Bethany told her. 'They're looking at their corporate responsibility programme and ways they can be more involved in the community. They're interested in cultural heritage; they feel that although their company is technology- and future-focused, it's only right to look at the past and the present and areas outside technology.'

'Good to hear,' said Deira.

'They want to set up a visitor centre in their offices,' said Bethany. 'They're going to devote a really large space to it. They want to have displays and readings and music. They need someone to head it up. They need you, Deira.'

'That's . . . interesting.'

'Their CEO has visited the Solas exhibitions a number of times,' said Bethany. 'He was very impressed. He checked out your profile on the company's website as well as on LinkedIn, and got in touch with me. We do all their executive hires.'

'I wasn't thinking of a move right now,' said Deira, although even as she spoke, the idea of moving away from Gavin was beginning to take hold. And yet she didn't want to be the one to leave. As though she was so broken by what had happened that she couldn't stay. Even if her actions over the previous few months could certainly have led people to think that.

'It would be really good if you'd be prepared to meet them and talk about it,' said Bethany. 'They're looking at an excellent offer for a person of your experience and calibre. There are stock options and other benefits too.'

Deira knew her current package was a good one. Would a tech company pay more? But did she really want to work for a business that might be considering their corporate responsibility as mere window-dressing? Would that be selling out? Still, she thought, what have I got to lose?

She explained to Bethany that she was away for a few days.

'Will you be back by Friday?' asked Bethany. 'I was hoping to make an appointment with you for then.'

'That's fine,' said Deira.

'I'll confirm it when it's set up and email you all the information I have about the post,' Bethany said. 'Good talking to you.'

'You too,' said Deira.

She was feeling slightly dazed by the turn of events as she put her phone back in her bag. But she was excited too. And her thoughts now turned to what she'd wear to the first interview she'd done in more than a decade.

On their final night in Spain, Grace suggested to Deira that they go to the Flor de la Esquina for dinner.

'Everywhere we've been so far has been pretty good,' Deira said. 'So whatever you suggest is fine by me.'

She'd packed most of her clothes, but had kept out a pair of wide white trousers and a black and white polka-dot top for dinner. She ran her brush through her hair and then applied her lipstick. She'd fallen in love with bright red. She wished she'd discovered it sooner.

Grace was already in the living room, wearing a cerise dress and looking utterly fabulous.

'Wow,' said Deira. 'You always put me to shame, but you look stunning tonight. And I know it's cheesy and sort of patronising to tell someone they don't look their age, but Grace, you're like . . . like Juliette Binoche! That woman has never aged and neither have you.'

'She's younger than me!' But Grace smiled. 'Come on, let's go.'

She led the way to the restaurant, which was a couple of streets back from the seafront. There were half a dozen tables on the street outside, another half a dozen on a covered terrace and the same again inside. When they told the waitress they didn't have a reservation, she brought them to the last unoccupied table on the covered terrace.

'This is pretty,' said Deira as she looked around. The decor was in shades of cream and pale green, and the walls were stencilled with flowers. 'Did you come here a lot with the professor?'

'No,' said Grace. 'He preferred to eat at the other end of town. This is my first visit, so I hope it's good.'

It was. Over their lobster dinner, the conversation turned to Deira's upcoming interview, and she told Grace of her fear that if she got the job, people would think she'd left Solas because she couldn't bear working with Gavin any more.

'Who cares what they think?' said Grace. 'You'll know the reason.'

'I know. But . . .' Deira snapped one of the breadsticks that had been left in a basket on the table. 'All my working life it's mattered to me how I've been perceived. It's why I am who I am. A senior executive. A person with responsibility. Someone in control.'

'You'd be all those things in the new place too,' Grace pointed out. 'As for being a person in control, I can't help thinking that's vastly overrated. It was what Ken always wanted, and when it was taken away from him because of his illness, he couldn't cope. Like I said before, he struggled when I had more influence in the relationship. It wasn't good, Deira. It really wasn't.'

'I'm talking about work,' Deira said. 'I'm not talking about Gavin and me personally.'

'But it all stems from a personal thing, doesn't it?' said Grace. 'And you feeling that he has something you don't. You don't want that to be the defining thing in the office either.'

Deira looked at her silently. Grace had put into words much of her feelings about her life since Gavin had left her.

'You're right,' she admitted. 'I don't want them feeling sorry for me. Thinking that he's all strong and virile and a baby-making machine, whereas I'm a sad old woman who's had to leave the job because of him and who can't even do what women are supposed to do.'

'Women aren't only here to have babies,' protested Grace.

'I know. I've always believed that. It's just that when you haven't . . . when you've decided you should have . . . when you've made a fool of yourself with a man over it . . .'

'Which man?' asked Grace. 'Gavin or Charlie?'

'Oh God, both of them.' Deira covered her face with her hands as she felt her colour rise.

'But how do you feel about it yourself?' asked Grace. 'Have you given up on the idea of going down the IVF route and doing it on your own?'

Deira let her hands fall to her lap again. 'It's such a hit-and-miss scenario,' she said. 'According to the HFEA – that's the Human Fertilisation and Embryo Authority – the birth rate for women trying to conceive from their frozen eggs is eighteen per cent. If someone came to me with a proposition for an event with that kind of success rate, I'd tell them to sod off. And only just over three per cent of women in my age group have a successful live birth. Those aren't odds, Grace. They're impossible numbers.'

'But lots of women do have babies over forty. You might be one of the lucky ones.'

'True,' said Deira. 'But I'd have to go through all that IVF entails for even the tiniest chance.'

'If it's what really matters to you, though . . .'

Deira put her fork on the table and looked thoughtfully at Grace. 'I honestly don't know if it's that I can't bear being the only one of Gavin's women who hasn't had a baby, or if I subconsciously clamped down on my desire to have a baby while I was with him and truly feel my life is incomplete without a child. If I don't know why I want something, how mad is it to be looking at ways of having it?'

'It's easy to second-guess yourself,' said Grace. 'You need to listen to your heart, Deira.'

'It was listening to my heart that landed me in a mess with Charlie,' said Deira. 'Or, being honest, it was listening to my damn hormones! There's a part of me that thinks I want a child because I'm supposed to want a child. And another part of me that longs for a baby of my own to hold. But is that just the same as me wishing my mother had bought me the same doll that she bought Gill when we were kids? I honestly don't know. And I don't have the time to think about it, because every second of every day my few remaining eggs are becoming more and more fragile.'

'I wish I could advise you.' Grace's words were heartfelt. 'I know that my children are my greatest achievement,' she continued, 'but sometimes I wonder if I lived some of my life through them instead of doing things for myself. I invested all of my own dreams in them, you know. I chose to be the best wife and mother I could be, but I wasn't always happy about it. I comforted myself with the achievements of my husband and my children. And yet doing this trip on my own – or at least with you – has made me wish that I'd done more things for myself and by myself when I was younger.' She gave Deira a rueful look. 'Maybe no matter what we do in life we look back and think things could have been better. Or different. Or that we should've chosen another path.'

'Do you wish that?' asked Deira.

'From time to time,' admitted Grace. 'Oh, I wouldn't change my kids for the world, but from where I am now, I wouldn't have been as flattered as I was that Ken wanted to marry me, and I wouldn't have believed myself so unworthy that I had to accept the first man who came along and asked me.'

'Do we ever get it right?' wondered Deira.

'We never get everything right,' said Grace. 'But we can adapt. We have to.'

The two women were contemplating each other's words in silence when Duncan Anderson walked over to their table, a wide smile on his face.

'You came,' he said to Grace. 'It's lovely to see you.'

Deira looked from one to the other.

'How could I not?' said Grace. 'I'm only a short walk away.'

'Did you enjoy your meal?'

'Delicious,' she assured him. 'Duncan, this is my friend Deira.'

'Pleased to meet you.' He smiled at her and then asked both of them if they'd like dessert.

'I couldn't manage it,' said Grace. 'But coffee, please. A decaf Americano.'

'Same for me,' said Deira.

'Right away.' Duncan went to get the coffees.

'I thought you said it was your first time here,' said Deira. 'But you seem to know him well.'

'It is,' said Grace. 'Oddly, I met him in Toledo and I couldn't believe the coincidence in him living near me. We got chatting that night you stayed in your room. I thought it would be nice to check out his restaurant.'

Deira gave her a speculative look as she commented that Duncan had seemed very pleased to see her.

'Of course he was,' said Grace. 'All the restaurant owners make a fuss of their regular customers.'

'But you're not a regular customer,' Deira reminded her.

'Well, no. But I'm sure he hopes I will be.'

'Ah, a customer. You think that's all he's hoping for?' Deira raised an eyebrow.

'I'm sure it is.' Grace felt the colour rise in her cheeks. 'I just thought—' She broke off as Duncan came back and placed the coffees in front of them.

'There's chemistry,' said Deira when he had gone. 'I can feel it.'

'You're being silly.'

'No,' said Deira. 'I'm not.'

When they asked for the bill and Duncan told them the meal was on the house, she gave Grace another pointed look that the older woman studiously ignored. And when Duncan gave them a double-cheek kiss in farewell, she noticed that he lingered slightly longer than necessary with Grace.

'I like him,' said Grace defensively when they were having a drink on the balcony later that night. 'But that's as far as it goes. I'm not looking for a replacement husband, Deira. No matter what you might think.'

Deira said nothing.

But she smiled into the darkness.

Chapter 34

Cartagena to Dublin: 2,729 km

She still hadn't driven through Paris in a sports car with the warm wind in her hair, thought Deira as she stepped off the plane at Dublin airport into a gusting wind and temperatures ten degrees lower than the south of Spain. But that didn't matter. She'd get around to it someday. However, having a child – would that ever happen? She still didn't know. Nevertheless, she realised that in the last few days she hadn't looked at a man and wondered if he could be the possible father of her child. She hadn't thought about getting pregnant every minute. She hadn't almost doubled over in pain every time she saw a mother and baby. Which wasn't to say that might not happen again. It was simply that right now, at this moment, she'd managed to put that particular desire and longing into a space in her head that didn't need to be accessed. And for the next few weeks, despite the precarious state of her eggs, she wasn't going to access it.

'It's weird to be back sooner than I expected,' said Grace after they'd collected their bags and gone through passport control. 'It goes to show, doesn't it, that you can make as many plans as you like, but they can come to nothing.'

Deira nodded and followed her into the arrivals hall, where, almost immediately, Grace gave a cry of delight and waved at a tall woman holding a toddler in her arms. The woman was a younger version of Grace herself. Less elegant, Deira thought, but with the same fine features and blue eyes. The toddler, when he saw Grace, squirmed in his mother's grip and held out his arms towards his grandmother.

'Who's my best boy!' cried Grace as she lifted him towards her and smothered him in kisses. 'Who's the person I've missed the most in the world?'

'Not me, I'm guessing.' The woman gave her an amused look. 'Hello, Mum.'

'Aline, sweetheart, it's lovely to see you. Thank you for coming to pick me up. This is my friend Deira.'

Aline held out her hand. 'Pleased to meet you,' she said. 'Mum's talked about you a lot.'

'And about you,' said Deira. 'It's nice to finally meet you.'

'Thank you for travelling with her,' said Aline.

'I was lucky she asked me,' Deira said. 'Otherwise I might have been stuck in Nantes for the duration. As it is, we had a fabulous trip together.'

'But you cut it short, Mum.' Aline frowned. 'You weren't terribly clear why in your phone call. Plus you'll still have to go back to bring the car home.'

'I know, I know,' said Grace. 'But that's not for over a month. I can be home for a few days in the meantime.'

'Of course you can,' said Aline. 'It's just—'

'We can talk about it later,' said Grace. 'Right now, I think we should make a move.' She turned to Deira. 'Are you absolutely sure you want to take a taxi? It's no trouble to drop you home.'

'It would be madness for you to even think about it,' said

Deira. 'It's close to rush hour and I'm on the other side of the city. Go home with your family and . . . well, we'll talk soon.'

'Absolutely,' said Grace. 'Take care of yourself.' She handed Declan back to Aline and hugged Deira. 'As soon as I have the USB, I'll call you.'

'OK.'

'You'll be all right, won't you?'

'Of course I will.'

'Talk soon.' Grace gave her another hug and then picked up her grandson again. 'My goodness, you're getting to be a big boy,' she said. 'Soon I won't be able to lift you at all.'

Deira watched as they walked out of the terminal building together, then made her way to the taxi rank.

Other than asking her for her address, the taxi driver didn't speak and, grateful for the silence, she tipped him generously when he pulled up outside the house. Before going in, she opened the post box and took out the accumulated mail. There wasn't much – she'd signed up to paperless billing for most things, and nobody sent personal letters any more. But she identified the documents from the insurance company straight away.

She put her key in the lock and stepped inside.

She walked past the tied bag of rubbish that Bex had left in the hallway and climbed the stairs. Another time she would have raged at her niece for not putting it in the bin outside, but now she didn't care.

Her bedroom door was open and the scent that lingered very faintly in the air was Gillian's. Her sister always wore strong fragrances. But apart from the traces of Black Opium, everything was exactly as she'd left it and there were no other signs that anyone had slept in her room. Even the sex toys that Gillian had commented on hadn't been disturbed, although Deira had a sudden wild image of her sister trying out one of the vibrators. She clamped down on it immediately before deciding that she was never going to be able to use any of them ever again.

Before starting to unpack, she rang the local Thai restaurant and ordered honey pepper chicken for delivery. When she'd finished eating, she opened the envelope from the insurance company, took out the forms and signed them.

She found it hard to believe that it was less than a fortnight ago that she'd sneaked into the car park of Gavin's building to take the Audi. She remembered thinking of herself as a spy back then. And now what was she?

A woman on her own who had decisions to make.

But who really wasn't sure how she was going to make them.

Even though the house had felt big and empty after Ken's death, Grace hadn't been bothered by it. But today, after Aline had kissed her goodbye and gone home, she was suddenly overwhelmed by the stillness and silence surrounding her. For the first time, her husband's passing seemed real to her; she accepted he was gone and wasn't coming back.

She pushed open the door to his office. The walls were lined with shelves crammed with books. His desk was piled with papers. Box files overflowing with even more papers were piled up on the floor. Everything about the room spoke of Ken.

She sat in the swivel chair beside the desk. It was the first time she'd ever sat in it, and it was more comfortable than she'd imagined. She wondered if, in the hours that Ken had been locked away in here supposedly working, he'd done what she was doing now: sat back in the comfortable chair, closed his eyes and propped his feet up on the desk.

'I'm busy!' She could hear his abrupt tone as she tapped on the door. 'Don't disturb me.'

But maybe he'd been busy enjoying the peace and quiet of his private space while she dealt with the competing demands of Aline, Fionn and Regan and whatever crisis had taken hold. She couldn't blame him if that was the case. She'd often wanted a private space herself.

She opened her eyes and stood up again, walking out of the office and through the house. It had been a perfect family home, with its four bedrooms, two reception rooms and extended kitchen, but she was no longer living as a family. She was a woman on her own. She was a woman in charge of her own life.

She was going to put it on the market straight away.

Deira dropped the signed forms at the insurance office on her way to her interview with the CEO of the tech company. As with her current job, she'd be able to walk to work if she took up a position there, a benefit of being so close to the city. Nevertheless, that depended on being able to continue living in the canalside mews, which would be in doubt if Gavin took an adversarial approach to their separation. She'd never really thought about what might happen if they split, because she'd never thought they would. And on the occasions when Gill had mentioned that she might be in a better position legally if she married Gavin, she'd dismissed the comments as further interfering in her life. Yet Gill could have had a point and she'd been a fool not to listen. Perhaps she'd misjudged her sister. Maybe she always had.

She turned towards Hanover Quay, where so many tech companies were now headquartered. Except for occasional visits to the contemporary theatre nearby, it wasn't a part of the city she usually visited, and she was struck by the energy of the glass and chrome buildings around her, somehow more dynamic and less forgiving than the warm terracotta of the Solas Life and Pensions offices.

Am I dynamic enough or modern enough for them? she wondered as she walked up the steps of Arc Tech. Or am I like my damn eggs, approaching my best-before date?

Yet she was enthused rather than dampened by the wide space inside the building that the young CEO told her was the designated area for the proposed visitor centre, and she couldn't help envisaging herself working there.

'We want to make it welcoming and accessible,' said Ardal Crane. 'We want to showcase art and culture. We want to make people feel that we're part of the community.'

She asked questions about the business itself as well as the ideas he had for the space, pushing against his thoughts for it and testing her own. He was as eager as she was to explore the possibilities, and she was surprised when she realised that they'd been talking for over an hour.

'I think you'd be a great fit for us,' he said. 'How about I chat to Bethany and see what sort of proposal I can put together to make this happen?'

'Sounds good,' she said, and shook his hand.

It was only after she'd left that she wondered if he could possibly be the one.

But she dismissed the thought almost as soon as she had it.

*

As Pat Rice lived on the other side of town, Grace had agreed to meet him in the city centre on Saturday morning. They both arrived at the Starbucks in College Green at exactly the same time, which made Pat observe that she was one of the few punctual women he'd ever met in his life.

Grace knew that he was divorced with two children and that he'd been living on his own for the past five years. She remembered Ken sympathising over his situation, arguing that men came off worst in most divorces, usually having to leave the family home while still having to pay for it. But Grace knew nothing of the circumstances of Pat's divorce, nor how old his children were.

'Twenty-five and twenty-two,' he told her when they'd sat at a table near the window and were exchanging pleasantries. 'Michael is a psychotherapist. Angelique is studying engineering. And how are yours?' he added. 'Ken was very proud of them.'

Grace smiled and told Pat that they were doing well. Then she decided there'd been enough chit-chat and asked about the USB. Pat took it out of his jacket pocket and put it on the table in front of them.

'I'm surprised you're here already,' he observed. 'Ken told me it might be some time before you came for it. If at all.'

'Did he give you any instructions for if I didn't contact you?' she asked.

For the first time, Pat, who until now had radiated a kind of urbane charm, looked uncomfortable.

'Well?' she asked.

'He told me that if you didn't contact me by the end of July, I was to get in touch with you and ask what had happened. And if you said you hadn't gone on the trip, or hadn't been able to solve the treasure hunt, I was to give you a different USB.'

'There's a second one!' She looked at him in surprise.

'There was,' he said. 'I destroyed it.'

She looked at him in surprise.

'That's what he told me to do if you called me first,' he explained.

'And you really did destroy it?'

'What else would I do?' he asked.

What else indeed. Grace was all too aware that in the same circumstances she – and every woman she knew – would have given it to the person it was intended for, regardless. She wondered if such a lack of curiosity was a male thing, or if academics generally were a special breed.

'I know Ken would be thrilled that you're here,' said Pat. 'He was excited about your treasure hunt.'

'Was he indeed.'

'He said it was to make you think,' said Pat. 'And to make you realise you could manage without him.'

'I knew that already,' said Grace.

'Ken told me that you were very capable and competent, but he wasn't sure you could think outside the box,' said Pat.

'You seem to have chatted rather a lot about me.'

'We talked about our wives from time to time. After my divorce, he told me that I should find someone like you.'

Grace was startled. 'Really?'

'Yes. He said you were the kind of wife every man should have.'

'I'm not entirely sure that's a compliment,' said Grace. 'It makes me sound far too much like a doormat. Which,' she added, 'I probably was.'

'I doubt that,' said Pat. 'I doubt you could ever be anything other than very lovely.'

'Excuse me?'

'You're a lovely woman,' Pat told her. 'Elegant, attractive, smart – Ken was right in everything he said about you.'

Grace felt herself blush.

'Anyway, he also asked me to keep an eye out for you,' Pat said. 'You know, if you needed anything done around the house or help with . . . well, anything at all you might need a man for. Advice on stuff.'

'So despite all my elegance, attractiveness and smartness, my late husband thought I needed a man to organise me?'

'That's not it at all,' Pat said. 'He told me you were very capable. But that he didn't want you to have to do it all alone.'

Grace said nothing.

'He wanted to make sure that you'd be OK after he'd gone,' said Pat.

'Yes. Yes, I get that.'

'So, if there's anything at all I can do . . .'

'You're kind to offer,' said Grace. 'But the truth is, I was the one who organised everything around the house. And if anyone needed advice, it was me who gave it.'

'I kind of suspected that might be the case,' said Pat. 'After all, I knew Ken.' He smiled at her, and Grace couldn't help smiling in return.

'It was nice to see you again,' she said after she'd drained her coffee cup. 'And thank you for carrying out your designated duty so conscientiously.'

'You're welcome.' He stood up and she did the same. 'I do realise that you're perfectly capable of coping on your own. But I also know there's more to life than coping. I've discovered that over the past few years. You have to get out and live it. I'd really like it if we could keep in touch. Perhaps meet up from time to time. Have dinner. Go to the theatre. That sort of thing.'

'Perhaps.' Should she feel complimented by the fact that Ken's friend seemed to be hitting on her? wondered Grace. Unless Ken had asked him to. In which case it was a bit insulting.

'I could call you later in the week,' he suggested.

'I'm not really in that frame of mind right now,' she said. 'Besides, I'm going back to Spain for a while.'

'Oh.' Pat looked disappointed. 'Tell you what, I'll send you a message if I see a play or a concert I think might interest you. If you're around, you can think about it. No commitment either way.'

'Sure,' said Grace. She shook hands and walked out of the café. Pat Rice was a decent man, she acknowledged. But she didn't want to form a relationship with another academic, no matter how decent he was. She'd done that already.

Nor was she going to let Ken manage her future relationships.

She could do that all by herself.

Chapter 35

As soon as she arrived home, Grace sat at the kitchen table and inserted the USB into the laptop.

There was a delay while the little wheel spun around and she was afraid that perhaps Ken had forgotten to leave her a final password clue. But eventually a screen opened with a link to yet another video.

Once again the light seemed to emphasise the lines on Ken's face and the fact that he was even more gaunt than in the last recording. His expression was serious. She hit pause, went to the fridge and took out a bottle of wine. She uncorked it, poured herself a large glass and took a gulp before she pressed play again.

'So,' Ken said. 'Here we are for the final time, Hippo. You and me. Face to face. I hope it hasn't taken you too long to work it all out. I gave you till July. Did you get it done more quickly? It infuriates me that I don't know. That I'll never know. But I've moved on, and so have you. I hope you won't forget me, though. I hope you'll always remember the good times we had together. I want to have been the most important man in your life.

'If I had to sum up my own life, Hippo, it's been good.

387

That's why I'm so frustrated by this cruel disease. I have so much more to offer and now I won't have the chance. I've done things I'm proud of. I had a successful career. I gave lectures in many different places. I'm a critically acclaimed author. And I have a wonderful family.

'A lot of that is down to you. I always knew that, but I never thanked you for making it the way it was. I suppose I should have. But I've never been much of a person for saying thanks.

'So somewhat late, I do thank you for being the person you are. For being the kind of person who puts other people ahead of herself. Me, the kids, even Brett, the dog I know you never wanted and that you ended up having to look after – whatever we wanted was always ahead of whatever you wanted. You let me be the man I wanted to be and you raised our children to be their own people too. And none of us ever thanked you enough.'

Ken started to cough, and reached out for the small bottle of water on the desk in front of him. Grace watched as he tried to bring it to his lips, wincing for him as the water dribbled down his chin and he wiped it clumsily away.

'I suppose the lack of thanks up to now is because I'm not an emotional person. You've known that from the start, of course, and I know it bothered you sometimes. I would've tried harder, but it's not who I am. I could never be an emoter rather than a thinker. It might be popular, but I don't like sentiment. Even now, knowing I don't have much time left, I find it hard to be emotional about it. Well, I'm angry, of course. I can do anger. I know I've lost my temper over this a number of times and I apologise if it upset you. I know you would have liked me to be more demonstrative. To tell you that I loved you more often. To hold your hand in public. I couldn't do that, Hippo. Even for you.

'But . . .' he took a deep breath, 'but I do love you. I loved you from the moment I first saw you at the door to the plane. I couldn't keep my eyes off you, even though I was supposed to be working on the paper I'd brought with me. I made a mess of editing it and spent the next day going over it again. I knew I had to be with you, Hippo. It was fate. Maybe these days you'd call it arrogance or privilege to think like that. I can see how you would. But I only thought that way because you mattered so much. I knew, you see, that you were the right person for me. I knew you'd make my life better. I knew you'd be a great wife.'

Grace paused the recording and got up from the table, taking her glass of wine with her. She walked out into the long garden filled with flowers and took deep breaths before sipping the wine. After a couple of minutes, when she felt more composed, she went back inside and hit the play icon again.

'I remember telling you that beautiful women had all the power.' Ken's voice continued seamlessly, although it was clear that it was becoming more of an effort for him to keep talking. 'I meant it, Hippo. You never knew the power you had over me. Not only because you're beautiful, but because you're such a strong person inside too. You never wielded that power, of course, even though you could have. I don't know why. You would have cowed me. But you never tried.

'And sometimes it made me wonder if you loved me as much as I loved you. I wondered if you simply couldn't be bothered to tell me not to do things because it didn't matter to you. I never asked that question because I was afraid of the answer. Afraid that maybe I didn't matter as much as I wanted to. Yet not asking was a form of arrogance too. I wasn't the best husband I could have been. And I'm sorry about that. I'm sorry I've only realised it now.

'If you're watching this, you've completed the task I set you. You did something for me when you didn't have to, because I'm not there to know. But that's the sort of woman you are. You're loyal and dependable and you were my rock. Have you scattered my ashes? I keep imagining you flinging them off the balcony on the ferry. I bet you weren't convinced about it. I bet you were worried about someone spotting you. About littering the sea. But I'm pretty sure you did it for me anyway. As for the remainder – I hope you held some back like I wanted – I'd quite like some left in Cartagena; you know how much I enjoyed going to the Roman theatre there. I don't suppose they'd let you scatter them in a historical monument, but maybe you could leave a small amount somewhere. I don't mind what you do with the rest. Your choice, Hippo. Whatever you want.'

He took another awkward sip from his water bottle. Grace took a much larger gulp of her wine.

'OK, now let's talk about the treasure hunt,' said Ken. 'I thought of it when you first suggested we take the ferry to France and Spain. I understood why you wanted to do it, but the more I thought about it, the more I knew I didn't want to take that trip, knowing it was for the last time. I didn't want to go to places I'd loved, knowing I wasn't ever going to see them again. And when I got a bit sicker and you said you'd do the driving, I couldn't bear the fact that you'd taken control of it. I felt useless. And then you said to me that if I wouldn't go, you'd go by yourself, remember?

I wasn't sure if you meant it then, but I suddenly thought it would be a good thing. I thought about your life after me, where you'd have to do so much on your own. I thought it might be nice to start with something different. So that's why I decided on the treasure hunt. That's what I've spent so much time doing in my office. You think I'm putting my affairs in order. Well, I am, I suppose, but not the way you think.

'In the end, I reckoned you'd go because I knew you wouldn't waste the ticket! You're not a woman who likes anything to go to waste. Even now, it makes me smile when I remember you feeding the children stuff after the best-before dates. Aline was always so dramatic – crying that she'd die of food poisoning. And you'd laugh at her and tell her she'd die of starvation first because it was the out-of-date food or nothing. You were so strong with them. You raised them well.

'Anyhow, Hippo, knowing you'd go, I wanted you to have something to do while you were there. Something to keep you anchored. Is that very arrogant of me too? I didn't do it from arrogance, though. I did it for you.

'I wanted you to see places we'd been through my eyes. To see the things I'd noticed but you hadn't. I wanted to share them with you. To share how I thought about them. So that's why I made you go to the Jules Verne museum in Nantes. I went there the year we stayed in Saint-Nazaire. It was the time Fionn fell out of the tree on the campsite and cut his leg, remember? After all the fuss of bringing him to the hospital and getting it stitched, I needed some time to myself, so I drove into town and found the museum. I never told you about it. I don't know why. But now you've been and I'm glad, because I really enjoyed it and I hope you did too.

We both loved La Rochelle, didn't we? I'm sorry there were so many times I went off wandering by myself. Especially that evening we took the kids into town for supper. They were acting up and I couldn't bear it, so I went for a walk. I remember leaving you with them in a pavement restaurant and wandering around the little book stalls near the port. I shouldn't have left you to deal with them, I know, but the book stalls were far more appealing. I used to think they'd be the perfect setting for a crime novel, and so every time we went to La Rochelle, I thought of murders and mystery and Simenon. You know when you'd sometimes ask me what I was thinking, and I'd say "nothing"? I was actually plotting my own murder-mystery novel. Never got around to it, of course. It was always going to be "some day". And now some day will never come. I regret that, Hippo. I don't want you to have regrets in the future.

'As for the Fleur d'Île, I ended up stopping there when I went for a walk the last year we visited La Rochelle. I had a drink there and I saw the dog. Isn't she a beauty? At least I hope she's still there and you saw her! I'm confident the plaque will be – and it must be because otherwise you wouldn't be looking at me now.

'I regret we didn't spend more time in Bordeaux. I always meant to go back and explore it properly, but it's too late now. The Spanish stretch – Pamplona, Alcalá de Henares and Toledo, all new to you; those are etched on my memory forever, and more than anything I wanted you to experience them as I experienced them. Because, of course, I wouldn't have gone on that first lecture tour without your encouragement.

Do you remember the evening at college? When the dean introduced the Spanish professor to us? You were more beautiful than ever that night, Hippo. Your hair was up – I always loved when you did it that way, you looked so elegant – and you were wearing a pale-yellow dress with beads around the collar. You'd bought a new pair of shoes to go with it. They had high heels and that meant you were taller than me. I kept trying to have someone standing between us so that you didn't tower over me. You were a true Amazon that night. And you talked to Professor Rodriguez for ages. I was quite jealous. But afterwards he told me that you'd spoken about my work on the influences of American writers in Europe. And how I believed it was important to look at the cultural implications of writers from different countries being published overseas. He was very impressed with you. I didn't say that, of course. Didn't want you getting a big head.

'Anyway, that's how the idea of the lecture tour came about. It started my love affair with Pamplona, too. I guess I saw myself as a modern-day Hemingway, although obviously – despite the fact that the critics liked my book – I wasn't. Still, I loved going there, and even though it was all thanks to you, when you asked me if you could come one year, I said no, because it was my thing. Mine alone. It was a place where I always felt good about myself. Alcalá de Henares and Toledo too. If you'd come, I wouldn't have been able to pretend that I was some kind of academic genius, because you'd have talked about everyday things that would have made me realise I wasn't.

'God, Hippo, thinking about all this now makes me feel as though I was the most selfish husband who ever lived. Was

I? I wish I could ask you that face to face. I wish we could have this conversation face to face. But I can't. I don't want to . . . well . . . it's bad enough that you're going to remember my broken body. I don't want you to remember my broken mind too.'

Grace paused the video again and closed her eyes, wrapping her arms around herself as she remembered the last time she'd seen him at the funeral home. Still Ken, but not Ken. He'd lost the arrogant look that had always been a part of him. And without it, he wasn't the man she'd known. Ken's body, without Ken's mind, wasn't Ken at all.

She started the video again. He was speaking more slowly now, taking care forming his words, trying hard not to slur them. Her heart ached for him.

'Granada,' he said, 'well, we had a couple of good stays there, didn't we? The thing I loved about our first trip was going around the Alhambra with you. I think we shared the enjoyment of that equally. I know you loved it, and so did I, possibly for different reasons.

'As for Lorca, naturally you weren't interested in his work. What I liked about him was that he didn't want to be type-cast as a certain type of poet and playwright. In the end, I guess he was. It's what we're all afraid of, isn't it? That people see us one way and one way only.

'I think I allowed you to see me only one way, Hippo. I don't know why that is. I know that if you love someone you're supposed to let your guard down in front of them. I did a bit with you, but never completely. I was always afraid that if you saw the real me, you'd stop loving me.

'I was a fool. I still am. A dying fool who can't tell his wife how much he loves her without a screen to separate us.

394

And who's now telling her after he's dead. You know, part of me still really wants to go on the trip with you, Hippo. Part of me thinks that I could drive a little bit of the way so I wouldn't be a total burden. Maybe I could give it a try. I could take the car for a short drive. Practise trying to park. That sort of thing.

'But if I go with you, you won't see this. And you won't get to hear me say that I love you. That I always loved you. That I always will. Because I still can't bear being emotional in front of you. I don't even know if you'd like me to be, Hippo. Women say they like men who can cry, but do they really?

'So let's move on.

'There's one more thing, and that's the treasure part of the treasure hunt. You need to go to the Safe Storage Company in Dundrum to find it. The details are in my contacts. I hope it's something you'll like. Something that makes you see how much I love you. The code to get into my storage locker is the dates our children were born. I'm picking something personal for once.

'By the way, Pat Rice has been a good friend and I've confided a lot in him. You might get close to him. I wouldn't mind it if you did. You've proved over and over again that you can look after yourself, but you deserve someone to look after you. I didn't do the best of jobs. Perhaps he can. Perhaps he will. I'd like that. I'd like you to have someone.

'I'm done now, Hippo. Totally done. So here's a little bit of Lorca by way of farewell. The poem is called "Es Verdad", which means "It's True", and this is my own translation of the Spanish. I did it especially for you, and I hope you like it. Poetry is never as good in translation, but I hope you appreciate the sentiment:

> Oh, how much it costs me
> To love you as I love you
> For in loving you
> The air hurts
> My heart hurts
> And my hat, it hurts me too.

'Goodbye, my darling Grace. I love you.'
  The screen faded.
  Grace continued to look at it.
  And then, for the first time since Ken's funeral, she cried.

Chapter 36

At the same time as Grace was watching Ken's final video, Deira was studying information on IVF and evaluating the competing statistics in front of her. She'd told Grace that at her age she had a 3 per cent chance of a successful pregnancy, but the site she was currently looking at gave the far more promising news that with continuing medical advances, her chances might actually be as high as 12 per cent. Nevertheless, she thought, a slightly more than one-in-ten chance of getting pregnant when she probably wouldn't be able to have more than three cycles of treatment was shockingly bad odds.

Was she out of her mind to even consider it?

Was it an impossible dream?

Was she being incredibly selfish?

Why did she want a baby?

The last question was the important one. None of the rest really mattered. But it was the one question she didn't know how to answer.

The doorbell buzzed and she went to answer it.

'Oh,' she said when she saw who was outside.

'Hello,' said Gavin.

'I wasn't expecting you.'

'You texted to say you'd hand-delivered the forms to the insurance company yesterday, so I knew you were back in Dublin. I came on the off chance you'd be home today. Because we need to talk about the future and we need to do it face to face.'

'You should have called,' said Deira. 'I'm not—'

'How many times have you barged in on me without asking first?' demanded Gavin. 'I'm here now, and I want to deal with this.'

Deira stepped back and he strode past her into the living room, where he sat on the arm of the sofa. His first question was when he'd be getting the insurance money.

'Hopefully they'll release the funds by the end of next week,' she replied. 'They're actually being very efficient.'

'What were you thinking?' His tone was suddenly less aggressive and he looked at her with real bemusement in his eyes. 'What possessed you to break into the apartment complex and take the car?'

'I'm not sure,' she confessed. 'I needed to get away and the journey was already booked. It seemed like a good idea.'

'Surely you realised I'd find out,' said Gavin. 'I mean, the original trip was nearly three weeks. You couldn't have thought I wouldn't notice the car missing for three weeks.'

'Of course not,' she said. 'I assumed you'd guess it was me.'

'And I'd have come looking and you wouldn't have been here.'

She shrugged.

'I worry about your mental health,' said Gavin.

'I've worried about it myself,' Deira said.

'You were always such an optimistic, clear-thinking person,' Gavin said. 'I don't know what happened to you.'

'You happened to me,' she said. 'You happened to me, and for a long time you brought out the best in me. And then you delivered your hammer blow and you brought out the worst.'

'I never thought you'd lose it like this,' said Gavin.

'Neither did I. But then I never thought you'd get another woman pregnant either.'

'Which bothers you more?' asked Gavin. 'That I met her or that she's pregnant?'

'That you shattered what I thought was our life together into a million pieces,' she replied.

They looked at each other in silence for a moment.

'I'm sorry it worked out that way,' said Gavin.

'Why didn't you tell me that you didn't love me any more? Why didn't you give us the chance to talk about it?'

'Because I'd been through that already with Marilyn and I wasn't prepared to do it all again,' said Gavin.

'It was cruel and heartless.'

'I didn't mean it to be. I thought it would be easier in the long run. I didn't know you'd go off at the deep end.'

'Lots of things about me you didn't know, apparently, despite our thirteen years together.'

'Look, I've said I'm sorry and I am,' said Gavin. 'But we need to put it all behind us. We need to talk about dividing our assets. I'm entitled to a share in this house.'

'Even though it's not a family home. Because you don't consider us a family.'

'We're back to that again?' His tone betrayed his exasperation with her. 'You're jealous of the fact that Afton's pregnant.'

'Jealous isn't the word,' she responded. 'I'm gutted that

you denied me a child yet you were prepared to cheat on me and get her pregnant.'

'I never denied you a baby,' said Gavin. 'If we were still together, you wouldn't even be thinking about it, would you?'

'I don't know,' she said.

'I do. I remember our conversations. You wanted to live your best, most successful life. And that didn't include children. You said they'd be inconvenient. That they wouldn't fit in with our lifestyle.'

'Of course I did. Because that was the way we were living. Because you said you'd already done the children thing. Because you didn't want Mae and Suzy to feel put out by another child.'

'You agreed with that.'

'You wanted me to!' cried Deira. 'I thought you were right.'

'I *was* right,' said Gavin. 'In our relationship, it was absolutely the right choice. But with Afton, it's different.'

'You don't mind Mae and Suzy being put out by Afton's baby, but you did about ours?'

'They're older now. They can handle it.'

'I'm older too,' said Deira. 'Maybe too old to have a baby of my own. And that's down to you.'

'You'd be a crap mother,' said Gavin. 'You're a career woman through and through.'

'A career wouldn't have stopped me from being a mother.'

'Don't fool yourself,' said Gavin. 'Nobody can have it all. Not even you.'

'I never wanted it all.'

'Deira . . .' His voice softened. 'I'm sorry. I really am. I thought we were OK together. I never meant for this to happen.'

'But you couldn't help yourself.'

'I really couldn't,' he said. 'I met Afton and I knew.'

'Exactly the way you met me and you knew.'

'Except that we're at different points in our lives now.'

'I was younger than Marilyn. Afton is younger than me.'

'That's got nothing to do with it.'

'Hasn't it?'

'No. It's about needing someone. Knowing they're right for you.'

'And junking the past because it doesn't suit you.'

'I didn't junk my past when we were together. I looked after my family.'

'But as I'm not your family, you don't have to look after me.'

'What do you want from me, Deira?' he asked. 'What will make you let me move on?'

She didn't answer.

Gavin stood up and walked into the kitchen. It took a moment for Deira to remember that she'd left her laptop open on the counter. She jumped up herself. She didn't want him to see that she'd been looking at IVF sites. She didn't want him to think she was totally obsessed.

But she was too late. He was standing in front of it.

'You're thinking about this?' he asked. 'Really?'

'It's my only option. Well, that or dragging in a random stranger off the street. Which I've also considered.'

'You're crazy.'

'You have two children and you're about to have a third by a different woman,' she said. 'What's so crazy about me wanting one of my own?'

He looked at her, and then back at the computer.

'You'd be in your forties before you'd have the kid. If you even did.'

'I know.'

'And yet you'd still do this?'

'What choice do I have?'

'Come upstairs,' he said abruptly. 'Come upstairs and we'll do it once, and if it works then it works and you won't have to go through all this crap.'

She stared at him.

'Before I change my mind,' he said.

'You're going to have sex with me?'

'I was going to say it's the only way you'll get pregnant, although clearly it isn't,' said Gavin. 'But it's the quickest way.'

'And if I did, how would you feel?'

'Like you said, I have my children. I'd be able to step away.'

'You would?'

'Deira, this is something you want, and because of our life together and because I'm not a bad person, I'm going to try to give it to you. It won't be my fault if it doesn't work.'

'I asked you before,' she said. 'You refused.'

'You came into my office and demanded it!' he cried. 'Of course I refused. This is your chance. Are we going to do it or not?'

She walked slowly across the room and up the stairs. She opened the door to the bedroom. She sat on the edge of the king-sized bed they'd once shared and pulled her T-shirt over her head while Gavin stood at the doorway and watched her.

I loved him once, she thought, as she slid her pleated skirt over her hips. Maybe I still do. But he doesn't love me. And

402

somehow that doesn't matter any more. What does matter is thinking of myself and what I want. And I want a baby. I want a baby, because if I don't have one now, I'll never have one. And I don't want to be the woman who never had a baby.

He's the one. He's always been the one.

And he's giving me what's mine by right.

Gavin unbuckled the belt of his trousers, just as he'd done thousands of times before, as he walked over to her.

'Does Afton know you're here?' she asked.

'I told her.' He pushed Deira gently backwards onto the bed. 'I told her we had unfinished business to deal with.'

'I don't expect she thought it was this, though.'

'Not the time to talk.' He unbuttoned the cotton shirt he was wearing.

She looked up at him and inhaled his scent. The familiarity of him came back to her. She closed her eyes, felt the weight of him on top of her. The heat of him. The maleness of him. She felt her body ready itself for him.

She opened her eyes and looked at him.

He shifted on top of her.

'Oh, hell,' she said, and rolled away from him.

'What—'

'I'm sorry,' she said. 'I've made a mistake. This isn't what I want to do.'

'For fuck's sake, Deira.' He stared at her. 'What the hell is wrong with you? You want a baby. I'm giving you the chance.'

'I know. But . . . but I don't want to.'

'What?'

'I don't want to have sex with you,' she said. 'Because this isn't the way I want it to be. I don't want to conceive a baby with someone who cheated on me. With someone who doesn't love me. I don't want a baby with you.'

'You're kidding me, aren't you?' He stared at her. 'Ever since you found out about Afton, you've been obsessed with having a baby. You've plagued me about it, and yes, I was angry with your behaviour in the office and angry about the car too, but I came here today to sort things out between us. When I saw that stuff on your computer, I felt bad about it all. I thought that perhaps by doing this for you, it would help. And now you're saying no?'

'I'm sorry,' she repeated. 'But you're right, I'm saying no.'

'In that case, I never want to hear another word about it again,' he told her as he did up his shirt. 'No more texts and no more trashing me in the office either.'

'You don't have to worry about anything like that,' she said. 'I've made my decision and I'm fine with it.'

'I used to love you,' he told her. 'Now all I feel is sorry for you. But not sorry enough that I won't get legal advice on our situation.'

'Right,' she said.

He picked up his jacket and walked out of the room.

A few moments later, she heard the front door slam.

She sat on the bed for a long time, wondering if she'd made the biggest mistake of her life. She'd had the chance (admittedly a 5 per cent chance in any given month), and she'd turned it down. Not only that, she'd turned down the possibility of getting pregnant with a man she'd loved for more than a decade. He was right to think she was off her head. Because she was. What better opportunity was going to come to her? What were the chances now that she'd ever have the baby she wanted?

She cupped her stomach in her hands.

He would've made her pregnant. It would've worked.

She was an idiot.

She'd made a mess of everything again.

It was nearly an hour before she got up and got dressed, this time in leggings and sweatshirt. She put on her trainers and began to jog, following the canal until she reached Hanover Quay. She looked up at the Arc Tech office, full of young people hoping for a wonderful career and a wonderful life. Would the youthful CEO offer her a job? And if so, would that job compensate her for having turned down an opportunity for a changed life?

'Hey, Deira.' The man walking down the steps waved at her. 'Are you scoping us out?'

'Ardal.' She smiled at the man who'd interviewed her the day before. 'Maybe I am. I came for a jog and ended up here.'

'I spoke to Bethany yesterday afternoon. We're working on a package for you. We really want to have you on the team.' The CEO smiled too. 'Would you like to see the space again?'

'OK,' she said.

She followed him back up the steps and inside the building.

'It's quiet today, being Saturday,' said Ardal. 'But we could have this area open on Saturdays too. I haven't really thought that through. I was also thinking we could incorporate a café. Make it a social centre, you know?'

She walked around the space, enjoying the sun as it came

through the glass walls but thinking about how any paintings would have to be protected from the light. And thinking about installation art exhibitions she'd done in the past and how much more effective they'd be here.

'I like it,' she said. 'It feels right.'

'That's what I thought too.' Ardal nodded 'I'm not the arty type, Deira. It's microprocessors that do it for me. But I don't want us to be a one-dimensional company.'

'You aren't,' she said. 'Not if you're thinking about this.'

'I have a dream of it being a wonderful place for people to come,' he said. 'And I hope you can deliver it for me.'

'I hope I can too,' she said. 'In fact, I know I can.'

Later that night, Tillie called around, bringing a couple of scented candles that she put on the coffee table in the living room. Soothing and inspiring, she said as she indicated them. Which would Deira like to light first?

'I'm not sure which I need more.'

'Soothing, I think,' said Tillie. 'You did the right thing today, Deira.'

Deira looked at her doubtfully. She'd phoned her friend after getting home and shared the whole saga with her.

'You did,' Tillie insisted as the scent of jasmine perfumed the air.

'I wanted something and I gave up the chance of it,' said Deira. 'Not particularly bright.'

'I honestly believe that if it's right for you, you'll find a way. Gavin clearly wasn't the right way. That's all.'

'It's weird, isn't it,' said Deira. 'Most people don't want to get pregnant after a quick shag, and yet he was looking at it as a kind of business transaction. In the end, I couldn't do that to myself. Or to any baby I might have wanted. But surely that means I mustn't have wanted it badly enough, because most women will do anything to get pregnant when they're desperate.'

'And are you? Still? Desperate?'

'I don't know,' she admitted. 'I have to be honest and confess that I don't feel quite as twangy in the womb department as I did a few weeks ago. Although it could just be that I'd been reading the stats again before Gavin came and thinking how hopeless it all was. And also thinking that if it really mattered to me, I wouldn't care about the hopelessness of it all, I'd do it anyway. It felt right to say no to him, and yet part of me is afraid I'll regret it.'

'We all have regrets,' said Tillie. 'The thing is not to let ourselves be taken over by them.'

Deira said nothing.

'And who knows, it might still happen,' Tillie added.

'I'm not holding my breath,' Deira said. 'I'll . . . Actually, no, I don't even want to think about it. Not now. Maybe not ever again.'

'OK,' said Tillie. 'Let's talk about something else. Tell me all the details of your trip.'

Even though she was closer to Tillie than anyone, Deira wasn't prepared to tell her everything. She left out her middle-of-the-night encounter with Charlie Mulholland – in fact she mentioned him only briefly and in passing. Instead she concentrated on Grace and her treasure hunt, which intrigued her friend.

'The poor woman,' said Tillie. 'Losing her husband like that must have been devastating, and then for him to have left her this to do . . .'

'Grace is so . . . so accepting as a person,' Deira said. 'She's always calm and relaxed about things, as though nothing can shake her out of herself. Even when she was telling me the worst of it, she had herself totally under control.'

'Doesn't mean she actually was,' Tillie pointed out.

'I know. But sometimes her self-control made me feel completely inadequate. Like I wasn't up to the task because I was far too emotional myself. I guess we just came at our problems a different way. Truth is, she's been really supportive, and I hope I helped her too.'

'I'm sure you did. Women can be so self-critical,' added Tillie. 'We judge ourselves for not being up to the task, even though we usually are. You especially.'

'I guess it depends on the task.' Deira looked thoughtful. 'I mean, I'm a hopeless case personally right now, but I'm really confident I can do a great job for Arc Tech if the offer they put together is a good one.'

'You'll definitely move if it's right?'

She nodded. 'Originally I thought it would be like running away from Gavin and Solas, but it's a potentially great move for me. And I'm better off in a new environment.'

'I think so too. At least you won't have to keep bumping into him every day and remembering that he offered to shag you and get you pregnant so that you'd piss off and leave him alone with his new girlfriend.'

'Tillie!'

But suddenly, Deira smiled.

Because Tillie, as always, was right.

Chapter 37

Dundrum, Dublin, Ireland: 53.2932°N 6.2462°W

Two days later, Grace and Deira stood in the storage ware-house and looked at the small locker unit that Ken had hired to stash the treasure.

'You finally made it,' said Deira.

'End of the line,' agreed Grace. 'When I think about it, he was nuts. Sending me all around France and Spain simply to bring me to the other side of Dublin. He could've left me the code for the locker from the start.'

'Was there a clue for it?' asked Deira.

'Not really,' replied Grace. 'It's the children's birthdays. Which . . .' she began pressing the keypad on the locker door, 'is 3 for Aline, 9 for Fionn and 21 for Regan.' As she finished speaking, the door swung open and the two women looked inside.

Facing them was a stack of old hardback books. Behind them was another stack of equally old paperbacks. On top of the hardback pile were four envelopes, propped up against a small plum-coloured jewellery box. Three were addressed to each of the children. One was addressed to Grace herself. She put the children's envelopes in her bag and then opened the one addressed to her. There was a card inside. She took it out.

The image on the card was of a woman sitting in a garden, reading. Her long blonde hair hid her face, and she was totally absorbed in the book in front of her. The writing inside was shaky, but Grace recognised it as Ken's. She read the message aloud.

'I know I never converted you to the authors I liked,' he'd written. 'But I hope you'll enjoy this hardback collection of the authors you do. Maybe one day they'll be as lauded as the rest of the editions in this locker. Either way, I bought them for you to keep and enjoy. Oh, and there's a little something in the box too. Love always, Ken.'

'Books.' Grace laughed. 'I might have guessed he'd think of books as treasure.'

'And a little something in the jewellery box,' Deira reminded her. 'Open it.'

Grace put the card in her bag, then opened the box. A ruby ring nestled against the purple velvet.

'Oh my goodness, it's an Adele Dahlia,' gasped Deira as Grace slid it out of the box. 'That's a classic ruby ring. We showed it in one of our displays at Solas. We had a number of Irish jewellery-makers and I didn't think we'd get anything from Warren's because they're so upmarket, but their owner loaned us pieces from their Dahlia, Snowdrop and Ice Dragon collections for the opening night. We had to have extra security and everything.'

Grace nodded slowly as she slipped it onto her finger. It fitted perfectly.

'I remember walking past Warren's with him one Christmas and seeing it in the window,' she told Deira. 'I said it was the most beautiful ring I'd ever seen and that if I ever had the money, I'd love to buy it. But that was years ago!'

'Obviously he remembered.'

'Oh Deira.' Grace's eyes glittered with tears. 'I've misjudged him in so many ways. I always thought he didn't listen to me, but he did. I thought he looked down on me, but he didn't . . . Well, maybe he did a bit, but . . . I wish he'd been as lovely to me when he was alive as he's been since he died. I wish he hadn't left it too late.'

Deira hugged her. 'You'll always remember him with love, Grace. That's important.'

Grace sniffed a couple of times and smiled wanly before taking a tissue from her bag and blowing her nose.

Deira allowed her a moment before picking up one of the books. 'It's an early Maeve Binchy,' she said. 'And Grace – it's signed by her.'

'Really?' Grace took it from her. The book, *Light a Penny Candle*, which had been published in 1982, was indeed signed by the author.

'And this one is too. It's Rosamunde Pilcher,' said Deira. '*The Shell Seekers*. I've heard of that, never read it, though.'

'It's one of my all-time favourite books,' said Grace. 'And the others – what are they?'

There were two more Maeve Binchys and another Rosamunde Pilcher, all signed, as well as signed editions of Edna O'Brien's Country Girls trilogy and Joanna Trollope's *The Rector's Wife*.

'I loved *The Rector's Wife* when it first came out,' said Grace. 'When I insisted he read it, Ken dismissed it as sentimental.'

'Hard to see anyone being more sentimental than him right now.'

'How did he manage to get all these signed copies?' wondered Grace. 'How long did it take him to find them?'

'I don't want to burst your bubble, but eBay is pretty good for everything,' said Deira. 'All the same, he went to a lot of trouble. Which shows how much he loved you, Grace. You know, when he went out in the car that night, I can't help thinking it was because he wanted to save you from the worst of his illness. That maybe he thought he was doing the right thing by you.'

Grace took a deep breath. 'Perhaps,' she said. 'And perhaps he didn't mean to do it at all, though that's unlikely.'

'Why would you think that?' asked Deira.

'Something he said in the video,' replied Grace. 'He talked about the fact that he didn't want to do the trip because we both knew it would be for the last time, and he didn't want to do something knowing it was for the last time. But then he said that part of him still wanted to go. That he thought he could drive part of the way so he wouldn't be a burden. He said he might practise. What if that night he'd gone out to practise but it all went horribly wrong?'

Deira hesitated before speaking. She thought that perhaps Grace was trying to rewrite history because of Ken's actions in sourcing the books and buying her a fabulous piece of jewellery. But if that was what she wanted to believe, who was Deira to stop her? So she said it was always possible.

'You should look at the video he left me,' said Grace.

'I couldn't possibly,' Deira said. 'I'm sure it's way too personal.'

'You've been part of my personal life for the last few weeks,' Grace said. 'I'd like you to see it.'

'If you're sure.' Deira herself wasn't. But she reckoned that despite Grace's inner strength, the older woman had been

412

shaken by Ken's last message and by his gift to her. 'What about these other books?' she asked. 'The paperbacks.'

'Gosh, yes.' Grace reached into the locker and took one out. 'Oh,' she said. 'Hemingway again. Another early edition. Actually,' she added, 'I think it's a first edition and – oh, wow – it's signed too.'

'Are you serious?' Deira leaned over her shoulder.

'I didn't know he even had these,' said Grace as she took out another book. 'Steinbeck. *The Grapes of Wrath*. Also signed.'

'Grace! This is a real treasure trove.'

'I guess he picked them up when he was in the States,' said Grace. 'There's an F. Scott Fitzgerald too. Oh my God, here's a Salinger – and an early Norman Mailer!'

'I'm sure a book collector would love them,' said Deira.

Grace laughed. 'Ken *was* a book collector,' she said. 'His study is overflowing with books. Maybe he wanted to keep the best of them safe here.'

'Will you keep them yourself, in that case?'

'I don't know,' said Grace. 'I have to think about it. Talk to the children. See what they'd like to do.'

'You can't leave them here, though.'

'It's as safe a place as anywhere for the moment,' said Grace. 'I'll go through the stuff in his office and give away as much as makes sense, then maybe have these at home. After all, they meant a lot to him. They should be on shelves, not locked away in storage.'

'Good idea,' said Deira. 'Oh!'

'Oh?'

'If you were willing, they could be part of my first exhibition with Arc,' she said, excitement bubbling at her sudden idea. 'Always provided I get the job, of course. I could do something about the evolution of sharing stories. Old books and modern technology. I could . . .' Her voice trailed off as she visualised how it might work out. It could be brilliant. And interactive. They could include readings . . .

'Earth to Deira.' Grace poked her in the side.

'Sorry.' Deira smiled. 'I was getting carried away.'

'Come back to the house with me,' said Grace. 'Have a look at the books in Ken's study. See what you could do.'

'I'd love to,' said Deira.

'In that case, let's lock up here and go.'

Grace stretched her hand out in front of her and looked at the deep-red ruby on her finger. Then she picked up one of the signed Maeve Binchys to take with her and shut the door of the storage unit.

Back at Grace's house, Deira stared at the mountain of books in her late husband's study.

'Oh my God,' she said. 'Less of a collector, more of a hoarder.'

'I know.' Grace edged her way past his desk. 'It'll take time to go through them all and see what might be worth keeping and what's not.'

'You need an expert to help you,' said Deira. 'Unfortunately, that's not me. D'you know anyone?'

'I suppose Pat Rice could help,' said Grace slowly.

'Maybe that's what the professor had in mind all along,' said Deira. 'That after you met him to get the USB stick, you'd realise that something had to be done about the books. And that you'd ask him. And one thing would lead to another.'

'Actually Ken did say in his video that he'd be OK with

414

me getting close to Pat,' Grace admitted. 'It's odd that on the one hand he realised I was an individual person with my own likes and dislikes, and on the other he was so terrified at the idea of me managing on my own that he wanted to choose the man to replace him.'

'I'm sure you'll manage perfectly well,' said Deira. 'And although the Professor seems to have been a bit of a control freak, I honestly think it was coming from a place of caring about you.'

'He did like to be in control,' agreed Grace. 'Maybe I allowed it too much.' She looked enquiringly at Deira. 'Would you like to see his video now?'

'If you're certain . . .'

Grace took the USB from where she'd left it in the drawer of Ken's desk and inserted it into the laptop. The two women watched in silence as once again, Ken began to speak to his wife.

Afterwards, Deira wiped the tears from her eyes.

'He loved you so much,' she said.

'And yet that was the first time he ever told me,' said Grace.

'Surely he must have said it from time to time.'

Grace shook her head. 'Not often,' she said. 'On our anniversary and on my birthday – he was good at dates; he always remembered. But day to day . . . hardly ever. Usually only as a reply if I said I loved him. And even then not always.'

'But he's even quoted poetry to you. I've never gone out with anyone who quoted poetry. Gavin certainly didn't; he wasn't a poetry fan.' Even though he'd green-lighted one of her exhibitions, which had showcased Irish poets.

'Did he tell you he loved you, though?'

I love you, Dee. He always called her Dee when he told her he loved her. He said it lots of times. Until he stopped. She should have realised something was wrong when he stopped. But she was too busy to even notice.

'Words don't matter if there isn't meaning behind them,' she said. 'I'd rather someone who never said it but who really loved me than someone who was always saying it but didn't.'

'Thing is,' said Grace, 'it's part of showing someone you care. He didn't say it and he didn't show it and I spent most of my life thinking I wasn't good enough for him because of that. And I sort of stopped saying it to him too. I regret that, Deira. Because if we'd talked a bit more, if we'd said how much we cared about each other, I'd never have felt the less important person in the relationship. And maybe he wouldn't have felt the way he did when he got ill.'

'It's bloody hard to get it right, isn't it,' Deira said. 'Telling someone they love them, not telling them. Doing the right thing, not doing it. How do we know?'

'We don't.' Grace gave her a wry smile. 'That's why the shelves of bookstores are groaning under the weight of self-help books. We never really know what we're doing. We're all faking it. Even the best of us.'

'Ken gave you more than the books and the ring,' said Deira. 'He gave you the chance to make new friendships. I hope we'll always be friends, Grace, because I love the fact that we met and we did the journey together and that we shared our problems and that even if everything hasn't turned out exactly how we wanted, we've ended up in . . . well, in my case a better place. In yours . . .'

'I'm definitely better than I was before we took the trip,'

416

Grace told her. 'I know my husband better, and even if I regret that we never had this conversation when he was alive, I'm glad to know how much he cared. I'm also glad that you were around, because without you, I mightn't have got any further than Nantes!'

'Friends forever.' Deira grinned.

'I sure hope so,' said Grace. 'Now, how about a cup of tea? Or,' she added, 'champagne. There's a bottle in the fridge that's been there for nearly a year. This seems like a good time to open it.'

'Champagne all the way,' said Deira, and followed her into the kitchen.

Chapter 38

Deira stood in the new visitor space of the Arc Tech building and breathed a sigh of satisfaction. Her first project, the exhibition of old books inspired by Professor Kenneth Harrington's collection, would shortly be opened by the newly appointed Minister for Arts and Heritage, and the guest list of attendees for the night was impressive. Apart from representatives from arts and culture organisations, it also included Grace Garvey and her three children, as well as Pat Rice, Gill, Bex and Tillie. Deira had also invited people who'd been involved in previous exhibitions with her, like Thelma Roache's niece, Jennifer. She'd contacted Jennifer to congratulate her on showing her work in Amaya's gallery, and Jennifer had come back to say how excited she was that six of her paintings had been sold. Deira was pleased for her, and pleased to keep the link with her very first successful project.

But now, in the moments before the exhibition was opened to the public for the first time, Deira was looking at it as a visitor and not someone who'd been intimately involved in designing the layout and selecting the books. She'd been almost overwhelmed by the professor's collection, but more than that, by the content, which included many first editions of famous works, especially by iconic Irish writers. She'd divided the project into different eras, drawing a route from the past to the present. She'd read many of the books herself in her student years, but there were others that had passed her by, and she was grateful for the opportunity to learn about them and to add them to her own reading list.

The last four months had been too busy for much reading. After handing in her notice to Solas Life and Pensions, she'd been obliged to take time off before starting with Arc. Accompanied by Bex, she'd gone to Paris, where she'd hired a sports car, dropped the roof and driven around the Arc de Triomphe with 'The Ballad of Lucy Jordan' blaring from the sound system. It hadn't been the most relaxing of experiences, as the Parisian traffic had been every bit as terrifying as Grace had promised, but it had been exhilarating all the same.

Bex had declared it one of the best times of her life. She'd been cheerful and positive throughout the stay, and even when she and Deira had a conversation about her decision to have an abortion, she didn't get upset.

'You might think differently,' she'd said to Deira the evening they'd discussed it. 'But it's my body, my choice and my right to make it.'

Deira would never say that she'd wished it had been different. Because even if her fantasy of raising Bex's baby had been fulfilled, it still would have changed her god-daughter's life in a way that she couldn't know. And so she simply said that she loved and supported Bex and that she'd always love and support her, which made the younger girl finally tear up and tell her that she'd always love Deira too.

They'd grown much closer on that trip, and Deira found that Bex's quirky sense of humour and determination to do what she wanted matched her own. She told her that she was always welcome to visit her in Dublin, and Bex said that she'd be taking her up on that, because there were concerts scheduled for later in the year that she wanted to go to, and there was always the shopping – and then she laughed and told her not to worry, she wouldn't land on her unannounced.

Neither Gill nor Bex was staying with her for their time in Dublin now, because although Gill had initially suggested it, she'd then messaged Deira to say she'd got a great deal on a two-night stay at the Clayton that would be better all round given that Deira would surely be busy with the exhibition and wouldn't have time to worry about them.

Deira was astonished but relieved. Nonetheless, she planned to have lunch with her sister and niece the following day. Not being obliged to do something made it so much easier to want to do it, she thought. And she wondered if she truly was a contrary madam, as Gill had often called her in the past, or if her perception of her relationship with her sister had finally shifted for the better.

'Deira. Looking amazing.' Ardal, Arc's CEO, bounded down the stairs to join her. 'I couldn't be happier with it.'

'Neither could I,' she admitted. 'It's exactly how I visualised it.'

'OK, I love the exhibition, but I also love that we're putting the company out there as being part of the community and part of the city,' said Ardal. 'And I know we have our corporate motives for wanting to do it, but it really matters to me personally too.'

'I'm glad,' said Deira. 'I've loved working on it.'

'I hope you'll be working on many more,' said Ardal.

'Me too.'

'Ah.' Ardal nodded towards the glass doors. 'Our first visitors have arrived. We're on.'

Grace was utterly blown away by the exhibition, which was bigger and better than she'd ever imagined. She wished that Ken could be here now to see people marvelling at his collection and talking about the books with such enthusiasm and eagerness. She wished he could have heard the speeches from the Minister and the Lord Mayor and Ardal and finally Deira, who recalled him as a lecturer passionate about words and literature who wanted his students to appreciate the power of the spoken and the written word.

'At college, he constantly tried to make us strive to use words better, to understand the nuances of language and to appreciate the joy that books can bring us,' she said. 'He liked challenging us and being challenged, and that never left him. I'm proud and honoured to have been able to bring his amazing collection to the public, and I'd like especially to thank his wife Grace and their children Aline, Fionn and Regan for being with us here today.'

Grace had been touched by Deira's remarks and had accepted a tissue from Aline when a tear rolled down her cheek. But after the speeches, she'd been uplifted by the innovative way the books were displayed, and the posters and artwork that Deira had sourced to go with them.

'I hope you don't mind,' Grace said when she got to speak to Deira afterwards. 'But I invited someone else along. He's only just arrived.'

'Of course not. I told you you could bring as many guests as you like,' Deira said. 'Who is it?'

'Duncan,' said Grace.

421

Deira frowned. 'Duncan?'

'From the restaurant in Spain,' said Grace. 'Duncan Anderson.'

'Grace!' Deira looked at her in astonishment. 'Are you and Duncan a thing?'

Grace smiled slowly.

'I don't believe it,' Deira said with delight. 'Well, I do, I thought he fancied you before, but . . . Oh Grace!'

'He came some of the way back with me in my car,' Grace explained. 'He was going to the UK for a couple of weeks and it suited him to get the ferry from Santander. So we drove through Spain together and I got to see Santander for the first time. Then I did France on my own.'

'You never said! You're a dark horse and an amazing woman, Grace Garvey,' said Deira. 'You take my breath away.'

'Well, it's early days, and a long-distance relationship, so we'll have to see how it works out.' Grace brushed her hair from her eyes and her huge Adele Dahlia ring flashed in the light. 'I'm not looking for someone to replace Ken, but even though we're in different countries at the moment, the companionship is nice. Duncan is a lovely man.'

'Good for you,' said Deira. 'What about Pat, though?'

Pat had been very helpful in sorting through Ken's collection, and over the last couple of months Deira had grown to like him.

'He's a decent guy, but he and Ken are very alike in many ways and I don't want to end up with Ken Mark 2,' said Grace. 'Duncan is different. I'm ready for different.'

Deira gave her a hug, then smiled as Duncan broke away from Fionn, who he'd been talking to, and made his way over.

'Congratulations,' he said. 'It's great.'

'Thank you.'

They spoke for a while about the exhibition and about the restaurant, and then Deira was claimed by Ardal, who told her that the PR people were keen to do a short video about the exhibition and that they'd managed to set it up for the following day.

'It's a pity we didn't think of it sooner,' he said. 'We could have filmed you at Grace's house, looking through the books. But let's see what they come up with.'

'Let's,' she said, and then went to spend some time with Gill and Bex.

It was after midnight by the time she got home.

She kicked off her shoes and flopped on the sofa, and was asleep before she had time to light the restful candle Tillie had given her to celebrate.

She woke up just before dawn, her neck aching from the odd angle at which she'd slept. But after she'd showered and changed into fresh clothes, she felt surprisingly refreshed. Arc Tech encouraged casual dressing, but Deira liked wearing the sharp suits she'd invested in during her time at Solas. Given that she'd be meeting the producer of the video that morning, and in case they wanted to do some recording there and then, she chose a red shift dress with matching jacket that brought out the warmth of her skin and the depth of her green eyes. She flicked her fingers through her hair and then added her newest red lipstick to her lips. She put her high-heeled Kurt Geiger shoes in her bag and slipped a pair of Skechers on her feet for the walk to the office.

As she locked the front door behind her, she felt a wave

of gratitude towards her new employers for the significant increase in salary that they'd offered her to take on the role. When Bethany Burke had called her back with the total package, she'd almost fallen off the chair, and had had to hold herself back from jumping at it straight away. But she'd been cool and collected and raised one or two (in her mind) trivial issues with the headhunter, who'd then come back with a revised and even better offer.

Because of that, Deira had been comfortably able to borrow enough to buy Gavin out of his share of the mews house. She smiled as she remembered his reaction to her handing in her notice at Solas – he'd called her and asked her to come to his office, where he'd asked what her plans were.

'It's not really your business any more, is it?' she asked.

'I'm concerned,' he said. 'I'm worried that you're not going to be in a position to deal with your responsibilities if you leave the company.'

'You don't have to worry about me in the slightest.' Her voice was serene. 'All you need to know is that I have a new job, I'm perfectly happy and there's no issue financially that you have to worry about. So let's get the valuation on the mews and see where we go from there.'

'OK.' He was clearly taken aback by her new-found positivity. 'And you're really all right?'

'Yes, and I'm sorry,' she said. 'Sorry that I gave you a hard time even though you deserved it. Sorry that I took the car without saying anything. Sorry about lots of things, really. I wasn't myself back then. Now I am.'

'Right. Thanks.' He was even more taken aback.

'I hope everything's OK with you,' she said. 'You look a bit tired, to be honest.'

'I didn't get a lot of sleep last night,' he said. 'Afton is—' and then he'd broken off and looked at her again. 'It's fine,' he said. 'I'm fine.'

A couple of weeks later, Afton gave birth to a baby girl, whom they named Jewel. Deira hadn't been sure how she'd feel when she heard the news, but although it initially upset her, she wasn't plunged into the depths of despair and resentment that she'd feared. And although she didn't send the new parents a card (they'd surely have thought that both inappropriate and slightly scary), she did send her congratulations to Gavin via her solicitor.

The early-morning sun filtered through the trees that lined the canal as she walked to Hanover Quay. There was a stillness about this time of the day that appealed to her, as did the knowledge that the hours ahead could be filled with interesting things (boring things too, she admitted to herself, but in the light of the morning sun, she was giving the nod to interesting).

Despite her early start, she wasn't the first person in the office. Depending on their role within the company, Arc Tech employees worked a flexible timetable, which allowed them to start any time from five thirty a.m. and finish up to midnight. Deira had never arrived at the office at five thirty, but in the days leading up to the exhibition opening, she'd been there close to midnight most nights.

The visitor space had been cleaned and tidied after the launch, and was now pristine and welcoming. She walked around it again, happy that every book was being showcased at its very best, still in awe of the professor's collection and aware that some of the books were indeed quite valuable and therefore more of a treasure than Grace had ever imagined.

She stopped in front of the rather dog-eared first edition of *The Sun Also Rises* that had been in the storage locker. The pages were yellowed and foxed with dark brown spots, but still readable. She'd downloaded a copy onto her Kindle app when she'd been given the go-ahead for the exhibition, but she had to admit that she hadn't really enjoyed it any more on this reading than she had on her first. Also included in the display were Grace's signed Maeve Binchy novels. Deira liked seeing their jaunty jackets among some of the more drab volumes. Light and shade, she thought. Always important.

She took the lift to the fourth floor. Although Arc Tech was generally an open-plan building, Deira had a spacious office of her own with floor-to-ceiling windows that gave her great views across the canal dock. It was a bigger office than Gavin's. And every time she thought of that, she smiled.

It was almost eleven when Rhona Maguire, the company's PR executive, dropped in to tell her that the video producer was waiting for her in the visitor space.

'I'll go down now.' Deira slipped on the Kurt Geigers – she'd changed from the Skechers after arriving at the building, but usually kicked off her shoes when she was at the desk – then checked her face in her compact mirror, reapplied her Pirate lipstick and tidied her hair before heading for the lift.

He was looking at a copy of James Plunkett's *Strumpet City*, his back to her, when she stepped out into the visitor space. But she recognised him straight away and her polite words of greeting froze on her lips, so that it was the sound of her heels clicking on the tiled floor that made him turn around.

'Hello, Deira,' he said.

'Charlie.' His name came out as a croak. 'Rhona didn't say . . . She told me it was a video recording . . . I wasn't expecting you.'

'I don't just get all the glam jobs interviewing people in France and Spain,' he said. 'Sometimes it's the corporate work that pays the best.'

She nodded, still at a loss for words.

'So what she wants is a piece with you talking about the idea for the exhibition. Maybe showing us one or two of the books. Talking about Arc's commitment to the community. I'll be doing a piece with Ardal later. It should be all wrapped and ready before the end of the week.'

'Right,' she said.

'You look great,' he told her. 'Very corporate.'

'You look good too.'

'I'm behind the camera. It doesn't matter how I look.' He gave her a short smile. 'Now, the way this works is that Rhona has given me a list of questions. I'll ask them off camera but I'll film you answering them. I've been looking at the light and I think we should go over there.' He indicated a corner of the visitor space. 'Obviously I'll be taking lots of shots of the exhibition generally. Sound OK?'

She was overwhelmed by his businesslike approach. By his apparent dismissal of the fact that the last time they'd met she'd humiliated herself in front of him and had forced him to make personal admissions to her that she knew he would have wanted to keep private. But he was behaving as though none of it had happened. As though this was the first time they'd met.

'OK?' he repeated.

He hadn't changed; not, she reminded herself, that a few

months should have wrought any great transformation in him. He was wearing the same scuffed leather jacket he'd worn on the ferry, and similar comfortable shoes. His jeans were stonewashed denim. His hair was still ever so slightly longer than was fashionable.

'Yes,' she said. 'Fine.'

'Great.'

Had he forgotten that night, or was he choosing to ignore it? She might have been the one in the wrong then, but she was the client now. So he couldn't afford to be offended by her. He couldn't afford to let any residual feelings he had about her behaviour back then show. She held a power over him that she felt uncomfortable with. She wanted to say something, but he was already getting her to sit on a particular seat and moving around her, checking the angle of the light and how much of the exhibition would be in the shot.

His phone rang and he had a brief conversation.

'The sound guy,' he told her when he'd finished. 'He'll be here shortly.'

'Would you like a coffee or anything while we're waiting?' she asked.

'No thanks. Plenty to be doing. Stay here, will you?' He left her sitting in his chosen place and walked through the exhibition, taking occasional snaps of the books. Then a younger man arrived and the two of them chatted for a while before returning to where Deira sat.

'I'm Jonah,' said the younger man. 'I'll be wiring you up for sound. D'you mind if I run this wire under your dress? We'll hide the box behind you. Perfect. Tell me what you had for breakfast.'

She looked at him, startled.

'To check the sound,' he clarified.

'Nothing, actually.'

'That's not helpful.' Charlie raised an eyebrow. 'You'll have to make it up. Cornflakes, toast?'

'Um . . . cornflakes, toast. Actually,' she said, as Jonah fiddled with some settings, 'I hate both of them. If I eat breakfast, I have fruit.'

'Someone once told me that fruit isn't good on an empty stomach,' Charlie remarked. 'Too acidic. I like toast myself. Smothered in chunky marmalade.'

'I'm a millennial, so it's smashed avocado toast for me,' said Jonah. 'OK, Deira. We're sorted.'

'Right,' Charlie said. 'We'll do the seated questions first. Then I'll ask you stuff as we walk around. It won't all make it into the recording, and don't worry if you make a mistake; we can do as many takes as we need. Don't forget, you won't hear my questions in the actual video, so remember to give as much information as you can. Ready?'

'Yes.'

'Let's go. First one. What gave you the idea for the *Written Words* exhibition and why did you think this was a good place to stage it?'

Rhona had emailed Deira the questions the previous evening so that she'd have some time to prepare her answers, but although she knew what she wanted to say, her mouth was dry with nerves.

Charlie took a small bottle of water from his rucksack and told her to take a slug. 'Take your time,' he told her. 'We're not in a rush.'

When she was ready, he asked the question again. This time she was able to give an answer that she hoped was coherent.

'Great,' he said. 'OK, next one. How did you source the books?'

Deira told him about the late professor's collection and how generous Grace had been in allowing her to look through it.

'How did you two meet?' asked Charlie.

'We joined forces on an unexpected road trip through France and Spain,' replied Deira. 'It was wonderful.'

'Can you show me some of the collection?'

Deira led him through the exhibition, growing in confidence as she shared her knowledge of the books and artwork.

'Sounds like you had a fun time putting it all together,' said Charlie.

'I did,' agreed Deira. 'I'm very lucky to have had the opportunity to bring this amazing collection to the public.'

At last Charlie told her that he thought they had enough material, and thanked her for being so helpful.

He looked at Jonah, who gave him a thumbs-up and checked his recording. Jonah then said he had another job to get to so he'd see Charlie later.

'Did you get everything you want?' asked Deira.

'Yes, thanks.'

She stood awkwardly beside him, unsure of what, if anything, she should say. He ignored her as he looked at various pieces of the video.

'I'm sorry.' She blurted it out and he paused the playback to look at her. 'About that night. I'm so, so sorry. It's been eating me up ever since.'

'Don't worry about it.'

'But I do,' she said. 'I realise that this opportunity for me to say something is as random as it may be unwelcome, but I'm not . . . I'm not really the sort of person I appeared to be. I—'

'You made a mistake. It's fine.'

'It's not.' She shook her head. 'You were absolutely right. I objectified you. I made it all about your body and what you could give me and not about you as a person. And you're a decent person, I know that. I tried to take advantage of you. I honestly can't apologise enough.'

His eyes met hers and held them for a moment.

'Apology accepted,' he said.

'I feel I have to justify myself, even though there's no justification.'

'Not to me you don't.'

'Mr Mulholland. Charlie. Please. I know I'm only trying to make myself feel better, but . . . could we have coffee or something?'

'Now?' he asked.

'Yes, if you like.'

'OK.'

She was surprised at his unequivocal acceptance. 'There's a good place around the corner,' she said. 'Can you give me five minutes? I need to get my bag.'

'OK,' he said again.

She took the lift to her office, grabbed her bag and was back in the lobby a couple of minutes later. Charlie had already packed away his gear and was waiting for her.

'This way.' She led him out of the building.

The coffee shop was almost empty, with only a few people sitting in booths, laptops open in front of them. Deira went to get the coffees, telling Charlie to pick a seat.

'How are your ribs, by the way?' he asked when she put an Americano in front of him.

431

'Good as new.'

'I'm glad to hear that,' he said. 'You really did flatten yourself on the floor at that service station.'

'I was in agony,' she said, 'but trying not to show it.'

'I could see it all the same. I was worried about you driving to Bordeaux.'

'I didn't make it that far.'

'No. But you got to Pamplona. And El Pozo de la Señora. I felt flattered when I saw you there. But obviously for the wrong reasons.'

'Look,' she said. 'You know from what I said that night that I was in a terrible place mentally. I was unhinged. Obsessed by what had happened with my boyfriend and his new girlfriend, obsessed with how devastated I felt, obsessed – as you know – by the fact that she was nearly half my age and going to have a baby, and what that represented for me. And I was obsessed in thinking that motherhood might have passed me by. It was physical, that obsession. It had taken me over.'

'It didn't seem that way in Pamplona.'

'It came to the surface in waves,' she said. 'But it was there all the time. Bubbling away. Ready to erupt. Unfortunately, you were in the firing line when it did.'

'I got the feeling that you put me in the firing line,' he said.

'Yes. I did. And I regret it very much. Most of all, I regret that you had to share information with me that you wouldn't have wanted to share. I embarrassed you as much as myself, and yes, all this is only to make me feel better, but I do want you to know that I was looking at *every* man I saw as a prospective father for my child. Every man who didn't look like a psycho was a possibility. No matter who, no matter where. I was a . . . a maternal predator stalking the country.'

'And now?'

'My ex and his partner have had their baby. I've agreed a settlement with him about our home. I've changed jobs. I've . . .' she glanced up from the mug she'd been staring into as she spoke, 'I've gone to a few counselling sessions, too.'

'Have they helped?'

'Yes,' replied Deira. 'Everything has helped. There's no point in me saying that I'm completely OK with all my choices. That I don't feel that perhaps I'd still like to be a mother eventually, even though I know that every passing day makes it less likely. But it's not the all-consuming passion it was before. And maybe I'll stop thinking that way too. I don't know. What I do know is that I've got my balance back.'

'I'm glad,' said Charlie. 'And I'm glad you got some help, too.'

'I don't expect you to understand completely,' she said, 'but it's really hard making the choices that women have to make. Especially when you suddenly realise that it's not an abstract thing and you're actually going to have to make them. It's a shock when you feel that your own body has betrayed you. It's still not an excuse for how I treated you, but it's an explanation of sorts.'

'I do understand the feeling of being betrayed by your own body,' said Charlie.

'Oh God. Of course. I—'

He interrupted her. 'Have you really been beating yourself up over our last encounter all this time?'

'Yes.'

He took a deep breath. 'I went out with a girl once and I told her I loved her and would do anything for her and that she was the most wonderful person in the world. We slept together and the next morning I deleted my name from her contacts before tiptoeing out of her flat and never seeing her again. You did what you did because you wanted what you wanted, Deira. At least you were upfront about it.'

'All the same . . .'

'All the same, nothing,' he said. 'Yes, I felt used by you. Yes, you wanted to use me. But in the whole realm of casting the first stone, we're standing side by side. If anything, all that you've said shows me how women take on board a whole heap of guilt that they really don't need to.'

'Does that mean you're OK about it?'

'I was OK about it around twenty-four hours after you'd gone,' said Charlie. 'And I wished I hadn't lost my temper with you, because I thought we got on well and I liked you. But I also knew that you wanted different things out of life than me, so there was no point trying to get in touch with you.'

'So . . . we're good?' asked Deira.

'Totally good.'

'And you won't make me look really stupid in the recording?'

'Is that what this is about?' asked Charlie. 'You're taking me to coffee because you're afraid I'll make you look dumb?'

'No. But I'm factoring that in.'

'You'll be great in it. And whatever I can do to make you look even greater, I will.'

'Thank you.'

They sat in silence for a moment, then Deira said she'd

better be getting back and Charlie agreed that he had a lot of work to do. To make her look wonderful, he added with a smile. She laughed.

They walked out of the coffee shop together. The sun was high in the sky now, reflecting off the water of the dock and dazzling them so that they hurried into the shade.

'I'll send the finished product to Rhona as soon as possible,' said Charlie.

'Great.'

'Unless you'd rather see it yourself first.'

She looked at him.

'In case you want me to make any changes.'

'There may be some,' she said.

'You could come to my place,' he suggested. 'Tomorrow? Seven-ish? I could cook.'

'You can cook?'

'Amaya taught me. She insisted I needed to learn. She said that I shouldn't starve when she was busy working. That everyone should know how to look after themselves and that didn't just mean phoning Deliveroo.'

'What sort of cooking?'

'Paella, if you like that,' he said. 'My pork steak is also a very acceptable dish. I'm not bad at Dover sole either.'

'I've never cooked any of those,' she said. 'When I was with Gavin, it was usually eating out, sending out or sandwiches.'

'You'll let me decide, so?'

'Totally.'

'I'll message you my details.'

He took out his phone.

'It's a no-strings thing,' he said. 'Just two people who know each other getting together.'

'No strings,' she agreed.

He nodded and headed down the street away from her.

She turned and walked back to her office.

When she was sitting at her desk, she called Grace.

'It seems we both may have found treasure thanks to Ken,' Grace said after Deira had told her about her meeting with Charlie.

'Maybe,' said Deira. 'I don't know how this will work out. If there even is anything to work out. If I want it to.'

'Sometimes the most unexpected things happen when you leave it all in the lap of the gods,' said Grace. 'Sometimes chance plays a far greater role in our lives than we think.'

Grace was right, thought Deira, just like Tillie so often was. Chance had brought them together, and their journey had ended in ways that neither of them had expected, ways that seemed to be sending both of them in a new direction.

The future isn't set in stone, she told herself as she pulled her keyboard towards her and started to type. But neither is it something I can be sure of shaping the way I want. All I can do is hang on for the ride, and grab whatever opportunities I can along the way.

With no regrets.

Acknowledgements

It takes more than just the author to turn an idea for a book into a finished novel that people might want to read, and the fact that Deira and Grace's story has made it to the shelves (and the digital downloads) is because I have some wonderful people looking after me along the way.

Enormous thanks to Marion Donaldson for her always thoughtful editorial suggestions. We've worked together for many years and technology has moved us away from reams of paper notes to colour-coded lists of queries on a screen. No matter which way they arrive, Marion's suggestions are always made with warmth and humour, and I'm very grateful that she always sees what I'm trying to say, no matter how inelegantly I sometimes say it.

Along with Marion, the book-loving people at Headline and Hachette are always a joy to work with. Special thanks to Ellie, Katie, Yeti and Alara in London, and to the entire Dublin team of Breda, Jim, Ruth, Elaine, Siobhan, Bernard, Joanna and the two Ciaras.

My agent Isobel Dixon and her fantastic colleagues at Blake Friedmann look after me and my books wonderfully well. Thank you all once again for everything you do on my behalf.

Extra thanks to Daisy, Sian, James and Resham for being unfailingly helpful even when I'm being particularly daft.

My copyeditor, Jane Selley, has saved me from myself on more than one occasion, and I thank her for doing it so brilliantly once again in this novel. Thanks also to my proof-reader, Kate Truman, for her work on the final manuscript.

For bringing me on the literary tour of France and Spain, doing most of the driving, parking in impossible carparks, finding hidden hotels and beautiful locations – as well as drafting the first version of the map and highlighting the not-so-deliberate errors in the manuscript – I truly can't thank Colm enough.

As always lots of thanks to my family who champion my books any time, any place and everywhere.

And finally – to you, the reader, whether this is the first of my books you've read or you've been with me for a lot of the journey, thank you for choosing *The Women Who Ran Away*. I hope you enjoyed reading about Deira and Grace as much as I enjoyed telling their story.